Critical acclaim for the thrillers of internationally bestselling author John Connolly

THE BOOK OF LOST THINGS

"A rousing series of adventures. . . . Connolly's novel should draw in both young and old fans to read happily ever after."

—*The Capital Times* (WI)

"Deliciously twisted."

—*Richmond Times-Dispatch*

"Enchanting, engrossing and enlightening."

—*The Sun-Sentinel* (Fort Lauderdale)

"An ambitious turn for Connolly. With his evocative style, he takes familiar themes . . . and tweaks them in clever, even perverse ways."

—*Los Angeles Times*

"Entertains and unnerves in equal measure."

—*The Washington Post*

"The Irish thriller writer breaks new ground with this extravagant fantasy."

—*Kirkus Reviews*

"The plot is brisk and the pages turn. [Connolly's] imagination is on full display as he creates a world rich with detail and dimensions."

—*The Globe and Mail* (Toronto)

"Enchanting.... Connolly echoes many great fairy tales and legends but cleverly twists them to his own purposes.... Consistently entertaining."

—*Publishers Weekly*

THE BLACK ANGEL

"Stylishly literate gore and terror."

—*Kirkus Reviews*

"Connolly, who resides in Ireland but writes about the U.S. like he's lived here all his life, once again blends the private-eye novel and the supernatural thriller in a way that's altogether unique."

—*Booklist*

"*The Black Angel* is by far Connolly's most ambitious work, a tale poetic in the telling that is global in scope and timeless in origin."

—Bookreporter.com

BAD MEN

"Powerful.... Connolly has quickly and decisively established himself as a unique voice."

—Michael Connelly, bestselling author of *The Narrows*

"Terrifying.... Think Thomas Harris by way of Stephen King.... Not for the faint of heart."

—*Publishers Weekly*

"A supernatural chiller.... A stylish darkness sucks you under."

—*Kirkus Reviews*

"An honest-to-goodness fright fest.... Connolly takes the chills to a new level."

—*Rocky Mountain News* (Denver)

THE WHITE ROAD

"Darkly brilliant, spellbinding, and disturbing, *The White Road* confirms John Connolly's position as one of the best thriller writers we have."

—Harlan Coben

"You don't want to miss a word of this near-perfect story."
—*Rocky Mountain News* (Denver)

"The malevolence here is almost palpable."
—*Publishers Weekly* (starred review)

"[A] complex, compelling read."
—*The Times-Picayune* (New Orleans)

THE KILLING KIND

"Unfolds with the force and logic of a nightmare."
—*The Washington Post*

"Connolly has that rare ability to hit you head-on with a great crime story while giving you goosebumps in the process."
—*Clarion-Ledger* (Jackson, Miss.)

"[A] marvelous mystery. Connolly is a master of actions and words, delivering both a compelling page-turner and a writing tour de force."
—*The Times-Picayune* (New Orleans)

"Few crime fiction writers can conjure up menace and chill as John Connolly."

—*Toronto Sun*

ALSO BY JOHN CONNOLLY

The
BOOK
of
LOST
THINGS

John Connolly

WASHINGTON SQUARE PRESS

New York   London   Toronto   Sydney

Washington Square Press
A Division of Simon & Schuster, Inc.
1230 Avenue of the Americas
New York, NY 10020

Grateful acknowledgment is made to the following for permission to reprint previously published material:

Extract from *The Greek Myths,* copyright © 2001 by Robert Graves. Used by permission of Carcanet Press Ltd.

Rubicon: The Last Years of the Roman Republic, copyright © 2003 by Tom Holland.

First Washington Square Press trade paperback edition October 2007

WASHINGTON SQUARE PRESS and colophon are registered trademarks of Simon & Schuster, Inc.

For information regarding special discounts for bulk purchases, please contact Simon & Schuster Special Sales at 1-800-456-6798 or business@simonandschuster.com.

Designed by Dana Sloan

Manufactured in the United States of America

10 9 8 7 6 5 4 3 2 1

Library of Congress Cataloging-in-Publication Data

ISBN-13: 978-0-7432-9885-8
ISBN-10:   0-7432-9885-3
ISBN-13: 978-0-7432-9890-2 (pbk)
ISBN-10:   0-7432-9890-X (pbk)

This book is dedicated to an adult, Jennifer Ridyard, and to Cameron and Alistair Ridyard, who will be adults all too soon.

For in every adult dwells the child that was, and in every child lies the adult that will be.

Deeper meaning resides in the fairy tales told to me in my childhood than in the truth that is taught by life.

—FRIEDRICH SCHILLER (1759–1805)

Everything you can imagine is real.

—PABLO PICASSO (1881–1973)

I

Of All That Was Found and All That Was Lost

NCE UPON A TIME—for that is how all stories should begin—there was a boy who lost his mother.

He had, in truth, been losing her for a very long time. The disease that was killing her was a creeping, cowardly thing, a sickness that ate away at her from the inside, slowly consuming the light within, so that her eyes grew a little less bright with each passing day, and her skin a little more pale.

And as she was stolen away from him, piece by piece, the boy became more and more afraid of finally losing her entirely. He wanted her to stay. He had no brothers and no sisters, and while he loved his father, it would be true to say that he loved his mother more. He could not bear to think of a life without her.

The boy, whose name was David, did everything that he could to keep his mother alive. He prayed. He tried to be good, so that she would not be punished for his mistakes. He padded around the house as quietly as he was able, and kept his voice down when he was playing war games with his toy soldiers. He created a routine, and he tried to keep to that routine as closely as possible, because he believed in part that his mother's fate was linked to the actions he performed. He would always get out of bed by putting his left foot on the floor first, then his right. He always counted up to twenty when he was brushing his teeth, and he always stopped when the count was completed. He always touched the faucets in the bathroom and the handles of the doors a certain number of times: odd numbers were bad, but even numbers were fine, with two, four, and eight being particularly favorable, although he didn't care for six because six was twice three and three was the second part of thirteen, and thirteen was very bad indeed.

If he bumped his head against something, he would bump it a second time to keep the numbers even, and sometimes he would have to do it again and again because his head seemed to bounce against the wall, ruining his count, or his hair glanced against it when he didn't want it to, until his skull ached from the effort and he felt giddy and sick. For an entire year, during the worst of his mother's illness, he carried the same items from his bedroom to the kitchen first thing in the morning, and then back again last thing at night: a small copy of Grimm's selected fairy tales and a dog-eared *Magnet* comic, the book to be placed perfectly in the center of the comic, and both to be laid with their edges lined up against the corner of the rug on his bedroom floor at night or on the seat of his favorite kitchen chair in the morning. In these ways, David made his contribution to his mother's survival.

After school each day, he would sit by her bedside, sometimes talking with her if she was feeling strong enough, but at other times merely watching her sleep, counting every labored, wheezing breath that emerged, willing her to remain with him. Often he would bring a book with him to read, and if his mother was awake and her head did not hurt too much, she would ask him to read aloud to her. She had books of her own—romances and mysteries and thick, black-garbed novels with tiny letters—but she preferred him to read to her much older stories: myths and legends and fairy tales, stories of castles and quests and dangerous, talking animals. David did not object. Although, at twelve, he was no longer quite a child, he retained an affection for these tales, and the fact that it pleased his mother to hear such stories told by him only added to his love for them.

Before she became ill, David's mother would often tell him that stories were alive. They weren't alive in the way that people were alive, or even dogs or cats. People were alive whether you chose to notice them or not, while dogs tended to make you notice them if they decided that you weren't paying them enough attention. Cats, meanwhile, were very good at pretending people didn't exist at all when it suited them, but that was another matter entirely.

Stories were different, though: they came alive in the telling. Without a human voice to read them aloud, or a pair of wide eyes following them by flashlight beneath a blanket, they had no real existence in our world. They were like seeds in the beak of a bird, waiting to fall to earth, or the notes of a song laid out on a sheet, yearning for an instrument to bring their music into being. They lay dormant, hoping for the chance to emerge. Once someone started to read them, they could begin to change. They could take root in the imagination, and transform the reader. Stories *wanted* to be read, David's mother would whisper. They needed it. It was the reason they forced themselves from their world into ours. They wanted us to give them life.

These were the things that his mother told David, before the illness took her. She would often have a book in her hand as she spoke, and she would run her fingertips lovingly across the cover, just as she would sometimes touch them to David's face, or to his father's, when he said or did something that reminded her of how much she cared for him. The sound of his mother's voice was like a song to David, one that was constantly revealing new improvisations or previously unheard subtleties. As he grew older, and music became more important to him (although never quite as important as books), he thought of his mother's voice less as a song and more as a kind of symphony, capable of infinite variations on familiar themes and melodies that changed according to her moods and whims.

As the years went by, the reading of a book became a more solitary experience for David, until his mother's illness returned them both to his early childhood but with the roles reversed. Nevertheless, before she grew sick, he would often step quietly into the room in which his mother was reading, acknowledging her with a smile (always returned) before taking a seat close by and immersing himself in his own book so that, although both were lost in their own individual worlds, they shared the same space and time. And David could tell, by looking at her face as she read, whether or not the story contained in the book was living inside her, and she in it, and he would recall again all that she had told him about stories and tales and the power that they wield over us, and that we in turn wield over them.

David would always remember the day his mother died. He was in school, learning—or not learning—how to scan a poem, his mind filled with dactyls and pentameters, the names like those of strange dinosaurs inhabiting a lost prehistoric landscape. The headmaster opened the classroom door and approached the English master, Mr. Benjamin (or Big Ben, as he was known to his pupils, because of his size and his habit of withdrawing his old pocket watch from the folds of his waistcoat and announcing, in deep, mournful tones, the slow passage of time to his unruly students). The headmaster whispered something to Mr. Benjamin, and Mr. Benjamin nodded solemnly. When he turned around to face the class, his eyes found David's, and his voice was softer than usual when he spoke. He called David's name and told him that he was excused, and that he should pack his bag and follow the headmaster. David knew then what had happened. He knew before the headmaster brought him to the school nurse's office. He knew before the nurse appeared, a cup of tea in her hand for the boy to drink. He knew before the headmaster stood over him, still stern in aspect but clearly trying to be gentle with the bereaved boy. He knew before the cup touched his lips and the words were spoken and the tea burned his mouth, reminding him that he was still alive while his mother was now lost to him.

Even the routines, endlessly repeated, had not been enough to keep her alive. He wondered later if he had failed to do one of them properly, if he had somehow miscounted that morning, or if there was an action he could have added to the many that might have changed things. It didn't matter now. She was gone. He should have stayed at home. He had always worried about her when he was in school, because if he was away from her then he had no control over her existence. The routines didn't work in school. They were harder to perform, because the school had its own rules and its own routines. David had tried to use them as a substitute, but they weren't the same. Now his mother had paid the price.

It was only then that David, ashamed at his failure, began to cry.

The days that followed were a blur of neighbors and relatives, of tall, strange men who rubbed his hair and handed him a shilling, and big women in dark dresses who held David against their chests while they wept, flooding his senses with the smell of perfume and mothballs. He sat up late into the night, squashed into a corner of the living room while the grown-ups exchanged stories of a mother he had never known, a strange creature with a history entirely separate from his own: a child who would not cry when her older sister died because she refused to believe that someone so precious to her could disappear forever and never come back; a young girl who ran away from home for a day because her father, in a fit of impatience at some minor sin she had committed, told her that he was going to hand her over to the gypsies; a beautiful woman in a bright red dress who was stolen from under the nose of another man by David's father; a vision in white on her wedding day who pricked her thumb on the thorn of a rose and left the spot of blood on her gown for all to see.

And when at last he fell asleep, David dreamed that he was part of these tales, a participant in every stage of his mother's life. He was no longer a child hearing stories of another time. Instead, he was a witness to them all.

David saw his mother for the last time in the undertaker's room before the coffin was closed. She looked different and yet the same. She was more like her old self, the mother who had existed before the illness came. She was wearing makeup, like she did on Sundays for church or when she and David's father were going out to dinner or to the movies. She was laid out in her favorite blue dress, with her hands clasped across her stomach. A rosary was entwined in her fingers, but her rings had been removed. Her lips were very pale. David stood over her and touched his fingers to her hand. She felt cold, and damp.

His father appeared beside him. They were the only ones left in the room. Everyone else had gone outside. A car was waiting to take David and his father to the church. It was big and black. The man who drove it wore a peaked cap and never smiled.

"You can kiss her good-bye, son," his father said. David looked up at him. His father's eyes were moist, and rimmed with red.

His father had cried that first day, when David returned home from school and he held him in his arms and promised him that everything would be all right, but he had not cried again until now. David watched as a big tear welled up and slid slowly, almost embarrassedly, down his cheek. He turned back to his mother. He leaned into the casket and kissed her face. She smelled of chemicals and something else, something David didn't want to think about. He could taste it on her lips.

"Good-bye, Mum," he whispered. His eyes stung. He wanted to do something, but he didn't know what.

His father placed a hand on David's shoulder, then lowered himself down and kissed David's mother softly on the mouth. He pressed the side of his face to hers and whispered something that David could not hear. Then they left her, and when the coffin appeared again, carried by the undertaker and his assistants, it was closed and the only sign that it held David's mother was the little metal plate on the lid bearing her name and the dates of her birth and death.

They left her alone in the church that night. If he could, David would have stayed with her. He wondered if she was lonely, if she knew where she was, if she was already in heaven or if that didn't happen until the priest said the final words and the coffin was put in the ground. He didn't like to think of her all by herself in there, sealed up by wood and brass and nails, but he couldn't talk to his father about it. His father wouldn't under-stand, and it wouldn't change anything anyway. He couldn't stay in the church by himself, so instead he went to his room and tried to imagine what it must be like for her. He drew the curtains on his window and closed the bedroom door so that it was as dark as he could make it inside, then climbed under his bed.

The bed was low, and the space beneath it was very narrow. It occupied one corner of the room, so David squeezed over until he felt his left hand touch the wall, then closed his eyes tightly shut and lay very still. After a while, he tried to lift his head. It bumped hard upon the slats that supported his mattress. He pushed against them, but they were nailed in place. He tried to lift the bed by pressing upward with his hands, but it was too heavy. He smelled dust and his chamber pot. He started to cough. His eyes watered. He decided to get out from under the bed, but it had been easier to shuffle into his current position than it was to pull himself out again. He sneezed, and his head banged painfully against the underside of his bed. He started to panic. His bare feet scrambled for some purchase on the wooden floor. He reached up and used the slats to pull himself along until he was close enough to the edge of the bed to squeeze out again. He climbed to his feet and leaned against the wall, breathing deeply.

That was what death was like: trapped in a small space with a big weight holding you down for all eternity.

His mother was buried on a January morning. The ground was hard, and all of the mourners wore gloves and overcoats. The coffin looked too short when they lowered it into the dirt. His mother had always seemed tall in life. Death had made her small.

In the weeks that followed, David tried to lose himself in books, because his memories of his mother were inextricably interwoven with books and reading. Her books, the ones deemed "suitable," were passed on to him, and he found himself trying to read novels that he did not understand, and poems that did not quite rhyme. He would ask his father about them sometimes, but David's father seemed to have little interest in books. He had always spent his time at home with his head buried in newspapers, little plumes of pipe smoke rising above the pages like signals sent by Indians. He was obsessed with the comings and goings of the modern world, more so than ever now that Hitler's armies were moving across Europe and the threat of attacks on their own land was growing ever more real. David's mother once said that his father used to read a lot of books but had fallen out of the habit of losing himself in stories. Now he preferred his newspapers, with their long columns of print, each letter painstakingly laid out by hand to create something that would lose its relevance almost as soon as it appeared on the newsstands, the news within already old and dying by the time it was read, quickly overtaken by events in the world beyond.

The stories in books *hate* the stories contained in newspapers, David's mother would say. Newspaper stories were like newly caught fish, worthy of attention only for as long as they remained fresh, which was not very long at all. They were like the street urchins hawking the evening editions, all shouty and insistent, while stories—real stories, proper made-up stories—were like stern but helpful librarians in a well-stocked library. Newspaper stories were as insubstantial as smoke, as long-lived as mayflies. They did not take root but were instead like weeds that crawled along the ground, stealing the sunlight from more deserving tales. David's father's mind was always occupied by shrill, competing voices, each one silenced as soon as he gave it his attention, only for its clamor to be instantly replaced by another. That was what David's mother would whisper to him with a smile, while his father scowled and bit his pipe, aware that they were talking about him but unwilling to give them the pleasure of knowing they were irritating him.

And so it was left to David to safeguard his mother's books, and he added them to those that had been bought with him in mind. They were the tales of knights and soldiers, of dragons and sea beasts, folk tales and fairy tales, because these were the stories that David's mother had loved as a girl and that he in turn had read to her as the illness gradually took hold of her, reducing her voice to a whisper and her breaths to the rasp of old sandpaper on decaying wood, until at last the effort was too much for her and she breathed no more. After her death, he tried to avoid these old tales, for they were linked too closely to his mother to be enjoyed, but the stories would not be so easily denied, and they began to call to David. They seemed to recognize something in him, or so he started to believe, something curious and fertile. He heard them talking: softly at first, then louder and more compellingly.

These stories were very old, as old as people, and they had survived because they were very powerful indeed. These were the tales that echoed in the head long after the books that contained them were cast aside. They were both an escape from reality and an alternative reality themselves. They were so old, and so strange, that they had found a kind of existence independent of the pages they occupied. The world of the old tales existed parallel to ours, as David's mother had once told him, but sometimes the wall separating the two became so thin and brittle that the two worlds started to blend into each other.

That was when the trouble started.

That was when the bad things came.

That was when the Crooked Man began to appear to David.

II

Of Rose and Dr. Moberley, and the Importance of Details

T WAS A STRANGE THING, but shortly after his mother died, David remembered experiencing a sense almost of relief. There was no other word for it, and it made David feel bad about himself. His mother was gone, and she was never coming back. It didn't matter what the priest said in his sermon: that David's mother was now in a better, happier place, and her pain was at an end. It didn't help when he told David that his mother would always be with him, even if he couldn't see her. An unseen mother couldn't go for long walks with you on summer evenings, drawing the names of trees and flowers from her seemingly infinite knowledge of nature; or help you with your homework, the familiar scent of her in your nostrils as she leaned in to correct a misspelling or puzzle over the meaning of an unfamiliar poem; or read with you on cold Sunday afternoons when the fire was burning and the rain was beating down upon the windows and the roof and the room was filled with the smell of woodsmoke and crumpets.

But then David recalled that, in those final months, his mother had not been able to do any of those things. The drugs that the doctors gave her made her groggy and ill. She couldn't concentrate, not even on the simplest of tasks, and she certainly couldn't go for long walks. Sometimes, toward the end, David was not even sure that she knew who he was anymore. She started to smell funny: not bad, just odd, like old clothes that hadn't been worn in a very long time. During the night she would cry out in pain, and David's father would hold her and try to comfort her. When she was very sick, the doctor would be called. Eventually she was too ill to stay in her own room, and an ambulance came and took her to a hospital that wasn't quite a hospital because nobody ever seemed to get well and nobody ever went home again. Instead, they just got quieter and quieter until at last there was only total silence and empty beds where they used to lie.

The not-quite-hospital was a long way from their house, but David's dad visited every other evening after he returned home from work and he and David had eaten their dinner together. David went with him in their old Ford Eight at least twice each week, even though the journey back and forth left him with very little time for himself once he'd completed his homework and eaten his dinner. It made his father tired too, and David wondered how he found the energy to get up each morning, make breakfast for David, see him off to school before heading to work, come home, make tea, help David with any schoolwork that was proving difficult, visit David's mother, return home again, kiss David good night, and then read the paper for an hour before taking himself off to bed.

Once, David had woken up in the night, his throat very dry, and had gone downstairs to fetch a drink of water. He heard snoring in the sitting room and looked in to find his father asleep in his armchair, the paper fallen apart around him and his head hanging unsupported over the edge of the chair. It was three o'clock in the morning. David hadn't been sure what to do, but in the end he woke his father up because he remembered how he himself had once fallen asleep awkwardly in the train on a long journey and his neck had hurt for days afterward. His father had looked a little surprised, and just slightly angry, at being woken up, but he'd roused himself from the chair and gone upstairs to sleep. Still, David was sure that it wasn't the first time he'd fallen asleep like that, fully clothed and nowhere near his bed.

So when David's mother died, it meant that there was no more pain for her but also no more long journeys to and from the big yellow building where people faded away to nothing, no more sleeping in chairs, no more rushed dinners. Instead, there was only the kind of silence that comes when someone takes away a clock to be repaired and after a time you become aware of its absence because its gentle, reassuring tick is gone and you miss it so.

But the feeling of relief went away after only a few days, and then David felt guilty for being glad that they no longer had to do all the things his mother's illness had required of them, and in the months that followed the guilt did not disappear. Instead it got worse and worse, and David began to wish that his mother was still in the hospital. If she had been there, he would have visited her every day, even if it meant getting up earlier in the mornings to finish his homework, because now he couldn't bear to think of life without her.

School became more difficult for him. He drifted away from his friends, even before summer came and its warm breezes scattered them like dandelion seeds. There was talk that all of the boys would be evacuated from London and sent to the countryside when school resumed in September, but David's father had promised him he would not be sent away. After all, his father had said, it was just the two of them now, and they had to stick together.

His father employed a lady, Mrs. Howard, to keep the house

clean and to do a little cooking and ironing. She was usually there when David came home from school, but Mrs. Howard was too busy to talk to him. She was training with the ARP, the Air Raid Precautions wardens, as well as taking care of her own husband and children, so she didn't have time to chat with David or to ask him how his day had been.

Mrs. Howard would leave just after four o'clock, and David's father would not return from work at the university until six at the earliest, and sometimes even later than that. This meant that David was stuck in the empty house with only the wireless and his books for company. Sometimes, he would sit in the bedroom that his father and mother had once shared. Her clothes were still in one of the wardrobes, the dresses and skirts lined up in such neat rows that they almost looked like people themselves if you squinted hard enough. David would run his fingers along them and make them swish, remembering as he did so that they had moved in just that way when his mother walked in them. Then he would lie back on the pillow to the left, for that was the side on which his mother used to sleep, and try to rest his head against the same spot on which she had once rested her head, the place obvious from the slightly dark stain upon the pillowcase.

This new world was too painful to cope with. He had tried so hard. He had kept to his routines. He had counted so carefully. He had abided by the rules, but life had cheated. This world was not like the world of his stories. In that world, good was rewarded and evil was punished. If you kept to the path and stayed out of the forest, then you would be safe. If someone was sick, like the old king in one of the tales, then his sons could be sent out into the world to seek the remedy, the Water of Life, and if just one of them was brave enough and true enough, then the king's life could be saved. David had been brave. His mother had been braver still. In the end, bravery had not been enough. This was a world that did not reward it. The more David thought about it, the more he did not want to be part of such a world.

He still kept to his routines, although not quite as rigidly as he once did. He was content merely to touch the doorknobs and taps twice, left hand first, then right hand, just to keep the numbers even. He still tried to put his left foot down first on the floor in the mornings, or on the stairs of the house, but that wasn't so difficult. He wasn't sure what would happen now if he didn't adhere to his rules to some degree. He supposed that it might affect his father. Perhaps, in sticking to his routines, he had saved his father's life, even if he hadn't quite managed to save his mother. Now that it was just the two of them, it was important not to take too many chances.

And that was when Rose entered his life, and the attacks began.

The first time was in Trafalgar Square, when he and his father were walking down to feed the pigeons after Sunday lunch at the Popular Café in Piccadilly. His father said that the Popular was due to close soon, which made David sad as he thought it was very grand.

David's mother had been dead for five months, three weeks, and four days. A woman had joined them to eat at the Popular that day. His father had introduced her to David as Rose. Rose was very thin, with long, dark hair and bright red lips. Her clothes looked expensive, and gold and diamonds glittered at her ears and throat. She claimed to eat very little, although she finished most of her chicken that afternoon and had plenty of room for pudding afterward. She looked familiar to David, and it emerged that she was the administrator of the not-quite-hospital in which his mother had died. His father told David that Rose had looked after his mother really, really well, although not, David thought, well enough to keep her from dying.

Rose tried to speak with David about school and his friends and what he liked to do with his evenings, but David could barely manage to respond. He didn't like the way that she looked at his father or the way that she called him by his first name. He didn't like the way that she touched his hand when he said something funny or clever. He didn't even like the fact that his father was try-ing to be funny and clever with her to begin with. It wasn't right.

Rose held on to his father's arm as they strolled from the restaurant. David walked a little ahead of them, and they seemed content to let him go. He wasn't sure what was happening, or that was what he told himself. Instead he silently accepted a bag of seeds from his father when they reached Trafalgar Square, and he used them to draw the pigeons to him. The pigeons bobbed obe-diently toward this new source of food, their feathers stained with the muck and soot of the city, their eyes vacant and stupid. His father and Rose stood nearby, talking quietly to each other. When they thought he wasn't looking, David saw them kiss briefly.

That was when it happened. One moment David's arm was outstretched, a thin line of seed spread along it and two rather heavy pigeons pecking away at his sleeve, and the next he was lying flat on the ground, his father's coat beneath his head and curious onlookers—and the odd pigeon—staring down at him, fat clouds scudding behind their heads like blank thought bal-loons. His father told him that he had fainted, and David sup-posed that he must have been right, except there were now voices and whispers in his head where no voices and whispers had been before, and he had a fading memory of a wooded landscape and the howling of wolves. He heard Rose ask if she could do any-thing to help, and David's father told her that it was all right, that he would take him home and put him to bed. His father hailed a cab to bring them back to their car. Before he left, he told Rose he would telephone her later.

That night, as David lay in his room, the whispers in his head were joined by the sound of the books. He had to put his pillow over his ears to drown out the noise of their chatter, as the oldest of the stories roused themselves from their night slumbers and began to look for places in which to grow.

Dr. Moberley's office was in a terraced house on a tree-lined street in the center of London, and it was very quiet. There were expensive carpets on the floors, and the walls were decorated with pictures of ships at sea. An elderly secretary with very white hair sat behind a desk in the waiting room, shuffling papers, typing letters, and taking telephone calls. David sat on a big sofa nearby, his father beside him. A grandfather clock ticked in the corner. David and his father didn't speak. Mostly it was because the room was so quiet that anything they said would have been overheard by the lady behind the desk, but David also felt that his father was angry with him.

There had been two more attacks since Trafalgar Square, each one longer than the last and each leaving David with more strange images in his mind: a castle with banners fluttering from the walls, a forest filled with trees that bled redly from their bark, and a half-glimpsed figure, hunched and wretched, who moved through the shadows of this strange world, waiting. David's father had taken him to see their family doctor, Dr. Benson, but Dr. Benson had been unable to find anything wrong with David. He sent David to a specialist at a big hospital, who shone lights in David's eyes and examined his skull. He asked David some questions, then asked David's father many more, some of them concerning David's mother and her death. David had then been told to wait outside while they talked, and when David's father came out, he looked angry. That was how they had ended up at Dr. Moberley's office.

Dr. Moberley was a psychiatrist.

A buzzer sounded beside the secretary's desk, and she nodded to David and his father. "He can go in now," she said.

"Off you go," said David's father.

"Aren't you coming in with me?" asked David.

David's father shook his head, and David knew that he had already spoken with Dr. Moberley, perhaps over the telephone.

"He wants to see you alone. Don't worry. I'll be here when you're finished."

David followed the secretary into another room. It was much bigger and grander than the waiting room, furnished with soft chairs and couches. The walls were lined with books, although they were not books like the ones David read. David thought that he could hear the books talking among themselves when he arrived. He couldn't understand most of what they were saying, but they spoke v-e-r-y s-l-o-w-l-y, as if what they had to impart was very important or the person to whom they were speaking was very stupid. Some of the books appeared to be arguing among themselves in blah-blah-blah tones, the way experts sometimes talked on the wireless when they were addressing one another, surrounded by other experts whom they were trying to impress with their intelligence.

The books made David very uneasy.

A small man with gray hair and a gray beard sat behind an antique desk that looked too big for him. He wore rectangular glasses with a gold chain to keep him from losing them. A red and black bow tie was knotted tightly at his neck, and his suit was dark and baggy.

"Welcome," he said. "I'm Dr. Moberley. You must be David."

David nodded. Dr. Moberley asked David to sit down, then flicked through the pages of a notebook on his desk, tugging on his beard while he read whatever was written on them. When he had finished, he looked up and asked David how he was. David said he was fine. Dr. Moberley asked him if he was sure. David said that he was reasonably sure. Dr. Moberley said David's dad was worried about him. He asked David if he missed his mum. David didn't answer. Dr. Moberley told David that he was worried about David's attacks, and they were going to try to find out together what was behind them.

Dr. Moberley gave David a box of pencils and asked him to draw a picture of a house. David took a lead pencil and carefully drew the walls and the chimney, then put in some windows and a door before he set to work adding little curved slates to the roof. He was quite lost in the act of drawing slates when Dr. Moberley told him that was quite enough. Dr. Moberley looked at the picture, then looked at David. He asked David if he hadn't thought of using colored pencils. David told him that the drawing wasn't finished, and that once the tiles were added to the roof he planned to color them red. Dr. Moberley asked David, in the v-e-r-y s-l-o-w way that some of his books spoke, why the slates were so important.

David wondered if Dr. Moberley was a real doctor. Doctors were supposed to be very clever. Dr. Moberley didn't seem terribly clever. V-e-r-y s-l-o-w-ly, David explained that without slates on the roof the rain would get in. In their way, they were just as important as walls. Dr. Moberley asked David if he was afraid of the rain getting in. David told him that he didn't like getting wet. It wasn't so bad outside, especially if you were dressed for it, but most people didn't dress for rain indoors.

Dr. Moberley looked a bit confused.

Next, he asked David to draw a tree. Again, David took the pencil, painstakingly drew the branches, then proceeded to add little leaves to each one. He was on only the third branch when Dr. Moberley asked him to stop again. This time, Dr. Moberley had the kind of expression on his face that David's father sometimes had when he managed to finish the crossword in the Sunday paper. Short of standing up and shouting "Aha!" with his finger pointing in the air, the way mad scientists did in cartoons, he couldn't have looked more pleased with himself.

Dr. Moberley then asked David a lot of questions about his home, his mum, and his dad. He asked again about the blackouts, and if David could remember anything about them. How did he feel before they happened? Did he smell anything strange before he lost consciousness? Did his head hurt afterward? Did his head hurt before? Did his head hurt now?

But he did not ask the most important question of all, in David's view, because Dr. Moberley chose to believe that the attacks caused David to black out entirely and that the boy could remember nothing of them before he regained consciousness. That wasn't true. David thought about telling Dr. Moberley of the strange landscapes that he saw when the attacks came, but Dr. Moberley had already begun asking about his mother again and David didn't want to talk about his mother, not any more and certainly not with a stranger. Dr. Moberley asked about Rose too, and how David felt about her. David didn't know how to answer. He didn't like Rose, and he didn't like his father being with her, but he didn't want to tell Dr. Moberley that in case he told David's father about it.

By the end of the session, David was crying and he didn't even know why. In fact, he was crying so hard that his nose began to bleed, and the sight of the blood frightened him. He started to scream and shout. He fell on the floor, and a white light flashed in his head as he began to tremble. He beat his fists on the carpet and heard the books tut-tutting their disapproval as Dr. Moberley called for help and David's dad came rushing in and then everything went dark for what seemed like only seconds but was in fact a very long time indeed.

And David heard a woman's voice in the darkness, and he thought it sounded like his mother. A figure approached, but it was not a woman. It was a man, a crooked man with a long face, emerging at last from the shadows of his world.

And he was smiling.

III

Of the New House, the New Child, and the New King

HIS IS how things came to pass.

Rose was pregnant. His father told David as they ate chips by the Thames, boats bustling by and the smell of oil and seaweed mixing in the air. It was November 1939. There were more policemen on the streets than before, and men in uniform were everywhere. Sandbags were piled against windows, and great lengths of barbed wire lay coiled around like vicious springs. Humpbacked Anderson shelters dotted gardens, and trenches had been dug in parks. There seemed to be white posters on every available space: reminders of lighting restrictions, proclamations from the king, all of the instructions for a country at war.

Most of the children David knew had by now left the city, thronging train stations with little brown luggage labels tied to their coats on their way to farms and strange towns. Their absence made the city appear emptier and increased the sense of nervous expectancy that seemed to govern the lives of all who remained. Soon, the bombers would come, and the city was shrouded in darkness at night to make their task harder. The blackout made the city so dark that it was possible to pick out the craters of the moon, and the heavens were crowded with stars.

On their way to the river, they saw more barrage balloons being inflated in Hyde Park. When these were fully inflated, they would hang in the air, anchored by heavy steel cables. The cables would prevent the German bombers from flying low, which meant that they would have to drop their payloads from a greater height. That way, the bombers would not be as certain of hitting their targets.

The balloons were shaped like enormous bombs. David's father said it was ironic, and David asked him what he meant. His father said it was just funny that something that was supposed to protect the city from bombs and bombers should look like a bomb itself. David nodded. He supposed that it was strange. He thought of the men in the German bombers, the pilots trying to avoid the anti-aircraft fire from below, one man crouched over the bombsight while the city passed beneath him. He wondered if he ever thought of the people in the houses and the factories before he released the bombs. From high in the air, London would look just like a model, with toy houses and miniature trees on tiny streets. Maybe that was the only way you could drop the bombs: by pretending that it wasn't real, that nobody would burn and die when they exploded below.

David tried to imagine himself in a bomber—a British one, perhaps a Wellington or a Whitley—flying over a German city, bombs at the ready. Would he be able to release the load? It was a war after all. The Germans were bad. Everybody knew that. They had started it. It was like a playground fight: if you started it, then you were to blame, and you couldn't really complain about what happened afterward. David thought that he would release the bombs, but he wouldn't think about the possibility that there might be people below. There would just be factories and shipyards, shapes in the darkness, and everyone employed in them would be safely tucked up in bed when the bombs fell and blew apart their places of work.

A thought struck him.

"Dad? If the Germans can't aim properly because of the balloons, then their bombs could drop just anywhere, right? I mean, they'll be trying to hit factories, won't they, but they won't be able to, so they'll just let them go and hope for the best. They're not going to go home and come back another night just because of the balloons."

David's father didn't reply for a moment or two.

"I don't think they care," he said at last. "They want people to lose their spirit and their hope. If they blow up airplane factories or shipyards along the way, then so much the better. That's how a certain type of bully works. He softens you up before going in for the killer blow."

He sighed. "We need to talk about something, David, something important."

They had just come from another session with Dr. Moberley, during which David was asked again if he missed his mother. Of course he missed her. It was a stupid question. He missed her, and he was sad because of it. He didn't need a doctor to tell him that. He had trouble understanding what Dr. Moberley was saying most of the time anyway, partly because the doctor used words that David didn't understand, but mostly because his voice was now almost entirely drowned out by the dronings of the books on his shelves.

The sounds made by books had become clearer and clearer to David. He understood that Dr. Moberley couldn't hear them the way he could, otherwise he couldn't have worked in his office without going mad. Sometimes, when Dr. Moberley asked a question of which the books approved, they would all say

"Hmmmmm" in unison, like a male voice choir practicing a single note. If he said something of which they disapproved, they would mutter insults at him.

"Clown!"

"Charlatan!"

"Poppycock!"

"The man's an idiot."

One book, with the name Jung engraved on its cover in gold letters, grew so irate that it toppled itself from the shelf and lay on the carpet, fuming. Dr. Moberley looked quite surprised when it fell. David was tempted to tell him what the book was saying, but he didn't think it would be a very good idea to let Dr. Moberley know that he heard books talking. David had heard of people being "put away" because they were "wrong in the head." David didn't want to be put away. Anyway, he didn't hear the books talking all of the time now. It was only when he was upset or angry. David tried to stay calm, to think about good things as much as he could, but it was hard sometimes, especially when he was with Dr. Moberley, or Rose.

Now he was sitting by the river, and his whole world was about to change again.

"You're going to have a little brother or sister," David's father said. "Rose is going to have a baby."

David stopped eating his chips. They tasted wrong. He felt pressure building in his head, and for a moment he thought he might topple from the bench and suffer another of his attacks, but somehow he made himself stay upright.

"Are you going to marry Rose?" he asked.

"I expect so," said his father. David had heard Rose and his father discussing the subject the previous week, when Rose had come to visit and David was supposed to be in bed. Instead, he had sat on the stairs and listened to them talking. He did that, sometimes, although he always went to bed when the talking ceased and he heard the smack of a kiss, or Rose laughing in a low, throaty way. The last time he'd listened, Rose had spoken about "people" and how these "people" were talking. She didn't like what they were saying. That was when the subject of marriage came up, but David didn't hear any more because his father left the room to put the kettle on and David only barely avoided being seen on the stairs. He thought his father might have suspected something because he came upstairs to check on David moments later. He kept his eyes closed and pretended to be asleep, which seemed to satisfy his father, but David was too nervous to go back to the stairs again.

"I just want you to know something, David," his father was saying to him. "I love you, and that will never change, no matter who else we share our life with. I loved your mum too, and I'll always love her, but being with Rose has helped me a lot these last few months. She's a nice person, David. She likes you. Try to give her a chance, won't you?"

David didn't reply. He swallowed hard. He had always wanted a brother or sister, but not like this. He wanted it to be with his mum and dad. This wasn't right. This wouldn't really be his brother or sister. It would come out of Rose. It wouldn't be the same.

His father placed his arm around David's shoulder. "Well, do you have anything to say?" he asked.

"I'd like to go home now," said David.

His father kept his arm around David for a second or two more, then let it drop. He seemed to sag slightly, as though some-one had just let a little air out of him.

"Fine," he said sadly. "Let's go home then."

Six months later, Rose gave birth to a little boy, and David and his father left the house in which David had grown up and went to live with Rose and David's new half brother, Georgie. Rose lived in a great big old house northwest of London, three stories high with large gardens at front and back and forest surrounding it. The house had been in her family for generations, according to David's father, and was at least three times as big as their own house. David had not wanted to move at first, but his father had gently explained the reasons to him. It was closer to his new place of work, and because of the war he was going to have to spend more and more time there. If they lived closer to it, then he would be able to see David more often, and perhaps even come home for his lunch sometimes. His father also told David that the city was going to become more dangerous, and that out here they would all be a little safer. The German planes were coming, and while David's father was sure that Hitler would be beaten in the end, things were going to get much worse before they got better.

David was not entirely sure what his father now did for a living. He knew that his dad was very good at math, and that he had been a teacher at a big university until recently. Then he had left the university and gone to work for the government in an old country house outside the city. There were army barracks nearby, and soldiers manned the gates that led to the house and patrolled its grounds. Usually when David asked his father about his work, he would just tell him that it involved checking figures for the government. But on the day that they finally moved from their house to Rose's, his father seemed to feel that David was owed something more.

"I know that you like stories and books," his father said, as they followed the moving van out of the city. "I suppose you wonder why I don't like them as much as you do. Well, I do like stories, in a way, and that's part of my job. You know how sometimes a story seems to be about one thing, but in fact it's about another thing entirely? There's a meaning hidden in it, and that meaning has to be teased out?"

"Like Bible stories," said David. On Sundays, the priest would often explain the Bible story that had just been read out loud. David didn't always listen because the priest was very dull indeed, but it was surprising what the priest could see in stories that seemed quite simple to David. In fact, the priest appeared to like making them more complicated than they were, probably because it meant that he could talk for longer. David didn't care much for church. He was still angry at God for what had happened to his mother, and for bringing Rose and Georgie into his life.

"But some stories aren't meant to have their meaning understood by just anyone," David's father continued. "They're meant for only a handful of people, and so the meaning is very carefully hidden. It can be done using words, or numbers, or sometimes both together, but the purpose is the same. It's to prevent anyone else who sees it from interpreting it. Unless you know the code, it has no meaning.

"Well, the Germans use codes to send messages. So do we. Some of them are very complicated, and some of them appear very simple, although often those are the most complicated of all. Someone has to try to figure them out, and that's what I do. I try to understand the secret meanings of stories written by people who don't want me to understand them."

He turned to David and laid a hand on his shoulder. "I'm trusting you with this," he said. "You must never tell anyone else what it is that I do."

He raised a finger to his lips. "Top secret, old chap."

David imitated the gesture.

"Top secret," he echoed.

And they drove on.

*   *   *

David's bedroom was at the very top of the house, in a little, low room that Rose had chosen for him because it was filled with books and bookshelves. David's own books found themselves sharing the shelves with other books that were older or stranger than they were. He made space for his books as best he could, eventually settling on ordering the books on the shelves according to size and color, because they looked better that way. It meant his books kept getting mixed up with those that were already there, so one book of fairy tales ended up squeezed between a history of communism and an examination of the last battles of the First World War. David had tried to read a little of the book on communism, mainly because he wasn't entirely sure what communism was (apart from the fact that his father seemed to think it was something very bad indeed). He managed to get about three pages into it before he lost interest, its talk of "workers' ownership of the means of production" and "the predation of capitalists" almost putting him to sleep. The history of the First World War was a little better, if only for the many drawings of old tanks that had been cut out of an illustrated magazine and stuck between various pages. There was also a dull textbook of French vocabulary, and a book about the Roman Empire that had some very interesting drawings in it and seemed to take a lot of pleasure in describing the cruel things that the Romans did to people and that other people did to the Romans in return.

David's book of Greek myths, meanwhile, was the same size and color as a collection of poetry nearby, and he would sometimes pull out the poems instead of the myths. Some of the poems weren't too bad, once he gave them a chance. One was about a kind of knight—except in the poem he was called a "Childe"—and his search for a dark tower and whatever secret it contained. The poem didn't really seem to end properly, though. The knight reached the tower and, well, that was it. David wanted to know what was in the tower, and what happened to the knight now that he'd reached it, but the poet obviously didn't think that was important. It made David wonder about the kinds of people who wrote poems. Anyone could see that the poem was really only getting interesting when the knight reached the tower, but that was the point at which the poet decided to go off and write something else instead. Perhaps he had meant to come back to it and had simply forgotten, or maybe he couldn't come up with a monster for the tower that was impressive enough. David had a vision of the poet, surrounded by bits of paper with lots of ideas for creatures crossed out or scribbled over.

~~Werewolf.~~
~~Dragon.~~
~~Really big dragon.~~
~~Witch.~~
~~Really big witch.~~
~~Small witch.~~

David tried to give a form to the beast at the heart of the poem but found that he could not. It was more difficult than it appeared, for nothing quite seemed to fit. Instead, he could only conjure up a half-formed being that crouched in the cobwebbed corners of his imagination where all the things that he feared curled and slithered upon one another in the darkness.

David was aware of a change in the room as soon as he began to fill the empty spaces on the shelves, the newer books looking and sounding uneasy beside these other works from the past. Their appearance was intimidating, and they spoke to David in dusty, rumbling tones. The older books were bound in calfskin and leather, and some of them contained knowledge that had long been forgotten, or that was found to be incorrect as science and the process of discovery uncovered new truths. The books that held this old knowledge had never come to terms with this relegation of their worth. They were now lower than stories, for stories were intended, at some level, to be made up and untrue, but these other books had been born for greater things. Men and women had worked hard on their creation, filling them with the sum total of all that they knew and all that they believed about the world. That they were misguided, and the assumptions they made were now largely worthless, was almost impossible for the books to bear.

A great book that claimed that the end of the world, based on a close examination of the Bible, would occur in 1783, had largely retreated into madness, refusing to believe that the present date was any later than 1782, for to do so would be to admit that its contents were wrong and that its existence therefore had no purpose beyond that of a mere curiosity. A slim work on the current civilizations of Mars, written by a man with a large telescope and an eye that discerned the paths of canals where no canals had ever flowed, gabbled constantly about how the Martians had retreated below the surface and were now building great engines in secret. It currently occupied a position among a number of books on sign language for the deaf, which, fortunately, could not hear anything that was being said to them.

But David also discovered books that were similar to his own. There were thick, illustrated volumes of fairy stories and folk tales, the colors still rich and full within, and it was to these works that David turned his attention in those first days in his new home, lying on the window seat and staring down occasionally upon the forest beyond, as though expecting the wolves and witches and ogres from the stories suddenly to materialize below, for the descriptions in the books matched so accurately the woods bordering the house that it was almost impossible to believe they were not one and the same, an impression strengthened by the nature of the books' construction, for some of their stories had been added to by hand and the drawings within had been carefully created by someone with no small talent for their art. David could find no name upon the books to identify the author of the additions, and some of the tales were unfamiliar to him while still retaining echoes of the tales he knew almost by heart.

In one story, a princess was forced to dance all night and sleep all day by the actions of a sorcerer, but instead of being rescued by the intervention of a prince or a clever servant, the princess died, only for her ghost to return and torment the sorcerer to such a degree that he threw himself into a chasm in the earth and was burned to death in its fires. A little girl was threatened by a wolf while walking through the forest, and as she fled from him she met a woodsman with an ax, but in this story the woodsman did not merely kill the wolf and restore the girl to her family, oh no. He cut off the wolf's head, then brought the girl to his cottage in the thickest, darkest part of the forest, and there he kept her until she was old enough to wed him, and she became his bride in a ceremony conducted by an owl, even though she had never stopped crying for her parents in all the years that he had kept her prisoner. And she had children by him, and the woodsman raised them to hunt wolves and to seek out people who strayed from the paths of the forest. They were told to kill the men and take what was valuable from their pockets, but to bring the women to him.

David read the stories by day and by night, his blankets drawn around him to protect him from the cold, for Rose's house was never warm. The wind found its way in through cracks in the window frames and the ill-fitting doors, rustling the pages of open books as though seeking within some piece of knowledge that it desperately required for its own purposes. The great sweeps of ivy that covered the house, front and back, had broken through the walls over the decades, so that tendrils crept from the upper corners of David's room, or bound themselves to the underside of the windowsill. At first, David had tried to cut them with his scissors, discarding the remnants, but after a few days the ivy would return, seemingly thicker and longer than before, clinging ever more tenaciously to the wood and the plaster. Insects exploited the holes too, so that the boundary between the natural world and the world of the house became blurred and unclear. He found beetles congregating in the closet, and earwigs exploring his sock drawer. At night, he heard mice scurrying behind the boards. It was as if nature was claiming David's room as its own.

Worse, when he slept he dreamed more often of the creature he had named the Crooked Man, who walked through forests very like the one beyond David's window. The Crooked Man would advance to the edge of the tree line, staring out at an expanse of green lawn to where a house just like Rose's stood. He would speak to David in his dreams. His smile was mocking, and his words made no sense to David.

"We are waiting," he would say. "Welcome, Your Majesty. All hail the new king!"

IV

Of Jonathan Tulvey and Billy Golding, and Men Who Dwell by Railway Tracks

AVID'S ROOM was curious in its construction. The ceiling was quite low and rather higgledy-piggledy, sloping in places where it should not have sloped and providing ample opportunity for industrious spiders to spin their webs. On more than one occasion David, in his urge to explore the darker corners of the bookshelves, had found himself wearing strands of spider silk in his face and hair, causing the web's resident to scuttle into a corner and crouch balefully, lost in thoughts of arachnid revenge. There was a wooden toy box in one corner, and a large wardrobe in the other. Between them stood a chest of drawers with a mirror on top. The room was painted light blue so that on a bright day it seemed like part of the world outside, especially with the ivy poking through the walls and the occasional insect providing food for the spiders.

The single small window overlooked the lawn and the woods. If he stood on his window seat, David could also see the spire of a church and the roofs of the houses in the nearby village. London lay to the south, but it might as well have been in Antarctica, so completely did the trees and the forest hide the house from the outside world. The window seat was David's favorite place in which to read. The books still whispered and spoke among themselves, but he was now able to hush them with a single word if his mood was right, and anyway they tended to remain quiet while he was reading. It was as if they were happy once he was consuming stories.

It was summer once again, so David had plenty of time to read. His father had tried to encourage him to make friends with the children who lived nearby, some of them evacuees from the city, but David did not want to mix with them, and they in turn saw something sad and distant in him that kept them away. Instead, the books took their place. The old books of fairy tales in particular, so strange and sinister with their handwritten additions and new paintings, had increased David's fascination with these stories. They still reminded him of his mother, but in a good way, and whatever reminded him of his mother equally helped to keep Rose and *her* son, Georgie, at a distance. When he was not reading, the window seat gave him a perfect view of one of the property's other curiosities: the sunken garden set into the lawn close to where the trees began.

It looked a little like an empty swimming pool, with a set of four stone steps leading down to a rectangle of green, bordered by a flagstoned pathway. While the grass was regularly mown by Mr. Briggs the gardener, who came every Thursday to tend the plants and lend nature a helping hand where necessary, the stone parts of the sunken garden had fallen into disrepair. There were large cracks in the walls, and in one corner the stonework had crumbled away entirely, leaving a gap big enough for David to squeeze through, if he had chosen to do so. David had never gone further than poking his head in, though. The space beyond was dark and musty, and filled with all kinds of hidden, scurrying things. David's father had suggested that the sunken garden might make a suitable site for an air-raid shelter, if they decided it should ever become necessary, but so far he had managed only to pile sandbags and sheets of corrugated iron in the garden shed, much to the annoyance of Mr. Briggs, who now had to navigate his way around them every time he wanted to reach his tools. The sunken garden became David's own place outside the house, especially when he wanted to get away from the whispering of the books or from Rose's well-intentioned but unwelcome intrusions into his life.

David's relations with Rose were not good. While he tried always to be polite, as his father had asked him to be, he did not like her, and he resented the fact that she was now part of his world. It was not merely that she had taken, or was trying to take, the place of his mother, although that was bad enough. Her attempts to cook meals that he liked for dinner, despite the pressures of rationing, irritated him. She wanted David to like her, and that made him dislike her even more.

But David believed that her presence also distracted his father from the memory of David's mother. He was forgetting about her already, so tied up was he with Rose and their new baby. Little Georgie was a demanding child. He cried a lot and always seemed to be ailing, so that the local doctor was a regular visitor to the house. His father and Rose doted on him, even as he deprived them of sleep almost every night, leaving them both short-tempered and weary. The result was that David was increasingly left to his own devices, which made him both grateful for the freedom offered by Georgie and resentful of the lack of attention to his own needs. In any case, it gave him more time to read, and that was no bad thing.

But as David's fascination with the old books grew, so did his desire to find out more about their former owner, for they had clearly belonged to someone who was just like him. He had at last found a name, Jonathan Tulvey, written inside the covers of two of the books, and he was curious to learn something about him.

So it was that one day David swallowed his dislike of Rose and went down to the kitchen, where she was working. Mrs. Briggs, the housekeeper and wife of Mr. Briggs, the gardener, was visiting her sister in Eastbourne, so Rose was taking care of the chores for the day. From outside came the clucking of hens in the chicken run. David had helped Mr. Briggs to feed them earlier, and to check the vegetable garden for damage from rabbits and the run for any holes that might allow a fox to enter. The week before, Mr. Briggs had trapped and killed a fox near the house using a snare. The fox had almost been decapitated by the trap, and David had said something about feeling sorry for it. Mr. Briggs had scolded him, pointing out that one fox would kill every hen they had if he managed to get into the run, but David had still been troubled by the sight of the dead animal, its tongue caught between its small, sharp teeth, its fur torn from where it had tried to bite itself free from the snare.

David made himself a glass of Borwick's lemon barley before sitting at the head of the table and asking Rose how she was. Rose stopped washing the dishes and turned around to speak with him, her face bright with pleasure and surprise. David had planned to try very hard to be nice in the hope of finding out more from her, but Rose, unused to any conversation with him that did not center on food or bedtime, or that was not conducted in surly monosyllables, immediately embraced the chance to build bridges between them, so David's acting abilities were not stretched very far. She dried her hands on a dishcloth and took a seat beside him.

"I'm fine, thank you," she said. "A little tired, what with Georgie and all, but that will pass. It's been a little strange this last while. I'm sure you feel the same way, the four of us all thrown together suddenly like this. I'm glad that you're here, though. This house is too big for one person, but my parents wanted to keep it in the family. It was . . . important to them."

"Why?" asked David. He tried to keep himself from sounding too interested. He didn't want Rose to realize that the only reason he was talking with her was to find out more about the house, and particularly his room and the books that it contained.

"Well," she said, "this house has been in our family for a very long time. My grandparents built it, and lived in it with their children. They hoped that it would stay in the family, and that there would always be children living in it."

"Did they own the books in my room?" asked David.

"Some of them," said Rose. "Others belonged to their children: my father, his sister, and—"

She paused for a moment.

"Jonathan?" suggested David, and Rose nodded. She looked sad.

"Yes. Jonathan. Where did you learn his name?"

"It was written in some of the books. I was wondering who he was."

"He was my uncle, my father's older brother, although I never met him. Your room was once his bedroom, and a lot of those books were his. I'm sorry if you don't like them. I thought it would be such a nice room for you. I know it's a little dark, but it had all those shelves and, of course, the books. I should have been more thoughtful."

David looked puzzled. "But why? I do like it, and I like the books too."

Rose turned away. "Oh, it's nothing," she said. "It doesn't matter."

"No," said David. "Please tell me."

Rose relented.

"Jonathan disappeared. He was only fourteen. It was a long time ago, and my grandparents kept his room exactly as it had always been, because they hoped that he would come back to them. He never did. Another child disappeared with him, a little girl. Her name was Anna, and she was the daughter of one of my grandfather's friends. He and his wife died in a fire, and my grandfather took Anna to live with his family instead. Anna was seven. My grandfather thought it would be good for Jonathan to have a little sister and for Anna to have a big brother to take care of her. Anyway, they must have wandered off and, oh, I don't know, something happened to them and they were never seen again. It was just very, very sad. They searched for them for so long. They looked in the woods and the river, and they asked after them in all of the nearby towns. They even went to London and placed drawings and descriptions of them anywhere that they could, but nobody ever came forward to say that they had seen them.

"In time, they had two more children, my father and his sister, Katherine, but my grandparents never forgot Jonathan, and never stopped hoping that he and Anna might someday come home. My grandfather in particular never recovered from their loss. He seemed to blame himself for what had happened. I suppose he thought he should have protected them. I think he died young because of it. When my grandmother was dying, she asked my father not to disturb the room, but to leave the books in their place just in case Jonathan should ever return. She never lost hope. She cared about Anna too, but Jonathan was her eldest son, and I don't think a day went by when she didn't stare out the window of her bedroom in the hope of seeing him walk up the garden path, older but still her son, with some wonderful tale to tell of his disappearance.

"My father did as she asked: he left the books as they were, and later, after my father and mother died, so did I. I always wanted a family of my own, and I suppose I just felt that Jonathan so loved his books that he would have liked to think there might be another little boy or girl in there someday who would appreciate them, instead of them being left to decay, unread. Now it's your room, but if you'd like us to move you to another one, we can. There's lots of space."

"What was Jonathan like? Did your grandfather ever tell you about him?"

Rose thought. "Well, I was as curious about him as you are, and I would ask my grandfather about him. I made quite a study of him, I suppose. My grandfather said that he was very quiet. He liked to read, as you can tell, just like you. It's funny, in a way: he loved fairy stories, but they scared him too, yet the ones that scared him the most were the ones that he most liked to read. He was afraid of wolves. I remember my grandfather telling me that, once. Jonathan would have nightmares in which wolves were chasing him, and not just ordinary wolves: because they came from the stories that he read, they could speak. They were clever, the wolves of his dreams, and dangerous. My grandfather tried to take his books away, his nightmares were so bad, but Jonathan hated being without them, so my grandfather would always relent in the end and return them to him. Some of the books were very old. They were old when Jonathan owned them. I suppose a few of them might even have been valuable, except someone else had written in them once upon a time. There were stories and drawings that didn't belong. My grandfather thought that it might have been the work of the man who sold them to him. He was a bookseller in London, a strange man. He sold a lot of books for children, but I don't think he liked children very much. I think he just liked scaring them."

Rose was staring out the window now, lost in memories of her grandfather and her missing uncle.

"My grandfather went back to that bookshop after Jonathan and Anna disappeared. I suppose he thought that people who had children of their own would come to buy books there, and that either they or their children might have heard something about the missing pair. But when he got to the street in question, he found that the bookshop was gone. It was boarded up. Nobody lived or worked there anymore, and no one could tell him what had happened to the little man who owned it. Perhaps he died. He was very old, my grandfather said. Very old, and very odd."

The doorbell rang, breaking the spell of harmony between David and Rose. It was the postman, and Rose went to greet him. When she returned, she asked David if he would like something to eat, but David said no. Already, he was feeling angry with himself for lowering his defenses against Rose, even if he had learned something as a result. He didn't want her to think that everything was now all right between them, because it wasn't, not at all. Instead, he left her alone in the kitchen and headed back to his bedroom.

On the way, he looked in on Georgie. The baby was fast asleep in his crib, his big gas helmet and the bellows for pumping air into it lying close by. It wasn't his fault that he was here, David tried to tell himself. He didn't ask to be brought into the world. Still, David couldn't rouse himself to care terribly for him, and something tore inside him each time he saw his father holding the new arrival. He was like a symbol of all that was wrong, of all that had changed. After his mother had died, it had been just David and his father, and they had become closer as a result because they had only each other to rely upon. Now his father had Rose too, and a new son. But David, well, he didn't have anyone else. It was just himself.

David left the baby and returned to his garret, where he spent the rest of the afternoon flicking through Jonathan Tulvey's old books. He sat in the window seat and thought that Jonathan had sat in this seat, once upon a time. He had walked the same hallways, had eaten in the same kitchen, played in the same living room, had even slept in the same bed as David. Perhaps, somewhere back in time, he was still doing all of those things, and both David and Jonathan were now occupying the same space but at different stages in history, so that Jonathan passed like an unseen ghost through David's world, unaware that he shared his bed each night with a stranger. The thought made David shiver, but it also gave him pleasure to think that two boys who were so much alike might somehow share such a connection.

He wondered what could have happened to Jonathan and to the little girl Anna. Perhaps they had run away, although David was old enough to understand that there was a great deal of difference between the kind of running away that happened in storybooks and the reality of what would face a boy of fourteen with a girl of seven in tow. It wouldn't have taken them long to become tired and hungry if something had made them run away, and to regret what they had done. David's father had told him that if he ever got lost, he was to find a policeman, or ask a grown-up to find one for him. He wasn't to approach men who were by themselves, though. He was always to ask a lady, or a man and woman together, preferably ones with a child of their own. You couldn't be too careful, his father would say. Was that what happened to Jonathan and Anna? Had they talked to the wrong person, someone who didn't want to help them get home but instead had spirited them away, hiding them in a place where no one would ever find them? Why would someone do that?

As he lay on his bed, David knew there was an answer to that question. Before his mother had finally left for the not-quite-hospital, he had heard her discussing with his father the death of a local boy named Billy Golding, who had disappeared on his way home from school one day. Billy Golding didn't go to David's school and he wasn't one of David's friends, but David knew what he looked like because Billy was a very good soccer player who played in the park on Saturday mornings. People said that a man from Arsenal had spoken to Mr. Golding about Billy joining the club when he was older, but someone else said that Billy had just made that up and it wasn't true at all. Then Billy went missing and the police came to the park two Saturdays in a row to talk to anyone who might know something about him. They spoke to David and his father, but David couldn't help them and, after that second Saturday, the police didn't come back to the park again.

Then, a couple of days later, David heard in school that Billy Golding's body had been found down by the railway tracks.

That evening, as he got ready for bed, he heard his mother and father talking in their bedroom, and that was how he learned that Billy had been naked when he was discovered and that the police had arrested a man who lived with his mother in a clean little house not far from where the body was found. David knew from the way they were talking that something very bad had happened to Billy before he died, something to do with the man from the clean little house.

David's mother had made a special effort that night to walk from her room in order to kiss David. She hugged him very tightly and warned him again about talking to strange men. She told him that he must always come straight home from school, and that if a stranger ever approached him and offered him sweets or promised to give him a pigeon for a pet if he would just go with him, then David was to keep on walking as fast as he could, and if the man tried to follow him, then David was to go up to the first house he came to and tell them what was happening. Whatever else he did, he must never, ever go with a stranger, no matter what the stranger said. David told her he would never do that. A question came to him as he made the promise to his mother, but he did not ask it. She looked worried enough as it was, and David didn't want her to worry so much that she wouldn't even let him go out to play. But the question stayed in his mind, even after she turned out the light and he was left in the darkness of his room. The question was:

But what if he made me go with him?

Now, in another bedroom, he thought of Jonathan Tulvey and Anna, and wondered if a man from a clean little house, a man who lived with his mother and kept sweets in his pockets, had made them go down with him to the railway tracks.

And there, in the darkness, he had played with them, in his way.

That evening at dinner, his father was talking about the war again. It still didn't feel to David as if there was a war on. All of the fighting was happening far away, even if they did get to see some of it on newsreels when they went to the pictures. It was a lot duller than David had expected. War sounded quite exciting, but the reality, so far, had been very different. True, squadrons of Spitfires and Hurricanes often passed over the house, and there were always dogfights over the Channel. German bombers had been carrying out repeated raids on airfields to the south, even dropping bombs on St. Giles, Cripplegate in the East End (which Mr. Briggs described as "typical Nazi behavior" but which David's father explained, rather less emotively, as a botched effort to destroy the Thameshaven oil refinery). Nevertheless, David felt removed from it all. It wasn't as if it was happening in his own back garden. In London, people were taking items from crashed German planes as souvenirs, even though nobody was supposed to approach the wrecks, and Nazi pilots who bailed out provided regular excitement for the citizenry. Here, even though they were barely fifty miles from London, it was all very sedate.

His father folded the *Daily Express* beside his plate. The newspaper was thinner than it used to be, down to six pages. David's father said that was because they had started rationing paper. *The Magnet* had stopped printing in July, depriving David of Billy Bunter, but there was still the *Boy's Own* paper every month, which David always filed carefully alongside his Aircraft of the Fighting Powers books.

"Will you have to go and fight?" David asked his father, once dinner was over.

"No, I shouldn't think so," his father replied. "I'm more use to the war effort where I am."

"Top secret," said David.

His father smiled at him.

"Yes, top secret," he said.

It still gave David a thrill to think that his father might be a spy, or at least know about spies. So far, it was the only interesting part of the war.

That night, David lay in his bed and watched the moonlight streaming through the window. The skies were clear, and the moon was very bright. After a time, his eyes closed, and he dreamed of wolves and little girls and an old king in a ruined castle, fast asleep on his throne. Railway tracks ran alongside the castle, and figures moved through the long grass that grew beside them. There was a boy and a girl, and the Crooked Man. They disappeared beneath the earth, and David smelled gumdrops and peppermints, and he heard a little girl crying before her voice was drowned out by the sound of an approaching train.

V

Of Intruders and Transformations

HE CROOKED MAN finally crossed over into David's world at the start of September.

It had been a long, tense summer. His father spent more time at his place of work than he did at home, sometimes not sleeping in his own bed for two or three nights in a row. It was often too difficult for him to return to the house anyway once night fell. All of the road signs had been removed to thwart the Germans if they invaded, and on more than one occasion David's father had managed to get lost while driving home in daylight. If he tried driving at night with his headlights off, who knew where he might end up?

Rose was finding motherhood difficult. David wondered if his own mother had found it as hard, if David had been as demanding as Georgie seemed to be. He hoped not. The stress of the situation had caused Rose's tolerance for David and his moods to sink lower and lower. They barely talked to each other now, and David could tell that his father's patience with both of them was almost extinguished. At dinner the night before, he had exploded when Rose had taken an innocuous remark of David's as an insult and the two of them had begun to bicker.

"Why can't you two just find a way to get along, for crying out loud!" his father had shouted. "I don't come home for this. I can get all the tension and shouting matches I want at work."

Georgie, seated in his high chair, started to cry.

"Now look what you've done," said Rose. She threw her napkin down on the table and went to Georgie.

David's father buried his head in his hands.

"So it's all my fault," he said.

"Well it's not mine," replied Rose.

Simultaneously, their eyes turned toward David.

"What?" he said. "You're blaming me. Fine!"

He stomped away from the table, leaving his dinner unfinished. He was still hungry, but the stew was mainly vegetables with some nasty pieces of cheap sausage spread through it to break the monotony. He knew that he'd have to eat the rest of it tomorrow, but he didn't care. It wasn't going to taste any worse reheated than it did already. As he headed for his room, he expected to hear his father's voice demanding that he return and finish his food, but nobody called him back. He sat down hard on his bed. He couldn't wait for the summer holidays to be over. A place had been found for David in a school not far from the house, which would at least be better than spending every day with Rose and Georgie.

David was not seeing Dr. Moberley quite as often, mainly because nobody had time to take him into London. Anyway, the attacks had stopped, or so it appeared. He no longer fell to the ground or experienced blackouts, but something far stranger and more unsettling was now occurring, stranger even than the whisperings of the books, to which David had grown almost accustomed.

David was experiencing waking dreams. That was the only way he could find to describe them to himself. It felt like those moments late in the evening when you were reading or listening to the radio and you grew so tired that for an instant you fell asleep and started dreaming, except obviously you didn't realize you'd fallen asleep so that the world suddenly seemed to become very strange. David would be playing in his room, or reading, or walking in the garden, and everything would shimmer. The walls would disappear, the book would fall from his hands, the garden would be replaced by hills and tall, gray trees. He would find himself in a new land, a twilight place of shadows and cold winds, heavy with the smell of wild animals. Sometimes, he would even hear voices. They were somehow familiar as they called to him, but as soon as he tried to concentrate on them, the vision would end and he would be back in his own world.

The strangest thing of all was that one of the voices sounded like his mother's. It was the one that spoke loudest and clearest. She called to him from out of the darkness. She called to him, and she told him that she was alive.

The waking dreams were always strongest near the sunken garden, but David found them so disturbing that he tried to stay away from that part of the property as much as possible. In fact, so troubled was David by them that he was tempted to tell Dr. Moberley about them, if his father could make time for an appointment. Perhaps he would finally tell him about the whispering of the books too, David thought. The two might be linked, but then he thought of Dr. Moberley's questions about David's mother and remembered once again the threat of being "put away." When David talked to him about missing his mother, Dr. Moberley would talk in turn about grief and loss, about how it was natural yet you had to try to get over it. But being sad about your mother dying was one thing; hearing her voice crying out from the shadows of a sunken garden, claiming to be alive behind the decaying brickwork, was quite another. David wasn't sure how Dr. Moberley would respond to that. He didn't want to be put away, but the dreams were frightening. He wanted them to stop.

It was one of his last days at home before school recommenced. Tiring of the house, David went for a walk in the woods at the back of the property. He picked up a big stick and scythed at the long grass. He found a spider's web in a bush and tried to tempt the spider out with fragments of small sticks. He dropped one close to the center of the web, but nothing happened. David realized it was because the stick wasn't moving. It was the struggles of the insect that alerted the spider, which made David think that perhaps spiders were a lot cleverer than anything so small had a right to be.

He looked back at the house and saw the window of his bedroom. The ivy growing on the walls almost surrounded the frame, making his room look more than ever like a part of the natural world. Now that he saw it from a distance, he noticed the ivy was thickest at his window and had barely touched any of the other windows on this side of the house. It had not spread across the lower parts of the wall either, the way ivy usually did, but had climbed straight and true along a narrow path to David's window. Like the beanstalk in the fairy tale that led Jack to the giant, the ivy seemed to know precisely where it was going.

And then a figure moved inside David's room. He saw a shape pass by the glass, dressed in forest green. For a moment, he was certain that it must be Rose, or perhaps Mrs. Briggs. But then David remembered that Mrs. Briggs had gone down to the village, while Rose rarely entered his room, and if she did she always asked his permission first. It wasn't his father either. The person in the room was the wrong shape for him. In fact, David thought, whoever was in his room was the wrong shape, period. The figure was slightly hunched, as though it had become so used to sneaking about that its body had contorted, the spine curving, the arms like twisted branches, the fingers clutching, ready to snatch at whatever it saw. Its nose was narrow and hooked, and it wore a crooked hat upon its head. It disappeared from sight for a moment before it reappeared holding one of David's books. The figure flicked through the pages before it found something that interested it, whereupon it paused and seemed to start reading.

Then, suddenly, David heard Georgie crying in his nursery. The figure dropped the book and listened. David saw its fingers extend into the air, as if Georgie were hanging before it like an apple ready to be plucked from the tree. It seemed to be debating with itself as to what to do next, for David saw its left hand move to its pointed chin and stroke it softly. While it was thinking, it glanced over its shoulder and down toward the woods below. It saw David and froze for an instant before dropping to the floor, but in that moment David saw coal black eyes set in a pale face so long and thin that it seemed to have been stretched on a rack. Its mouth was very wide, and its lips were very, very dark, like old, sour wine.

David ran for the house. He burst into the kitchen, where his father was reading the newspaper. "Dad, there's someone in my room!" he said.

His father looked up at him curiously. "What do you mean?"

"There's a *man* up there," insisted David. "I was walking in the woods, and I looked up at my window and he was there. He wore a hat, and his face was really long. Then he heard the baby crying and he stopped whatever he was doing and listened. He saw me looking at him, and he tried to hide. Please, Dad, you've got to believe me!"

His father's brow furrowed, and he put the paper down. "David, if you're joking . . ."

"I'm not, honestly!"

He followed his father up the stairs, the stick still clutched in his hand. The door to his room was closed, and David's father paused before opening it. Then he reached down and twisted the knob. The door opened.

For a second, nothing happened.

"See," said David's father. "There's nothing—"

Something struck his father in the face, and he shouted loudly. There was a panicked fluttering, and a banging as whatever it was bounced against the walls and the window. Once the initial shock had gone away, David peered around his father and saw that the intruder was a magpie, its feathers a blur of black and white as it tried to escape from the room.

"Stay outside and keep the door closed," said his father. "They're vicious birds."

David did as he was told, although he was still frightened. He heard his father open the window and shout at the magpie, forcing it toward the gap, until finally he could hear the bird no longer and his father opened the door, sweating slightly.

"Well, that gave both of us a fright," he said.

David looked into the room. There were some feathers on the floor, but that was all. There was no sign of the bird, or of the strange little man he had seen. He went to the window. The magpie was perched on the crumbling stonework of the sunken garden. It seemed to be staring back at him.

"It was only a magpie," said his father. "That's what you saw."

David was tempted to argue, but he knew his father would just tell him that he was being silly if he insisted that something else had been in here, something far bigger and far nastier than a magpie. Magpies didn't wear crooked hats, or reach out for crying babies. David had seen its eyes, and its hunched body, and its long, grasping fingers.

He looked back at the sunken garden. The magpie was gone.

His father sighed theatrically. "You still don't believe that it was only a magpie, do you?" he said.

He went down on his knees and checked under the bed. He opened the wardrobe and looked in the bathroom next door. He even peered behind the bookcases, where there was a gap barely large enough to accommodate David's hand.

"See?" said his father. "It was just a bird."

But he could see that David remained unconvinced so, together, they searched all of the rooms on the top floor and then the floors below, until it became clear that the only people in the house were David, his father, Rose, and the baby. Then David's father left him and returned to his newspaper. Back in his room, David picked up a book from the floor by his window. It was one of Jonathan Tulvey's storybooks, and it lay open at the tale of Red Riding Hood. The story was illustrated by a picture of the wolf towering over the little girl, Grandma's blood on its claws, and its teeth bared to consume her granddaughter. Someone, presumably Jonathan, had scribbled over the figure of the wolf with a black crayon, as though disturbed by the threat it represented. David closed the book and returned it to its shelf. As he did so, he noticed the silence in his room. There was no whispering. All the books were quiet.

I suppose a magpie could have dislodged that book, thought David, but a magpie couldn't enter a room through a locked window. Someone else had been there, of that he was sure. In the old stories, people were always transforming themselves, or being transformed, into animals and birds. Couldn't the Crooked Man have changed himself into a magpie in order to escape discovery?

He hadn't gone far, though, oh no. He had flown only as far as the sunken garden, and then he had disappeared.

As David lay in bed that night, caught between sleeping and

waking, his mother's voice carried to him from the darkness of the sunken garden, calling his name, demanding that she not be forgotten.

And David knew then that the time was quickly approaching when he would have to enter that place and face at last what lay within.

VI

Of the War, and the Way Between Worlds

AVID AND ROSE had their worst fight the next day.

It had been coming for a long time. Rose was breast-feeding Georgie, which meant that she was forced to rise during the night in order to take care of his needs. But even after he was fed, Georgie would toss and turn and cry, and there was little that David's father could do to help even when he was around. This sometimes led to arguments with Rose. They usually began with a little thing—a dish that his father forgot to put away, or dirt tracked through the kitchen on the soles of his shoes—and quickly developed into shouting matches that would end with Rose in tears and Georgie echoing his mother's cries.

David thought that his father looked older and more tired than before. He worried about him. He missed his father's presence. That morning, the morning of the big fight, David stood at the bathroom door and watched his father shave.

"You work really hard," he said.

"I suppose so."

"You're tired all the time."

"I'm tired of you and Rose not getting along."

"Sorry," said David.

"Hmmmph," said his father.

He finished shaving, wiped the lather from his face with water from the sink, then dried himself with a pink towel.

"I don't see you that much anymore," said David, "that's all. I miss having you around."

His father smiled at him, then cuffed him gently on the ear. "I know," he said. "But we all have to make sacrifices, and there are men and women out there who are making much greater sacrifices than we are. They're putting their lives at risk, and I have a duty to do all I can to help them. It's important that we find out what the Germans are planning and what they suspect about our people. That's my job. And don't forget that we're lucky here. They're having a much harder time of it in London."

The Germans had struck hard at London the day before. At one point, according to David's father, there had been a thousand aircraft battling over the Isle of Sheppey. David wondered what London looked like now. Was it filled with burned-out buildings, with rubble where streets used to be? Were the pigeons still in Trafalgar Square? He supposed that they were. The pigeons weren't clever enough to move somewhere else. Perhaps his father was right, and they were lucky to be away from it, but a part of David thought again that it must be quite exciting to live in London now. Scary, sometimes, but exciting.

"In time, it will come to an end, and then we can all go back to living normal lives," said his father.

"When?" asked David.

His father looked troubled. "I don't know. Not for a while."

"Months?"

"Longer, I think."

"Are we winning, Dad?"

"We're holding on, David. At the moment, that's the best we can do."

David left his father to get dressed. They all ate breakfast together before his father left, but Rose and his dad said little to each other. David knew that they had been fighting again, so when his father left for work he decided to stay out of Rose's way even more than usual. He went to his room for a while and played with his soldiers, then later lay in the shade at the back of the house to read his book.

It was there that Rose found him. Although his book was open upon his chest, David's attention was focused elsewhere. He was staring at the far end of the lawn, where the sunken garden lay, his eyes fixed on the hole in the brickwork as though expecting to see movement within.

"So there you are," said Rose.

David looked up at her. The sun was in his eyes, so he was forced to squint. "What do you want?" he asked.

He hadn't meant it to come out the way it did. It sounded as if he was being disrespectful and rude, but he wasn't, or no more than he ever was. He supposed that he could have asked "What can I do for you?" or even have prefixed "Yes" or "Certainly" or just "Hello" to what he had said, but by the time he thought of this it was too late.

Rose had red marks under her eyes. Her skin was pale, and it looked like there were more lines on her forehead and face than there had previously been. She was heavier too, but David supposed that this was to do with having the baby. He had asked his father about it, and his father had told him never, ever to mention it to Rose, no matter what. He had been very serious about it. In fact, he'd used the words "more than our lives are worth" to stress how important it was that David keep such opinions to himself.

Now Rose, fatter and paler and more tired, was standing

beside David, and even with the sun in his eyes he could see the anger rising in her.

"How *dare* you speak to me like that!" she said. "You sit around all day with your head buried in your books and you contribute nothing to life in this house. You can't even keep a civil tongue in your head. Who do you think you are?"

David was about to apologize, but he didn't. What she was saying wasn't fair. He had offered to help with things, but Rose nearly always turned him down, mostly because he seemed to catch her when Georgie was acting up, or when she had her hands full with something else. Mr. Briggs took care of the garden, and David always tried to assist him with the sweeping and raking, but that was out-of-doors, where Rose couldn't see what he was doing. Mrs. Briggs did all of the cleaning and most of the cooking, but whenever David tried to lend her a hand, she shooed him out of the room, claiming that he was just one more thing for her to trip over. It had simply seemed to him that the best option was to stay out of everyone's way as much as possible. And anyway, these were the last days of his summer holidays. The village school had postponed opening for a couple of days because of a shortage of teachers, but his father seemed certain that David would be behind his new desk by the start of the following week at the very latest. From then until half-term he would be in school during the day and doing homework in the evenings. His working day would be nearly as long as his father's. Why shouldn't he take it easy while he could? Now his anger was growing to match Rose's. He stood up and saw that he was now just as tall as she was. The words poured from his mouth almost before he knew that he was speaking them, a mixture of half-truths and insults and all of the rage that he had suppressed since the birth of Georgie.

"No, who do *you* think you are?" he said. "You're not my

mother, and you can't talk to me like that. I didn't want to come here to live. I wanted to be with my dad. We were doing just fine by ourselves, and then you came along. Now there's Georgie too, and you think I'm just someone who's in your way. Well, you're in *my* way, and you're in my dad's way. He still loves my mum, just like I do. He still thinks of her, and he's never going to love you the way he loved her, not ever. It doesn't matter what you do or what you say. He still loves her. He. Still. Loves. *Her.*"

Rose hit him. She struck him on the cheek with the palm of her hand. It wasn't a hard slap, and she pulled the blow as soon as she realized what she was doing, but the impact was still enough to rock David on his heels. His cheek smarted, and his eyes watered. He stood, openmouthed with shock, then brushed past Rose and ran to his room. He didn't look back, not even when she called after him and said that she was sorry. He locked the door behind him and refused to open it to her when she knocked on it. After a while, she went away and did not return.

David stayed in his room until his father came home. He heard Rose speak to him in the hallway. His father's voice grew louder. Rose tried to calm him down. There were footsteps on the stairs. David knew what was coming.

The door to his room was almost blown off its hinges by the force of his father's fists upon it.

"David, open this door. Open it *now.*"

David did as he was told, turning the key once in the lock, then stepped back hurriedly as his father entered. His father's face was almost purple with fury. He raised his hand as if to hit David, then seemed to think better of it. He swallowed once, took a deep breath, then shook his head. When he spoke again, his voice was strangely calm, which worried David more than the previous show of anger.

"You have no right to speak to Rose in that way," said his

father. "You will show respect to her, just as you show respect to me. Things have been hard for all of us, but that does not excuse your behavior today. I haven't decided yet what I'm going to do with you, or how you're to be punished. If it wasn't already too late, I'd pack you off to boarding school and then you'd realize just how fortunate you are to be here."

David tried to speak. "But Rose hi——"

His father raised his hand. "I don't want to hear about it. If you open your mouth again, it will go hard with you. For now you will stay in your room. You will not go outside tomorrow. You will not read and you will not play with your toys. Your door will remain open and if I catch you reading or playing then, so help me, I will take a belt to you. You will sit there on your bed and you will think about what you said and about how you're going to make it up to Rose when you're eventually allowed to return to life with civilized people. I'm disappointed in you, David. I brought you up to behave better than that. We both did, your mum and I."

With that, he left. David sank back on his bed. He didn't want to cry, but he couldn't stop himself. It wasn't fair. He had been wrong to talk to Rose that way, but she had been wrong to hit him. As his tears fell, he became aware of the murmuring of the books on the shelves. He had grown so used to it that he had almost ceased to notice it, like birdsong or the wind in the trees, but now it was growing louder and louder. A burning smell came to him, like matches igniting and tram wires sparking. He clenched his teeth as the first spasm came, but there was nobody to witness it. A great fissure appeared in his room, ripping apart the fabric of this world, and he saw another realm beyond. There was a castle, with banners waving from its battlements and soldiers marching in columns through its gates. Then that castle was gone and another took its place, this one surrounded by fallen trees. It was darker than the first, its shape unclear, and it was dominated by a single great tower that pointed like a finger toward the sky. Its topmost window was lit, and David felt a presence there. It was at once both strange and familiar. It called to him in his mother's voice. It said:

David, I am not dead. Come to me, and save me.

David did not know how long he had been unconscious, or if sleep had at some point taken over, but his room was dark when he opened his eyes. There was a foul taste in his mouth, and he realized that he had been sick on his pillow. He wanted to go to his father and tell him of the attack, but he felt certain there would be little sympathy for him from that quarter. There was not a sound to be heard in the house, so he assumed everyone was in bed. The waiting moon shone upon the rows of books, but they were now quiet again, apart from the occasional snore that arose from the duller, more boring volumes. There was a history of the coal board, abandoned and unloved upon a high shelf, that was particularly uninteresting and had the nasty habit of snoring very loudly and then coughing thunderously, at which point small clouds of black dust would appear to rise from its pages. David heard it cough now, but he was aware of a certain wakefulness among some of the older books, the ones that contained the strange, dark fairy stories he loved so much. He sensed that they were waiting for an event to occur, although he could not tell what it might be.

David was certain that he had been dreaming, although he could not quite recall the substance of the dream. Of one thing he was sure: the dream had not been a pleasant one, but all that remained was a lingering feeling of unease and a tingling on the palm of his right hand, as though it had been stroked with poison ivy. There was the same sensation on the side of his face, and he could not shake off the feeling that something unpleasant had touched him while he was lost to the world.

He was still wearing his day clothes. He climbed out of bed and undressed in the dark, changing into clean pajamas. He returned to his bed and wrestled with his pillow, turning this way and that in an effort to find a comfortable position in which to go to sleep, but no rest came. As he lay with his eyes closed, he noticed that his window was open. He didn't like it to be open. It was hard enough to keep the insects out even when it was closed, and the last thing he wanted was for the magpie to return while he was sleeping.

David left his bed and carefully approached the window. Something curled over his bare foot, and he raised it in shock. It was a tendril of ivy. There were shoots of it along the inner wall, and green fingers extended over the wardrobe and the carpet and the chest of drawers. He had spoken to Mr. Briggs about it, and the gardener had promised to get a ladder and trim back the ivy from the outside wall, but so far that hadn't happened. David didn't like touching the ivy. The way it was encroaching on his room made it seem almost alive.

David found his slippers and placed them on his feet before walking across the ivy to the glass. As he did so, he heard a woman's voice speak his name.

"David."

"Mum?" he asked uncertainly.

"Yes, David, it's me. Listen. Don't be afraid."

But David was afraid.

"Please," said the voice. *"I need your help. I'm trapped in here. I'm trapped in this strange place and I don't know what to do. Please come, David. If you love me, come across."*

"Mum," he said. "I'm frightened."

The voice spoke again, but it was fainter now.

"David," it said, *"they're taking me away. Don't let them take me from you. Please! Follow me, and bring me home. Follow me through the garden."*

And with that, David overcame his fear. He grabbed his dressing gown and ran, as quickly and as quietly as he could, down the stairs and out onto the grass. He paused in the darkness. There was a disturbance in the night sky, a low, irregular put-putting noise that came from high above. David looked up and saw something glowing faintly, like a meteor falling. It was an airplane. He kept the light in view until he came to the steps that led into the sunken garden, taking them as fast as he could. He didn't want to pause, because if he paused he might think about what he was going to do, and if he began thinking about it, he might become too afraid to do it. He felt the grass crumple beneath his feet as he ran to the hole in the wall, even as the light in the sky grew brighter. The plane was now flaming redly, and the noise of its sputtering engines tore through the night. David stopped and watched it descend. It was dropping fast, shedding burning shards as it came. It was too big to be a fighter. This was a bomber. He thought he could make out the shape of its wings lit by fire and hear the desperate thrumming of the remaining engines as the plane fell to earth. It grew larger and larger, until at last it seemed to fill the sky, dwarfing their house, lighting up the night with red and orange fire. It was heading straight for the sunken garden, flames licking at the German cross on its fuselage, as though something in the heavens above was determined to stop David from moving between realms.

The choice had been made for him. David could not hesitate. He forced himself through the gap in the wall and into the darkness just as the world that he had left behind became an inferno.

VII

Of the Woodsman and the Work of His Ax

HE BRICKS AND MORTAR were gone. There was now rough bark beneath David's fingers. He was inside the trunk of a tree, before him an arched hole, beyond which lay shadowy woods. Leaves fell, descending in slow spirals to the forest floor. Thorny bushes and stinging nettles provided low cover, but there were no flowers that David could see. It was a landscape composed of greens and browns. Everything appeared to be illuminated by a strange half-light, as though dawn was just approaching or the day was at last drawing to its close.

David stayed in the darkness of the trunk, unmoving. His mother's voice was gone, and now there was only the barely heard sound of leaf glancing against leaf and the distant rushing of water over rocks. There was no sign of the German plane, no indication that it had ever even existed. He was tempted to turn back, to run to the house and wake his father in order to tell him of what he had seen. But what could he say, and why would his father believe him after all that had occurred that day? He needed proof, some token of this new world.

And so David emerged from the hollow of the tree trunk. The sky above was starless, the constellations hidden by heavy clouds. The air smelled fresh and clean to him at first, but as he breathed deeply he caught a hint of something else, something less pleasant. David could almost taste it upon his tongue: a metallic sensation composed of copper and decay. It reminded him of the day he and his father had found a dead cat by the side of the road, its fur torn and its insides exposed. The cat had smelled a lot like the night air in the new land. David shivered, and only partly from the cold.

Suddenly he was aware of a great roaring noise from behind him, and a sensation of heat at his back. He threw himself to the ground and rolled away as the trunk of the tree began to distend, the hollow widening until it resembled the entrance to a great, bark-lined cave. Flames flickered deep within it, and then, like a mouth expelling a tasteless piece of food, it spit forth part of the burning fuselage of the German bomber, the body of one of its crew still trapped in the wreckage of the gondola beneath, its machine gun pointing at David. The wreckage tore a blackened, burning path through the undergrowth before it came to rest in a clearing, still spewing smoke and fumes as the flames fed upon it.

David stood, brushing leaves and dirt from his clothing. He tried to approach the burning plane. It was a Ju 88; he could tell from the gondola. He could see the remains of the gunner, now almost entirely wreathed in flames. He wondered if any of the crew had survived. The body of the trapped aviator lay pressed against the cracked glass of the gondola, his mouth grinning white in his charred skull. David had never seen death up close before, not like this, not violent and smelly and turning to black. He could not help thinking of the German's final moments, trapped in the searing heat, his skin burning. He experienced a wave of pity for the dead man, whose name he would never know.

Something whizzed past his ear like the warm passage of a night insect, followed almost immediately by a cracking noise. A second insect buzzed past, but by then David was already lying flat on the ground, crawling for cover as the ammunition for the .303 ignited. He found a depression in the earth and threw himself into it, covering his head with his hands and trying to keep himself as flat as he could until the hail of bullets had ceased. Only when he was certain that the ammunition was entirely spent did he dare to raise his head again. He stood warily and watched as flames and sparks shot into the skies above. For the first time, he got some sense of how huge were the trees in this forest, taller and wider than even the oldest of oaks in the woods back home. Their trunks were gray and entirely without branches until, at least one hundred feet above his head, they exploded into massive, mostly bare crowns.

A black, boxlike object had separated from the main body of the shattered plane and now lay, smoking slightly, not far from where David stood. It looked like an old camera, but with wheels on its side. He could make out the word "Blickwinkel" marked on one of the wheels. Beneath it was a label reading "Auf Farbglas Ein."

It was a bombsight. David had seen pictures of them. This was what the German fliers had used to pick out their targets on the ground. Perhaps that had even been the task of the man who now lay burning in the wreckage, for the city would have passed beneath him as he lay prone in the gondola. Some of David's pity for the dead man seeped away. The bombsight made what they had been doing seem more real, somehow, more awful. He thought of the families huddled in their Anderson shelters, the children crying and the adults hoping that whatever descended would strike far away from them, or the crowds gathered together in the Underground stations, listening to the explosions, dust and dirt falling on their heads as the bombs shook the ground above.

And they would be the lucky ones.

He kicked out hard at the bombsight, connecting with a perfect right foot shot, and felt a surge of satisfaction as he heard the sound of broken glass from within and knew the delicate lenses had shattered.

Now that the excitement was over, David put his hands in the pockets of his dressing gown and tried to take in a little more of his surroundings. Some four or five steps beyond where he was, four bright purple flowers stood tall above the grass. They were the first signs of real color he had seen so far. Their leaves were yellow and orange, and the hearts of the flowers themselves looked to David like the faces of sleeping children. Even in the murk of the forest, he thought he could discern their closed eyelids, the slightly opened mouths, the twin holes of their nostrils. They were unlike any flower that he had ever seen before. If he could take one and give it to his father, then he might be able to convince him that this place truly existed.

David approached the flowers, dead leaves crunching beneath his feet. He was almost upon them when the eyelids of one of the flowers opened, revealing small yellow eyes. Then its lips parted and it emitted a shriek. Instantly, the other flowers awoke, and then, almost as one, they closed their leaves around themselves, revealing hard, barbed undersides that glistened faintly with a sticky residue. Something told David that it would be a bad idea to touch those barbs. He thought of nettles, and poison ivy. They were bad enough, but who knew what poisons the plants here might use to defend themselves?

David's nose wrinkled. The wind was blowing the stink of the burning aircraft away from him, and its stench had now been replaced by another. The metallic smell that he had detected earlier was stronger here. He took a few steps deeper into the forest and saw an uneven formation under the fallen leaves, spots of blue and red suggesting something lay barely concealed beneath. It was roughly the shape of a man. David drew closer and saw clothing, and fur beneath it. His brow furrowed. It was an animal, an animal wearing clothes. It had clawed fingers and legs like those of a dog. David tried to glimpse its face, but there was none. Its head had been cleanly severed from the body, and recently too, for a long spray of arterial blood still lay upon the forest floor.

David covered his mouth so that he would not be sick. The sight of two corpses in as many minutes was making his stomach churn. He stepped away from the body and turned back toward his tree. As he did so, the great hole in the trunk disappeared, the tree shrinking to its previous size and the bark seeming to grow over the gap while he watched, entirely covering the passage back to his own world. It became just one more tree in a forest of great trees, each hardly different from the next. David touched his fingers to the wood, pressing and knocking, hoping to find some way of reopening the portal back to his old life, but nothing happened. He almost cried, but he knew that if he began crying, all would be lost. He would be just a small boy, powerless and afraid, far from home. Instead, he looked around him and found the tip of a large, flat rock erupting from the dirt. He dug it free and, using its sharpest edge, he chipped at the trunk of the tree: once, then again, over and over until the bark fragmented and fell to the ground. David thought that he felt the tree shudder, the way a person might if he had suddenly experienced a severe shock. The whiteness of the inner pulp turned to red, and what looked very much like blood began to seep from the wound, flowing down the channels and crevasses of the bark and dripping onto the ground beneath.

A voice said: "Don't do that. The trees don't like it."

David turned. There was a man standing in the shadows a short distance from him. He was big and tall, with broad shoulders and short, dark hair. He wore brown boots of leather that came almost to his knees and a short coat made from skins and hides. His eyes were very green, so that he seemed almost like a part of the forest itself given human form. Over his right shoulder, he carried an ax.

David dropped the stone. "I'm sorry," he said. "I didn't know."

The man regarded him silently. "No," he said at last. "I don't suppose you did."

He advanced toward David, and the boy instinctively took a couple of steps back until he felt his hands graze the tree. Once again, it seemed to shiver beneath his touch, but the feeling was less pronounced than before, as though it were gradually recovering from the injury it had received and was certain now, in the presence of the approaching stranger, that no such hurt would be visited on it again. David was not so reassured by the man's approach: he had an ax, the kind of ax that looked as if it could sever a head from a body.

Now that the man had emerged from the shadows, David was able to examine his face more closely. He thought that the man looked stern, but there was kindness there too, and the boy felt that here was someone who could be trusted. He began to relax a little, although he kept a wary eye on the big ax.

"Who are you?" said David.

"I might ask you the same question," said the man. "These woods are in my care, and I have never seen you in them before. Still, in answer to you, I am the Woodsman. I have no other name, or none that matters."

The Woodsman approached the burning airplane. The flames were dying down now, leaving the framework exposed. It looked like the skeleton of some great beast, abandoned to the fire after the roasted meat had been stripped from its bones. The gunner could no longer be seen clearly. He had become just another dark shape in a tangle of metal and machine parts. The Woodsman shook his head in wonder, then walked away from the wreckage and returned to David. He reached past the boy and laid his hand upon the trunk of the wounded tree. He looked closely at the damage David had inflicted upon it, then patted the tree as one might pat a horse or a dog. Kneeling down, he removed some moss from the nearby stones, which he packed into the hole.

"It's all right, old fellow," he said to the tree. "It will heal soon enough."

Far above David's head, the branches moved for a moment, even though all of the other trees remained still.

The Woodsman returned his attention to David. "And now," he said, "it's your turn. What is your name, and what are you doing here? This is no place for a boy to be wandering alone. Did you come in this . . . *thing*?"

He gestured toward the airplane.

"No, that followed after me. My name is David. I came through the tree trunk. There was a hole, but it disappeared. That was why I was chipping at the bark. I was hoping to cut my way back in, or at least to mark the tree so I would be able to find it again."

"You came through the tree?" he asked. "From where did you come?"

"A garden," said David. "There was a little gap in a corner, and I found a way through from there to here. I thought I heard my mother's voice, and I followed it. Now the way back is gone."

The Woodsman pointed again at the wreckage. "And how did you come to bring that with you?"

"There was fighting. It fell from the sky."

If the Woodsman was surprised by this information, he didn't show it.

"There is the body of a man inside," said the Woodsman. "Did you know him?"

"He was the gunner, one of the crew. I'd never seen him before. He was a German."

"He is dead now."

The Woodsman touched his fingers to the tree once again, lightly tracing its surface as though hoping to find the telltale cracks of a doorway beneath his skin. "As you say, there is no longer a door here. You were right to try to mark this tree, though, even if your methods were clumsy."

He reached into the folds of his jacket and removed a small ball of rough twine. He unraveled it until he was satisfied that he had the correct length, then tied it around the trunk of the tree. From a small leather bag he produced a gray, sticky substance that he smeared on the twine. It didn't smell at all nice.

"It will keep the animals and birds from gnawing upon the rope," explained the Woodsman. He picked up his ax. "You'd better come with me," he said. "We'll decide what to do with you tomorrow, but for now we need to get you to safety."

David didn't move. He could still smell blood and decay on the air, and now that he had seen the ax at close quarters, he thought he spotted drops of red along its length. There were red marks too on the man's clothing.

"Excuse me," he said, as innocently as he could, "but if you care for the woods, why do you need an ax?"

The Woodsman looked at David with what might almost have been amusement, as though he saw through the boy's efforts to conceal his concerns yet was impressed by his guile nonetheless.

"The ax isn't for the woods," said the Woodsman. "It's for the things that *live* in the woods."

He raised his head and sniffed the air. He pointed the ax in the direction of the headless corpse. "You smelled it," he said.

David nodded. "I saw it too. Did you do it?"

"I did."

"It looked like a man, but it wasn't."

"No," said the Woodsman. "Not a man. We can talk about it later. You have nothing to fear from me, but there are other creatures that we both have reason to fear. Come now. Their time is near, and the heat and the smell of burning flesh will draw them to this place."

David, realizing that he had no other choice, followed the Woodsman. He was cold, and his slippers were damp, so the Woodsman gave him his jacket to wear and raised David up onto his back. It had been a long time since someone had carried David upon his back. He was too heavy for his father now, but the Woodsman did not appear troubled by the burden. They passed through the forest, the trees seeming to stretch endlessly before them. David tried to take in the new sights, but the Woodsman moved quickly and it was all David could do to hang on. Above their heads, the clouds briefly parted, and the moon was revealed. It was very red, like a great hole in the skin of the night. The Woodsman picked up the pace, his long steps eating up the forest floor.

"We must hurry," he said. "They'll be coming soon."

And as he spoke, a great howling arose from the north, and the Woodsman began to run.

VIII

Of Wolves, and Worse-Than-Wolves

HE FOREST PASSED in a blur of gray and brown and fading winter green. Briars tore at the Woodsman's jacket and the trousers of David's pajamas, and on more than one occasion David had to duck down to prevent his face from being raked by high bushes. The howling had ceased, but the Woodsman had not slowed his pace, not for a moment. Neither did he speak, so David too stayed silent. He was frightened, though. He tried to look back over his shoulder once, but the effort almost caused him to lose his balance and he did not try again.

They were still in the depths of the forest when the Woodsman stopped and seemed to be listening. David almost asked him what was wrong but then thought better of it and remained quiet, trying to hear what it was that had caused the Woodsman to pause. He felt a prickling sensation at his neck as his hairs stood on end, and he was certain that they were being watched. Then, faintly, he heard a brushing of leaves to his right, and a snapping of twigs to his left. There was movement behind them, as though presences in the undergrowth were trying to close in on them as softly as possible.

"Hold on tight," said the Woodsman. "Almost there."

He sprinted to his right, leaving the easy ground and breaking through a thicket of ferns, and instantly David heard the woods erupt into noise behind them as the pursuit recommenced in earnest. A cut opened upon his hand, dripping blood onto the ground, and a large hole was ripped in his pajamas from the knee to the ankle. He lost a slipper, and the night air bit at his bare toes. His fingers ached with the cold and the effort of holding on tightly to the Woodsman, but he did not release his grip. They passed through another patch of bushes, and now they were on a rough trail that wound its way down a slope toward what looked like a garden beyond. David glanced behind him and thought he saw two pale orbs gleaming in the moonlight, and a patch of thick, gray fur.

"Don't look back," said the Woodsman. "Whatever you do, don't look back."

David faced forward again. He was terrified, and was now very sorry that he had followed the voice of his mother into this place. He was just a boy wearing pajamas, one slipper, and an old blue dressing gown under a stranger's jacket, and he did not belong anywhere but in his own bedroom.

Now the trees were thinning, and David and the Woodsman emerged into a patch of lovingly tended land, sown with row upon row of vegetables. Before them stood the strangest cottage that David had ever seen, surrounded by a low wooden fence. The dwelling was built of logs hewn from the forest, with a door at the center, a window on either side, and a sloping roof with a stone chimney stack at one end, but that was where any resemblance to a normal cottage ended. Its silhouette against the night sky was like that of a hedgehog, for it was covered in spikes of wood and metal, where sharpened sticks and rods of iron had been inserted between, or through, the logs. As they drew closer, David could also make out pieces of glass and sharp stone in the walls and even on the roof, so that it shone in the moonlight as though sprinkled with diamonds. The windows were heavily barred, and great nails had been driven through the door from the inside, so that to fall heavily against it would be to risk instant impalement. This was not a cottage: this was a fortress.

They passed through the fence and were approaching the safety of the house when a form appeared from behind its walls and advanced toward them. It resembled a large wolf in shape, except that it wore an ornate shirt of white and gold on its upper body and bright red breeches on its lower half. And then, as David watched, it rose on its hind legs and stood like a man, and it became clear that this was more than an animal, for its ears were roughly human in shape, although tufted with points of hair at the tips, and its muzzle was shorter than a wolf's. Its lips were drawn back from its fangs, and it growled at them in warning, but it was in its eyes that the struggle between wolf and man was clearest. These were not the eyes of an animal. They were cunning but also self-aware, and they were filled with hunger and desire.

Other similar creatures were now emerging from the forest, some wearing clothing, mostly tattered jackets and torn trousers, and they too rose up and stood on their hind legs, but there were many more who were just like ordinary wolves. They were smaller and stayed on all fours, and looked savage and unthinking to David. It was the ones who bore traces of men upon them that frightened David the most.

The Woodsman lowered David to the ground. "Stay close to me," he said. "If anything happens, run for the cottage."

He patted David on the lower back, and David felt something fall into the pocket of the jacket. As discreetly as he could, he allowed his hand to drift toward the pocket, trying to pretend it was the cold that made him seek its comfort. He put his hand inside and felt the shape of a large iron key. David closed his fist upon it and held it as though his very life depended on it, which, he was starting to realize, might very well have been the case.

The wolf-man by the house regarded David intently, and so terrifying was his gaze that David was forced to look to the ground, to the back of the Woodsman's neck, anywhere but into those eyes that were both familiar and alien. The wolf-man touched a long claw to one of the spikes on the cottage's walls, as though testing its power to harm, and then it spoke. Its voice was deep and low, and filled with spittle and growls, but David could clearly understand every word that it said.

"I see you have been busy, Woodsman," it said. "You have been fortifying your lair."

"The woods are changing," the Woodsman replied. "There are strange creatures abroad."

He shifted the ax in his hands in order to improve his grip upon it. If the wolf-man noticed the implicit threat, he did not show it. Instead he merely growled in agreement, as if he and the Woodsman were neighbors whose paths had crossed unexpectedly while walking in the woods.

"The whole land is changing," said the wolf-man. "The old king can no longer control his kingdom."

"I am not wise enough to judge such matters," said the Woodsman. "I have never met the king, and he does not consult with me about the care of his realm."

"Perhaps he should," said the wolf-man. He seemed almost to smile, except there was no friendliness to it. "After all, you treat these woods as though they were your own kingdom. You should not forget that there are others who would contest your right to rule them."

"I treat all living creatures in this place with the respect they deserve, but it is in the order of things that man should rule over all."

"Then perhaps it is time for a new order to rise," said the wolf-man.

"And what order would that be?" asked the Woodsman. David could hear mockery in his tone. "An order of wolves, of predators? The fact that you walk on hind legs doesn't make you a man, and the fact that you wear gold in your ear doesn't make you a king."

"There are many kingdoms that might exist, and many kings," said the wolf-man.

"You will not rule here," said the Woodsman. "If you try, I will kill you and all of your brothers and sisters."

The wolf-man opened its jaws and snarled. David trembled, but the Woodsman did not move an inch.

"It seems that you have already begun. Was that your handi-work back in the forest?" asked the wolf-man, almost carelessly.

"These are my woods. My handiwork is all over them."

"I am referring to the body of poor Ferdinand, my scout. He appears to have lost his head."

"Was that his name? I never had a chance to ask. He was too intent upon tearing out my throat for us to engage in idle chitchat."

The wolf-man licked his lips. "He was hungry," he said. "We are all hungry."

His eyes flicked from the Woodsman to David, as they had done for much of the conversation, but this time they lingered a little longer on the boy.

"His appetites will no longer trouble him," said the Woods-man. "I have relieved him of their burden."

But Ferdinand was forgotten. The wolf-man's attention was now entirely focused on David.

"And what have you found on your travels?" said the wolf-man. "It seems that you have discovered a strange creature of your own, new *meat* from the forest."

A long, thin thread of saliva dripped from its muzzle as it spoke. The Woodsman placed a protective hand on David's shoulder, drawing him closer, while his right hand held firmly on to the ax.

"This is my brother's son. He has come to stay with me."

The wolf fell to all fours, and the hackles on its back rose high. It sniffed the air.

"You lie!" it growled. "You have no brother, no family. You live alone in this place, and you always have. This is no child of our land. He brings with him new scents. He is . . . *different*."

"He is mine, and I am his guardian," said the Woodsman.

"There was a fire in the forest. Something strange was burning there. Did it come with him?"

"I do not know anything about it."

"If you do not, then perhaps the boy does, and he can explain to us where this came from."

The wolf-man nodded to one of its fellows, and a dark shape flew through the air and landed close to David.

It was the head of the German gunner, all cindery black and charred red. His flight helmet had melted into his scalp, and once again David glimpsed his teeth still locked in their death grimace.

"There was little eating on him," said the wolf-man. "He tasted of ash, and sour things."

"Man does not eat man," said the Woodsman in disgust. "You have shown your true nature through your actions."

The wolf-man crouched, its front paws almost on the ground.

"You cannot keep the boy safe. Others will learn of him. Give him to us, and we will offer him the protection of the pack."

But the wolf-man's eyes gave the lie to its words, for everything about the beast spoke of hunger and want. Its ribs stuck out against its gray fur, visible beneath the white of its shirt, and its limbs were thin. The others with it were also starving. They were now slowly closing in on David and the Woodsman, unable to resist the promise of food.

Suddenly, there was a blur of movement to the right, and one of the lower order of wolves, overcome by its appetites, leaped. The Woodsman spun, the ax rose, and there was a single sharp yelp before the wolf fell dead upon the ground, its head almost severed from its body. A howling arose from the assembled pack, the wolves twisting and turning in excitement and distress. The wolf-man stared at the fallen animal, then turned on the Woodsman, every sharp tooth in its mouth visible, every hackle raised upon its back. David thought that it must certainly fall on them, and then the rest would follow and they would be torn apart, but instead the side of the creature that bore traces of something human seemed to overcome the animal half, and it brought its rage under control.

It rose once again on its hind legs and shook its head. "I warned them to keep their distance, but they are starving," it said. "There are new enemies, and new predators who compete with us for food. Still, this one was not like us, Woodsman. We are not animals. These others cannot control their urges."

The Woodsman and David were backing toward the cottage, trying to get closer to the promise of safety that it offered.

"Do not fool yourself, beast," said the Woodsman. "There is no 'us.' I have more in common with the leaves on the trees and the dirt on the ground than I do with you and your kind."

Already, some of the wolves had advanced and begun to feed on their fallen comrade, but not the ones who wore clothes. They looked longingly at the corpse but, like their leader, they tried to maintain a veneer of self-control. It did not run deep, however. David could see their nostrils twitching at the scent of blood, and he felt certain that were the Woodsman not there to protect him, the wolf-men would have already torn him to pieces. The lower wolves were cannibals, content to feed upon their own kind, but the appetites of the ones who resembled men were much worse than those of the rest.

The wolf-man considered the Woodsman's answer. Masked by the Woodsman's body, David had already taken the key from his pocket and was preparing to insert it into the lock.

"If there is no bond between us," it said, thoughtfully, "then my conscience is clear."

It looked to the assembled pack and howled.

"It is time," it snarled, "to *feed*."

David fitted the key into the hole and began to turn it, just as the wolf-man fell to all fours, its body tensing and ready to spring.

A sudden yelp of warning came from one of the wolves at the edge of the forest. The animal turned to face some threat as yet unseen, and it drew the attention of the rest of the pack, so that even their leader was distracted for crucial seconds. David risked a glance and saw a shape moving against the trunk of a tree, coiling around it like a snake. The wolf backed away from it, whining softly. While it was distracted, a length of green ivy extended itself from a low branch and looped itself around the wolf's neck. It cinched tight upon the fur and then yanked the wolf high into the air, the animal's legs kicking in vain as it began to choke.

Now the whole forest appeared to come alive in a blur of twisting strands of green, the tendrils curling around legs and muzzles and throats, hauling wolves and wolf-men into the air or trapping them upon the ground, drawing tighter and tighter around them until all struggles ceased. The wolves immediately began to fight back, snapping and snarling, but they were powerless against an enemy like this, and those that could were already trying to retreat. David felt the key turn in the lock as the pack leader's head jerked to and fro, torn between its desire for flesh and its urge to survive. Lengths of ivy were moving in its direction now, creeping across the damp earth of the vegetable patch. It had to choose quickly between fight and flight. With a final growl of fury at the Woodsman and David, the wolf-man turned tail and ran south, even as the Woodsman pushed David through the gap and into the safety of the cottage, the door closing firmly behind them and sealing off the sounds of howling and dying from the edge of the forest.

IX

Of the Loups and How They Came into Being

AVID MOVED to one of the barred windows as a warm orange glow crept through the little cottage. The Woodsman had made sure that the door was securely bolted and the wolves had fled before piling logs into the stone fireplace and preparing the fire. If he was troubled by what had occurred outside, then he wasn't showing it. In fact, he seemed remarkably calm, and some of that calm had spread to David. He should have been terrified, even trauma- tized. After all, he had been threatened by talking wolves, wit- nessed an attack by living ivy, and the charred head of a German flier had landed at his feet, half gnawed by sharp teeth. Instead, he was merely bewildered, and more than a little curious.

David's fingers and toes tingled. His nose began to run in the growing warmth, and he discarded the Woodsman's jacket. He wiped his nose on the sleeve of his dressing gown and then felt a little ashamed. The dressing gown, now looking decidedly sorry for itself, was the only item of outer clothing that he possessed, and it seemed unwise to add to its current state of disrepair in any way. Apart from the gown, he had one slipper, a pair of torn, muddy pajama bottoms, and a pajama shirt, which, compared with the other items, was almost as good as new.

The window at which he stood had been blocked by internal shutters behind the bars, with a narrow horizontal slit to allow those inside to see out. Through the gap he saw the corpses of wolves being dragged into the forest, some leaving trails of blood behind.

"They are growing ever bolder and more cunning, and that makes them harder to kill," said the Woodsman. He had joined David at the window. "A year ago they would not have risked such an attack upon me or upon another under my protection, but now there are more of them than ever before, and their numbers are swelling with each passing day. Soon they may try to make good on their promise to take the kingdom."

"The ivy attacked them," said David. He still could not quite believe what he had seen.

"The forest, or this forest at least, has ways of protecting itself," said the Woodsman. "Those beasts are unnatural, a threat to the order of things. The forest wants no part of them. It is to do with the king, I think, and the fading of his powers. This world is coming apart, and it grows stranger with each passing day. The Loups are the most dangerous creatures yet to have arisen, for they have the worst of man and beast fighting for supremacy within them."

"Loups?" said David. "Is that what you call those wolf things?"

"They are not wolves, although wolves run with them. Neither are they men, although they walk on two legs when it suits their purposes, and their leader decks himself in jewels and fine clothes. He calls himself Leroi, and he is as intelligent as he is ambitious, and as cunning as he is cruel. Now he would war with the king. I hear stories from travelers through these woods. They talk of great packs of wolves moving across the land, white wolves from the north and black wolves from the east, all heeding the call of their brothers, the grays, and their leaders, the Loups."

And while David sat by the fire, the Woodsman told him a story.

THE WOODSMAN'S FIRST TALE

Once upon a time there was a girl who lived on the outskirts of the forest. She was lively and bright, and she wore a red cloak, for that way if she ever went astray she could easily be found, since a red cloak would always stand out against the trees and bushes. As the years went by, and she became more woman than girl, she grew more and more beautiful. Many men wanted her for their bride, but she turned them all down. None was good enough for her, for she was cleverer than every man she met and they presented no challenge to her.

Her grandmother lived in a cottage in the forest, and the girl would visit her often, bringing her baskets of bread and meat and staying with her for a time. While her grandmother slept, the girl in red would wander among the trees, tasting the wild berries and strange fruits of the woods. One day, as she walked in a dark grove, a wolf came. It was wary of her and tried to pass without being seen, but the girl's senses were too acute. She saw the wolf, and she looked into its eyes and fell in love with the strangeness of it. When it turned away, she followed it, traveling deeper into the forest than she had ever done before. The wolf tried to lose her in places where there were no trails to follow, no paths to be seen, but the girl was too quick for it, and mile after mile the chase continued. At last, the wolf grew weary of the pursuit, and it turned to face her. It bared its fangs and growled a warning, but she was not afraid.

"Lovely wolf," she whispered. "You have nothing to fear from me."

She reached out her hand and placed it upon the wolf's head. She ran her fingers through its fur and calmed it. And the wolf saw what beautiful eyes she had (all the better to see him with), and what gentle hands (all the better to stroke him with), and what soft, red lips (all the better to taste him with). The girl leaned forward, and she kissed the wolf. She cast off her red cloak and put her basket of flowers aside, and she lay with the animal. From their union came a creature that was more human than wolf. He was the first of the Loups, the one called Leroi, and more followed after him. Other women came, lured by the girl in the red cloak. She would wander the forest paths, enticing those who passed her way with promises of ripe, juicy berries and spring water so pure that it could make skin look young again. Sometimes she traveled to the edge of a town or village, and there she would wait until a girl walked by and she would draw her into the woods with false cries for help.

But some went with her willingly, for there are women who dream of lying with wolves.

None was ever seen again, for in time the Loups turned on those who had created them and they fed upon them in the moonlight.

And that is how the Loups came into being.

When his tale was done, the Woodsman went to an oak chest in the corner by the bed and found a shirt that would fit David, as well as a pair of trousers that were just a little too long, and shoes that were just a little too loose, although the addition of an extra pair of coarse wool socks made them wearable. The shoes were leather and had clearly not been worn in a great many years. David wondered where they had come from, for they had obviously belonged to a child once, but when he tried to ask the Woodsman about them, he just turned away and busied himself with laying out bread and cheese for them to eat.

While they ate, the Woodsman questioned David more closely about how he came to enter the forest, and about the world that he had left behind. There was so much to tell, but the Woodsman seemed less interested in talk of war and flying machines than he was in David and his family, and the story of his mother.

"You say that you heard her voice," he said. "Yet she is dead, so how can this be?"

"I don't know," said David. "But it was her. I know it was."

The Woodsman looked doubtful. "I have seen no woman pass through the woods for a long time. If she is here, she found another way into this world."

In return, the Woodsman told David much about the place in which he now found himself. He spoke of the king, who had reigned for a very long time but had lost control of his kingdom as he grew old and tired and was now a virtual recluse in his castle to the east. He spoke more of the Loups and their desire to reign over others as men did, and of new castles that had appeared in distant parts of the kingdom, dark places of hidden evil.

And he spoke of a trickster, the one who had no name and was unlike any other creature in the kingdom, for even the king feared him.

"Is he a crooked man?" asked David, suddenly. "Does he wear a crooked hat?"

The Woodsman stopped chewing his bread. "And how would you know that?" he said.

"I've seen him," said David. "He was in my bedroom."

"That is him," said the Woodsman. "He steals children, and they are never seen again."

And there was something so sad and yet so angry about the way the Woodsman spoke of the Crooked Man that David wondered if Leroi, the leader of the Loups, was wrong. Perhaps the Woodsman had had a family, once, but something very bad had happened and now he was entirely alone.

X

Of Tricksters and Trickery

AVID SLEPT that night upon the Woodsman's bed. It smelled of dried berries and pinecones and the animal scent of the Woodsman's leathers and furs. The Woodsman dozed in a chair by the fire, his ax close to hand and his face cast in flickering shadows by the light of the dying flames.

It took David a long time to get to sleep, even though the Woodsman assured him that the cottage was secure. The slits in the windows had been covered up, and there was even a metal plate, pierced with small holes, set halfway up the chimney to prevent the creatures of the forest from entering that way. The woods beyond were silent, but it was not the quiet of peace and rest. The Woodsman had told David that the forest changed at night: half-formed creatures, beings from deep beneath the ground, colonized it once the half-light faded, and most of the nocturnal animals were dead or had learned to be even warier of predation than before.

The boy was aware of a strange mixture of feelings. There was fear, of course, and an aching regret that he had ever been foolish enough to leave the security of his own home and enter this new world. He wanted to return to the life he knew, however difficult it might be, but he also wanted to see a little more of this land, and he had not yet found an explanation for the sound of his mother's voice. Was this what happened to the dead? Did they travel into this land, perhaps on the way to another place? Was his mother trapped here? Could a mistake have been made? Maybe she wasn't meant to die, and now she was trying to hold on here in the hope that someone would find her and bring her back to those whom she loved. No, David could not return, not yet. The tree was marked, and he would find his way home, once he had discovered the truth about his mother and the part this world now played in her existence.

He wondered if his father had missed him yet, and the thought made his eyes water. The impact of the German plane would have woken everyone, and the garden was probably already sealed off by the army or the ARP. David's absence would have been quickly noticed. They would be looking for him at this very moment. He felt a kind of satisfaction in the knowledge that, by his absence, he had made himself more important in his father's life. Now perhaps his dad would be worried more about him and less about work and codes and Rose and Georgie.

But what if they didn't miss him? What if life became easier for them now that he was gone? His father and Rose could start a new family, untroubled by the remnant of the old, except once a year, perhaps, when the anniversary of his disappearance came around. In time, though, even that would fade, and then he would be largely forgotten, remembered only in passing, just as the memory of Rose's uncle, Jonathan Tulvey, had been resurrected only by David's own questions about him.

David tried to push such thoughts aside and closed his eyes. At last he fell asleep, and he dreamed of his father, and of Rose and his new half brother, and of things that burrowed up from beneath the earth, waiting for the fears of others to give them shape.

And in the dark corners of his dreams, a shadow capered, and it threw its crooked hat in the air with glee.

David woke to the sound of the Woodsman preparing food. They ate hard white bread at the little table by the far wall and drank strong black tea from crudely made mugs. Outside, only the faintest trace of light showed in the sky. David assumed that it was very early in the morning indeed, so early that the sun had not yet dawned, but the Woodsman said the sun had not been truly visible for a very long time and this was as much light as was ever seen in the world. It made David wonder if he had somehow traveled far to the north, to a place where night lasted for months and months in winter, but even in the Arctic north the long, dark winters were balanced by days of endless light in summer. No, this was no northern land. This was Elsewhere.

After they had eaten, David washed his face and hands in a bowl and tried to clean his teeth with his finger. When he had finished, he performed his little rituals of touching and counting, and it was only when he became aware of a silence in the room that he realized the Woodsman was watching him quietly from his chair.

"What are you doing?" asked the Woodsman.

It was the first time that the question had ever been posed to David, and he was stumped for a moment as he tried to provide a plausible excuse for his behavior. In the end, he settled on the truth.

"They're rules," he said simply. "They're my routines. I started doing them to try to keep my mother from harm. I thought that they would help."

"And did they?"

David shook his head. "No, I don't think so. Or maybe they did, but just not enough. I suppose you think they're strange. I suppose you think *I'm* strange for doing them."

He was afraid to look at the Woodsman, fearful of what he might see in the man's eyes. Instead he stared into the bowl and saw his reflection distort upon the water.

Eventually the Woodsman spoke. "We all have our routines," he said softly. "But they must have a purpose and provide an outcome that we can see and take some comfort from, or else they have no use at all. Without that, they are like the endless pacings of a caged animal. If they are not madness itself, then they are a prelude to it."

The Woodsman stood and showed David his ax. "See here," he said, pointing with his finger at the blade. "Every morning, I make certain that my ax is clean and keen. I look to my house and check that its windows and doors remain secure. I tend to my land, disposing of weeds and ensuring that the soil is watered. I walk through the forest, clearing those paths that need to be kept open. Where trees have been damaged, I do my best to repair what has been harmed. These are *my* routines, and I enjoy doing them well."

He laid a hand gently on David's shoulder, and David saw understanding in his face. "Rules and routines are good, but they must give you satisfaction. Can you truly say you gain that from touching and counting?"

David shook his head. "No," he said, "but I get scared when I don't do them. I'm afraid of what might happen."

"Then find routines that allow you to feel secure when they are done. You told me that you have a new brother: look to him each morning. Look to your father, and your stepmother. Tend to the flowers in the garden, or in the pots upon the windowsill. Seek others who are weaker than you are, and try to give them comfort where you can. Let these be your routines, and the rules that govern your life."

David nodded, but he turned his face from the Woodsman's to

hide what might be read upon it. Perhaps the Woodsman was right, but David could not bring himself to do those things for Georgie and Rose. He would try to take on some other, easier duties, but to keep safe these intruders into his life was beyond him.

The Woodsman took David's old clothes—his torn dressing gown, his dirty pajamas, his single muddy slipper—and placed them in a rough sack. He slung the sack over his shoulder and unlocked the door.

"Where are we going?" said David.

"We're going to return you to your own land," said the Woodsman.

"But the hole in the tree disappeared."

"Then we will try to make it appear again."

"But I haven't found my mother," said David.

The Woodsman looked at him sadly. "Your mother is dead. You told me so yourself."

"But I heard her! I heard her voice."

"Perhaps, or something like it," said the Woodsman. "I don't pretend to know every secret of this land, but I can tell you that it is a dangerous place, and becoming more so with every day that passes. You must go back. The Loup Leroi was right about one thing: I can't protect you. I can barely protect myself. Now come: this is a good time to travel, for the night beasts are in their deepest sleep, and the worst of the daylight ones are not yet awake."

So David, perceiving that he had little choice in the matter, followed the Woodsman from the cottage and into the forest. Time and again the Woodsman would stop and listen, his hand raised as a signal to David that he should remain silent and still.

"Where are the Loups and the wolves?" David asked eventually, after they had walked for perhaps an hour. The only signs of life that he had seen were birds and insects.

"Not far away, I fear," replied the Woodsman. "They will scavenge for food in other parts of the forest, where they are less at risk of attack, and in time they will try once again to steal you away. That is why you must leave here before they return."

David shivered at the thought of Leroi and his wolves descending upon him, their jaws and claws tearing at his flesh. He was beginning to understand the cost that might be paid in searching this place for his mother, but it seemed as if the decision to return home had already been made for him, at least for now. He could always come back here again, if he chose. After all, the sunken garden still remained, assuming the German plane had not entirely destroyed it when it crashed.

They came to the glade of enormous trees through which he had first entered the Woodsman's world. As they reached it, the Woodsman stopped so suddenly that David almost ran into him. Cautiously, he peered around the man's back in order to glimpse what it was that had caused him to stop.

"Oh no," gasped David.

Every tree, as far as the eye could see, was marked with string, and every string, David's nose told him, was daubed with the same foul-smelling substance that the Woodsman had used to keep the animals from gnawing upon it. There was no way of telling which tree was the one that marked the doorway from David's world to this one. He walked on a little, trying to find the hollow from which he had emerged, but every tree was similar, every bark smooth. It seemed even the hollows and gnarls that made each one distinctive had been filled in or altered, and the little path that once wound through the forest was now entirely gone, so the Woodsman had no bearings to follow. Even the wreckage of the German bomber was nowhere to be seen, and the furrow it had carved through the earth had been filled in. It must have taken hundreds of hours, and the work of many, many hands, to achieve such an end, thought David. How could it have

THE BOOK OF LOST THINGS

been done in a single night, and without leaving even one footprint upon the ground?

"Who would so such a thing?" he asked.

"A trickster," said the Woodsman. "A crooked man in a crooked hat."

"But why?" said David. "Why didn't he just take away the string that you had tied. Wouldn't that have worked just as well?"

The Woodsman thought for a moment before answering. "Yes," he said, "but it wouldn't have been so amusing to him, and it wouldn't have made such a good story."

"A story?" asked David. "Whatever do you mean?"

"You're part of a story," said the Woodsman. "He likes to create stories. He likes to store up tales to tell. This will make a very good story."

"But how will I get home?" asked David. Now that his means of returning to his own world was gone, he suddenly wanted very much to be there, whereas when it had seemed that the Woodsman was trying to force him to return against his will, David had wanted nothing more than to stay in the new land and look for his mother. It was all very peculiar.

"He doesn't *want* you to get home," said the Woodsman.

"I've never done anything to him," said David. "Why is he trying to keep me here? Why is he being so mean?"

The Woodsman shook his head. "I don't know," he said.

"Then who does?" said David. He almost shouted in frustration. He was starting to wish there was someone around who knew a little more than the Woodsman. The Woodsman was fine for decapitating wolves and giving unwanted advice, but he didn't seem to be keeping up with developments in the kingdom.

"The king," said the Woodsman at last. "The king might know."

"But I thought you told me that he wasn't in control anymore, that no one had seen him in a long time."

"That doesn't mean he isn't aware of what's happening," said the Woodsman. "They say that the king has a book, a Book of Lost Things. It is his most prized possession. He keeps it hidden in the throne room of his palace, and no one is permitted to look upon it but him. I have heard it said that it contains in its pages all of the king's knowledge, and that he turns to it in times of trouble or doubt to give him guidance. Perhaps there is an answer within it to the question of how to get you home."

David tried to read the expression on the Woodsman's face. He wasn't sure why, but he had a strong feeling that the Woodsman wasn't telling him the entire truth about the king. Before he could question him further, the Woodsman tossed the sack containing David's old clothes into a copse of bushes and started to walk back in the direction they had come.

"It will be one fewer thing to carry on our journey," he said. "We have a long way to go."

With a last, longing look at the forest of anonymous trees, David turned and followed the Woodsman back to the cottage.

When they were gone, and all was quiet, a figure emerged from the beneath the spreading roots of a great and ancient tree. Its back was hunched, its fingers were twisted, and it wore a crooked hat upon its head. It moved quickly through the undergrowth until it came to a copse of bushes dotted with swollen, frost-sweetened berries, but it ignored the fruits in favor of the rough, dirty sack that lay amid the leaves. It reached inside, removed the top of David's pajamas, and held the clothing to its face, sniffing deeply.

"Boy lost," it whispered to itself, "and child lost to come."

And with that it grabbed the sack and was swallowed up by the shadows of the forest.

XI

Of the Children Lost in the Forest and What Befell Them

AVID AND THE WOODSMAN returned to the cottage without incident. There they packed food into two leather bags and filled a pair of tin canteens from the stream that ran behind the house. David saw the Woodsman kneel by the water's edge and examine some marks upon the damp ground, but he said nothing to David about them. David glanced at them in passing and thought that they looked like the tracks left by a big dog, or a wolf. There was a little water at the bottom of each, so David knew that they were recent.

The Woodsman armed himself with his ax, a bow and a quiver of arrows, and a long knife. Finally, he took a short-bladed sword from a storage chest. After only the slightest pause to blow some of the dust from it, he gave the sword to David, and a leather belt upon which to wear it. David had never held a real sword before, and his knowledge of swordsmanship did not extend much further than playing pirates with wooden sticks, but having the sword at his side made him feel stronger and a little braver.

The Woodsman locked the cottage, then laid his hand flat upon the door and lowered his head, as though praying. He looked sad, and David wondered if, for some reason, the Woodsman thought that he might not see his home again. Then they moved into the forest, heading northeast, and kept up a steady pace while the sickly luminescence that passed for daylight lit their way. After a few hours, David grew very tired. The Woodsman allowed him to rest, but only for a little while.

"We must be clear of the woods before nightfall," he told David, and the boy did not have to ask him why. Already he feared to hear the silence of the woods shattered by the howling of wolves and Loups.

As they walked, David had a chance to examine his surroundings. He was unable to name any of the trees that he saw, although aspects of some were familiar to him. A tree that looked like an old oak had pinecones dangling beneath its evergreen leaves. Another was the size and shape of a large Christmas tree, the bases of its silver leaves dotted with clusters of red berries. Most of the trees, though, were bare. Occasionally, David would catch sight of some of the childlike flowers, their eyes wide and curious, although at the first sign of the approaching Woodsman and boy, they would draw their leaves protectively around themselves and quake gently until the threat had passed.

"What are those flowers called?" he asked.

"They have no name," said the Woodsman. "Sometimes, children stray from the path and become lost in the forest, and they are never seen again. They die there, consumed by beasts or slain by evil men, and their blood soaks into the ground. In time, one of these flowers will spring up, often far from where the child breathed his last. They cluster together, just like frightened children might. They are the forest's way of remembering them, I think. The forest feels the loss of a child."

David had learned that the Woodsman generally did not speak unless spoken to first, so it was left to him to ask questions, which the Woodsman would answer as best he could. He tried to give David some sense of the geography of this place: the king's castle lay many miles to the east, and the area in between was sparsely populated, with only the occasional settlement to disturb the landscape. A deep chasm separated the Woodsman's forest from the territories farther to the east, and they would have to cross it to continue their journey to the king's castle. To the south was a great, black sea, but few ever ventured far upon it. It was the domain of sea beasts, dragons of the waters, and constantly wracked by storms and huge waves. North and west lay ranges of mountains, but they were impassable for most of the year, their peaks topped with snow.

While they walked, the Woodsman spoke more to David of the Loups. "In the old days, before the coming of the Loups, wolves were predictable creatures," he explained. "Each pack, rarely numbering more than fifteen or twenty wolves, had a territory where it would live and hunt and breed. Then the Loups began to appear, and everything changed. The packs began to grow; allegiances were formed; territories grew larger, or ceased to have meaning at all; and cruelty raised its head. In the past, perhaps half of all wolf pups died. They needed more food than their parents, for their size, and if food was scarce, then they starved. Sometimes they were killed by their own parents, but only if they showed signs of disease or madness. For the most part, wolves were fine parents, sharing their kills with the young, guarding them, giving them care and affection.

"But the Loups brought with them a new way of dealing with the young: only the strongest are now fed, never more than two or three to a litter, and sometimes not even that. The weak are eaten. In that way, the pack itself remains strong, but it has altered their nature. Now they turn upon one another, and there is no loyalty between them. Only the rule of the Loups keeps them under control. Without the Loups, they would be as they once were, I think."

The Woodsman told David how to tell the females from the males. The females had narrower muzzles and foreheads. Their necks and shoulders were thinner, their legs shorter, yet they were faster when young than males of a similar age and for that reason made better hunters and deadlier enemies. In normal wolf packs, the females were often the leaders, but once again the Loups had usurped this natural order of things. There were females among them, but it was Leroi and his lieutenants who made the important decisions. Perhaps that was one of their weaknesses, suggested the Woodsman. Their arrogance had led them to turn their backs on thousands of years of female instinct. Now they were driven only by the desire for power.

"Wolves will not give up on prey," said the Woodsman, "not unless they are exhausted. They can run for ten or fifteen miles at speeds far faster than a man can travel, and trot for five miles more before they have to rest. The Loups have slowed them somewhat, for they choose to walk on two legs and are no longer as fleet as they once were, but on foot we are still no match for them. We must hope that, when we reach our destination tonight, there are horses to be found. There is a man there who deals in them, and I have gold enough to buy us a mount."

There were no trails to follow. Instead, they relied upon the Woodsman's knowledge of the forest, although as they traveled farther and farther from his home, he stopped more frequently, examining growths of moss and the shapes the wind had carved from the trees in order to satisfy himself that they had not strayed. In all that time they passed only one other dwelling, and that lay in brown ruins. It appeared to David to have melted rather than fallen into disrepair, and only its stone chimney remained standing, blackened but intact. He could see where molten droplets had cooled and hardened upon the walls, and the buckled spaces where the windows had collapsed in upon themselves. The route they were taking brought him close enough to touch the structure, and now it was clear that there were chunks of a lighter brown substance embedded in the walls. He rubbed his hand upon the doorframe, then chipped away at it with a nail. He recognized the texture, and the faint smell that arose.

"It's chocolate," he exclaimed. "And gingerbread."

He broke off a larger piece and was about to taste it when the Woodsman knocked it from his hands.

"No," he said. "It may look and smell sweet, but it hides its own poison yet."

And he told David another story.

THE WOODSMAN'S SECOND TALE

Once upon a time, there were two children, a boy and a girl. Their father died and their mother married again, but their stepfather was an evil man. He hated the children and resented their presence in his home. He came to despise them even more when the crops failed and famine came, for they ate valuable food, food that he would rather have kept for himself. He begrudged them every meager bite that he was forced to give them, and as his own hunger grew, he began to suggest to his wife that they might eat the children and thereby save themselves from death, for she could always give birth to more children when times improved. His wife was horrified, and she feared what her new husband might do to them when her back was turned. Yet she realized that she could no longer afford to feed them herself, so she took them deep, deep into the forest, and there she abandoned them to fend for themselves.

The children were very frightened, and they cried themselves to sleep that first night, but in time they grew to understand the forest. The girl was wiser and stronger than her brother, and it was she who learned to trap small animals and birds, and to steal eggs from nests. The boy preferred to wander or to daydream, waiting for his sister to provide whatever she could catch to feed them both. He missed his mother and wanted to return to her. Some days he did nothing but cry from dawn until dusk. He desired his old life back, and he made no effort to embrace the new.

One day, he did not return when his sister called his name. She went in search of him, leaving a trail of blossoms behind her so that she would be able to find her way back to their little supply of food, until she came to the edge of a small clearing, and there she saw the most extraordinary house. Its walls were made of chocolate and gingerbread. Its roof was slated with slabs of toffee, and the glass in its windows was formed from clear sugar. Embedded in its walls were almonds and fudge and candied fruits. Everything about it spoke of sweetness and indulgence. Her brother was picking nuts from the walls when she found him, and his mouth was dark with chocolate.

"Don't worry, there's nobody home," he said. "Try it. It's delicious."

He held out a piece of chocolate to her, but she did not take it at first. Her brother's eyelids were half closed, so overcome was he by the wonderful taste of the house. His sister tried to open the door, but it was locked. She peered through the glass, but the curtains were drawn and she could not see inside. She did not want to eat, for something about the house made her uneasy, but the smell of the chocolate was too much for her, and she allowed herself to nibble on a piece. It tasted even better than she had imagined, and her stomach cried out for more. So she joined her brother, and together they ate and ate until they had consumed so much that, in time, they fell into a deep sleep.

When they awoke, they were no longer lying on the grass beneath the trees of the forest. Instead, they were inside the house, trapped in a cage that hung from the ceiling. A woman was fueling an oven with logs. She was old and foul-smelling. Piles of bones lay stacked on the floor by her feet, the remains of the other children who had fallen prey to her.

"Fresh meat!" she whispered to herself. "Fresh meat for old Gammer's oven!"

The little boy began to cry, but his sister hushed him. The woman came to them and peered at them through the bars of the cage. Her face was covered with black warts, and her teeth were worn and crooked like old gravestones.

"Now which of you will be first?" she asked.

The boy tried to hide his face, as though by doing so he might avoid the attentions of the old woman. But his sister was braver.

"Take me," she said. "I am plumper than my brother, and will make a better roast for you. While you eat me you can fatten him up, so that he will feed you for longer when you cook him."

The old woman cackled with joy.

"Clever girl," she cried. "Although not so clever as to avoid Gammer's plate."

She opened the cage and reached in, grabbing the girl by the scruff of the neck and dragging her out. Then she locked the cage once again and brought the girl to the oven. It was not yet hot enough, but it soon would be.

"I will never fit in there," said the girl. "It's too small."

"Nonsense," said the old woman. "I've put bigger than you in there, and they've cooked just fine."

The girl looked doubtful. "But I have long limbs, and fat upon them. No, I will never manage to get into that oven. And if you do squeeze me in, you'll never get me out again."

The old woman took the girl by the shoulders and shook her. "I was wrong about you," she said. "You're an ignorant, foolish girl. Look, I'll show you how big this oven is."

She climbed up and stuck her head and shoulders into the mouth of the oven.

"See?" she said, and her voice echoed within. "There's room to spare for me, let alone a girl like you."

The little girl ran at her and with a great push she shoved her into the oven and slammed the door closed. The old woman tried to kick it open again, but the girl was too quick for her, slamming the bolt on it (for the old woman did not want a child to break free once the roasting had begun) and leaving her trapped inside. Then she fed more logs to the fire, and slowly the old woman began to cook, all the time screaming and wailing and threatening the girl with the most awful of tortures. So hot was the oven that the fats of her body began to melt, creating a stench so terrible that the little girl felt ill. Still the old woman fought, even as her skin parted from her flesh, and her flesh from her bones, until at last she died. Then the little girl drew wood from the fire and scattered burning logs around the cottage. She led her brother away by the hand as the house melted behind them, leaving only the chimney standing tall, and they never went back there again.

In the months that followed, the girl grew happier and happier in the forest. She built a shelter, and over time the shelter became a little house. She learned to fend for herself, and as the days went by she thought less and less of her old life. But her brother was never happy and yearned always to be back with his mother. After a year and a day, he left his sister and returned to his old home, but by then his mother and his stepfather were long gone, and no one could tell him where they were. He came back to the forest, but not to his sister, for he was jealous and resentful of her. Instead, he found a path in the woods that was well-tended and cleared of roots and briars, the bushes beside it thick with juicy berries. He followed it, eating some of the berries as he went, never noticing that the path behind him was disappearing with every step that he took.

And after a time he came to a clearing, and in the clearing was a pretty little house, with ivy on the walls and flowers by the door and a trail of smoke rising from its chimney. He smelled bread baking, and a cake lay cooling on the windowsill. A woman appeared at the door, bright and merry, as his mother had once been. She waved to him, inviting him to come to her, and he did.

"Come in, come in," she said. "You look tired, and berries are not enough

to fill a growing boy. I have food roasting over the fire, and a soft place for you to rest. Stay as long as you wish, for I have no children, and have long wanted a son to call my own."

The boy cast the berries aside as the path behind him vanished forever, and he followed the woman into the house, where a great cauldron bubbled on the fire and a sharp knife lay waiting on the butcher's block.

And he was never seen again.

XII

Of Bridges and Riddles, and the Many Unappealing Characteristics of Trolls

HE LIGHT was changing as the Woodsman's story ended. He looked up at the sky, as if in hope that darkness might be held back for a little longer, and suddenly he stopped walking. David followed his gaze. Above their heads, just at the level of the forest's crown, David saw a black shape circling and thought that he heard a distant cawing.

"Damnation," hissed the Woodsman.

"What is it?" asked David.

"A raven."

The Woodsman removed his bow from his back and notched an arrow to its string. He knelt, sighted, then released the arrow. His aim was true. The raven jerked in the air as the arrow pierced its body, then tumbled to the ground not far from where David stood. It was dead, the point of the arrow red with its blood.

"Foul bird," said the Woodsman, as he lifted the corpse and pulled the arrow through its body.

"Why did you kill it?" asked David.

"The raven and the wolf hunt together. This one was leading the pack to us. They would have fed our eyes to it as its reward."

He looked back in the direction they had come.

"They will have to rely on scent alone now, but they are closing on us, make no mistake. We must hurry."

They continued on their way, moving now at a slight trot, as though they themselves were tired wolves at the end of a hunt, until they reached the edge of the forest and emerged onto a high plateau. Ahead of them lay a great chasm, hundreds of feet deep and a quarter of a mile wide. A river, thin as a length of silver thread, wound through it, and David heard the cries of what might have been birds echoing from the canyon's walls. Carefully, he peered over the edge of the crevasse in the hope of getting a better look at what was making the noise. He saw a shape, much larger than any bird that he had ever seen, gliding through the air, supported by the updrafts from the canyon. It had bare, almost human legs, although its toes were strangely elongated and curved like an eagle's talons. Its arms were outstretched, and from them hung the great folds of skin that served as its wings. Its long white hair flowed in the wind, and as David listened, he heard it start to sing. The creature's voice was very high and very beautiful, and its words were clear to him:

What falls is food,
What drops will die,
Where lives the Brood,
Birds fear to fly.

Its song was taken up and echoed by other voices, and David could make out many more of the creatures moving through the canyon. The one nearest to him performed a loop in the air, at once both graceful and strangely menacing, and David glimpsed its naked body. He looked away immediately, ashamed and embarrassed.

It had a female form: old, and with scales instead of skin, yet still female for all that. He risked another look and saw the creature descending now in diminishing circles, until suddenly its wings folded in, streamlining its form, and it fell rapidly, its clawed feet extended as it seemed to head directly for the canyon wall. It struck the stone, and David saw something struggle in its claws: it was a little brown mammal of some kind, scarcely bigger than a squirrel. Its paws flailed at the air as it was plucked from the rocks. Its captor changed direction and headed for an outcrop beneath David in order to feed, shrieking in triumph. Some of its rivals, alerted by its cries, approached in the hope of stealing its meal, but it struck at the air with its wings in warning and they drifted away. David had an opportunity to examine its face as it hovered: it resembled a woman's but was longer and thinner, with a lipless mouth that left its sharp teeth permanently exposed. Now those teeth tore into its prey, ripping great chunks of bloody fur from its body as it fed.

"The Brood," said the Woodsman from nearby. "Another new evil that blights this part of the kingdom."

"Harpies," said David.

"You've seen such creatures before?" asked the Woodsman.

"No," said David. "Not really."

But I've read about them. I've seen them in my book of Greek myths. For some reason, I don't think they belong in this story, yet here they are . . .

David felt ill. He moved away from the edge of the canyon, which was so deep that it gave him vertigo. "How do we get across?" he asked.

"There is a bridge about a half mile downriver," said the Woodsman. "We'll make it before the light fades."

He led David along the canyon, keeping close to the edge of

the forest so that there was no danger of them losing their foot-
ing and falling into that awful abyss where the Brood waited.
David could hear the beating of their wings and, on more than
one occasion, he thought he saw one of the creatures briefly
ascend above the rim of the canyon and regard them balefully.

"Don't be afraid," said the Woodsman. "They are cowardly
things. Were you to fall, they would pluck you from the air and
tear you apart as they fought over you, but they would not dare to
attack you on the ground."

David nodded, but he did not feel reassured. In this land, it
seemed that hunger inevitably overwhelmed cowardice, and the
harpies of the Brood, as thin and emaciated as the wolves, looked
very hungry indeed.

After they had walked for a little while, their footsteps echoed by
the beating of the harpies' wings, they saw a pair of bridges span-
ning the gorge. The bridges were identical. They were made
from rope, with uneven slats of wood for the base, and they did
not look terribly safe to David.

The Woodsman stared at them in puzzlement. "Two bridges,"
he said. "There was only ever one bridge at this spot."

"Well," said David, matter-of-factly, "now there are two." It
didn't seem like such a terrible imposition to have a choice of two
ways to cross. Perhaps this was a busy spot. After all, there didn't
seem to be any other way to get across the chasm, unless you were
able to fly and were prepared to take your chances with the
harpies.

He heard flies buzzing nearby and followed the Woodsman to
a small hollow just out of sight of the chasm. The remains of a
cottage and some stables stood there, but it was clear that the
property was deserted. Outside one of the stables lay the carcass
of a horse, most of the meat already picked from its bones. David

watched as the Woodsman peered into the stables, then looked through the open doorway of the house itself. With his head lowered, he walked back to David.

"The horse dealer is gone," he said. "It looks as if he fled with whatever horses survived."

"The wolves?" asked David.

"No, something else did this."

They returned to the chasm. One of the harpies hung in the air nearby, watching them, her wings beating a fast cadence to keep her in place. She stayed in that position for just an instant too long, for suddenly her body spasmed and the barbed silver tip of a harpoon shot through her chest, a length of rope anchoring the shaft to a point lower down on the canyon wall. The harpy grasped the harpoon, as if she could somehow wrest her body from it and escape, but then the beating of her wings began to fail and she plummeted down, twisting and turning until the rope reached the end of its length and she was brought up short, her corpse striking against the rock with a dull, thudding sound. From the edge of the chasm, David and the Woodsman watched the dead harpy being hauled up toward a hollow in the wall, the barbs of the harpoon preventing the corpse from sliding off. Finally, the body reached the entrance to the cave and was pulled inside.

"Ugh," said David.

"Trolls," said the Woodsman. "That explains the second bridge."

He approached the twin structures. Between them was a slab of stone into which words had been laboriously, if crudely, carved:

One lies in truth,
One's truth is lies.

One path is death,
One path is life.
One question asked,
The path to guide.

"It's a riddle," said David.

"But what does it mean?" asked the Woodsman.

The answer quickly became apparent. David had never imagined that he might see a troll, although he had always been fascinated by them. In his mind, they existed as shadowy figures who dwelled beneath bridges, testing travelers in the hope of eating them when they failed. The figures that climbed over the lip of the canyon, flaming torches in their hands, were not quite what he had expected. They were smaller than the Woodsman but very broad, and their skin was like that of an elephant, tough and wrinkled. Raised plates of bone, like those on the backs of some dinosaurs, ran along their spines, but their faces were similar to those of apes; very ugly apes, admittedly, and ones that seemed to be suffering from severe acne, but apes nonetheless. Each troll took up a position in front of one of the bridges and smiled grimly. They had small red eyes that glowed sinisterly in the gathering darkness.

"Two bridges, and two paths," said David. He was thinking aloud, but he caught himself before he gave anything away to the two trolls and resolved to keep his thoughts to himself until he had come to some conclusion. The trolls already had all the advantages. He didn't want to give them any more.

The riddle clearly meant that one bridge was unsafe, and to take it would lead to death, at the hands of either the harpies or the trolls themselves, or, assuming both parties failed to act quickly enough, by falling a very long distance and landing hard on the ground below. Actually, David thought both bridges looked pretty ramshackle, but he had to assume that the riddle had some truth to it, otherwise, well, there was hardly any point in having a riddle at all.

One lies in truth, one's truth is lies. David knew that one. He'd encountered it somewhere before, probably in a story. Oh, he had it! One could tell only lies, and the other could tell only the truth. So you could ask one troll which bridge to follow, but he—or she, as David wasn't entirely sure if the trolls were male or female—might not be telling the truth. There was a solution to it as well, except that David couldn't remember it. What was it?

The light faded entirely at last, and a great howling arose from the forest. It sounded very close.

"We have to cross," said the Woodsman. "The wolves have found our trail."

"We can't cross until we've chosen a bridge," explained David. "I don't think those trolls will let us pass unless we do, and if we try to force our way through and choose the wrong one—"

"Then we won't have to worry about the wolves," the Woodsman said, finishing the sentence for him.

"There's a solution," said David. "I know there is. I just have to remember how it goes."

They heard a thrashing in the woods. The wolves were drawing ever nearer.

"One question," muttered David.

The Woodsman hefted his ax in his right hand and with his left drew his knife. He was facing the line of trees, ready to take on whatever emerged from the woods.

"Got it!" said David. "I think," he added, softly.

He approached the troll on the left. It was slightly taller than the other, and smelled slightly better, which wasn't saying much.

David took a deep breath. "If I asked the other troll to point to the right bridge, which bridge would it choose?" he asked.

There was silence. The troll knit its brow, causing some of the sores upon its face to ooze unpleasantly. David didn't know how recently the bridge had been constructed, or how many other travelers had passed this way, but he got the feeling the troll had never been asked that question before. Finally, the troll seemed to give up trying to understand David's logic and pointed to its left.

"It's the one on the right," said David to the Woodsman.

"How can you be sure?" he asked.

"Because if the troll I asked is the liar, then the other troll is the truth teller. The truth teller would point to the correct bridge, but the liar would lie about it, so if the truthful one would have pointed to the bridge on the right, then the liar would lie about it and tell me that it was the one on the left.

"But if the troll I asked has to tell the truth, then the other is the liar, and he would point to the wrong bridge. Either way, the one on the left is the false bridge."

Despite the approach of the wolves, the presence of the bewildered trolls, and the shrieking of the harpies, David couldn't help but grin with pleasure. He'd remembered the riddle and recalled the solution. It was like the Woodsman had said: someone was trying to create a story and David was a part of it, but the story was itself made up of other stories. David had read about trolls and harpies, and lots of old stories had woodsmen in them. Even talking animals, like the wolves, cropped up in them.

"Come on," said David to the Woodsman. He approached the bridge on the right, and the troll standing before it stepped to one side to allow David to pass. David put a foot on the first of the boards and held on tight to the ropes. Now that his life depended on his choice, he felt a little less certain of himself, and the sight of the harpies gliding just beneath his feet made him even more anxious. Still, he had chosen, and there was no going back. He took a second step, then another, always keeping a grip on the rope supports and trying not to look down. He was making good progress when he realized that the Woodsman was not following. David stopped on the bridge and looked back.

The forest was alive with wolf eyes. David could see them shining in the torchlight. Now they were moving, emerging from the shadows, advancing slowly on the Woodsman, the more primitive ones leading, the others, the Loups, staying back, waiting for their lesser brothers and sisters to overpower the armed man before they approached. The trolls had vanished, clearly realizing that there was little point in discussing riddles with wild animals.

"No!" cried David. "Come on! You can make it."

But the Woodsman did not move. Instead, he called out to David. "Go now, and go quickly. I will hold them off for as long as I can. When you get to the other side, cut the ropes. Do you hear me? Cut the ropes!"

David shook his head. "No," he repeated. He was crying. "You have to come with me. I need you to come with me."

And then, almost as one, the wolves pounced.

"Run!" shouted the Woodsman, as his ax swung and his knife flashed. David saw a fine spray of blood fountain into the air as the first wolf died, and then they were all around the Woodsman, snapping and biting, some trying to find a way past him to pursue the boy. With one last look over his shoulder, David ran. He was still not quite halfway across the bridge, and it swung sickeningly with each movement that he made. The pounding of his feet echoed through the gorge. Soon, it was joined by the sound of paws on wood. David looked to his left and saw that three of his pursuers had taken the other bridge in the hope of cutting him off on the far side, for they could not find a way around the Woodsman, who was guarding the first bridge. The creatures were gaining ground quickly. One of them, a Loup bringing up the rear, wore the remains of a white dress, and droplets of gold dangled from its ears. Saliva dripped from its jaws as it ran, and it licked at it with its tongue.

"Run," it said, in a voice that was almost girlish, "for all the good that it will do you." It snapped at the air. "You'll taste just as good on the other side."

David's arms ached from holding on to the ropes, and the swaying of the bridge made him feel dizzy. The wolves were already almost level with him. He would never make it to the other side before they did.

And then some of the slats on the false bridge collapsed, and the lead wolf plunged through the hole. David heard the whistling of a harpoon, and the wolf was speared through its belly and yanked toward the trolls in the canyon wall.

The other wolf stopped in its tracks so suddenly that the female Loup almost knocked it over from behind. A great hole, six or seven feet wide at least, now gaped where their brother had fallen. More harpoons shot through the air, for the trolls were no longer prepared to wait for their prey to fall. The wolves had set foot on the wrong bridge and in doing so had doomed them- selves. Another barbed blade found its mark, and the second wolf was pulled through the gaps in the ropes, writhing in torment upon the steel as it died. Now only the Loup remained. It tensed its body and leaped across the gap in the bridge, landing safely on the other side. It slid for a moment, then recovered itself before it rose on its hind legs and, now out of range of the trolls' weapons, howled in triumph, even as a shadow descended upon it.

The harpy was larger than any of the others that David had seen, taller and stronger and more ancient than the rest. It hit the Loup with enough force to send it toppling over the support ropes, and only the firm grasp of the harpy's claws, which had buried themselves deep in the Loup's flesh as they struck, prevented it from tumbling to its death. The Loup's paws flailed and its jaws snapped at empty space as it tried to bite the harpy, but the fight was already lost. As David watched in horror, a second harpy joined the first, sinking its claws into the Loup's neck. The two monstrous females pulled in opposite directions, their wings beating rapidly, and the Loup was torn in two.

The Woodsman was still trying to hold back the pack, but he was fighting a losing battle. David saw him slash and cut again and again at what seemed like a moving wall of fur and fangs, until finally he fell, and the wolves descended upon him.

"No!" cried David, and although he was overcome by rage and sadness, he somehow found it in himself to begin running again, even as he saw two Loups leap over the Woodsman's body to lead a pair of wolves onto the bridge. He could hear their paws rattling the struts, and the weight of their bodies made the bridge sway. David reached the far side of the chasm, drew his sword, and faced the approaching animals. They were now more than halfway across, and closing fast. The four support ropes of the bridge were fixed to a pair of thick poles set deep into the stone beneath David's feet. David took his sword and swung at the first of the ropes, cutting about halfway through. He struck again, and the rope shot away, causing the bridge to topple suddenly to the right and sending the two wolves into the canyon. David heard the harpies cry with delight, and the beating of their wings grew louder.

There were still two Loups on the bridge, and they had somehow managed to hook their limber paws around the remaining support rope. Now, standing on their two hind legs, and keeping to the ropes on the left, they were continuing to close on David. He brought his sword down on the second rope and heard the Loups bay in alarm. The bridge shook, and strands unraveled beneath his blade. He laid the sword edge on the rope, looked to the Loups, then raised his arms and slashed with all the force that he could muster. The rope broke, and now there was nothing for the Loups to hold on to and only the wooden slats of the bridge beneath their feet. With loud yelps, they fell.

David stared over at the far side of the chasm. The Woodsman was gone. There was a trail of blood on the ground where he had been dragged into the forest by the wolves. Now only their leader, the dandy Leroi, remained. He stood upright in his red trousers and his white shirt, staring at David with undisguised hatred. He raised his head and howled for the lost members of his pack, but he did not leave. Instead, he continued to watch David until the boy at last left the bridge and disappeared over a small rise, crying softly for the Woodsman who had saved his life.

XIII

Of Dwarfs and Their Sometimes Irascible Nature

AVID WAS ON a raised white road, paved with gravel and stones. It was not straight but wound according to the obstacles it encountered: a small stream here, a rocky outcrop there. A ditch ran along each side, and from there an area of weed and grass led to the tree line. The trees were smaller and more scattered than in the forest he had recently left, and he could see the outlines of small, rocky hills rising beyond them. He was suddenly very tired. Now that the chase was over, all of his energy was gone. He wanted very badly just to fall asleep, but he was afraid to do so out in the open, or to remain too close to the chasm. He needed to find shelter. The wolves would not forgive him for what had happened at the bridges. They would find another way to cross, and then they would seek out his trail once again. Instinctively, he raised his eyes to the sky, but he could see no birds following his path from above, no traitorous ravens waiting to reveal his presence to the hunters at his back.

To give himself some energy, he ate a little bread from his bag and drank deeply from his water. It made him feel better for a moment, but the sight of the bag and the carefully packed food reminded him of the Woodsman. His eyes grew teary again, but he refused to allow himself the luxury of crying. He got to his feet, put his pack on his shoulder, and almost fell over a dwarf who had just climbed up on the road from the low ditch on the left.

"Mind where you're going," said the dwarf. He was about three feet tall and wore a blue tunic, black trousers, and black boots that came up to his knees. There was a long blue hat on his head, at the end of which was a little bell that no longer made any sound. His face and hands were grubby with dirt, and he carried a pickax over one shoulder. His nose was quite red, and he had a short white beard. The beard appeared to have pieces of food trapped in it.

"Sorry," said David.

"So you should be."

"I didn't see you."

"Oh, and what's that supposed to mean?" said the dwarf. He waved his pick threateningly. "Are you sizeist? Are you saying I'm *small*?"

"Well, you are small," said David. "Not that there's anything wrong with that," he added hurriedly. "I'm small too, compared to some people."

But the dwarf was no longer listening and had commenced shouting at a column of squat figures heading for the road.

"Oy, comrades!" said the dwarf. "Bloke over here says I'm small."

"Bloody cheek!" said a voice.

"Hold him till we get there, comrade," said another, who then appeared to reconsider. "Hang on, how big is he?"

The dwarf examined David. "Not very big," he said. "Dwarf and a half. Dwarf and two-thirds at most."

"Right, we'll 'ave him" came the reply.

Suddenly, it seemed as if David was surrounded by short, unhappy men muttering about "rights" and "liberties" and having enough of "this sort of thing." They were all filthy, and they all wore hats with broken bells. One of them kicked David in the shin.

"Ow!" said David. "That hurt."

"Now you know how our feelings, er, feel," said the first dwarf.

A small, grubby hand tugged at David's pack. Another tried to steal his sword. A third appeared to be poking him in his soft places just for the fun of it.

"That's enough!" shouted David. "Stop it!"

He swung his pack wildly and was rather pleased to feel it connect with a pair of dwarfs, who immediately fell into the ditch and rolled around theatrically for some time.

"What did you do that for?" asked the first dwarf. He looked quite shocked.

"You were kicking me."

"Was not."

"Were so too. And someone tried to steal my bag."

"Did not."

"Oh, this is just ridiculous," said David. "You did and you know it."

The dwarf lowered his head and kicked idly at the road, sending a little puff of white dust into the air. "Oh, all right then," it said. "Maybe I did. Sorry."

"That's all right," said David.

He reached down and helped the dwarfs raise their two fellows from the ditch. Nobody was badly hurt. In fact, now that it was all over, the dwarfs seemed rather to have enjoyed the whole encounter.

"Reminder of the Great Struggle, that was," said one. "Right, comrade?"

"Absolutely, comrade," replied another. "The workers must resist oppression at every turn."

"Um, but I wasn't really oppressing you," David said.

"But you could have, if you'd wanted to," said the first dwarf. "Right?"

He looked up at David quite pathetically. David could tell that he really, really would have liked someone to try unsuccessfully to oppress him.

"Well, if you say so," said David, just to make the dwarf happy.

"Hurrah!" shouted the dwarf. "We have resisted the threat of oppression. The workers will not be shackled!"

"Hurrah!" shouted the other dwarfs in unison. "We have nothing to lose but our chains."

"But you don't have any chains," said David.

"They're *metaphorical* chains," explained the first dwarf. He nodded once, as if he had just said something very profound.

"Riiight," said David. He wasn't certain what a metaphorical chain was, exactly. In fact, David wasn't entirely sure what the dwarfs were talking about at all. Still, there were seven of them altogether, which seemed about right.

"Do you have names?" asked David.

"Names?" said the first dwarf. "*Names?* Course we have names. I"—he gave a little, self-important cough—"am Comrade Brother Number One. These are Comrade Brothers Numbers Two, Three, Four, Five, Six, and Eight."

"What happened to Seven?" asked David.

There was an embarrassed silence.

"We don't talk about Former Comrade Brother Number Seven," said Comrade Brother Number One, eventually. "He has been officially excised from the Party's records."

"He went to work for his mum," explained Comrade Brother Number Three, helpfully.

"A *capitalist*!" spit Brother Number One.

"A baker," Brother Number Three corrected him.

He stood on his tiptoes and whispered to David. "We're not allowed to talk to him now. We can't even eat his mum's buns, not even the day-old ones that she sells for half price."

"I heard that," said Brother Number One. "We can make our own buns," he added huffily. "Don't need buns made by a class traitor."

"No we can't," said Brother Number Three. "They're always hard, and then *she* complains."

Instantly, the dwarfs' relative good humor disappeared. They picked up their tools and prepared to leave.

"Got to be on our way," said Brother Number One. "Pleasure to have met you, comrade. Er, you are a comrade, aren't you?"

"I suppose so," said David. He wasn't sure, but he wasn't about to risk getting into another fight with the dwarfs. "Can I still eat buns if I'm a comrade?"

"As long as they're not baked by Former Comrade Brother Number Seven—"

"Or his mum," added Brother Number Three sarcastically.

"—you can eat anything you like," concluded Brother Number One, as he raised a finger of warning to Brother Number Three.

The dwarfs started marching back down the ditch on the other side of the road, following a rough trail that led into the trees.

"Excuse me," said David. "I don't suppose I could stay with you for the night, could I? I'm lost, and very tired."

Comrade Brother Number One paused.

"She won't like it," said Brother Number Four.

"Then again," said Brother Number Two, "she's always complaining that she has nobody to talk to. Might put her in a good mood to see a new face."

"A good mood," said Brother Number One wistfully, as though

it was a wonderful flavor of ice cream that he'd tasted a long, long time ago. "Right you are, comrade," he said to David. "Come with us. We'll see you straight."

David was so happy he could have skipped.

While they walked, David learned a little more about the dwarfs. At least, he thought that he might be learning more about them, but he didn't quite catch everything he was being told. There was a lot of stuff about "workers' ownership of the methods of production" and "the principles of the Second Congress of the Third Committee" but not the Third Congress of the Second Committee, which had apparently ended in a fight over who was going to wash the cups afterward.

David had some idea of who "she" might be as well, but it seemed polite to check, just in case.

"Does a lady live with you?" he asked Brother Number One.

The buzz of conversation from the other dwarfs instantly ceased.

"Yes, unfortunately," said Brother Number One.

"All seven of you?" David continued. He wasn't sure why, but there was something slightly odd about a woman who lived with seven little men.

"Separate beds," said the dwarf. "No funny business."

"Gosh, no," said David. He tried to wonder what funny business the dwarf could be referring to, then decided that it might be better not to think about it. "Er, her name wouldn't be Snow White, would it?"

Comrade Brother Number One stopped suddenly, causing a minor pileup of comrades behind him.

"She's not a friend of yours, is she?" he asked suspiciously.

"Oh no, not at all," said David. "I've never met the lady. I might have heard about her, that's all."

"Huh," said the dwarf, apparently satisfied, and started walking again. "Everybody's heard of her: 'Ooooh, Snow White who lives with the dwarfs, eats them out of house and home. They couldn't even kill her right.' Oh yes, everybody knows about Snow White."

"Er, kill her?" asked David.

"Poisoned apple," said the dwarf. "Didn't go too well. We underestimated the dose."

"I thought it was her wicked stepmother who poisoned her," said David.

"You don't read the papers," said the dwarf. "Turned out the wicked stepmother had an alibi."

"We should really have checked first," said Brother Number Five. "Seems she was off poisoning someone else at the time. Chance in a million, really. It was just bad luck."

Now it was David's turn to pause. "So you mean *you* tried to poison Snow White?"

"We just wanted her to nod off for a while," said Brother Number Two.

"A *very* long while," said Number Three.

"But why?" said David.

"You'll see," said Brother Number One. "Anyway, we feed her an apple: chomp-chomp, snooze-snooze, weep-weep, 'poor Snow White, we-will-miss-her-so-but-life-goes-on.' We lay her out on a slab, surround her with flowers and little weeping bunny rabbits, you know, all the trimmings, then along comes a bloody prince and kisses her. We don't even *have* a prince around here. He just appeared out of nowhere on a bleeding white horse. Next thing you know he's climbed off and he's onto Snow White like a whippet down a rabbit hole. Don't know what he thought he was doing, gadding about randomly kissing strange women who happened to be sleeping at the time."

"Pervert," said Brother Number Three. "Ought to be locked up."

"Anyway, so he bounces in on his white horse like a big perfumed tea cozy, getting involved in affairs that are none of his business, and next thing you know she wakes up and—ooooh!—was she in a bad mood. The prince didn't half get an earful, and that was after she clocked him one first for 'taking liberties.' Five minutes of listening to that and, instead of marrying her, the prince gets back on his horse and rides off into the sunset. Never saw him again. We blamed the local wicked stepmother for the whole apple business, but, well, if there's a lesson to be learned from all this, it's to make sure that the person you're going to wrongfully blame for doing something bad is actually available for selection, as it were. There was a trial, we got suspended sentences on the grounds of provocation combined with lack of sufficient evidence, and we were told that if anything ever happened to Snow White again, if she even chipped a nail, we'd be for it."

Comrade Brother Number One did an impression of choking on a noose, just in case David didn't understand what "it" meant.

"Oh," said David. "But that's not the story I heard."

"Story!" The dwarf snorted. "You'll be talking about 'happily ever after' next. Do we look happy? There's no happily ever after for us. Miserably ever after, more like."

"We should have left her for the bears," said Brother Number Five, glumly. "They know how to do a good killing, do the bears."

"Goldilocks," said Brother Number One, nodding approvingly. "Classic that, just classic."

"Oh, she was awful," said Brother Number Five. "You couldn't blame them, really."

"Hang on," said David. "Goldilocks ran away from the bears' house and never went back there again."

He stopped talking. The dwarfs were now looking at him as if he might have been a little slow.

"Er, didn't she?" he added.

"She got a taste for their porridge," said Brother Number One, tapping the side of his nose gently as though he were confiding a great secret to David. "Couldn't get enough of it. Eventually, the bears just got tired of her, and, well, that was that. 'She ran away into the woods and never went back to the bears' house again.' A likely story!"

"You mean . . . they killed her?" asked David.

"They *ate* her," said Brother Number One. "With porridge. That's what 'ran away and was never seen again' means in these parts. It means 'eaten.' "

"Um, and what about 'happily ever after'?" asked David, a little uncertainly. "What does that mean?"

"Eaten quickly," said Brother Number One.

And with that they reached the dwarfs' house.

XIV

Of Snow White, Who Is Very Unpleasant Indeed

OU'RE LATE!"*

David's eardrums rang like bells as Comrade Brother Number One opened the front door of the cottage and cried, very nervously, "Coo-ee, we're home!" in that singsong voice that David's father had sometimes used on David's mother when he got back late from the pub and knew he was in trouble.

"Don't 'we're home' me" came the reply. "Where have you been? I'm *starvin'*. Me stomach's like an empty barrel."

David had never heard a voice quite like it. It was a woman's voice, but it managed to be both deep and high at the same time, like those huge trenches that were supposed to lie at the bottom of the ocean, only not quite so wet.

"Ooooooh, I can 'ear it rumbling," said the voice. " 'Ere, you, listen to it."

A big white hand reached out and grabbed Brother Number One by the scruff of the neck, lifting him off his feet and yanking him inside.

"Oh, yeph," said Brother Number One, after a moment or two. His voice sounded slightly muffled. "I can hear iff now."

David allowed the other dwarfs to enter the cottage ahead of him. They walked like prisoners who had just been told that the executioner had a little extra time on his hands and could fit in a few more beheadings before he went home for his tea. David cast a lingering glance back at the dark forest and wondered if he shouldn't just take his chances outside.

"Close that door!" said the voice. "I'm freezin'. Me teeth are chatterin'."

David, feeling that he had no other choice, stepped into the cottage and closed the door firmly behind him.

Standing before him was the biggest, fattest lady that David had ever seen. Her face was caked with white makeup. Her hair was black, held back by a brightly colored cotton band, and her lips were painted purple. She wore a pink dress large enough to house a small circus. Brother Number One was pressed hard against its folds, the better to hear the strange noises that the great stomach beneath was currently making. His little feet almost, but not quite, touched the ground. The dress was decorated with so many ribbons and buttons and bows that David was quite at a loss as to how the lady could remember which ones actually released her from the dress and which were merely for show. Her feet were squashed into a pair of silk slippers that were at least three sizes too small, and the rings on her fingers were almost lost in her flesh.

"Who are you, then?" she said.

"He'ph comfany," said Brother Number One.

"Company?" said the lady, dropping Brother Number One like an unwanted toy. "Well, why didn't you say you were bringin' company?" She patted her hair and smiled, exposing lipstick-smeared teeth. "I'd have dressed up. I'd have put me face on."

David heard Brother Number Three whisper to Brother Number Eight. The words "anything" and "improvement" were barely audible. Unfortunately, they were still too loud for the lady's liking, and Brother Number Three received a smack across the head for his trouble.

"Careful," she said. "Cheeky sod."

She then extended a large pale hand toward David and gave a little curtsy.

"Snow White," she said. "Pleased to make your acquaintance, I'm sure."

David shook hands and watched with alarm as his fingers were swallowed up in Snow White's marshmallow palm.

"I'm David," he said.

"That's a nice name," said Snow White. She giggled and buried her chin in her chest. The action created so many ripples of fat that her head looked as if it was melting. "Are you a prince?"

"No," said David. "Sorry."

Snow White looked disappointed. She released David's hand and tried to play with one of her rings, but the ring was so tight that it wouldn't budge.

"A nobleman, maybe?"

"No."

"Son of a nobleman, with a great inheritance waiting for you on your eighteenth birthday?"

David pretended to think about the question.

"Er, no again," he said.

"Well, what are you then? Don't tell me you're another one of their *booorrrring* friends come here to talk about workers and oppression. I warned them, I did: no more talk about revolutions, not until I've had me tea."

"But we *are* oppressed," protested Brother Number One.

"Of course you're oppressed!" said Snow White. "You're only

three feet tall. Now go and get me tea started, before I lose me good humor. And take your boots off. I don't want you lot puttin' muck on me nice clean floor. You only cleaned it yesterday."

The dwarfs removed their boots and left them at the door along with their tools, then lined up to wash their hands in the little sink before preparing the evening meal. They sliced bread and cut vegetables while two rabbits roasted over the open fire. The smell made David's mouth water.

"I suppose you'll be wantin food an' all," said Snow White to David.

"I am rather hungry," David admitted.

"Well, you can share their rabbit. You ain't 'avin' any of mine."

Snow White plopped herself down in a big chair by the fire. She puffed her cheeks and sighed loudly.

"I 'ate it 'ere," she said. "It's so *booorrrinnng*."

"Why don't you just leave?" asked David.

"Leave?" said Snow White. "And where would I leave *to*?"

"Don't you have a home?" said David.

"Me dad and stepmum moved away. They say their place is too small for me. Anyway, they're just *booorrinnnng*, and I'd rather be bored here than bored with 'em."

"Oh," said David. He wondered if he should bring up the subject of the court case and the dwarfs' attempt to poison Snow White. He was very interested in it, but he wasn't sure that it would be polite to ask. After all, he didn't want to get the dwarfs into any more trouble than they were already in.

In the end, Snow White made the decision for him. She leaned forward and whispered, in a voice like two rocks rubbing together: "Anyway, they 'ave to look after me. Judge told them they 'ad to, on account of how they tried to poison me."

David didn't think he'd want to live with someone who had already tried to poison him once, but he supposed that Snow

White wasn't worried about the dwarfs trying again. If they did, they'd be killed, although the look on Brother Number One's face made David suspect that death might almost be welcomed after living with Snow White for a while.

"But don't you want to meet a handsome prince?" he asked.

"I've met a handsome prince," said Snow White. She stared dreamily out of the window. "He woke me with a kiss, but then he 'ad to leave. He told me he'd be back, though, once he'd gone off and killed some dragon or other."

"Should have stayed here and taken care of the one we have first," muttered Brother Number Three. Snow White threw a log at him.

"See what I have to put up with?" she said to David. "I'm left alone all day while they work down't mine, and then I have to listen to them complain as soon as they get home. I don't even know why they bother with that all that minin'. They never find anything!"

David saw the dwarfs exchange some looks when they heard what Snow White was saying. He even thought he heard Brother Number Three give a little laugh, until Brother Number Four kicked him in the shin and told him to be quiet.

"So I'm going to stay 'ere with this lot until me prince returns," said Snow White. "Or until another prince comes along and decides to marry me, whichever happens first."

She bit a hangnail from her little finger and spit it into the fire.

"Now," she said, bringing the subject to a close, *"WHERE'S. ME. TEA?"*

Every cup, pot, pan, and plate in the cottage rattled. Dust fell from the ceiling. David saw a family of mice evacuate their mouse hole and leave through a crack in the wall, never to return.

"I always get a bit shouty when I'm 'ungry, me," said Snow White. "Right. Somebody 'and me that rabbit . . ."

*　　*　　*

They ate in silence, apart from the slurping, scraping, chewing, and belching coming from Snow White's end of the table. She really did eat an awful lot. She stripped her own rabbit to the bones and then began picking meat from Brother Number Six's plate without even a by-your-leave. She devoured an entire loaf of bread, and half a block of very smelly cheese. She drank tankard after tankard of the ale the dwarfs brewed in their shed, and polished it all off with two chunks of fruitcake baked by Brother Number One, although she complained when a raisin chipped one of her teeth.

"I told you it was a bit dry," whispered Brother Number Two to Brother Number One. Brother Number One just scowled.

Once there was nothing left to eat, Snow White staggered from the table and flopped down in her chair by the fire, where she instantly fell asleep. David helped the dwarfs to clear the table and wash the dishes, then joined them in a corner where they all began smoking pipes. The tobacco reeked as if someone was burning old, damp socks. Brother Number One offered to share his pipe with David, but David very politely declined the offer.

"What do you mine?" he asked.

There was some coughing from a number of the dwarfs, and David noticed that none of them wanted to catch his eye. Only Brother Number One seemed willing to try to answer the question.

"Coal, sort of," he said.

"Sort of?"

"Well, it's a kind of coal. It's stuff that used to be, sort of, in a way, coal."

"It's coal*ish*," said Brother Number Three helpfully.

David considered this. "Er, do you mean diamonds?"

Seven small figures instantly leaped on him. Brother Number

One covered David's mouth with a little hand and said, "Don't say that word in here. Ever."

David nodded. Once the dwarfs were sure that he understood the gravity of the situation, they climbed off him again.

"So you haven't told Snow White about the, er, *coalish* stuff," he said.

"No," said Brother Number One. "Never, um, quite got round to it."

"Don't you trust her?"

"Would you?" asked Brother Number Three. "Last winter, when food was hard to come by, Brother Number Four woke up to find her nibbling on his foot."

Brother Number Four nodded solemnly to let David know that this was nothing less than the truth.

"Still have the marks," he said.

"If she found out the mine was working, she'd take us for every gem we were worth," continued Brother Number Three. "Then we'd be even more oppressed than we are already. And poorer."

David looked around the cottage. It wasn't very much to write home about. There were two rooms: the one in which they now sat, and a bedroom that Snow White had taken for her own. The dwarfs slept together in one bed in a corner beside the fire, three at one end and four at the other.

"If she wasn't around, we could do the place up a bit," said Brother Number One. "But if we start spending money on it then she'll get suspicious, so we have to keep it the way it is. We can't even buy another bed."

"But aren't there people nearby who know about the mine? Doesn't anybody suspect?"

"Oh, we've always let people know that we make a little from mining," said the dwarf. "Just enough to keep us going. It's hard work, mining, and nobody wants to do it unless they're sure of getting wealthy from it. As long as we keep our heads down and don't go wild spending money on fancy clothes or gold chains—"

"Or beds," said Brother Number Eight.

"Or beds," agreed Brother Number One, "then everything will be fine. It's just that none of us is getting any younger, and now it would be nice to take things a bit easier and perhaps treat ourselves to some luxuries."

The dwarfs looked at Snow White snoring in her chair, and all of them sighed as one.

"Actually, we're hoping to bribe someone to take her off our hands," admitted Brother Number One at last.

"You mean, pay someone to marry her?" asked David.

"He'd have to be really desperate, of course, but we'd make it worth his while," said Brother Number One. "Well, I'm not sure there are enough diamonds in the whole land to make living with her worthwhile, but we'd give him a pile to ease the burden. He could buy some really nice earplugs, and a really big bed."

By now some of the dwarfs were nodding off. Brother Number One took a long stick and nervously approached Snow White.

"She doesn't like being woken up," he explained to David. "We find this is easiest for everyone."

He poked at Snow White with the end of the stick. Nothing happened.

"I think you'll have to do it harder," said David.

This time, the dwarf hit Snow White a good, strong prod. It seemed to work, because she instantly grabbed the stick and gave it a sharp tug, almost flicking Brother Number One straight into the fireplace before he remembered to let go and landed in the coal scuttle instead.

"Unk," said Snow White. "Arfle."

She wiped some drool from her mouth, rose from her chair,

and staggered to her bedroom. "Bacon in the morning," she said. "Four eggs. And a sausage. No, make that eight sausages."

With that, she slammed the door behind her, fell on her bed, and was immediately sound asleep.

David sat curled up in the chair by the fire. The house rumbled with the snoring of Snow White and the dwarfs, a complex arrangement of snorts, whistles, and dusty coughs. David thought of the Woodsman, and the trail of blood leading into the woods. He remembered Leroi, and the look in the Loup's eyes. David knew that he could not afford to remain with the dwarfs for longer than one night. He had to keep moving. He had to make his way to the king.

He got up from his chair and walked to the window. He could see nothing outside, so thick and heavy was the darkness. He listened, but he could hear only the hooting of an owl. He had not forgotten what had brought him to this place, but his mother's voice had not come to him again since he had entered the new world. Only if she called to him would he be able to find her.

"Mum," he whispered. "If you're out there, I need your help. I can't find you if you don't guide me."

But there was no reply.

He went back to his chair and closed his eyes. He fell asleep and dreamed of his bedroom at home, and of his father and his new family, but they were not alone in the house. In his dream, the Crooked Man stalked the hallway until he came to Georgie's bedroom, where he stood for a long time looking at the child before departing the house and returning to his own world.

XV

Of the Deer-Girl

NOW WHITE was still snoring in her bed when David and the dwarfs departed the next morning, and the spirits of the little men seemed to lift significantly the farther behind they left her. They walked with him as far as the white road, then they all stood around rather awkwardly as everyone tried to find the best way to say good-bye.

"We can't tell you where the mine is, obviously," said Brother Number One.

"Obviously," said David. "I quite understand."

"Because it's secret, like."

"Yes, of course."

"Don't want every Tom, Dick, and Harry snooping around it."

"That seems very sensible."

Brother Number One tugged pensively at his ear.

"It's just beyond the big hill on the right," he said quickly. "There's a trail that leads up to it. It's well-hidden, mind, so you'll need to keep watching out for it. It's marked by an eye carved in a tree. At least, we think it's carved. You never can tell with those trees. Just in case, you know, you ever need a little company."

His face brightened. "Ha!" he said. "A 'little company'! See what I did there? You know, a little company, like friends, and a *little company,* like a band of dwarfs. See?"

David did see, and laughed dutifully.

"Now remember," said Brother Number One, "if you come across a prince or a young nobleman, in fact if you see anyone who looks desperate enough to marry a big woman for money, you send him to us, right? Make sure he waits on this road until we appear. We don't want him making his own way to the cottage and, well, you know . . ."

"Being scared off," finished David for him.

"Yes, quite. Well, good luck, and stay on the road. There's a village a day or two from here, and there's bound to be someone there who can help you on your way, but don't be tempted to stray from the path, no matter what you see. There's a lot of nasty things in these woods, and they have their ways of luring folk into their clutches, so mind how you go."

And with that the little company of the little company was lost to David as the dwarfs disappeared into the forest. He heard them singing a song as they marched, one that Brother Number One had made up for them as they went on their way to work. It didn't have much of a tune, and Brother Number One seemed to have encountered some difficulty in finding suitable rhymes for "collectivization of labor" and "oppression by the capitalist running dogs," but David was still sad when the song faded away and he was left alone on the silent road.

He had quite liked the dwarfs. He often had no idea what they were talking about, but for a group of homicidal, class-obsessed small people, they were really rather good fun. After they left him, he felt very alone. Although this was clearly a major road, David appeared to be the only person traveling upon it. Here and there he found traces of others who had passed that way—the remains of a fire, now long cold; a leather strap, gnawed at one end by a hungry animal—but that was as close as it appeared he was going to come to another human being that day. The constant twilight, which altered significantly only early in the morning and late in the evening, sapped his energy and subdued his spirits, and he found his attention drifting. At times, he seemed to fall asleep on his feet, for he had flashes of dreams, visions in which Dr. Moberley stood over him and seemed to be speaking to him, and periods of darkness during which he thought that he heard his father's voice. Then he would awaken suddenly as his feet strayed from the path, his legs almost tangling beneath him as he moved from stone to grass.

He realized that he was very hungry. He had eaten with the dwarfs that morning, but now his stomach was rumbling and aching. There was still food in his pack, and the dwarfs had added to his supplies a little by giving him some pieces of dried fruit, but he had no idea how far he might have to travel before he reached the castle of the king. Even the dwarfs were of no help there. As far as David could tell, the king didn't have very much to do with the running of his kingdom at all. Brother Number One told David that someone had once come to the cottage claiming to be a royal tax collector, but after an hour in the company of Snow White, he left without his hat and never returned again. The only facts about the king that Brother Number One could confirm were that there was a king (probably) and that there was a castle, somewhere at the end of the road upon which David was traveling, although Brother Number One had never seen it. And so David walked on, his mind drifting, his stomach hurting, and the road glowing whitely before him.

It was during one of his near tumbles into the ditch that David saw apples hanging from the branches of a tree in a clearing near the edge of the forest. They looked green and almost ripe, and he felt his mouth begin to water. He remembered the dwarfs' injunction, their warning that he should remain on the path always and not be tempted by the gifts of the forest. But what harm could it do to take some apples from a tree? He would still be able to see the road from it, and with the help of a fallen branch he could probably dislodge enough fruit to keep him going for a day, perhaps more. He stopped and listened but heard nothing. The forest was quiet.

David left the road. The ground was soft, and his feet made an unpleasant squelching noise with each step that he took. As he drew nearer to the tree, he saw the fruit at the farthest ends of the branches was smaller and less ripe than the apples higher up at the heart of the tree, where each one was as big as a man's fist. He could reach them if he climbed up, and climbing trees was something that David was very good at indeed. It was the work of only a few minutes to scale the trunk, and soon he was seated in the crook of a branch, munching on an apple that tasted incredibly sweet to him. It had been weeks since he'd eaten an apple, not since a local farmer had quietly slipped Rose a couple "for the lit- tle 'uns." Those apples had been small and sour, but these were wonderful. The juice trickled down his chin, and the flesh was firm in his mouth.

He devoured the last of the first apple and discarded the core, then picked another. He ate this one more slowly, recalling his mother's warnings about eating too many apples. They gave you stomach pains, she had said. David supposed that stuffing your- self with too much of anything was a recipe for feeling ill, but he wasn't sure how that applied if you hadn't eaten for almost an entire day. All he knew for certain was that the fruit tasted good and his stomach was grateful for it.

He was halfway through the second apple when he heard a disturbance below. Something was approaching fast from his left. He could see movement in the bushes, and a flash of tan hide. It looked like a deer, although David could not see its head, and it was clearly fleeing from some threat. Instantly, David thought of the wolves. He cowered closer to the trunk of the tree and tried to shield himself with it. Even as he did so, he wondered if the wolves would detect his scent upon the ground as they passed, or if the lure of the deer might be enough to blind their senses to it.

Seconds later, the deer broke from cover and entered the clearing beneath David's tree. It paused for a moment, as if uncertain of which direction to take, and in that moment he got his first clear look at its head. The sight made him gasp, for it was not the head of a deer but that of a young girl with blond hair and dark green eyes. He could see where her human neck ended and the body of the deer began, for a red welt marked the place where the two beings had been joined. The girl glanced up, startled by the sound, and her eyes met David's.

"Help me!" she begged. "Please."

And then the sounds of pursuit drew nearer, and David saw a horse and rider bearing down upon the clearing, the rider's bow drawn and ready to release its arrow. The deer-girl heard them too, for her back legs tensed and she bounded toward the cover of the forest. She was still in midair when the arrow struck her neck. The blow threw her body to the right, where it lay twitching upon the ground. The deer-girl's mouth opened and closed as she tried to speak her final words. Her back legs kicked at the dirt, her body trembled, and then she stopped moving.

The rider trotted into the clearing upon a huge black horse. He was hooded and dressed in the colors of the autumn forest, all greens and ambers. In his left hand he held a short bow, and a quiver of arrows hung across his shoulder. He dismounted from the horse, drew a long blade from a scabbard upon his saddle, and approached the body on the ground. He raised the blade and struck once, then again, at the neck of the deer-girl. David looked away after the first blow, his hand against his mouth and his eyes squeezed shut. When he dared to glance back again, the girl's head had been severed from the deer's body and the hunter was carrying it by the hair, dark blood dripping from the neck onto the forest floor. Using the hair, he tied the head to the horn of his saddle so that it hung against the flank of his horse, then placed the carcass of the deer across the horse before preparing to remount. His left foot was already raised when he paused and stared at the ground. David followed his gaze and saw the discarded core of the apple at the horse's hooves. The hunter lowered his foot and stared at the core, and then in one swift movement drew an arrow from his quiver and notched it to the bow. The tip of the arrow was raised toward the apple tree and came to rest pointing straight at David.

"Come down," said the hunter, his voice muffled slightly by a scarf across his mouth. "Come down or I'll shoot you down."

David had no choice but to comply. He felt himself start to cry. He tried desperately to stop himself, but he could smell the deer-girl's blood on the air. His only hope was that the hunter had enjoyed his sport for the day and might see fit to spare him as a result.

David reached the base of the tree. He was tempted for an instant to run and take his chances in the forest, but it was an idea that he rejected almost immediately. A hunter who could kill a leaping deer with an arrow while riding on horseback would surely be able to hit a fleeing boy with greater ease. He had no choice but to hope for mercy from the hunter, but as he stood before the hooded figure, he looked into the deer-girl's sightless eyes and wondered if there was any hope of mercy from someone who could do such a thing.

"Lie down," said the hunter. "On your belly."

"Please, don't hurt me," said David.

"Lie down!"

David knelt on the ground, then forced himself to lie flat. He heard the hunter approach, and then his arms were wrenched behind his back and his wrists bound with coarse rope. His sword was taken from him. His legs were tied at the ankles, and he was lifted into the air and slung over the back of the great horse, his body lying upon that of the deer, his left side resting painfully against the saddle. But David did not think about the pain, not even when they began to trot and the ache in his side became a regular, rhythmic pounding, like the blade of a dagger being forced between his ribs.

No, all that David could think about was the head of the deer-girl, for her face rubbed against his as they rode, her warm blood smeared his cheek, and he saw himself reflected in the dark green mirrors of her eyes.

XVI

Of the Three Surgeons

HEY RODE FOR what seemed to David like an hour, perhaps more. The hunter did not speak. David felt dizzy from hanging across the horse, and his head hurt. The smell of the deer-girl's blood was very strong, and as their journey drew on, the touch of her skin against his grew colder and colder.

At last they came to a long stone house in the forest. It was plain and unadorned, with narrow windows and a high roof. To one side was a large stable, and there the rider tethered his horse. There were other animals here too. A doe stood in a stall, chewing on some straw and blinking at the new arrivals. There were chickens in a wire run and rabbits in hutches. Nearby a fox clawed at the bars of its cage, its attention torn between the hunter and the tasty prey just beyond its reach.

The hunter dismounted and detached the deer-girl's head from the saddle. With his other hand he lifted David and slung him over his shoulder, then carried him to the house. The deer-girl's head made a soft thudding noise against the door as the hunter raised the latch, and then they entered and David was thrown upon the stone floor. He landed on his back and lay there, dazed and frightened, as, one by one, lamps were lit, and he was at last able to see the hunter's lair.

The walls were covered with heads, each mounted upon a wooden board and fixed to the stone. Many of the heads came from animals—deer, wolves, even a Loup, which seemed to have been given pride of place at the center of the display on one wall—but others were human. Some came from young adults, and three came from very old men, but most seemed to belong to children, boys and girls, their eyes replaced with glass equivalents that glittered in the lamplight. There was a fireplace at one end of the room, and a single pallet bed beside it. Against another wall stood a small desk and a single chair. David turned his head and saw dried meat hanging from hooks at the other end of the room. He could not tell if it came from animals or people.

But the room was dominated by two great oak tables, so huge that they must have been assembled within the house itself, piece by piece. They were stained with blood, and from where he lay David could see chains and manacles on them, and leather restraints. To one side of the tables was a rack of knives, blades, and surgical tools, all clearly old but kept sharp and clean. Above the tables hung an array of metal and glass tubes on ornate frames, half of them as thin as needles, the others as thick as David's arm.

Bottles of all shapes and sizes, some filled with clear liquid while the rest had been used to store body parts, stood on shelves. One bottle was filled almost to the top with eyeballs. They seemed alive to David, as though being wrenched from their sockets had not deprived them of the capacity to see. Another contained a woman's hand, a gold ring upon its wedding finger, red varnish flaking slowly from its nails. A third contained half a brain, its inner workings exposed and marked by colored pins.

And there were worse things than those, oh, much worse . . .

He heard footsteps approaching. The hunter stood over him,

the hood now lowered and the scarf removed to reveal the face beneath. It was the face of a woman. Her skin was ruddy and unadorned, her mouth slim and unsmiling. Her hair was tied loosely upon her head. It was black and white and silver, like the fur of a badger. While David watched, she released her tresses, so that they fell in an avalanche across her shoulders and down her back. She knelt and gripped David's face with her right hand, turning his head back and forth as she examined his skull. She then released his face and tested his neck, and the muscles in his arms and legs.

"You'll do," she said, more to herself than to David, and then she left him to lie upon the floor while she worked on the head of the deer-girl. She did not say another word to him until her work was complete, many hours later. She raised David and placed him upon a low chair before displaying to him the fruits of her labors.

The deer-girl's head had been mounted upon a piece of dark wood. Her hair had been washed and spread out on the block, held in place by a thin glue. Her eyes had been removed and replaced with ovals of green and black glass. Her skin had been coated with a waxy substance to preserve it, and her head made a hollow sound when the huntress rapped upon it with her knuckles.

"She's pretty, don't you think?" said the huntress.

David shook his head but said nothing. This girl had had a name once. She'd had a mother and father, maybe sisters and brothers. She would have played and loved and been loved in return. She might have grown up and given birth to children of her own. Now all of that was lost.

"You disagree?" asked the huntress. "Perhaps you feel sorry for her. But think: in years to come she would have grown old and ugly. Men would have used her. Children would have burst forth from her. Her teeth would have rotted from her head, her skin would have wrinkled and aged, and her hair would have grown thin and white. Now, she will always be a child, and she will always be beautiful."

The huntress leaned forward. She touched her hand to David's cheek, and for the first time she smiled. "And soon, you too will be like her."

David twisted his head away.

"Who are you?" he asked. "Why are you doing this?"

"I am a hunter," she replied simply. "A hunter must hunt."

"But she was a little girl," said David. "A girl with the body of an animal, but still a girl. I heard her speak. She was frightened. And then you killed her."

The huntress stroked the deer-girl's hair.

"Yes," she said, softly. "She lasted longer than I expected. She was more cunning than I thought. Perhaps a fox's body might have been more appropriate, but it is too late now."

"You made her that way?" David gasped. Even though he was frightened, his disgust at what the huntress had done suffused every word. The huntress looked surprised at the venom in his voice and seemed to feel that some justification of her actions was required.

"A hunter is always seeking new prey," she said. "I grew tired of hunting beasts, and humans make poor game. Their minds are sharp, but their bodies are weak. And then I thought how wonderful it would be if I could combine the body of an animal with the intelligence of a human. What a test it would be for my skills! But it was hard, so hard, to create such hybrids: both animals and humans would die before I could bring them together. I could not stem the bleeding for long enough to make the union possible. Their brains died, their hearts stopped, and all my hard work would turn to nothing, drop by red drop.

"And then I had some good fortune. Three surgeons were traveling through the forest, and I came upon them and captured them and brought them here. They told me of a salve that they had created, one that could fuse a severed hand back upon its wrist, or a leg to its torso. I made them show me what they could do. I cut the arm from one of them and the others repaired it, just as they said they could. Then I cut another in half, and his friends made him whole again. Finally, I severed the head of the third, and they fixed it again upon his neck.

"And they became the first of my new prey," she said, pointing to the heads of the three elderly men on the wall, "once they had told me how to make the salve for myself. Now each prey is different, for each child brings something of itself to the animal that I fuse with it."

"But why children?" asked David.

"Because adults despair," she answered, "while children do not. Children accommodate themselves to their new bodies and their new lives, for what child has not dreamed of being an animal? And, in truth, I prefer to hunt children. They make better sport, and better trophies for my wall, for they are beautiful."

The huntress stepped back and regarded David carefully, as though only now becoming aware of the nature of his questions.

"What is your name, and where have you come from?" she asked. "You are not from these lands. I can tell from your scent and your speech."

"My name is David. I came from another place."

"What place?"

"England."

"*Eng-land,*" repeated the huntress. "And how did you get here?"

"There was a passageway between my land and this one. I came through, but now I can't get back."

"So sad, so sad," said the huntress. "And are there many children in *Eng-land*?"

David did not reply. The huntress grabbed his face and dug her nails into his skin. "Answer me!"

"Yes," he said, reluctantly.

The huntress released him.

"Perhaps I will make you show me the way. There are so few children here now. They do not wander as they once did. This one"—she gestured at the head of the deer-girl—"was the last that I had, and I had been saving her. Now, though, I have you. So . . . Should I use you as I used her, or should I make you take me to Eng-land?"

She stepped away from David and thought for a time.

"I am patient," she said, at last. "I know this land, and I have weathered its changes before. The children will come again. Soon it will be winter, and I have food enough to keep me. You will be my last hunt before the snows descend. I will make you a fox, for I think you are even brighter than my little deer. Who knows, you may escape me and live out your life in some hidden part of the forest, although none has yet managed it. There is always hope, my David, always hope. Now, sleep, for tomorrow we begin."

With that, she cleaned David's face with a cloth and kissed him softly on the lips. Then she carried him to the great table and chained him there in case he tried to escape during the night, before extinguishing all of the lamps. In the firelight she undressed herself, then lay naked upon her pallet and fell asleep.

But David did not sleep. He thought about his situation. He recalled his tales and returned to the memory of the Woodsman telling him of the gingerbread house. In every story, there was something to be learned.

And, in time, he began to plan.

XVII

Of Centaurs and the Vanity of the Huntress

ARLY THE NEXT MORNING, the huntress awoke and dressed herself. She roasted some meat on the fire and ate it with a tea made from herbs and spices, then came to David and raised him up. His back and limbs ached from the hard table and the constraints placed upon his movement by the chains, and he had slept only a little, but he now had a sense of purpose. Up to this point, he had been largely dependent upon the goodwill of others—the Woodsman, the dwarfs—for his care and safety. Now he was on his own, and the possibility of survival lay entirely in his own hands.

The huntress gave him some of the tea, then tried to make him eat the meat, but he would not open his mouth to it. It smelled strong and gamy.

"It is venison," she said. "You must eat. You will need your strength."

But David kept his mouth tightly closed. He could think only of the deer-girl, and the feel of her skin against his. Who knew what child had once been part of this animal's body, human and beast becoming one? Perhaps this was even the flesh of the deer-girl, torn bloodied from her body to provide fresh fare for the huntress's breakfast. He could not, would not, eat of it.

The huntress gave up and offered David bread instead. She even freed one of his hands so that he could feed himself. While he ate, she brought the caged fox from the stables and laid it on the table beside David. The fox watched the boy, almost as though it were aware of what was to come. While they regarded each other, the huntress began to assemble all that she would need. There were blades and saws, swabs and bandages, long needles and lengths of black thread, tubes and vials, and a jar of clear, viscous lotion. She attached bellows to some of the tubes—"to keep the blood flowing, just in case"—and adjusted the restraints so that they would fit the small legs of the fox.

"So what do you think of your new body to come?" she said to David once her preparations were complete. "It is a fine fox, young and nimble."

The fox tried to bite at the wire of its cage, revealing sharp white teeth.

"What will you do with my body and its head?" asked David.

"I will dry your flesh, and I will add it to my winter store. I have found that while it is possible successfully to fuse the head of a child with the body of an animal, the opposite does not hold true. The animal brains are unable to adjust to the new bodies. They cannot move properly and make poor prey. In the beginning, I would set them free for fun and nothing more, but now I do not even waste my time doing that. Still, they are out in the forest, those that have survived. They are sickly creatures. Sometimes, I kill them out of pity when they cross my path."

"I was thinking about what you said last night," said David carefully, "about how all children dream of being animals."

"And is it not true?" asked the huntress.

"I think so," said David. "I always wanted to be a horse."

The huntress looked interested.

"And why a horse?"

"In the stories that I read when I was little, I came across a creature called a centaur. It was half horse and half man. Instead of a horse's neck, it had the torso of a man, so it could hold a bow in its hands. It was beautiful and strong, and it was the perfect hunter because it combined all of the strength and speed of a horse with the skill and cunning of a man. You were fast on your mount yesterday, but you were still not one with your horse. I mean, doesn't your horse trip sometimes, or move in ways that you hadn't expected? My father used to ride as a boy, and he told me that even the finest of horsemen can be unsaddled. If I was a centaur, then I would be the best of both horse and man in one, and if I hunted, then nothing would ever be able to escape me."

The huntress looked from the fox to David, then back again. She turned her back on him and walked to her desk. She found a scrap of paper and a quill pen, and began drawing. From where he sat, David saw diagrams, and figures, and the shapes of horses and men, drawn with all the care of an artist. He did not disturb the huntress. He simply watched her patiently, and when he looked to the fox, he found that it was watching her too. So boy and fox remained that way, united in anticipation, until at last the huntress's work was done.

She rose, returned to the great operating tables, and without another word bound David's free hand once again so that he could not move. He felt a moment of panic. Perhaps his plan had not worked and she was now about to operate on him, severing his head and transplanting it to the body of a wild animal, creating a new being out of blood and salve and agony. Would she decapitate him with a single sweep of an ax, or cut and saw her way through gristle and bone? Would she give him something to put him to sleep, so that before he closed his eyes he would be one thing and when he awoke he would be another entirely, or was there a part of her that enjoyed the infliction of pain? As her hands worked upon him, he wanted to cry out, but he did not. Instead, he was quiet, swallowing his fear, and his self-discipline was rewarded.

Once he was secure, the huntress put on her hooded cloak and left the house. After a few minutes had gone by, David heard the clopping of a horse's hooves, and then they faded as she rode off into the forest, leaving David alone with the fox, two beasts on the verge of becoming one.

David dozed for a while and woke only to the sound of the huntress returning. This time, the horse's hooves sounded very close. The door to the house opened, and the huntress appeared, leading her mount by the reins. At first, the horse seemed reluctant to enter, but she spoke softly to it, and eventually it followed her through the door. David could see the horse's nose responding to the smells in the house, and he thought its eyes looked panicked and fearful. She tethered it to a ring in the wall, then approached David.

"I will make a bargain with you," she said. "I have been thinking about this creature, this *centaur*. You are right: such a beast would be the perfect hunter. I wish to become one. If you help me, I give you my word that I will set you free."

"How do I know that you won't kill me as soon as you become a centaur?" David asked.

"I will destroy my bow and arrows, and I will draw you a map to guide you back to the road. Even if I chose to pursue you, what threat would I pose without a bow with which to hunt? In time I will make more, but by then you will be long gone, and if you ever pass through my forest again, I will give you free passage in recognition of all that you have done for me."

Then the huntress leaned over and whispered in David's ear. "But if you do not agree to help me, then I will make you one with the fox, and I guarantee that you will not live out this day. I will chase you through these forests until you fade from exhaustion, and when you can run no longer, I will skin you alive and wear you on cold winter days. You may live or die. The choice is yours."

"I want to live," said David.

"Then we are agreed," said the huntress. With that, she fed her bow and arrows to the fire and drew David a detailed map of the forest, showing him the way back to the road, which he tucked carefully into his shirt. The huntress then instructed him in what he had to do. She brought from the stable a pair of huge blades, heavy and sharp as guillotines, then raised them above the operating tables using a system of ropes and pulleys. The huntress adjusted one of these so that it would sever her body in half when it fell, then showed David how to apply the salve immediately so that she would not bleed to death before her torso could be attached to the horse's body. She went over the procedures with him again and again, until he knew them by rote. Then the huntress stripped herself naked, took a long, heavy blade in her hands, and with two strokes severed her horse's head from its body. There was a great deal of blood at first, but David and the huntress quickly poured the salve over the red, exposed flesh of the horse's neck, the wounds smoking and sizzling as the mixture did its work. Instantly the ejections from the veins and arteries ceased. The horse's body lay on the floor, its heart still beating, while its head lay nearby, the eyes rolling in the sockets, the tongue lolling from its mouth.

"We don't have long," said the huntress. "Hurry, hurry!"

She lay upon the table beneath the blade. David tried not to look at her nakedness and instead concentrated on the preparations for the release of the blade, as he had been instructed. While he checked the ropes once again, the huntress gripped his arm. In her right hand, she held a sharp knife.

"If you try to run away, or if you betray me, this knife will leave my hand and find your body before you can get an arm's length from me. Do you understand?"

David nodded. One of his ankles was tied to the leg of the table. He couldn't run far, even if he wanted to take his chances. The huntress released her grip upon him. Beside her stood one of the glass jars containing the miraculous salve. It would be David's task to pour it on her wounded body, then haul her from the table to the floor. From there, he would help her to crawl to the horse. Once the two wounds were touching, he would have to pour more salve upon them, causing the huntress and the horse to fuse together, creating one living creature.

"Then do it, and be quick."

David stepped back. The rope holding the guillotine in place was taut. To avoid any accidents, he simply had to sever it with his sword blade, causing it to drop down upon the huntress and split her body into two pieces.

"Ready?" asked David.

He laid the blade upon the rope. The huntress gritted her teeth.

"Yes. Do it! Do it now!"

David raised the blade above his head and brought it down on the rope with all of his strength. The rope snapped and the blade fell, cutting the huntress in two. She screamed in agony, writhing upon the table as the blood poured from both halves of her being.

"The salve!" she cried. "Apply it quickly!"

But instead David raised the blade again and cut off the huntress's right hand. It fell to the floor, the knife still held tightly in its grasp. Finally, with a third stroke, David broke the rope holding him to the table. He jumped over the horse's body and ran for the door, while all the time the huntress's screams of rage and pain filled the room. The door was locked, but the key remained in the keyhole. David tried to turn it, but it would not move.

Behind him, the huntress's screams rose in pitch, followed suddenly by a smell of burning. David turned to see the the great wound in her upper body smoking and bubbling as the salve repaired her injuries. Her right arm too was covered in the salve, and she was pouring more on the floor so that it pooled over the wrist of her severed hand, healing the wound. Using the stump and the power of her left hand, she forced herself off the table and onto the floor.

"Come back here!" she hissed. "We're not done yet. I'll eat you alive."

She touched her stump to her right hand, then doused both with salve. Instantly, the two halves reconnected, and she raised the knife to her mouth, clasping the blade between her teeth. The huntress began to pull herself across the floor, drawing closer and closer to David. Her hand touched the end of his trouser leg as the key turned in the lock and the door opened. David pulled his leg free and ran out into the open air, then stopped dead.

He was not alone.

The clearing before the house was filled with an assemblage of creatures with the bodies of children and the heads of beasts. There were foxes and deer and rabbits and weasels, the features of the smaller animals sitting incongruously on the larger human shoulders, their necks narrowed by the actions of the salve. The hybrids moved awkwardly, as though not in control of their own limbs. They shuffled and staggered, their faces filled with confusion and pain. Slowly, they approached the house, just as the huntress dragged herself through the doorway and on to the grass. The knife dropped from her mouth, and she grasped it in her fist.

"What are you doing here, you foul creatures? Get away from this place. Go back to skulking in the shadows."

But the beasts did not respond. They just kept shambling forward, their gaze fixed on the huntress. The huntress looked up at David. She was frightened now.

"Take me back inside," she said. "Quickly, before they reach me. I forgive you for all that you have done. You are free to go. Only do not leave me here with . . . *them*."

David shook his head. He moved away from her as a creature with the body of a boy but the head of a squirrel twitched its nose at him.

"Don't desert me," cried the huntress. She was now almost surrounded, the knife striking out feebly at thin air as the beasts she had created encircled her.

"Help me!" she shouted to David. "Please help me."

And then the animals fell upon her, tearing and biting, ripping and shredding, as David turned away from the grisly sight and fled into the forest.

XVIII

Of Roland

AVID WALKED for many hours through the forest, trying as best he could to follow the huntress's map. There were trails marked upon it that either had ceased to exist or had never existed in the first place. Cairns of stones that had been used for generations as primitive signposts were often obscured by long grass, were overgrown by moss, or had been demolished by passing animals or vindictive travelers, so that David was forced again and again to go back over old ground, or slash at the undergrowth with his sword in order to find the markers. From time to time he wondered if the huntress had been planning to trick him by constructing a false map, a ruse that would have left him trapped in her forest, easy prey for her once she became a centaur.

Then, suddenly, he glimpsed a thin line of white through the trees, and moments later he was standing on the edge of the forest with the road before him. David had no idea where he was. He could have been back at the dwarfs' crossing or farther east along the road, but he didn't care. He was just glad to be out of the woods and once again on the path that would take him to the king's castle.

He walked on, until the dim light of this world began to fade, then sat on a rock and ate a piece of dry bread and some of the dried fruit that the dwarfs had pressed upon him, washed down with cool water from the little brook that always ran alongside the path.

He wondered what his dad and Rose were doing. He supposed that they must be very worried about him by now, but he had no idea what would happen if they looked in the sunken garden, or even if anything remained of the garden itself. He recalled the fire of the burning bomber illuminating the night sky, and the desperate roar of the plane's engines as it descended. It must have torn the garden apart when it struck, scattering bricks and airplane parts across the lawn and setting fire to the trees beyond. Perhaps the crack in the wall through which David had escaped had collapsed in the aftermath of the crash, and the path from his world to this one was no more. There would be no way for his father to know if David had been in the garden when the plane fell, or what had become of him if he was there when it happened. He imagined men and women sifting through the remains of the plane, searching for charred bodies in the wreckage, fearful of finding one that was smaller than the rest . . .

Not for the first time, David worried about whether he was doing the right thing by moving farther and farther away from the doorway through which he had entered this world. If his father or others found a way through and came looking for him, then wouldn't they arrive in the same place? The Woodsman had seemed so certain that the best thing to do was travel to the king, but the Woodsman was gone. He hadn't been able to save himself from the wolves, and he had not been able to protect David. The boy was alone.

David glanced down the road. He couldn't go back now. The wolves were probably still looking for him, and even if he did manage to find his way to the chasm, he would then have to seek out another bridge. There was nothing for it but to keep going in the hope that the king might be able to help him. If his father came looking for him, well, David hoped that he would keep himself safe. But just in case he or someone else came this way, David took a flat rock from beside the brook and, using a sharp stone, he carved his name upon it and an arrow pointing in the direction he was taking. Beneath it, he wrote: "To see the king." He made a little cairn of stones by the side of the road, just like the ones used to mark the forest trails, and placed his message on top of it. It was the best that he could do.

As he was packing away the remains of his food, he saw a figure approaching on a white horse. David was tempted to hide, but he knew that if he could see the horseman, then the horseman could also see him. The figure drew nearer, and David could see that he was wearing a silver breastplate decorated with twin symbols of the sun, and he had a silver helmet upon his head. A sword hung from one side of his belt, and a bow and a quiver of arrows lay on his back: the weapons of choice in this world, it seemed. A shield, also bearing the device of the twin suns, hung from his saddle. He pulled his horse up when he was alongside David and looked down at the boy. He reminded David of the Woodsman, because there was something similar about the horseman's face. Like the Woodsman, he looked both serious and kind.

"And where are you going, young man?" he asked David.

"I'm going to see the king," said David.

"The king?" The horseman did not look very impressed. "What use would the king be to anyone?"

"I'm trying to return home. I was told that the king had a book, and in that book might be a way for me to get back to where I'm from."

"And where would that be?"

"England," said David.

"I don't think I've heard that name before," said the horseman. "I can only suppose that it is far from here. Everywhere is far from here," he added, almost as an afterthought.

He shifted slightly on his horse and glanced around him, scanning the trees, the hills beyond them, and the road ahead and behind.

"This is no place for a boy to be walking alone," he said.

"I came across the chasm two days ago," said David. "There were wolves, and the man who was helping me, the Woodsman, was—"

David broke off. He didn't want to say aloud what had become of the Woodsman. He saw again his friend falling beneath the weight of the wolf pack, and the trail of blood that led into the forest.

"You crossed the chasm?" said the horseman. "Tell me, was it you who cut the ropes?"

David tried to read the expression on the horseman's face. He didn't want to get into trouble, and he supposed he must have caused no end of harm by destroying the bridge. Still, he did not want to lie, and something told him that the horseman would call him on it if he did.

"I had to," he said. "The wolves were coming. I had no choice."

The horseman smiled. "The trolls were most unhappy," he said. "They will have to rebuild the bridge now if they are to continue their game, and the harpies will harass them at every turn."

David shrugged his shoulders. He didn't feel sorry for the trolls. Forcing travelers to gamble their lives on the solution to a silly riddle wasn't a decent way to behave. He rather hoped that the harpies decided to eat some of the trolls for dinner, although he didn't imagine trolls would taste very nice.

"I came from the north, so your antics did not interfere with my plans," said the horseman. "But it seems to me that a young man who manages to irritate trolls and escape from both harpies and wolves might be worth having around. I'll make a bargain with you: I will take you to the king if you will accompany me for a time. I have a task to complete, and have need of a squire to help me along the way. It should not require more than a few days of service, and in return I will make sure that you have safe passage to the royal court."

It didn't seem to David as if he had very much choice in the matter. He didn't believe that the wolves would forgive him for the deaths he had caused at the bridge, and by now they must have found another way to cross the canyon. They were probably already on his trail. He had been lucky at the bridge. He might not be so fortunate a second time. Traveling alone on this road, he was always at the mercy of those, like the huntress, who might wish to do him harm.

"I'll go with you, then," he said. "Thank you."

"Good," said the horseman. "My name is Roland."

"And I am David. Are you a knight?"

"No, I am a soldier, nothing more."

Roland reached down and offered David his hand. When David took it, he was instantly lifted off the ground and hoisted onto the back of Roland's horse.

"You look tired," said Roland, "and I can afford to spare a little dignity by sharing my horse with you."

He tapped the horse's flanks with his heels, and they took off at a trot.

David was not used to sitting on a horse. He found it hard to adjust to her movements, so his bottom bounced against the saddle with painful regularity. It was only when Scylla—for that was the horse's name—broke into a gallop that he began to enjoy the experience. It was almost like floating along the road, and even with the added burden of David on her back, Scylla's hooves ate up the ground beneath her feet. For the first time, David began to fear the wolves a little less.

They had been riding for some time when the landscape around them began to change. The grass was charred, the ground broken and churned up as though by great explosions. Trees had been cut down, the trunks sharpened to points and driven into the ground in what looked like an effort to create defenses against some enemy. There were pieces of armor scattered upon the earth, and battered shields and shattered swords. It seemed they were staring at the aftermath of a great battle, but there were no bodies that David could see, although there was blood on the ground, and the muddy pools that pitted the battlefield were more red than brown.

And in the midst of it all was something that did not belong there, something so strange that it caused Scylla to halt in her tracks and worry at the ground with one of her hooves. Even Roland stared at it with undisguised fear. Only David knew what it was.

It was a Mark V tank, a relic of the Great War. Its squat six-pounder gun still protruded from the turret on its left, but it bore no markings of any kind. In fact, it was so clean, so pristine, that it looked to David as if it had just rolled out of a factory some-where.

"What is it?" asked Roland. "Do you know?"

"It's a tank," said David.

He realized that this was unlikely to make the nature of the thing any more understandable to Roland, so he added: "It's a ma-chine, like a big, um, covered cart in which men can travel. This"— he pointed at the six-pounder—"is a gun, a kind of cannon."

David clambered up onto the body of the tank, using the rivets for handholds and footholds. The hatch was open. Inside he could see the system of brakes and gears by the driver's seat, and the workings of the big Ricardo engine, but there were no men to crew it. Once again, it seemed as if it had never been used. From his perch atop the tank, David looked around and could see no sign of tracks on the muddy field. It was as if the Mark V had just appeared there from out of nowhere.

He climbed down from it, jumping the last couple of feet so that he landed on the ground with a splash. Blood and mud instantly stained his trousers, and he was reminded again that they were standing in a place where men had been injured and perhaps had died.

"What happened here?" he asked Roland.

The horseman shifted in the saddle, still uneasy in the presence of the tank.

"I do not know," he said. "A battle of some kind, from the signs. The fight was recent. I can still smell blood on the air, but where are the bodies of the fallen? And if they were buried, then where are the graves?"

A voice spoke from behind them. It said: "You are looking in the wrong place, travelers. There are no bodies on the field. They are . . . elsewhere."

Roland turned Scylla, drawing his sword as he did so. He helped David to climb up behind him. As soon as he was settled, David reached for his own small sword and pulled it from its scabbard.

The remains of an old wall, all that was left of some larger structure now long gone from the world, stood by the roadside. Upon the stones sat an old man. He was completely bald, and thick blue veins ran across his exposed scalp like rivers on a map of some barren, cold place. His eyes were crisscrossed with blood vessels, and the sockets seemed too big for them, so that the red flesh beneath his skin hung loose and exposed under each eyeball. His nose was long, and his lips were pale and dry. He wore an old brown robe, rather like a monk's habit, that ended just above his ankles. His feet were bare, and his toenails were yellow.

"Who fought here?" asked Roland.

"I did not ask them their names," said the old man. "They came, and they died."

"To what purpose? They must have been fighting for some cause."

"No doubt. I am sure that they believed their cause was the right one. *She,* unfortunately, did not."

The smell from the battlefield was making David queasy, and it added to his sense that the old man was not to be trusted. Now the way he spoke of the "she" who had done this, and the manner in which he smiled at the mention of her, made it very clear to David that the men who had died here had died very badly indeed.

"And who is 'she'?" asked Roland.

"She is the Beast, the creature that lives beneath the ruins of a tower deep in the forest. She has slept for a long time, but now she is awake once more." The old man made a gesture toward the trees at his back. "They were the king's men, trying to maintain control over a dying kingdom, and they paid the price. They made their stand here and were overwhelmed. They retreated to the cover of the woods behind me, dragging their dead and injured with them, and there she had her way with them."

David cleared his throat. "How did the tank get here?" he asked. "It doesn't belong."

The old man grinned, revealing purple gums dotted with ruined teeth. "Perhaps the same way you did, boy," he replied. "You don't belong here either."

Roland urged Scylla toward the forest, keeping his distance from the old man. Scylla was a brave horse, and after only a moment's hesitation she did her master's bidding.

The smell of blood and decomposition grew stronger. There was a copse of broken, stunted trees ahead, and David knew that this was the true source of the stench. Roland told David to dismount, then instructed him to keep his back against a tree and his eyes on the old man, who remained upon the little wall, watching them over his shoulder.

David knew that Roland didn't want him to see what lay beyond the bushes, but he could not resist the urge to look as he heard the soldier parting the bushes to enter the copse. David caught a brief glimpse of bodies hanging from trees, the remains reduced to little more than bloodied bones. He quickly looked away—

And found himself staring straight into the eyes of the old man. David had no idea how he had moved so quickly and so silently from his perch on the wall, but now here he was, so close that the boy could smell his breath. It stank of sour berries. David grasped the sword tightly in his hand, but the old man did not even blink.

"You are a long way from home, boy," he said. He raised his right hand and touched his fingers to a stray strand of David's hair. David shook his head furiously and pushed at the old man. It was like pushing at a wall. The old man might have looked frail, but he was far stronger than David.

"Do you still hear your mother calling?" said the old man. He put his left hand to his ear as though trying to catch the sound of a voice on the air. *"Da-vid,"* he sang, in a high voice. *"Oh, Da-vid."*

"Stop it!" said David. "You stop it now."

"Or you'll do what?" said the old man. "A little boy, far, far from home, crying for his dead mother. What can you do?"

"I'll hurt you," said David. "I mean it."

The old man spit on the ground. The grass sizzled where the spittle landed. The liquid expanded, forming a frothy pool upon the ground.

And in the pool David saw his father, and Rose, and the baby Georgie. They were all laughing, even Georgie, who was being tossed high in the air by his father just as David had once been.

"They don't miss you, you know," said the old man. "They don't miss you one little bit. They're glad that you're gone. You made your father feel guilty because you reminded him of your mother, but he has a new family now, and with you out of the way he no longer has to worry about you or your *feelings*. He has forgotten you already, just as he has forgotten your mother."

The image in the pool changed, and David saw the bedroom his father shared with Rose. Rose and his father were standing beside the bed, kissing each other. Then, as David watched, they lay down together. David looked away. His face was stinging, and he felt a great rage rising up inside. He didn't want to believe it, and yet the evidence was before him in a pool of steaming spittle ejected from the mouth of a poisonous old man.

"See," said the old man. "There's nothing for you to go back to now."

He laughed, and David struck at him with the sword. He was not even aware that he was doing it. He was just so angry, and so sad. He had never felt so betrayed. Now it was as if control of his body had been taken over by something else, something outside himself, so that he seemed to have no will of his own. His arm rose of its own volition and slashed at the old man, tearing through his brown robe and drawing a bloody line across the skin beneath.

The old man retreated. He put his fingers to the wound on his chest. They came back red. His face began to change. It extended and assumed the shape of a half-moon, the chin curving up so sharply that it almost met the bridge of his crooked nose. Clumps of rough, black hair sprouted from his skull. He cast aside the robe, and David saw a green and gold suit, tied with an ornate gold belt, and a gold dagger that curved like the body of a snake. There was a rip in the fabric of the suit, where David's sword had cut through the beautiful material. Last of all, a flat black disk appeared in the man's hand. He flicked with it at the air, and it became a crooked hat, which he placed upon his head.

"You," said David. "You were in my room."

The Crooked Man hissed at David, and the dagger at his waist twisted and writhed as though it really were a snake. His face was contorted with fury and pain.

"I have walked through your dreams," he said. "I know everything that you think, everything that you feel, everything that you fear. I know what a nasty, jealous, hateful child you are. And despite all that, I was still going to help you. I was going to help you find your mother, but then you cut me. Ooooh, you're a horrid boy. I could make you very sorry, so sorry you'd wish you'd never been born, but—"

The tone of his voice suddenly changed. It became quiet and reasonable, which frightened David even more.

"I won't, because you'll have need of me yet. I can take you to the one you seek, and then I can get you both home. I'm the only one who really can. And I'll just ask for one small thing in return, so small that you won't even miss it . . ."

But before he could proceed, he was disturbed by the sound of Roland returning.

The Crooked Man wagged a finger in David's face. "We'll talk again, and perhaps you'll be a little more appreciative when we do!"

The Crooked Man began spinning in a circle, and he spun so

fast and so hard that he dug a hole in the earth and disappeared from view, leaving only the brown robe behind. His spittle had dried into the ground, and the images from David's world could no longer be seen.

David felt Roland arrive beside him, and the two of them peered into the dark hole left by the Crooked Man.

"Who, or what, was that?" asked Roland.

"He disguised himself as the old man," said David. "He told me that he could help me to get back home, and that he was the only one who could. I think he was the one the Woodsman spoke of. He called him a trickster."

Roland saw the blood dripping from the blade of David's sword.

"Did you cut him?"

"I was angry," said David. "It happened before I could stop myself."

Roland took the sword from David's hands, plucked a large green leaf from a bush, and used it to clean the blade.

"You must learn to control your impulses," he said. "A sword wants to be used. It wants to draw blood. That is why it was forged, and it has no other purpose in the world. If you do not control it, then it will control you."

He handed the sword back to David. "Next time you see that man, don't just cut him, kill him," said Roland. "Whatever he may say, he means you no good."

They walked together to where Scylla stood nibbling upon the grass.

"What did you see back there?" asked David.

"Much the same as you saw, I suspect," said Roland. He shook his head in mild annoyance at the fact that David had disobeyed his instructions. "Whatever killed those men sucked the flesh from their bones, then left their remains hanging from trees. The forest is filled with bodies, as far as the eye can see. The ground is still wet with blood, but they injured this 'Beast,' or whatever it is, before they died. There is a foul substance on the ground, black and putrid, and the tips of some of their spears and swords have been melted by it. If it can be wounded, then it can be killed, but it will take more than a soldier and a boy to do it. This is none of our concern. We ride on."

"But—" said David. He wasn't sure what to say. It wasn't like this in the stories. Soldiers and knights slew dragons and monsters. They weren't afraid, and they didn't run away from the threat of death.

Roland was already astride Scylla. His hand was outstretched, waiting for David to take it. "If you have something to say, then say it, David."

David tried to find the right words. He did not want to offend Roland.

"These men all died, and whatever killed them is still alive, even if it is wounded," he said. "It will kill again, won't it? More people will die."

"Perhaps," said Roland.

"So shouldn't something be done?"

"What would you suggest: that we hunt it down with one and a half swords to our names? This life is filled with threats and danger, David. We face those that we have to face, and there will be times when we must make the choice to act for a greater good, even at risk to ourselves, but we do not lay down our lives needlessly. Each of us has only one life to live, and one life to give. There is no glory in throwing it away where there is no hope. Now, come. The twilight grows thicker. We need to find a place to shelter for the night."

David hesitated for a moment more, then took Roland's hand and was hoisted into the saddle. He thought of all those dead men, and wondered at the kind of creature that could inflict such harm upon them. The tank still stood in the midst of the battle-field, marooned and alien. Somehow, it had found its way from his world to this one, but without a crew and apparently without even being driven.

As they left it behind, he remembered the visions in the Crooked Man's pool of spittle, and the words that had been spo-ken to him: *"They don't miss you one little bit. They're glad that you're gone."*

It couldn't be true, could it? And yet David had seen the way his father doted on Georgie, and the way he looked at Rose and held her hand as they walked, and he guessed at the things they did together when the bedroom door closed each night. What if he found a way to return home and they didn't want him back? What if they really were happier without him?

But the Crooked Man had told him that he could make things right, that he could restore his mother to him and bring them both home in return for just one small favor. And David won-dered what that favor might be, even as Roland spurred Scylla, urging her on.

Meanwhile, far to the west, out of sight and out of hearing, a cho-rus of triumphant howls rose into the air.

The wolves had found another bridge across the chasm.

XIX

Of Roland's Tale and the Wolf Scout

OLAND WAS RELUCTANT to pause for the night, for he was anxious to continue his quest and he was concerned about the wolves that were pursuing David, but Scylla was tiring and David was so exhausted that he could barely hold on to Roland's waist. Eventually, they came to the ruins of what looked like a church, and there Roland agreed to rest for a few hours. He would not allow a fire, even though it was cold, but he gave David a blanket in which to wrap himself, and he allowed him to sip from a silver flask. The liquid inside burned David's throat before filling him with warmth. He lay down and stared at the sky. The spire of the church loomed over him, its windows empty as the eyes of the dead.

"The new religion," said Roland dismissively. "The king tried to make others follow it when he still had the will to do so, and the power to enforce that will. Now that he broods in his castle, his chapels lie empty."

"What do you believe in?" asked David.

"I believe in those whom I love and trust. All else is foolishness. This god is as empty as his church. His followers choose to attribute all of their good fortune to him, but when he ignores their pleas or leaves them to suffer, they say only that he is beyond their understanding and abandon themselves to his will. What kind of god is that?"

Roland spoke with such anger and bitterness that David wondered if he had once followed the "new religion," only to turn his back upon it when something bad happened to him. David had felt that way himself at times as he sat in church in the weeks and months after his mother's death, listening to the priest talking of God and how much He loved his people. He had found it hard to equate the priest's God with the one who had left his mother to die slowly and painfully.

"And who do you love?" he asked Roland.

But Roland pretended not to hear him.

"Tell me about your home," he said. "Talk to me of your people. Talk to me of anything but false gods."

And so David told Roland of his mother and his father, of the sunken garden, of Jonathan Tulvey and his old books, of hearing his mother's voice and following it into this strange land, and, finally, of Rose and the arrival of Georgie. As he spoke, he could not hide his resentment of Rose and her baby. It made him feel ashamed, and more like a child than he wished to appear in front of Roland.

"That is hard indeed," said Roland. "So much has been taken from you, but so much has been given too, perhaps."

He did not say any more, for fear that the boy might think he was preaching to him. Instead, Roland lay back against Scylla's saddle and told David a tale.

ROLAND'S FIRST TALE

Once upon a time, there was an old king who promised his only son in marriage to a princess in a land far away. He bade his son farewell and entrusted to him a golden cup that had been in his family for many generations. This, he told his son, would be part of his dowry to the princess, and a symbol of the bond between her family and their own. A servant was told to travel with the prince and to care for his every need, and so the two men set out together for the princess's lands.

After they had traveled for many days, the servant, who was jealous of the prince, stole the goblet from him while he was sleeping and dressed himself in the prince's finest clothing. When the prince awoke, the servant made him vow, on pain of his own death and the deaths of all those whom he loved, that he would inform no man of what had transpired and told him that in future the prince would serve him in all things. And so the prince became the servant, and the servant the prince, and in that way they came to the castle of the princess.

When they arrived, the false prince was treated with great ceremony and the true prince was given a job herding pigs, for the false prince told the princess that he was a bad and unruly servant and could not be trusted. So her father sent the true prince out to herd swine and sleep in the mud and straw, while the impostor ate the finest food and rested his head on the softest of pillows.

But the king, who was a wise old man, heard others speak well of the swineherd, of how gracious were his manners and how kind he was to the animals under his charge and to the servants whom he met, and he went to him one day and asked him to tell him something of himself. But the true prince, bound by his vow, told the king that he was unable to obey his command. The king grew angry, for he was not used to being disobeyed, but the true prince fell to his knees and said: "I am bound by a death vow not to tell any man the truth about myself. I beg you to forgive me, for I mean Your Majesty no disrespect, but a man's word is his bond, and without it he is no better than an animal."

So the king thought for a time, and then he said to the true prince: "I can see that the secret you keep inside is troubling to you, and perhaps you would feel happier once you have spoken it aloud. Why don't you tell it to

*the cold hearth in the servants' quarters, and then you may rest easier
because of it."*

*The true prince did as the king asked, but the king hid in the darkness
behind the hearth, and he heard the true prince's tale. That night, he held a
great banquet, for the princess was due to marry the impostor the next day,
and he invited the true prince to sit on one side of his throne as a masked guest,
and on the other side he placed the false prince. And he said to the false prince:
"I have a test of your wisdom, if you will agree to take it." The false prince
readily agreed, and the king told him the tale of an impostor who took on the
identity of another man, and as a result claimed all the wealth and privileges
that were due to another. But the false prince was so arrogant, and so certain
of his position, that he did not recognize the tale as being about himself.*

"What would you do with such a man?" asked the king.

*"I would strip him naked and place him inside a barrel studded with
nails," said the false prince. "Then I would tie the barrel behind four horses,
and I would drag it through the streets until the man inside was ripped to
death."*

*"That that shall be your punishment," said the king, "for such is your
crime."*

*And the true prince was restored to his position, and he married the
princess and lived happily ever after, while the false prince was torn to pieces
in a barrel of nails, and nobody wept for him, and nobody spoke his name
after he was gone.*

When the story was done, Roland looked at David.

"What did you think of my tale?" he asked.

David's brow was furrowed. "I think I read a story like it once
before," he said. "But my story was about a princess, not a prince.
The ending was the same, though."

"And did you like the ending?"

"I did when I was little. I thought that was what the false
prince deserved. I liked it when the bad were punished to death."

"And now?"

"It seems cruel."

"But he would have done the same to another, had it been in his power to do so."

"I suppose so, but that doesn't make the punishment right."

"So you would have shown mercy?"

"If I was the true prince, then, yes, I think so."

"But would you have forgiven him?"

David thought about the question.

"No, he did wrong, so he deserved some punishment. I would have made him herd the pigs and live the way the true prince had been forced to live, and if he ever hurt one of the animals, or hurt another person, then the same thing would be done to him."

Roland nodded approvingly. "That is a fit punishment, and merciful. Sleep now," he said. "We have wolves snapping at our heels, and you must rest while you can."

David did as he was told. With his head upon his pack, he closed his eyes and instantly fell fast asleep.

He did not dream, and awoke only once before the false dawn that marked the coming of day. He opened his eyes and thought that he heard Roland speaking softly to someone. When he glanced over at the soldier, he saw that he was staring at a small silver locket. Inside was a picture of a man, younger than Roland and very handsome. It was to this image that Roland was whispering, and although David could not understand everything that was said, the word "love" was spoken clearly more than once.

Embarrassed, David drew his blanket closer to his head to block out the words until sleep returned.

Roland was already up and moving about when David woke again. David shared some of his food with the soldier, although there was only a little left. He washed himself in a brook and almost began to perform one of his counting routines, but he stopped himself, remembering the Woodsman's advice, and instead cleaned his sword and sharpened its blade against a rock. He checked that his belt was still strong and that the loop holding the scabbard in place was undamaged, then asked Roland to teach him how to saddle Scylla and to tighten her reins and bridle. Roland did so, and also taught him how to check the horse's legs and hooves for any signs of injury or discomfort.

David wanted to ask the soldier about the picture in the locket, but he did not want Roland to think that he had been spying on him in the night. Instead, he asked the other question that had been troubling him since the two had met, and by doing so was given an answer to the mystery of the man in the locket as well.

"Roland," David asked, as the soldier placed the saddle on Scylla's back once again. "What task have you set yourself?"

Roland drew the straps tight around the horse's belly.

"I had a friend," he said, without looking at David. "His name was Raphael. He wanted to prove himself to those who doubted his courage and spoke ill of him behind his back. He heard a tale of a woman bound to sleep by an enchantress in a chamber filled with treasures, and he vowed to release her from her curse. He set out from my land to find her, but he never returned. He was closer to me than a brother. I vowed that I would discover what had befallen him, and avenge his death if such had been his fate. The castle in which she lies is said to move with the cycles of the moon. It now rests at a place not more than two days' ride from here. After we have discovered the truth within its walls, I will take you to see the king."

David climbed onto Scylla's back, and then Roland led the horse by the reins back to the road, testing the ground in front for hidden hollows that might injure his mount. David was growing used to the horse and the rhythm of her movements, although he still ached from the long ride of the day before. He held on to the horn of the saddle, and they left the ruins of the church as the first faint light of morning scratched at the sky.

But they did not leave unobserved. In a patch of brambles beyond the ruins, a pair of dark eyes watched them. The wolf's fur was very dark, and its face had more of man than beast about it. It was the fruit of the union between a loup and a she-wolf, but it favored its mother in looks and instincts. It was also the largest and most ferocious of its kind, a mutant of sorts, big as a pony with jaws capable of encircling a man's chest. The scout had been sent on by the pack to look for signs of the boy. It had picked up his scent upon the road, following it to a little house deep in the woods. There it had almost met its end, for the dwarfs had set traps around their home: deep pits with sharpened poles at their base, disguised with sticks and sods of grass. Only the wolf's reflexes had prevented it from falling to its death, and it had been more careful in its approaches thereafter. It had found the boy's scent mingled with that of the dwarfs and had then traced it back to the road again, losing it for a time until it reached a little stream, where the boy's spoor was replaced by the strong odor of a horse. This told the wolf that the boy was no longer on foot, and probably not alone. It marked the place with its urine, as it had marked each step of its hunt, so that the pack might follow it more easily when it came.

The scout knew what Roland and David could not: the pack had ceased its advance shortly after crossing the chasm, for more wolves were arriving to join it in its march upon the king's castle. The scout had been entrusted by Leroi with the task of finding the boy. If possible, it was to bring him back to the pack for Leroi to deal with. If this could not be achieved, then it was to kill him and return with only a token—the boy's head—to prove that the deed had been done. The scout had already decided the head would be sufficient. It would feed on the rest of the boy, for it was a long time since it had eaten fresh man-flesh.

The wolf hybrid had again detected traces of the boy by the battlefield, along with a stench of something unknown that stung its delicate nose and made its eyes water. The starving scout had fed upon the bones of one of the soldiers, sucking the marrow from deep within, and its belly was now fuller than it had been in many months. Its energy renewed, it had followed the horse's scent once more, and had arrived at the ruins just in time to see the boy and the rider depart.

With its massive back legs, the scout was capable of long, high leaps, and its bulk had driven many a rider from the saddle of a horse, forcing him to the ground and allowing the scout to tear his throat out with its long, sharp teeth. Taking the boy would be easy. If the scout judged its leap right, it could have the boy in its jaws and be ripping him apart before the horseman even realized what was happening. Then the scout would flee, and if the horseman chose to follow, well, it would draw him straight into the jaws of the waiting pack.

The rider was leading his mount at a slow pace, carefully negotiating low branches and thick patches of briar. The wolf shadowed them, waiting for its chance. Ahead of the horseman was a fallen tree, and the wolf guessed that the horse would pause there for a moment as it tried to work out the best way to overcome the obstacle. The wolf would seize the boy when the horse stopped. Quietly, it padded on, overtaking the horse so that it would have time to find the best position from which to strike. It reached the tree and found, in the bushes to its right, a slab of elevated stone perfect for its purpose. Saliva dripped from its jaws, for it was already tasting the boy's blood in its mouth. The horse came into view, and the scout tensed, ready to strike.

A sound came from behind the wolf: the faintest hint of metal against stone. It turned to face the threat, but not quickly enough. It saw the flash of a blade, and then there was a burning deep in its throat, so deep that it could not even make a sound of pain or surprise. It began to smother in its own blood, its legs giving out beneath it as it fell upon the rock, its eyes bright with panic as it began to die. Then that brightness began to fade, and the scout's body spasmed and twitched, until finally it lay still.

In the darkness of its pupil, the Crooked Man's face was reflected. With the blade of his sword, he cut off the scout's nose and placed it in a little leather pouch on his belt. It was another trophy for his collection, and its absence would give Leroi and the pack pause when they found the remains of their brother. They would know who they were dealing with, oh yes, for no other mutilated his prey in this way. The boy was his, and his alone. No wolf would feed upon his bones.

So the Crooked Man watched as David and Roland passed by, Scylla pausing for a second before the fallen tree, just as the scout had guessed that she would, and then jumping it with a single leap before taking the rider and the boy toward the road beyond. Then the Crooked Man descended into the briars and thorns, and was gone.

XX

Of the Village, and Roland's Second Tale

AVID AND ROLAND encountered no one on the road that morning. It still surprised David that so few should walk upon it. After all, the road was well-kept, and it seemed to him that others must use it to get from here to there.

"Why is it so quiet?" he asked. "Why are there no people?"

"Men and women fear to travel, for this world has grown passing strange," said Roland. "You saw what was left of those men yesterday, and I have told you of the sleeping woman and the enchantress who binds her. There have always been dangers in these lands, and life has never been easy, but now there are new threats and no one can tell where they have come from. Even the king is uncertain, if the stories from his court are true. They say his time is almost done."

Roland raised his right hand and pointed to the northeast. "There is a settlement beyond those hills, and there we will spend our last night before we reach the castle. Perhaps we will learn more from those who live there of the woman and of what fate befell my companion."

After another hour had passed, they came upon a party of men emerging from the woods. The men carried dead rabbits and voles tied to sticks. They were armed with sharpened staffs and short, crude swords. When they saw the horse approaching, they raised their weapons in warning.

"Who are you?" called one. "Come no closer until you have identified yourselves."

Roland reined Scylla in while they were still out of reach of the men's staffs.

"I am Roland. This is my squire, David. We are heading for the village, in the hope that we may find food and rest there."

The man who had spoken lowered his sword. "Rest you may find," he said, "but little food."

He raised one of the sticks of dead animals. "The fields and forests are almost bare of life. This is all we have for two days of hunting, and we lost a man for it."

"Lost him how?" asked Roland.

"He was bringing up the rear. We heard him cry out, but when we went back his body was gone."

"You saw no trace of what took him?" asked Roland.

"None. The earth was disturbed where he had stood, as though some creature had burst through from below, but above there was only blood and some filthy stuff that did not come from any animal we know. He was not the first to die in such a way, for we have lost others, but we have yet to see the thing responsible. Now we venture out only in numbers, and we wait, for most believe that it will soon attack us in our beds."

Roland looked back down the road, in the direction from which he and David had come.

"We saw the remains of soldiers, about half a day's ride from here," said Roland. "From their insignia, it appears that they were the king's men. They had no luck against this Beast, and they were well-trained and well-armed. Unless your fortifications are high and strong, you might be advised to leave your homes until the threat has passed."

The man shook his head. "We have farms, livestock. We live where our fathers lived, and their fathers too. We will not abandon all that we have worked so hard to build."

Roland said nothing more, but David could almost hear what he was thinking: *Then you will die.*

David and Roland rode alongside the men, talking with them and sharing what was left of the alcohol in Roland's flask. The men were grateful for the kindness, and in return they confirmed the changes in the land and the presence of new creatures in the forests and fields, all of them hostile and hungry. They spoke too of the wolves, who had become ever more daring of late. The hunters had trapped and killed one during their time in the woods: a Loup, an interloper from far away. Its fur was a perfect white, and it wore breeches made from the skin of a seal. Before it died it told them that it had traveled from the distant north, and others were coming who would avenge its death at their hands. It was as the Woodsman had told David: the wolves wanted the kingdom for themselves, and they were assembling an army with which to take it over.

As they rounded a bend in the road, the settlement was revealed to them. It was surrounded by clear space upon which cattle and sheep grazed. A wall of tree trunks had been built around it, the tops sharpened to white points, and elevated platforms behind allowed men to watch all the approaches. Thin streams of smoke were rising from the houses within, and the spire of another church was visible above the top of the wall. Roland did not look pleased to see it.

"Here, perhaps, they still practice the new religion," he said to

David softly. "For the sake of peace, I will not trouble them with my views."

A cry went up from within the walls as they drew closer to the village, and the gates were opened to admit them. Children gathered to greet their fathers, and women arrived to kiss sons and husbands. They stared curiously at Roland and David, but before anyone had a chance to question them, a woman began wailing and crying, unable to find the one whom she sought among the hunters. She was young and very pretty, and in between her sobs she called a name over and over again: "Ethan! Ethan!"

The leader of the hunters, whose name was Fletcher, approached David and Roland. His wife hovered nearby, grateful that her husband had returned safely.

"Ethan was the man that we lost along the way," he said. "They were to have been married. Now, she does not even have a grave at which to mourn him."

The other women gathered around the weeping girl, trying to console her. They brought her to one of the little houses nearby, and the door closed behind them.

"Come," said Fletcher. "I have a stable behind my house. You may sleep there, if you wish, and I will feed you from my table for tonight. After that, I will have little enough to feed my own family, and you must ride on."

Roland and David thanked him and followed him through the narrow streets until they came to a wooden cottage, its walls painted white. Fletcher showed them to the stable and pointed out where they could find water, and fresh straw and a few stale oats for Scylla. Roland removed Scylla's saddle and made sure that she was comfortable before he and David washed themselves in a trough. Their clothes smelled, and although Roland had other garments that he could wear, David had none. When she heard this, Fletcher's wife brought David some of her son's old clothes, for he was now seventeen and had a wife and son of his own. Feeling much better than he had in a long time, David went with Roland to Fletcher's house, where the table was laid and Fletcher and his family were waiting for them. Fletcher's son looked a lot like his father, for he also had long red hair, although his beard was not as thick and lacked the gray that marked the older man's. His wife was small and dark, and said little, all of her attention fixed on the baby in her arms. Fletcher had two more children, both girls. They were younger than David, although not by much, and they cast sly glances at him and giggled softly.

Once Roland and David were seated, Fletcher shut his eyes, bent his head, and gave thanks for the food—David noticed that Roland neither closed his eyes nor prayed—before inviting all at the table to eat.

The conversation drifted from village matters to the hunting trip and the disappearance of Ethan, before finally reaching Roland and David, and the purpose of their journey.

"You are not the first to have passed through here on the way to the Fortress of Thorns," said Fletcher, once Roland had told him of his quest for it.

"Why do you call it that?" asked Roland.

"Because that is what it is: it is surrounded entirely by thorny creepers. Even to approach its walls is to risk being torn apart. You will need more than a breastplate to breach them."

"You have seen it, then?"

"A shadow passed across the village perhaps half a month ago. When we looked up to see what it was, we saw the castle moving through the air without sound or support. Some of us followed it and saw where it had landed, but we did not dare approach. Such things are best left alone."

"You said others have tried to find it," said Roland. "What happened to them?"

"They did not return," replied Fletcher.

Roland reached beneath his shirt and took out the locket. He opened it and showed the image of the young man to Fletcher. "Was he one of those who did not come back?"

Fletcher examined the picture in the locket. "Yes, I recall him," he said. "He watered his horse here and drank ale at the inn. He left before nightfall, and that was the last we saw of him."

Roland closed the locket and placed it near to his heart once more. He did not speak again until they had finished their meal. When the table was cleared, Fletcher invited Roland to take a seat by the fire, and they shared some tobacco.

"Tell us a story, Father," said one of the little girls, who had seated herself at her father's feet.

"Yes, please do, Father!" echoed the other.

Fletcher shook his head. "I have no more stories to tell. You have heard them all. But perhaps our guest might have a tale that he could share with us?"

He looked inquiringly at Roland, and the faces of the little girls turned toward the stranger. Roland thought for a moment, then he laid down his pipe and began to speak.

ROLAND'S SECOND TALE

Once upon a time there was a knight named Alexander. He was all that a knight should be. He was brave and strong, loyal and discreet, but he was also young and anxious to prove himself by feats of daring. The land in which he lived had been at peace for a very long time, and Alexander had been given few opportunities to gain greater renown on the field of battle. So one day he informed his lord and master that he wished to travel to new and strange lands, to test himself and find out if he was truly worthy to stand alongside the greatest of his fellow knights. His lord, recognizing that Alexander would not be content until he was granted permission to leave, gave him his blessing, and so the knight prepared his horse and weapons and set out alone to seek his destiny, without even a squire to tend to his needs.

In the years that followed, Alexander found the adventures of which he had long dreamed. He joined an army of knights that journeyed to a kingdom far to the east, where they marched against a great sorcerer named Abuchnezzar, who had the power to turn men to dust with his gaze, so that their remains blew like ash across the fields of his victories. It was said that the sorcerer could not be slain by the arms of men, and all those who had attempted to kill him had died. Yet the knights believed that there might yet prove to be a way to end his tyranny, and the promise of great rewards from the true king of the land, who was in hiding from the sorcerer, spurred them on.

The sorcerer met the knights with his ranks of vicious imps on the empty plain before his castle, and there a fierce and bloody conflict commenced. As his comrades fell to the claws and teeth of demons, or were transformed into ash by the sorcerer's gaze, Alexander battled his way through the enemy's ranks, hiding always behind his shield and never looking in the direction of the sorcerer, until at last he was within earshot of him. He called Abuchnezzar's name, and when the sorcerer turned his gaze toward Alexander, the knight quickly spun his shield around so that its inner surface faced his enemy. Alexander had stayed awake all through the previous night polishing the shield so that it now shone brightly in the hot midday sun. Abuchnezzar looked upon it and saw his own reflection, and in that instant he was turned to ash, and his army of imps vanished into thin air and were never seen in the kingdom again.

The king was true to his word and lavished gold and jewels upon Alexander, and offered him the hand of his daughter in marriage so that Alexander might become the heir to his kingdom. Yet Alexander turned down all these things and asked only that word might be sent back to his own lord telling him of the great deed he had performed. The king promised him that it would be done, and so Alexander left him and continued on his travels. He killed the oldest and most terrible dragon in the western lands and made a cloak from its skin. He used the cloak to guard himself against the heat of the underworld, where he journeyed to rescue the son of the Red Queen, who had been abducted by a demon. With every feat that he accomplished, word was sent back to his lord, and so Alexander's reputation grew and grew.

Ten years passed, and Alexander became weary of wandering. He bore the scars of his many adventures, and he felt certain that his reputation as the greatest of knights was now secure. He decided to return to his own lands and so began his long journey home. But a band of thieves and brigands fell upon him on a dark road, and Alexander, worn down by battles uncountable, was barely able to fight them off, suffering grievous injuries at their hands. He rode on, but he was weak and ailing. Upon a hill before him he spied a castle, and he rode to its gates and called out for help, for it was the custom in those lands that people offered help to strangers in need, and that a knight in particular should never be turned away without being given all that was in the power of another to offer him.

But there was no reply, even though a light burned in the upper reaches of the castle. Alexander called out again, and this time a woman's voice said: "I cannot help you. You must leave this place and seek comfort elsewhere."

"I am wounded," answered Alexander. "I fear that I may die if my injuries are not seen to."

But the woman again replied: "Go. I cannot help you. Ride on. In a mile or two you will reach a village, and there they will tend to your wounds."

With no choice but to do as she said, Alexander turned his horse away from the castle gates and prepared to follow the road to the village. As he did so, his strength failed him. He fell from his horse and lay upon the cold, hard ground, and the world grew dark around him.

When he awoke, he found himself on clean sheets in a large bed. The room in which he lay was very grand but layered with dust and cobwebs, as if it had not been used in a very long time. He rose and saw that his wounds had been cleaned and dressed. His weapons and armor were nowhere to be seen. There was food by his bedside, and a jug of wine. He ate and drank, then dressed himself in a robe that hung from a hook on the wall. He was still weak, and he ached when he walked, but he was no longer at risk of death. He tried to leave the room, but the door was locked. Then he heard the woman's voice again. It said: "I have done more than I wished for you, but I will not allow you to roam my house. None has entered this place in many years. It is my domain. When you are strong enough to travel, then I will open the door and you must leave and never return."

"Who are you?" asked Alexander.

"I am the Lady," she said. "I no longer have any other name."

"Where are you?" asked Alexander, for her voice seemed to come from somewhere beyond the walls.

"I am here," she said.

At that moment, the mirror on the wall to his right shimmered and grew transparent, and through the glass he saw the shape of a woman. She was dressed all in black and was seated on a great throne in an otherwise empty room. Her face was veiled, and her hands were covered in velvet gloves.

"Can I not look upon the face of the one who has saved my life?" asked Alexander.

"I choose not to allow it," the Lady replied.

Alexander bowed, for if it was the Lady's will, then so it should be.

"Where are your servants?" asked Alexander. "I would like to be sure that my horse is being tended to."

"I have no servants," said the Lady. "I have looked to your horse myself. He is well."

Alexander had so many questions to ask that he was not sure where to begin. He opened his mouth, but the Lady raised a hand to silence him. "I will leave you now," she said. "Sleep, for I wish you to recover quickly and be gone from this place as soon as you can."

The mirror shimmered, and the Lady's image was replaced with

Alexander's own. With nothing else to do, Alexander returned to his bed and slept.

The next morning, he awoke to find fresh bread beside him, and a jug of warm milk. He had heard no one enter during the night. Alexander drank some of the milk, and while he ate the bread he walked to the mirror and gazed upon it. Although the image did not change, he was certain that the Lady was behind the glass, watching him.

Now Alexander, like many of the greatest knights, was not merely a warrior. He could play both the lute and the lyre. He could compose poems, and even paint a little. He had a love of books, for in books was recorded the knowledge of all those who had gone before him. And so, when next the Lady appeared in the glass that night, he asked for some of these things in order to pass the time while he recovered from his injuries. When he woke up the next morning, he was greeted by a pile of old books, a slightly dusty lute, and a canvas, paints, and some brushes. He played the lute, then began to work his way through the books. There were volumes of history and philosophy, astronomy and morals, poetry and religion. As he read them in the days that followed, the Lady began to appear more often behind the glass, questioning him about all that he had read. It was clear to him that she had read them all many times and knew their contents intimately. Alexander was surprised, for in his own land women were not allowed access to such books, yet he was grateful for the conversation. The Lady then asked him to play for her on the lute, and he did so, and it seemed to him that the sounds he made pleased her.

Thus the days turned to weeks, and the Lady spent more and more time on the other side of the glass, talking with Alexander of art and books, listening to him play, and inquiring after what it was that he was painting, for Alexander refused to show it to her and obtained a promise from her that she would not look upon it while he slept, for he did not want her to see it until it was finished. And although Alexander's wounds had almost healed, the Lady no longer seemed to wish him to leave, and Alexander no longer wanted to leave, for he was falling in love with this strange, veiled woman behind the glass. He spoke to her of the battles he had fought, and the reputation he had gained from his conquests. He wanted her to understand that he was a great knight, a knight worthy of a great lady.

After two months had passed, the Lady came to Alexander and sat in her usual place.

"Why do you look so sad?" she asked, for it was clear to her that the knight was unhappy.

"I cannot finish my painting," he said.

"Why? Do you not have brushes and paints? What more do you need?"

Alexander turned the canvas away from the wall, so that the Lady might see the image upon it. It was a painting of the Lady herself, yet the face was blank, for Alexander had yet to look upon it.

"Forgive me," he said. "I am in love with you. In these months we have spent together, I have learned so much about you. I have never met a woman like you, and I fear that if I leave here I may never do so again. Can I hope that you might feel the same way about me?"

The Lady lowered her head. She seemed about to speak, but then the mirror shimmered and she disappeared from view.

Days went by, and the Lady did not reappear. Alexander was left alone to wonder if he had offended her by what he had said and done. Each night he slept soundly, and each morning food appeared, but he never caught sight of the Lady who brought it.

Then, after five days, he heard the key turning in the lock of his door, and the Lady entered. She was still veiled and still dressed all in black, but Alexander sensed something different about her.

"I have thought about what you have said," she said. "I too have feelings for you. But tell me, and tell me truly: Do you love me? Will you always love me, no matter what may occur?"

Somewhere deep in Alexander the hastiness of youth still lived, for he answered, almost unthinkingly: "Yes, I will always love you."

Then the Lady raised her veil, and Alexander looked upon her face for the first time. It was the face of a woman crossed with that of a beast, a wild thing of the woods, like a panther or a tigress. Alexander opened his mouth to speak, but he could not, so shocked was he by what he saw.

"My stepmother made me this way," said the Lady. "I was beautiful, and she envied me my beauty, so she cursed me with the features of an animal and told me that I would never be loved. And I believed her, and I hid myself away in shame, until you came."

The Lady advanced toward Alexander, her hands outstretched, and her eyes were filled with hope and love and a faint flicker of fear, for she had opened herself to him as she had never before opened herself to another human being, and now her heart lay exposed as it would before a sharp blade.

But Alexander did not come to her. He backed away, and in that moment his fate was sealed.

"Foul man!" cried the Lady. "Fickle creature! You told me that you loved me, but you love only yourself."

She raised her head and bared her sharp teeth at him. The tips of her gloves split as long claws emerged from her fingers. She roared at the knight, then sprang upon him, biting him, scratching him, ripping him with her claws, the taste of his blood warm in her mouth, the feel of it hot upon her fur.

And she tore him apart in the bedchamber, and she wept as she devoured him.

The two little girls looked rather shocked when Roland finished his tale. He rose, thanked Fletcher and his family for the meal, then indicated to David that they should leave. At the door, Fletcher laid a hand gently on Roland's arm.

"A word, if you please," he said. "The elders are worried. They believe that the village has been marked by the Beast of which you spoke, for it is surely nearby."

"Do you have weapons?" asked Roland.

"We do, but you have seen the best of them. We are farmers and hunters, not soldiers," said Fletcher.

"Perhaps that is fortunate," said Roland. "The soldiers did not fare so well against it. You may have better luck."

Fletcher looked at him quizzically, unable to tell if Roland was being serious or was taunting him. Even David was not sure.

"Are you jesting with me?" asked Fletcher.

Roland laid his hand upon the older man's shoulder. "Only a little," he said. "The soldiers approached the Beast's destruction as they would that of another army. They fought of necessity on unfamiliar ground, against an enemy that they did not understand. They had time to build some defenses, for we saw what was left of them, but they were not strong enough to hold them. They were forced to retreat into the forest, and there they were finished off. Whatever it is, this creature is big, and heavy, for I saw where its bulk had flattened trees and shrubs. I doubt if it can move fast, but it is strong and can withstand the injuries inflicted by spears and swords. Out in the open, the soldiers were no match for it.

"But you and your fellows are in a different position. This is your land, and you know it. You need to look upon this thing as you would a wolf or a fox that is threatening your animals. You must lure it to a place of your own choosing, and there trap it and kill it."

"You're suggesting a decoy? Livestock, perhaps?"

Roland nodded. "That might work. It is coming, for it likes the taste of meat, and there is little of that between the site of its last meal and this village. You may huddle here and hope that your walls can withstand it, or you can plan for its destruction, but you may have to sacrifice more than some cattle to achieve that end."

"What do you mean?" asked Fletcher. He looked fearful.

Roland wet his finger in a flask of water, then knelt and drew a circle on the stone floor, leaving a small gap instead of completing it.

"This is your village," said Roland. "Your walls are built to repel an attack from outside." He drew arrows pointing away from the circle. "But what if you were to allow your enemy in, and then close the gates upon him?" Roland completed the circle, and this time he drew arrows pointing inward. "Then your walls become a trap."

Fletcher stared at the drawing, which was already drying upon the stone, fading away to nothing.

"And what do we do once it's inside?" he asked.

"Then you set fire to the village, and everything within," said Roland. "You burn it alive."

That night, as Roland and David slept, a great blizzard arose, and the village and all that surrounded it was blanketed with snow. The snow continued to fall throughout the day, so thickly that it was impossible to see more than a few feet ahead. Roland decided that they would have to stay in the village until the weather improved, but neither he nor David had food left, and the villagers had barely enough for themselves. So Roland asked to meet the elders, and he spent time with them in the church, for that was where the villagers met to discuss matters of great importance. He offered to help them kill the Beast if they would give shelter to him and to David. David sat at the rear of the church as Roland told them of his plan, and the arguments for and against it went back and forth. Some of the villagers were unwilling to sacrifice their houses to the flames, and David didn't really blame them. They wanted to wait in the hope that the walls and defenses would save them when the Beast came.

"And if they do not hold?" asked Roland. "What then? By the time you realize they have failed you, it will be too late to do anything but die."

In the end, a compromise was suggested. As soon as the weather cleared, the women, children, and old men would leave the village and take shelter in the caves on the nearby hills. They would bring with them everything of value, even their furniture, leaving only the shells of the houses behind. Barrels of pitch and oil would be stored in the cottages near the heart of the village. If the Beast attacked, the defenders would try to repel it or kill it from behind the walls. If it broke through, they would retreat, drawing it into the center. The fuses would be lit, and the Beast would be trapped and killed, but only as a last resort. The villagers took a vote, and all agreed that this was the best plan.

Roland stormed out of the church. David had to run to catch up with him.

"Why are you so angry?" asked David. "They agreed to most of your plan."

"Most isn't enough," said Roland. "We don't even know what we're facing. What we do know is that trained soldiers, armed with hardened steel, couldn't kill this thing. What hope do farmers have against it? Had they listened to me, then the Beast might have been defeated without any loss of life to them. Now men will die needlessly because of sticks and straw, because of hovels that could be rebuilt in weeks."

"But it's their village," said David. "It's their choice."

Roland slowed down, then stopped. His hair was white with snow. It made him look much older than he was.

"Yes," he said, "it's their village. But our fortunes are now tied up with theirs, and if this fails, then there is a good chance that we may die alongside them for our troubles."

The snow fell, and the fires burned in the cottages, and the wind carried the smell of the smoke into the darkest depths of the forest.

And in its lair the Beast smelled the smoke upon the air, and it began to move.

XXI

Of the Coming of the Beast

LL THAT DAY and the next, preparations were made for the evacuation of the village. The women, children, and old men gathered up everything that they could carry, and every cart and every horse was pressed into service, except for Scylla, for Roland would not let her out of his sight. Instead, he rode beside the wall, both inside and out, checking it for weaknesses. He did not look pleased by what he saw. The snow still fell, numbing fingers and freezing feet. It made the task of reinforcing the village's defenses harder, and the men grumbled among themselves, asking if all these preparations were really necessary and suggesting that they might have been better off fleeing with the women and children. Even Roland seemed to have his doubts.

"We might as well set splinters and firewood against this creature," David heard him tell Fletcher. They had no idea from which direction the attack would come, so over and over again Roland instructed the defenders in their lines of retreat if the wall was breached and in their tasks once the Beast was in the village. He did not want the men to panic and flee blindly when the creature broke through—as he was sure it would—or all would be lost, but he had little faith in their willingness to stand and face the Beast if the tide of battle turned against them.

"They are not cowards," Roland told David while they sat by a fire and rested, drinking milk still warm from the cow. All around them men were sharpening staffs and sword blades, or using oxen and horses to drag tree trunks into the compound in order to support the walls from within. There was little conversation now, for the day was drawing to a close and night was approaching. Everyone was tense and frightened. "Each of these men would lay down his life for his wife and children," Roland continued. "Faced by bandits or wolves or wild beasts, they would meet the threat, and live or die according to the outcome. But this is different: they don't know or understand what they are about to confront, and they are not disciplined or experienced enough to fight as one. While they will all stand together, each in his way will face this thing alone. They will be united only when the courage of one falters and he runs, and the others follow after him."

"You don't have much faith in people, do you?" said David.

"I don't have much faith in anything," Roland replied. "Not even in myself."

He drank the last of his milk, then cleaned the cup in a bucket of cold water.

"Come now," he said. "We have sticks to sharpen, and blunt swords to make keen."

He smiled emptily. David did not smile back.

It had been decided that they would marshal the main part of their little force near the gates, in the hope that this would draw the Beast to them. If it breached the defenses, it would then be lured into the center of the village, where the trap would be sprung. They would then have one chance, and one chance only, to contain it and to kill it.

When not even the barest sliver of pale moon was visible in the sky, a convoy of people and animals quietly left the village, with a small escort of men to make sure that they reached the caves safely. Once the men had returned, a formal watch was placed upon the walls, each man taking it in turn to spend a few hours guarding the approaches. Altogether, they numbered about forty men, and David. Roland had asked David if he wished to enter the caves with the others, but, although he was frightened, David said that he wanted to stay. He was not sure why. Partly he felt safer with Roland, who was the only person he trusted in this place, but also he was curious. David wanted to see the Beast, whatever it was. Roland seemed to know this and, when the villagers asked him why he had allowed David to stay, he told them that David was his squire and was as valuable to him as his sword or his horse. His words made David blush with pride.

They tethered an old cow in the clearing before the gates, hoping that it would lure the Beast, but nothing happened on that first night of the watch, or the second, and the men grew ever more grouchy and tired. The snow kept falling and freezing, falling and freezing. The watchers on the walls found it hard to see the forest because of the blizzard. A few began muttering among themselves.

"This is foolishness."

"This creature is as cold as we are. It will not attack us in this weather."

"Perhaps there is no Beast at all. What if Ethan was attacked by a wolf, or a bear? We have only this vagabond's word that he saw the bodies of soldiers."

"The blacksmith is right. What if all of this is a trick?"

It was Fletcher who tried to make them see reason. "And what purpose would such a trick serve?" he asked them. "He is one man, with a boy by his side. He cannot murder us in our sleep, and we have nothing worth stealing. If he is doing it for food, then there is poor eating for him here. Have faith, my friends, and be patient and watchful."

Their grumblings ceased then, but they were still cold and unhappy, and they missed their wives and their families.

David spent all of his time with Roland, sleeping beside him during their periods of rest and walking the perimeter with him when their time came to take the watch. Now that the defenses had been strengthened as well as they could be, Roland took time to talk and joke with the villagers, shaking them awake when they dozed and encouraging them when their spirits grew low. He knew that this was the hardest time for them, for the watch was both dull and hard on their nerves. Watching him move among them, and seeing the way in which he had supervised the defense of the village, David wondered if Roland really was only a soldier, as he claimed. He seemed more like a leader to David, a natural captain of men, yet he was riding alone.

On the second night, they sat in the light of a big fire, huddled beneath thick cloaks. Roland had told David that he was free to sleep in one of the cottages nearby, but none of the others had chosen to do so and David did not want to appear weaker than he already seemed by taking up the offer, even if his refusal meant sleeping outdoors, cold and exposed. Thus he chose to remain with Roland. The flames illuminated the soldier's features, casting shadows across his skin, enhancing the bones in his cheeks, and deepening the darkness in the sockets of his eyes.

"What do you think happened to Raphael?" David asked him.

Roland did not answer. He just shook his head.

David knew that he should probably remain silent, but he did not want to. He had questions and doubts of his own, and somehow he knew that Roland shared them. It was not chance that had brought them together. Nothing in this place seemed bound by the rules of chance alone. There was a purpose to all that was happening, a pattern behind it, even if David could catch only glimpses of it in passing.

"You think he's dead, don't you?" he said softly.

"Yes," answered Roland. "I feel it in my heart."

"But you have to find out what happened to him."

"I will know no peace until I do."

"But you may die as well. If you follow his path, you could end up just as he did. Aren't you afraid of dying?"

Roland took a stick and poked at the fire, sending sparks flying upward into the night. They fizzled out before they got very far, like insects that were already being consumed by the flames even as they struggled to escape them.

"I am afraid of the pain of dying," he said. "I have been wounded before, once so badly that it was feared I would not survive. I can recall the agony of it, and I don't wish to endure it again.

"But I feared more the death of others. I did not want to lose them, and I worried about them while they were alive. Sometimes, I think that I concerned myself so much with the possibility of their loss that I never truly took pleasure in the fact of their existence. It was part of my nature, even with Raphael. Yet he was the blood in my veins, the sweat on my brow. Without him, I am less than I once was."

David stared into the flames. Roland's words resonated within him. That was how he had felt about his mother. He had spent so long being terrified at the thought of losing her that he had never really enjoyed the time they spent together toward the end.

"And you?" said Roland. "You're only a boy. You don't belong here. Aren't you frightened?"

"Yes," said David. "But I heard my mother's voice. She's here, somewhere. I have to find her. I have to bring her back."

"David, your mother is dead," said Roland gently. "You told me so."

"Then how can she be here? How can I have heard her voice so clearly?"

But Roland had no answer, and David's frustration grew.

"What is this place?" he demanded. "It has no name. Even you can't tell me what it's called. It has a king, but he might as well not exist. There are things here that don't belong: that tank, the German plane that followed me through the tree, the harpies. It's all wrong. It's just . . ."

His voice trailed off. There were words forming in his brain like a dark cloud building on a clear summer's day, filled with heat and fury and confusion. The question came to him, and he was almost surprised to hear his own voice ask it.

"Roland, are you dead? Are we dead?"

Roland looked at him through the flames.

"I don't know," he replied. "I think I am as alive as you are. I feel cold and warmth, hunger and thirst, desire and regret. I am conscious of the weight of a sword in my hand, and my skin bears the marks of the armor that I wear when I remove it at night. I can taste bread and meat. I can smell Scylla upon me after a day in the saddle. If I were dead, such things would be lost to me, would they not?"

"I suppose so," said David. He had no idea how the dead felt once they passed from one world to the next. How could he? All he knew was that his mother's skin had been cold to the touch, but David could still feel the warmth of his own body. Like Roland, he could smell and touch and taste. He was aware of pain and discomfort. He could feel the heat from the fire, and he was sure that if he put his hand to it, his skin would blister and burn.

And yet this world remained a curious mix of the strange and the familiar, as though by coming here he had somehow altered its nature, infecting it with aspects of his own life.

"Have you ever dreamed of this place?" he asked Roland. "Have you ever dreamed of me, or of anything else in it?"

"When I met you on the road, you were a stranger to me," said Roland, "and although I knew there was a village here, I had never seen it until now, for I have never traveled these roads before. David, this land is as real as you are. Do not start believing that it is some dream conjured up from deep within yourself. I have seen the fear in your eyes when you speak of the wolf packs and the creatures that lead them, and I know that they will eat you if they find you. I smelled the decay of those men on the battlefield. Soon we will face whatever wiped them out, and we may not survive the encounter. All of these things are real. You have endured pain here. If you can endure pain, then you can die. You can be killed here, and your own world will be lost to you forever. Never forget that. If you do, you are lost."

Perhaps, thought David.

Perhaps.

It was deep in the third night when a cry went up from one of the lookouts at the gates.

"To me, to me!" said the young man whose job it was to watch the main road to the settlement. "I heard something, and I saw movement on the ground. I am certain of it."

Those who were sleeping awoke and joined him. Those who were far from the gates heard the cry and were about to come running too, but Roland called to them and told them to stay where they were. He arrived at the gates and began to climb a ladder to the platform at the top of the walls. Some of the other men were already waiting for him, while others stood on the ground and stared through the slits that had been cut into the tree trunks at eye level. Their torches hissed and sputtered as the snow fell upon them and melted instantly.

"I can see nothing," said the blacksmith to the young man. "You woke us for no good reason."

They heard the cow lowing nervously. It rose from its sleep and tried to pull itself free from the post to which it was tethered.

"Wait," said Roland. He took an arrow from a pile against the wall, each one with a rag soaked in oil at its tip. He touched the wrapped point to one of the torches, and it exploded into flame. He took careful aim and fired where the guard on the wall said that he had seen movement. Four or five of the other men did the same, the arrows sailing like dying stars through the night air.

For a moment, there was nothing to be seen but falling snow and shadowy trees. Then something moved, and they saw a massive yellow body erupting from beneath the earth, ridged like that of a great worm, each ridge embedded with thick black hairs, each hair ending in a razor-sharp barb. One of the arrows had lodged itself in the creature, and a foul smell of burning flesh arose, so horrible that the men covered their noses and mouths to block the stink. Black fluid bubbled from the wound, spitting in the heat of the arrow's flame. David could see the shafts of broken arrows and spears stuck in its skin, relics of its earlier encounter with the soldiers. It was impossible to tell how long it was, but its body was ten feet high at least. They saw the Beast twist and turn as it pulled itself free from the dirt, and then a terrible face was revealed. It had clusters of black eyes like a spider, some small, some large, and a sucking mouth beneath them that was ridged with row upon row of sharp teeth. Between eyes and mouth, openings like nostrils quivered as it smelled the men in the village and the warm blood beneath their skin. There were two arms at either side of its jaws, each one ending in a series of three hooked claws with which it could pull its prey into the maw. It did not seem able to make any sound from its mouth, but there was a wet, sucking noise as it began to move across the forest floor, and clear, sticky strands of mucus dripped from its upper body as it raised itself up like a huge, ugly caterpillar reaching for a tasty leaf. Its head was now twenty feet above the ground, revealing its lower parts and the twin rows of black, spiny legs with which it propelled itself along the ground.

"It's higher than the wall!" yelled Fletcher. "It won't need to break through. It can just climb over!"

Roland didn't reply. Instead, he told all of the men to light arrows and aim for the Beast's head. A rain of flames shot toward the creature. Some missed their mark, while more bounced off the thick, spiny hairs on its skin. But still others struck home, and David saw an arrow land in one of the creature's eyes, bursting it instantly. The smell of rotting, burning flesh grew stronger. The Beast shook its head in pain, then began to move toward the walls. They could now see clearly how big it was: thirty feet long from its jaws to its rear. It was moving much faster than even Roland had expected, and only the thick snow prevented it from moving faster still. Soon it would be upon them.

"Keep firing for as long as you can, then retreat once you've drawn it to the walls!" cried Roland. He grabbed David's arm. "Come with me. I need your help."

But David could not move. He was drawn by the dark eyes of the Beast, unable to tear his gaze from it. It was as though a fragment of his own nightmares had somehow come to life, the thing that lay in the shadows of his imagination finally given form.

"David!" shouted Roland. He shook the boy's arm, and the spell was broken. "Come now. We have little time."

They climbed down from the platform and headed for the gates. These consisted of two thick masses of planks, locked from within by half a tree trunk that could be raised by pressing hard upon one end. When they reached the trunk, Roland and David began to push down with all of their strength.

"What are you doing?" shouted the blacksmith. "You'll damn us to death!"

And then the great head of the Beast appeared above the blacksmith, and one of its clawed arms shot out and grasped the man, lifting him high into the air and straight into its waiting jaws. David looked away, unable to watch the blacksmith die. The other defenders were using spears and swords now. Fletcher, who was bigger and stronger than any of the others, raised a sword and with a single blow tried to sever one of the Beast's arms from its body, but it was as thick and hard as the trunk of a tree, and the sword barely broke its skin. Still, the pain distracted it for long enough to allow the villagers to begin their retreat from the walls, just as David and Roland managed to raise the barrier from the gates.

The Beast was attempting to climb over the wall, but Roland had instructed the men to force sticks tipped with hooks through the gaps if the Beast got close enough. They tore at the Beast's hide, and it writhed and twisted upon them. The hooks slowed it down, but it continued to try to push itself over the defenses, even at the cost of great injury to itself. Just then, Roland opened the gates and appeared outside the walls. He drew an arrow and fired it at the side of the Beast's head.

"Hey!" shouted Roland. "This way. Come on!"

He waved his arms, then fired again. The Beast pulled its body from the wall and flopped down onto the ground, the ooze from its wounds staining the snow black. It turned on Roland, pushing itself through the gates, its arms trying to grab him as he ran ahead of it, its head thrusting forward, its jaws snapping at his heels. It paused as it crossed the threshold, taking in the twisting streets, the fleeing men.

Roland waved his torch and sword. "Here!" he cried. "Here I am!"

Roland loosed another arrow, barely missing the Beast's jaws, but it was no longer interested in him. Instead, its nostrils opened and closed as it lowered its head, sniffing, searching. David, hiding in the shadows outside the blacksmith's forge, saw his face reflected in the depths of its eyes as the Beast found him. Its jaws opened, dripping saliva and blood, and then one of its sharp claws swiped the roof from the forge as it reached for the boy. David threw himself backward just in time to avoid being swept up in the creature's grasp. Dimly, he heard Roland's voice.

"Run, David! You must lure it for us!"

David rose to his feet and began to sprint through the narrow streets of the village. Behind him, the Beast crushed the walls and roofs of cottages as it followed him, its head lunging at the little figure fleeing before it, its claws raking at the air. Once David stumbled, and the claws tore at the clothes on his back as he rolled out of their reach and got to his feet again. Now he was just a stone's throw from the center of the village. There was a square around the church, where markets had been held in happier times. Channels had been dug through it by the defenders so that the oil would flow into the square, surrounding the Beast. David raced across the open space toward the doors of the church, the Beast just feet behind him. Roland was already in the doorway, urging David forward.

Suddenly, the Beast stopped. David turned and stared at it. In the nearby houses, the men were preparing to send the oil into the channels, but they too ceased what they were doing and watched the Beast. It began to shudder and shake. Its jaws grew impossibly wide, and it spasmed as if in great pain. Suddenly it fell to the ground as its belly began to swell. David could see movement inside. A shape pressed itself against the Beast's skin from within.

She. The Crooked Man had said the Beast was a female.

"It's giving birth!" shouted David. "You have to kill it now!"

It was too late. The Beast's belly split open with a great ripping sound, and her offspring began to pour out, miniatures of herself, each as big as David, their eyes clouded and unseeing but their jaws gaping and hungry for food. Some were chewing their way out of their own mother, eating her flesh as they freed themselves from her dying body.

"Pour the oil!" shouted Roland to the other men. "Pour it, then light the fuses and run!"

Already, the young were pushing themselves across the square, the instincts to hunt and kill already strong within them. Roland pulled David inside the church and locked the door behind them. Something thrust against it from outside, and the door trembled in its frame.

Roland took David by the hand and led him toward the bell tower. They ascended the stone steps until they reached the very top, where the bell itself hung, and from there they looked down upon the square.

The Beast was still lying on her side, but she had stopped moving. If she was not already dead, then she soon would be. Most of her offspring continued to feed upon her, chewing at her insides and gnawing at her eyes. Others were squirming across the square, or searching the surrounding cottages for food. The oil was running through the channels, but the young did not seem troubled by it. In the distance, David saw the surviving defenders running for the gates, desperate to escape the creatures.

"There are no flames," cried David. "They haven't lit the fires."

Roland drew one of the oil-soaked arrows from his quiver. "Then we will have to do it for them," he said.

He lit the arrow from his flaming torch, then aimed for one of the channels of oil below. The arrow shot from the bow and struck the black stream. Instantly, flames arose, the fire racing across the square, following the patterns that had been cut into it. The creatures in its path began to burn, sizzling and writhing as they died. Roland took a second arrow and fired into a cottage through its window, but nothing happened. Already, David could see some of the young trying to escape from the square and the flames. They could not be allowed to return to the forest.

Roland notched a final arrow to his bow, drew it against his cheek, and released it. This time there was a loud explosion from inside the cottage, and its roof was lifted off by the force of the blast. Flames shot up into the air, and then there were more explosions as the system of barrels that Roland had created inside the houses ignited one after the other, showering burning liquid all over the square and killing everything within reach. Only Roland and David were saved, high in their perch in the bell tower, for the flames could not reach the church. There they stayed, the stink of the burning creatures and the smell of acrid smoke filling the air, until there was only the dying crackle of the flames and the soft whisper of snow melting in fire to disturb the silence of the night.

XXII

Of the Crooked Man and the Sowing of Doubt

AVID AND ROLAND left the village next morning. By then the snow had ceased falling, and although thick drifts still masked the lay of the land, it was possible to pick out the route that the concealed road took between the tree-covered hills. The women, children, and old men had returned from their hiding places in the caves. David could hear some of them crying and wailing as they stood before the smoldering ruins of what were once their homes, or mourning those who had been lost, for three men had died fighting the Beast. Others had gathered in the square, where the horses and oxen were once again being pressed into service, this time to haul away the charred carcasses of the Beast and her foul offspring.

Roland had not asked David why he thought the Beast had chosen to pursue him through the village, but David had seen the soldier looking at him thoughtfully as they prepared to depart. Fletcher, too, had seen what occurred, and David knew that he also was curious. David was not sure how he would answer the question if it was asked. How could he explain his sense that the Beast was familiar to him, that there was a corner of his imagination where the creature had found an echo of herself? What frightened him most of all was the feeling that he had somehow been responsible for her creation, and the deaths of the soldiers and the villagers were now on his conscience.

When Scylla was saddled, and they had scraped together some food and fresh water, Roland and David walked through the village to the gates. Few of the villagers came to wish them well. Most chose instead to turn their backs upon the departing travelers or stared balefully at them from the ruins.

Only Fletcher seemed truly sorry to see them go. "I apologize for the behavior of the rest," he said. "They should show more gratitude for what you have done."

"They blame us for what happened to their village," said Roland to Fletcher. "Why should they be grateful to those who took the roofs from above their heads?"

Fletcher looked embarrassed.

"There are those who say that the Beast followed you, and that you should never have been allowed to enter the village in the first place," he said. He glanced at David quickly, unwilling to meet his eye. "Some have spoken about the boy and how the Beast attacked him instead of you. They say that he is cursed, and we are well rid of him and you."

"Are they angry with you for bringing us here?" asked David, and Fletcher seemed thrown slightly by the boy's solicitude.

"If they are, then they will soon forget. Already we are planning to send men into the forest to cut down trees. We will rebuild our homes. The wind saved most of the houses to the south and west, and we will share our living spaces with one another until we have rebuilt. In time, they will come to realize that, had it not been for you, there would be no village at all, and many more would have died in the jaws of the Beast and her young."

Fletcher handed Roland a sack of food.

"I can't take this," said Roland. "You will all have need of it."

"With the Beast dead, the animals will return, and we will have prey to hunt once again."

Roland thanked him and prepared to turn Scylla to the east.

"You are a brave young man," Fletcher said to David. "I wish there was something more that I could give to you, but all I could find was this."

In his hand he held what looked like a blackened hook. He gave it to David. It was heavy, and had the texture of bone.

"It is one of the Beast's claws," said Fletcher. "If anyone ever questions your bravery, or you feel your courage ebb, take it in your hand and remember what you did here."

David thanked him and stored the claw in his pack. Then Roland spurred Scylla on, and they left the ruins of the village behind them.

They rode in silence through the twilight world, its appearance rendered more spectral yet by the fallen snow. Everything seemed to glow with a bluish tinge, and the land appeared both brighter and yet more alien. It was very cold, and their breath hung heavily in the air. David felt the little hairs in his nostrils freeze, and the moisture from his breath formed crystals of ice upon his eyelashes. Roland rode slowly, taking care to keep Scylla away from ditches and drifts for fear that she might injure herself.

"Roland," said David at last. "There's something that's been bothering me. You told me that you were just a soldier, but I don't think that's true."

"Why do you say that?" asked Roland.

"I saw how you gave orders to the villagers and how they obeyed you, even the ones who weren't sure they liked you. I have seen your armor and your sword. I thought that the decoration on them was just bronze or colored metal, but when I looked more closely, I could see that it was gold. The sun symbol on your breastplate and your shield is made of gold, and there is gold on your scabbard and on the hilt of your sword. How can that be, if you are just a soldier?"

Roland did not answer for a time, then he said, "I was once more than a soldier. My father was lord of a vast estate, and I was his eldest son and heir. But he did not approve of me or of the way that I lived my life. We argued, and in a fit of anger he banished me from his presence and from his lands. It was not long after our fight that my quest for Raphael began."

David wanted to ask more, but he sensed that whatever lay between Roland and Raphael was private and very personal. To pursue it further would have been rude, and would have been hurtful to Roland.

"And you?" asked Roland. "Tell me more about yourself and your home."

And David did. He tried to explain some of the wonders of his own world to Roland. He told him of airplanes and radio, of cinemas and cars. He spoke of the war, of the conquest of nations and the bombing of cities. If Roland thought these things were extraordinary, he did not show it. He listened to them the way an adult might listen to a child's constructed tales, impressed that a mind could create such fantasies but reluctant to share their creator's belief in them. He seemed more interested in what the Woodsman had told David of the king, and of the book that held his secrets.

"I too have heard that the king knows a great deal about books and stories," said Roland. "His realm may be falling to pieces around him, but he always has time for talk of tales. Perhaps the Woodsman was right to try to lead you toward him."

"If the king is weak, as you say, then what will happen to his kingdom when he dies?" asked David. "Does he have a son or a daughter who will succeed him?"

"The king has no children," said Roland. "He has ruled for a very long time, since before I was born, but he has never taken a wife."

"And before him?" asked David, who had always been interested in kings and queens and kingdoms and knights. "Was his father king?"

Roland struggled to remember.

"There was a queen before him, I think. She was very, very old, and she announced that a young man, one whom nobody had ever seen before but who was soon to come, would rule the realm in her place. That was what happened, according to those who were alive then. Within days of the young man's arrival, he was king, and the queen went to her bed and fell asleep and never woke again. They say that she seemed almost . . . *grateful* to die."

They came to a stream, frozen over by the plummeting temperature, and there they decided to rest for a short while. Roland used the hilt of his sword to break the ice so that Scylla could drink from the water beneath. David wandered along the edge of the stream while Roland ate. He was not hungry. Fletcher's wife had given him great slabs of homemade bread and jam for breakfast that morning, and they were still sitting in his stomach. He sat on a rock and dug in the snow for stones to throw upon the ice. The snow was deep, and soon his arm was buried in it. His fingers touched some pebbles—

And a hand shot out of the snow beside him and gripped him just above the elbow. It was white and thin, with long, jagged nails, and with enormous force it pulled him from the rock and into the snow. David opened his mouth to yell for help, but a second hand appeared and clamped itself across his lips. He was dragged beneath the drift, the snow falling on top of him so that he could no longer see the trees and sky above, the hands never loosening their hold upon him. He felt hard ground at his back and was overcome by a terrible sense of suffocation, and then the earth too collapsed and he found himself in a hollow of dirt and stone. The hands released him, and a light shone through the darkness. Tree roots hung down from above, gently caressing his face, and David saw the openings of three tunnels, their mouths converging on this one spot. Yellowing bones lay in one corner, the flesh that once covered them long since rotted or consumed. There were worms and beetles and spiders all around, scurrying and fighting and dying in the moist, cold earth.

And there was the Crooked Man. He squatted in a corner, one of those pale hands that had dragged David down now holding a lamp while the other gripped a huge black beetle. As David watched, the Crooked Man put the struggling insect into his mouth, head first, and bit it in half. He chewed on the beetle, all the time watching David. The bottom half of the insect kept moving for a few seconds, then stopped. The Crooked Man offered it to David. David could see part of its insides. They were white. He felt very sick.

"Help me!" he shouted. "Roland, please help me!"

But there was no reply. Instead, the vibrations of his cries merely dislodged dirt from the roof of the hollow. It fell on his head and into his mouth. David spit it out, then prepared to shout again.

"Oh, I wouldn't do that," said the Crooked Man. He picked at his teeth and extracted a long, black beetle leg that had lodged close to his gums. "The ground here isn't stable, and with all that snow above, well, I don't like to think what would happen if it came down on top of you. You'd die, I expect, and not very pleasantly."

David closed his mouth. He did not want to be buried alive

down there with the insects and the worms and the Crooked Man.

The Crooked Man worked on the lower half of the beetle, removing its back to expose its innards entirely.

"Are you sure you don't want any?" he asked. "They're very good: crunchy on the outside, soft on the inside. Sometimes, though, I find that I don't want crunchy. I just want soft."

He lifted the insect's body to his mouth and sucked at its flesh, then threw the husk into a corner.

"I thought that you and I should have a talk," he said, "without the risk of your, um, 'friend' up there interrupting us. I don't think you've fully grasped the nature of your predicament. You still seem to think that allying yourself with every passing stranger will help you, but it won't, you know. I'm the reason you're still alive, not some ignorant Woodsman or disgraced knight."

David couldn't bear to hear the men who had helped him dismissed like that. "The Woodsman wasn't ignorant," he said. "And Roland argued with his father. He isn't a disgrace to anyone."

The Crooked Man grinned unpleasantly. "Is that what he told you? Tut, tut. Have you seen the picture he carries in his locket? Raphael, isn't that the name of the one whom he seeks? Such a nice name for a young man. They were very close, you know. Oooh, *very* close."

David didn't know quite what the Crooked Man meant, but the way he spoke made David feel dirty and soiled.

"Perhaps he would like you to be his new friend," continued the Crooked Man. "He looks at you in the night, you know, when you're asleep. He thinks you're beautiful. He wants to be close to you, and closer than close."

"Don't talk about him that way," warned David. "Don't you dare."

The Crooked Man sprang from the corner, leaping like a frog, and landed in front of David. His bony hand grasped the boy's jaw painfully, the nails digging into his skin.

"Don't tell me what to do, *child,*" he said. "I could tear your head off if I chose, and use it to adorn my dinner table. I could bore a hole in your skull and stick a candle in it, once I'd eaten my fill of whatever was inside—which wouldn't be much, I expect. You're not a very bright boy, are you? You enter a world you don't understand, chasing the voice of someone you know is dead. You can't find your way back again, and you insult the only person who can help you return, namely me. You are a very rude, ungrateful, and ignorant little boy."

With a snap of his fingers, the Crooked Man produced a long, sharp needle, threaded with coarse black string made from what looked like the knotted legs of dead beetles.

"Now why don't you work on your manners before you force me to sew your lips shut?"

He released his grip on David's face, then patted his cheek gently.

"Let me show you a proof of my good intentions," he purred. He reached into the leather pouch upon his belt and drew from it the snout that he had severed from the wolf scout. He dangled it in front of David.

"It was following you, and it found you as you emerged from the church in the forest. It would have killed you, too, had I not intervened. Where it went, others will follow. They are on your trail, and growing ever greater in number. More and more of them are transforming now, and they cannot be stopped. Their time is coming. Even the king knows it, and he does not have the strength to stand in their way. It would be well for you to be back in your own world before they find you again, and I can help you. Tell me what I want to know and you will be safe in your bed before nightfall. All will be well in your house, and your problems will have been solved. Your father will love you, and you alone. This I can promise you if you answer just one question."

David didn't want to bargain with the Crooked Man. He couldn't be trusted, and David felt certain that he was keeping many things from him. No deal made with him could ever be simple, or without cost. Yet David also knew that much of what he was saying was true: the wolves were coming, and they would not stop until they found David. Roland would not be able to kill them all. Then there was the Beast: terrible though she was, she was only one of the horrors that this land seemed to conceal. There would be others, perhaps worse than Loups or Beast. Wherever David's mother now was, in this world or another, she seemed beyond his reach. He could not find her. He had been foolish ever to think he could, but he had wanted so badly for it to be true. He had wanted her to be alive again. He missed her. Sometimes he would forget her, but in forgetting he would remember her again, and the ache for her would return with a vengeance. Yet the answer to his loneliness did not lie in this place. It was time to go home.

And so David spoke. "What do you want to know?" he said.

The Crooked Man leaned toward him and whispered. "I want you to tell me the name of the child in your house," he said. "I want you to name for me your half brother."

David's fear was replaced by puzzlement. "But why?" he said. If the Crooked Man was the same figure he had seen in his bedroom, then wasn't it possible that he had been in other parts of the house too? David remembered how he had awoken at home with the unpleasant sensation that something or someone had touched his face while he was asleep. A strange smell had sometimes hung about Georgie's bedroom (stranger, at least, than the smell that usually came from Georgie). Could that have been an indication of the Crooked Man's presence? Was it possible that the Crooked Man had failed to hear Georgie's name spoken during his incursions into their house, and why was it so important to him to know the name anyway?

"I just want to hear it from your lips," said the Crooked Man. "It's such a small thing, such a tiny, tiny favor. Tell me, and all this will be over."

David swallowed hard. He so badly wanted to go home. All he had to do was speak Georgie's name. What harm could that do? He opened his mouth to speak, but the next name spoken was not Georgie's but his own.

"David! Where are you?"

It was Roland. David heard the sound of digging from above. The Crooked Man hissed his displeasure at the intrusion.

"Quickly!" he said to David. "The name! Tell me the name!"

Dirt fell on David's head, and a spider scurried across his face.

"Tell me!" shrieked the Crooked Man, and then the ceiling of earth over David's head fell in, blinding and burying him. Before his sight failed, he saw the Crooked Man scurry for one of the tunnels to escape the collapse. There was earth in David's mouth and nose. He tried to breathe, but it caught in his throat. He was drowning in dirt. He felt strong hands grip his shoulders as he was pulled from the earth and into the clean, crisp air above. His vision cleared, but he was still choking on soil and bugs. Roland's hands pumped at David's body, forcing the earth and insects from his throat. David coughed up dirt and blood and bile and crawling things as his airways cleared, then lay on his side in the snow. The tears froze on his cheeks, and his teeth were chattering.

Roland knelt by his side. "David," he said. "Talk to me. Tell me what happened."

Tell me. Tell me.

Roland touched his hand to David's face, and David felt himself recoil. Roland, too, registered his response, for instantly he withdrew his hand and moved away from the boy.

"I want to go home," David whispered. "That's all. I just want to go home."

And he curled into himself upon the snow and cried until he had no tears left to shed.

XXIII

Of the March of the Wolves

AVID SAT on Scylla's back. Roland was not riding with him but once more led the horse by her reins along the road. There was an unspoken tension between Roland and David, and while the boy was able to recognize both Roland's hurt and its source, he could not find a way to connect the two with an apology. The Crooked Man had hinted at something about the relationship between Roland and the lost Raphael that David felt might be true, but he was less convinced by the implication that Roland now had similar feelings for David himself. Deep down, he was certain that it was false; Roland had shown him nothing but kindness, and if there had been any ulterior motive to his actions, it would have revealed itself long before now. He was sorry that he had recoiled from Roland's touch of solicitude, but to make the admission would have forced him to acknowledge that, even for just the blink of an eye, the Crooked Man's words had found their mark.

It had taken David a long time to recover himself. His throat hurt when he spoke, and he could still taste dirt in his mouth even after he had washed it out with icy water from the stream. It was only after riding in silence for a long time that he was able to tell Roland of what had taken place beneath the ground.

"And that is all he asked of you?" said Roland, when David had repeated to him most of what had been uttered. "He wanted you to tell him your half brother's name?"

David nodded. "He told me I could go back home if I did."

"Do you believe him?"

David thought about the question. "Yes," he said. "I think he could show me the way, if he wanted to."

"Then you must decide for yourself what to do. Remember, though, that nothing comes without cost. The villagers learned that as they sifted through the remains of their homes. There is a price to be paid for everything, and it is a good idea to find out that price before you make the agreement. Your friend the Woodsman called this fellow a trickster, and if that is what he is, then nothing he says is entirely to be trusted. Be careful in striking a bargain with him and listen closely to his words, for he will say less than he means and conceal more than he reveals."

Roland did not look back at David as he spoke, and these were the last words that they exchanged for many miles. When they stopped to rest that night, they sat at opposite sides of the small fire Roland had made, and they ate in silence. Roland had removed the saddle from Scylla's back and placed it against a tree, far from the spot where he had laid out David's blanket.

"You can rest easy," he said. "I am not tired, and I will keep watch on the forest while you sleep."

David thanked him. He lay down and closed his eyes, but he could not fall asleep. He thought of wolves and Loups, of his father and Rose and Georgie, of his lost mother and the offer that the Crooked Man had made. He wanted to leave this place. If all that was required was to share Georgie's name with the Crooked Man, then perhaps that was what he should do. But the Crooked Man would not come back now that Roland was keeping watch, and David felt his anger at Roland begin to grow. Roland was using him: his promise of protection and of guidance to the king's castle had come at too great a price. David was being dragged along on a quest for a man whom he had never met, a man for whom only Roland had feelings, and those feelings, if the Crooked Man was to be believed, were not natural. There were names for men like Roland where David came from. They were among the worst names that a man could be called. David had always been warned to keep away from such people, and now here he was keeping company with one of them in a strange land. Well, soon their ways would part. Roland reckoned that they would reach the castle the following day, and there they would finally learn the truth of Raphael's fate. After that, Roland would lead him to the king, and then their arrangement would be over.

While David slept, and Roland brooded, the man named Fletcher knelt at the walls of his village, his bow in his hand, a quiver of arrows by his side. Others crouched alongside him, their faces lit by torches once again, just as they had been when they prepared to face the Beast. They gazed out at the forest before them, for even in the darkness it was clear to them that it was no longer empty and still. Shapes moved through the trees, thousands upon thousands of them. They padded on all fours, gray and white and black, but among them were those that walked on two legs, dressed like men but with faces that bore traces of the animals they once were.

Fletcher shivered. This, then, was the wolf army of which he had heard. He had never seen so many animals moving as one before, not even when he had looked to the late summer skies and witnessed the migration of birds. Yet they were now more than animals. They moved with a purpose beyond merely the desire to hunt or breed. With the Loups at their head to impose discipline and plan the campaign, they represented a fusion of all that was most terrifying about men and wolves. The king's forces would not be strong enough to defeat them on a field of battle.

One of the Loups emerged from the pack and stood at the edge of the forest, staring at the men hunched behind the defenses of their little village. He was more finely dressed than the others, and even from this distance Fletcher could tell that he seemed more human than the others, although he could not yet be mistaken for a man.

Leroi: the wolf who would be king.

During the long wait for the coming of the Beast, Roland had shared with Fletcher what he knew of the wolves and the Loups, and how David had bested them. Although Fletcher wished the soldier and the boy only health and happiness, he was very glad that they were no longer within the walls of the village.

Leroi knows, thought Fletcher. He knows they were here, and if he suspected they were still with us, he would attack with the full fury of his army.

Fletcher raised himself to his feet and stared across the open ground to the place where Leroi stood.

"What are you doing?" whispered someone from close by.

"I will not cower before an animal," said Fletcher. "I will not give that *thing* the satisfaction."

Leroi nodded, as though in understanding of Fletcher's gesture, then slowly drew a clawed finger across his throat. He would be back once the king was dealt with, and they would see how brave Fletcher and the others truly were. Then Leroi turned away to rejoin the pack, leaving the men to watch impotently as the great wolf army passed through the woods on its way to seize the kingdom.

XXIV

Of the Fortress of Thorns

AVID AWOKE the next morning to find Roland gone. The fire was dead, and Scylla was no longer tethered to her tree. David rose and stood where the horse's tracks disappeared into the forest. He felt concern at first, then a kind of relief, followed by anger at Roland for abandoning him without even a word of good-bye, and, finally, the first twinge of fear. Suddenly, the prospect of confronting the Crooked Man alone again was not so appealing, and the possibility of the wolves coming across him was less appealing yet. He drank from his canteen. His hand was shaking. It caused him to spill water over his shirt. He wiped at it and caught the jagged end of a fingernail on the coarse material. A thread unraveled, and as he tried to free it, his nail tore still further, causing him to yelp in pain. He threw the canteen at the nearest tree in a fit of rage, then sat down hard on the ground and buried his head in his hands.

"And what purpose did that serve?" said Roland's voice.

David looked up. Roland was watching him from the edge of the woods, seated high on Scylla's back.

"I thought you'd left me," said David.

"Why would you think that?"

David shrugged. Now he was ashamed of his display of petulance and his doubts about his companion. He tried to hide it by going on the attack. "I woke up and you were gone," he replied. "What was I supposed to think?"

"That I was scouting the way ahead. I did not leave you for very long, and I believed that you were safe here. There is stone not far below the ground here, so our friend could not use his tunnels against you, and at all times I was within earshot. You had no reason to doubt me."

Roland dismounted and walked to where David sat, leading Scylla behind him.

"Things have not been the same with us since that foul little man dragged you beneath the ground," said Roland. "I think I may have some inkling of what he said to you about me. My feelings for Raphael are mine, and mine alone. I loved him, and that is all anyone needs to know. The rest is no business of any man's.

"As for you, you are my friend. You are brave, and you are both stronger than you look and stronger than you believe yourself to be. You are trapped in an unfamiliar land with only a stranger for company, yet you have defied wolves, trolls, a beast that had destroyed a force of armed men, and the tainted promises of the one you call the Crooked Man. Through it all I have never yet seen you in despair. When I agreed to take you to the king, I thought you would be a burden on me, but instead you have proved yourself worthy of respect and trust. I hope that I in turn have proved myself worthy of *your* respect and trust, for without it we are both lost. Now, will you come with me? We have almost reached our destination."

He extended his hand to David. The boy took it, and Roland raised him to his feet.

"I'm sorry," said David.

"You have nothing to be sorry for," said Roland. "But gather your belongings, for the end is near."

They rode for only a short time, but as they traveled the air around them changed. The hairs on David's head and arms stood on end. He could feel the static when he touched his hand to them. The wind blew a strange scent from the west, musty and dry, like the interior of a crypt. The land rose beneath them until they came to the brow of a hill, and there they paused and looked down.

Before them, like a stain upon the snow, was the dark shape of a fortress. David thought of it as a shape rather than a fortress itself, because there was something very peculiar about it. He could make out a central tower, and walls and outbuildings, but they were slightly blurred, like the lines of a watercolor painting made on damp paper. It stood at the center of the forest, but all of the trees around it had been felled as though by some great explosion. Here and there David saw the glinting of metal upon its battlements. Birds hovered above it, and the dry smell grew stronger.

"Carrion birds," said Roland, pointing. "They feed upon the dead."

David knew what he was thinking: Raphael had entered that place, and had not returned.

"Perhaps you should stay here," said Roland. "It will be safer for you."

David looked around. The trees here were different from the others he had seen. They were twisted and ancient, their bark diseased and pitted with holes. They looked like old men and women frozen in agony. He did not want to remain alone among them.

"Safer?" queried David. "There are wolves following me, and who knows what else lives in these woods? If you leave me here, I'll just follow you on foot anyway. I might even be useful to you in there. I didn't let you down in the village when the Beast came after me, and I won't let you down now," he said with determination.

Roland did not argue with him. Together they rode toward the fortress. As they moved through the forest, they heard voices whispering. The sounds seemed to come from within the trees, emerging through the openings in their trunks, but whether they were the voices of the trees themselves or those of unseen things that dwelled within them David could not say. Twice he believed that he saw movement in the holes, and once he was certain that eyes had stared back at him from deep inside the tree, but when he told Roland, the soldier said only: "Don't be afraid. Whatever they are, they have nothing to do with the fortress. They are not our concern, unless they choose to make themselves so."

Nevertheless, he slowly withdrew his sword as he rode and let it hang by Scylla's side, ready to be used.

The forest was so thick with trees that the fortress was lost from sight as they passed through them, so it came as something of a shock to David when they finally emerged into the blasted landscape of fallen trunks. The force of the explosion, or whatever it had been, had torn the trees from the ground, so that their roots lay exposed above deep hollows. At the epicenter lay the fortress, and now David could see why it had appeared blurred from a distance. It was completely covered by brown creepers that wound around the central tower and covered the walls and battlements, and from the creepers emerged dark thorns, some easily a foot long and thicker than David's wrist. It might have been possible to attempt to climb the walls using the creepers, but make even the slightest misstep and an arm or a leg or, worse, the head or the heart would be impaled upon the waiting spikes.

They rode around the perimeter of the fortress until they came to the gates. They were open, but the creepers had formed a barrier across the entrance. Through the gaps between the thorns, David could see a courtyard, and a closed door at the base of the central tower. A suit of armor lay upon the ground before it, but there was no helmet, and no head.

"Roland," said David. "That knight . . ."

But Roland was not looking at the gates, or at the knight. His head was raised, and his eyes were fixed on the battlements. David followed his gaze and discovered what it was that had gleamed upon the walls from a distance.

The heads of men had been impaled upon the topmost thorns, facing out over the gates. Some still wore their helmets, although their face guards were raised or torn off so that their expressions could be seen, while others had no armor left at all. Most were little more than skulls, and, while there were three or four that were still recognizable as men, they looked as though they had no flesh left on their faces, just a thin covering of gray, papery skin over the bone. Roland examined each one in turn until, at last, he had stared into the faces of every dead man upon the battlements. He looked relieved when he was done. "Raphael is not among those that I can identify," he said. "I see neither his face nor his armor."

He dismounted and approached the entrance. Drawing his sword, he sliced off one of the thorns. It fell to the ground, and instantly another grew in its place, even longer and thicker than the one that had been severed. It grew so fast that it almost stabbed Roland in the chest before he managed, just in time, to step out of its way. Roland next tried to hack through the creeper itself, but his sword made only the slightest of cuts upon it, and the damage once again repaired itself before his eyes.

Roland stepped back and returned his sword to its sheath.

"There must be a way inside," he said. "How else did that knight gain admittance before he died? We will wait. We will wait, and we will watch. In time, perhaps it will reveal its secrets to us."

They settled down after building a small fire to keep the cold at bay and maintained a silent, uneasy vigil on the Fortress of Thorns.

Night fell, or the greater darkness that merely deepened the shadows of the day and served as night in that world. The whispering from the forest, which had continued while they circled the fortress, abruptly ceased with the coming of the moon. The carrion birds disappeared. David and Roland were alone.

A faint light appeared in the topmost window of the tower and then was blocked as a figure passed before the opening. It paused and seemed to stare down upon the man and boy below, then disappeared.

"I saw it," said Roland, before David could open his mouth.

"It looked like a woman," said David.

It was the enchantress, he thought, watching over the sleeping lady in the tower. The moonlight shone upon the armor of the dead men impaled on the battlements, reminding him of the danger he and Roland now faced. They must all have been armed when they approached the fortress, yet still they had died. The body of the knight that lay inside the gates was huge, taller than Roland by a foot at least, and almost as broad as him again. Whoever guarded the tower was strong and fast and very, very cruel.

Then, as they watched, the creepers and thorns blocking the gates began to move. They unraveled slowly, creating an entrance through which a man could pass. It gaped like an open mouth, the long thorns poised like teeth waiting to bite.

"It's a trap," said David. "It must be."

Roland stood.

"What choice do I have?" he said. "I must discover what happened to Raphael. I have not come all this way to sit on the ground and stare at walls and thorns."

He placed his shield upon his left arm. He did not look frightened. In fact, he looked happier to David than he had been at any point since they had met. He had traveled from his own land to find an answer to his friend's disappearance, tormented by what might have befallen him. Whatever now happened within the fortress walls, and whether he lived or died as a result, he would at last discover the truth about the end of Raphael's journey.

"Stay here, and keep the fire burning," said Roland. "If I have not returned by daybreak, take Scylla and ride as fast as you can from this place. Scylla is as much your horse now as mine, for I think she loves you just as she loves me. Remain on the road, and it will lead you eventually to the castle of the king."

He smiled down upon David. "It has been an honor to travel these roads with you. If we do not see each other again, I hope that you find your home and the answers you seek."

They shook hands. David did not shed a tear. He wanted to be as brave as he thought Roland to be. It was only later that he wondered if Roland was truly brave. He knew that Roland believed Raphael was dead, and that he wanted revenge upon whomever had killed him. But he also felt, as Roland walked toward the waiting fortress, that part of the knight did not want to live without Raphael, and that death, for him, would be preferable to a life alone.

David accompanied Roland to the gates. As they approached, Roland gazed up at the waiting thorns in apprehension, as though he feared they would close upon him as soon as he was within their reach. But they did not move, and Roland passed through the gap without incident. He stepped over the armor of the knight and pushed open the door of the tower. He looked back at David, raised his sword in a final farewell, and walked into the shadows. The creepers on the gates twisted, and the thorns extended, restoring the barrier across the entrance to the courtyard, and then all was still once more.

*   *   *

The Crooked Man watched what had transpired from his perch on the topmost branch of the tallest tree in the forest. The presences that dwelled within the tree trunks did not trouble him, for they were more scared of the Crooked Man than of almost any other being that dwelled in this land. The thing in the fortress was ancient and cruel, but the Crooked Man was older and crueler still. He stared down upon the boy seated by the fire, Scylla standing close by him, untethered, for she was a brave, intelligent horse and would not easily take fright or abandon her rider. The Crooked Man was tempted to approach David once again and ask him for the child's name, but he thought better of it. A night alone at the edge of the forest, facing the Fortress of Thorns and watched over by the heads of dead knights, would make him more willing to bargain with the Crooked Man come morning.

For the Crooked Man knew that the knight Roland would never come out of the fortress alive, and David was, once more, alone in the world.

Time passed slowly for David. He fed the fire with sticks and waited for Roland to return. Sometimes, he felt Scylla nuzzle his neck gently, reminding him that she was close. He was glad of the horse's presence. Her strength and her loyalty were reassuring to him.

But tiredness began to overcome him, and his mind played tricks upon him. He would fall asleep for a second or two and instantly begin to dream. He glimpsed flashes of home, and incidents from the last few days replayed themselves in his mind, their stories overlapping as wolves and dwarfs and the young of the Beast all became part of the same tale. He heard the voice of his mother crying out for him, as she sometimes had when the pain had grown too great for her in her last days, and then her face was replaced by Rose's, just as his place in his father's affections had been taken by Georgie.

But was that true? He realized suddenly that he missed Georgie, and the feeling was so surprising to him that he almost awoke. He remembered the way the baby would smile at him, or grasp his finger in his chubby fist. True, he was noisy and smelly and demanding, but all babies were like that. It wasn't Georgie's fault, not really.

Then the image of Georgie faded, and David saw Roland, sword in hand, advancing down a long, dark hallway. He was inside the tower, but the tower itself was a kind of illusion, and hidden within it were a great many rooms and corridors, each one containing traps for the unwary. Roland entered a large circular chamber, and in his dream David saw Roland's eyes widen in disbelief, and the walls ran red as something in the shadows called David's name . . .

David awoke abruptly. He was still by the fire, but the flames had almost died out. Roland had not returned. David got up and walked toward the gates. Scylla whinnied nervously as he moved away, but she remained by the fire. David stood before the gates, then reached out and touched his finger warily to one of the thorns. Immediately, the creepers retreated, the thorns retracted, and an opening in the barrier was revealed. David looked back at Scylla and the dying embers of the fire. *I should go now,* he thought. *I should not even wait for the dawn. Scylla will take me to the king, and he will tell me what I should do.*

But still he lingered before the gates. Despite what Roland had told him to do if he did not return, David did not want to abandon his friend. And as he stood facing the thorns, uncertain of how to proceed, he heard a voice calling to him.

"David," it whispered. *"Come to me, please come to me."*

It was his mother's voice.

"This is the place to which I was brought," the voice continued. *"When the sickness took me I fell asleep, and I passed from our world to this one. Now she watches over me. I cannot awake, and I cannot escape. Help me, David. If you love me, please help me . . ."*

"Mum," said David. "I'm afraid."

"You've come so far, and you've been so brave," said the voice. *"I've been watching you in my dreams. I'm so proud of you, David. Just a few steps further. Just a little more courage, that's all I ask."*

David reached into his pack and found the claw of the Beast. He gripped it tightly in his hand before slipping it into his pocket and thought of Fletcher's words. He had been brave once, and he could be brave again for his mother. The Crooked Man, still watching from the trees, realized what was happening and began to move. He leaped from his perch, descending from branch to branch and landing like a cat upon the ground, but he was too late. David had passed into the fortress, and the barrier of thorns had closed behind him.

The Crooked Man howled with rage, but David, already lost to the fortress, did not hear him.

XXV

Of the Enchantress and What Became of Raphael and Roland

HE COURTYARD was cobbled with black and white stones stained by droppings from the carrion birds that hovered above the fortress by day. Carved stairs led up to the battlements; racks of weapons stood beside them, but the spears, swords, and shields were rusted and useless. Some of the weaponry had fantastic designs, intricate spirals and delicate interwoven chains of silver and bronze that were echoed on the hilts of the swords and the faces of the shields. David could not equate the beauty of the craftsmanship with the sinister place that now held them. It suggested that the castle had not always been as it now was. It had been taken over by a malevolent entity, a cuckoo that had turned it into a spiked, creepered nest, and its original inhabitants had either died or fled when it came.

Now that he was inside, David could see signs of damage: hollow pits, mostly, where the walls and courtyard had absorbed the force of cannon fire. It was clear that the castle was very old, yet the fallen trees surrounding it suggested that what Roland had heard and what Fletcher claimed to have seen, however strange, was in fact the case. The castle could move through the air, traveling to new locations with the cycles of the moon.

Beneath the walls were stables, but they were empty of hay and bore no trace of the healthy animal smells such places built up over time. Instead there were only the bones of horses left to starve after the deaths of their masters, and the lingering stench from within was a reminder of their slow decay. Across from them, and at either side of the central tower, were what might once have been guards' quarters and kitchens. Carefully, David peered through the windows of each, but both were entirely devoid of life. There were bare bunks in the guards' building and cold, empty ovens in the kitchens. Plates and mugs lay upon the tables, as though a meal had been disturbed and those who were eating had never been given the chance to return to their food.

David walked to the door of the tower. The body of the knight lay at his feet, a sword still gripped in his great hand. The sword had not rusted, and the knight's armor still shone. In addition, he wore a sprig of some white flower tucked into a hole in his shoulder armor. It had not yet withered fully, so David guessed that his body had not been lying there for very long. There was no blood on his neck or on the ground around him. David did not know a great deal about the mechanics of cutting off a man's head, but he imagined that there would be some blood at least. He wondered who the knight was and whether he, like Roland, bore some device on his breastplate to identify him. The huge knight was lying chest down, and David wasn't sure that he would be able to turn him over. Still, he decided that the identity of the dead knight should not remain unknown, just in case he found a way to tell anyone of what had happened to him.

David knelt down and took a deep breath, then pushed hard against the armor. To his surprise, the knight's remains moved quite easily. True, the armor was heavy, but not as heavy as it should have been with the body of a man inside it. Once he had managed to turn the knight over, David could see the sign of an eagle on his breastplate, a snake writhing in its talons. He rapped upon the armor with the knuckles of his right hand. The sound echoed within; it was like tapping on an empty can. It seemed that the suit of armor was empty.

But, no, that was not the case, for David both heard and felt something move as he rolled the armor, and when he examined the hole at the top, where the head had been separated from the body, he saw bone and skin within. The top of the spinal column was white where the head had been severed from the body, but even here there was no blood. Somehow, the knight's remains had been reduced to a husk inside the armor, rotting away to almost nothing so quickly that the flower he'd worn, perhaps for luck, had not yet had time to die.

David considered fleeing the fortress, but he knew that even if he tried to do so, the thorns would not part for him. This was a place to be entered but not to be left, and despite his doubts, he had heard, once again, his mother's voice calling to him. If she was truly here, then he could not abandon her now.

David stepped over the fallen knight and entered the tower. A set of stone stairs wound upward in a spiral. He listened intently but could hear no sound from above. He wanted to call his mother's name, or to cry out for Roland, but he was afraid of alerting the presence in the tower to his approach. Perhaps, though, whatever waited in the tower already knew that he was in the fortress and had parted the thorns to enable him to pass through. Still, it seemed wiser to be quiet than to be noisy, and so he did not speak. He recalled the figure that had passed across the lighted window, and the tale of the enchantress who kept a woman in thrall, dooming her to an eternal, ageless sleep in a chamber of treasures unless she could be awakened by a kiss. Could that woman be his mother? The answer lay above.

He drew his sword and started to climb. There were small, narrow windows every ten steps, and these allowed a little light to filter into the tower, enabling David to see where he was going. He counted a dozen such windows before he reached the stone floor at the top of the tower. A hallway stretched before him, with open doorways on either side. From outside, the tower appeared to be twenty or thirty feet wide, but the corridor in front of him was so long that the end of it was lost in shadow. It must have been hundreds of feet in length, lit by flaming torches set into the walls, yet somehow it was contained within a tower only a fraction of that size.

David walked slowly down the hallway, glancing into each room as he did so. Some were bedrooms, opulently furnished with enormous beds and velvet drapes. Others contained couches and chairs. One housed a grand piano and nothing else. The walls of another were decorated with hundreds of similar versions of one painting: a picture of two male children, identical twins, with a painting of themselves in the background that was an exact replica of the picture they occupied, so that they stared out at infinite versions of themselves.

Halfway down the hall was a vast dining room, dominated by a huge oak table with one hundred chairs around it. Candles were lit along its length, and their light shone upon a great feast: there were roast turkeys and geese and ducks, and a huge pig with an apple in its mouth as the centerpiece. There were platters of fish and cold meats, and vegetables steamed in big pots. It all smelled so wonderful that David was drawn into the room, unable to resist the urgings of his growling stomach. Someone had started carving one of the turkeys, for its leg had been removed and slivers of white meat had been cut from its breast and now lay, tender and moist, upon a plate. David picked up one of the pieces and was about to take a great bite from it when he saw an insect crawling across the table. It was a large red ant, and it was making its way toward a fragment of skin that had fallen from the turkey. It clasped the crisp, brown morsel in its jaws and prepared to carry it away, but suddenly it seemed to totter on its feet, as though its burden was heavier than it had expected. It dropped the skin, wobbled a little more, then ceased moving entirely. David poked at it with his finger, but the insect did not respond. It was dead.

David dropped his piece of turkey on the table and quickly wiped his fingers clean. Now that he looked more closely, he could see that the table was littered with the remains of dead insects. The corpses of flies and beetles and ants dotted the wood and the plates, all poisoned by whatever was contained in the food. David backed away from the table and returned to the hallway, his appetite entirely gone.

But if the dining room disgusted him, the next room into which he looked was more troubling still. It was his bedroom in Rose's house, perfectly re-created down to the books upon the shelves, although neater than David's room had ever been. The bed was made, but the pillows and sheets were slightly yellowed and covered in a thin layer of dust. There was dust on the shelves as well, and when David stepped inside, he left footprints on the floor. Ahead of him was the window facing onto the garden. It was open, and noises could be heard from outside, the sounds of laughter and singing. He walked over to the glass and looked out. In the garden below, three people were dancing in a circle: David's father, Rose, and a boy whom David did not recognize but whom he knew instantly to be Georgie. Georgie was older now, perhaps four or five, but still a chubby child. He was smiling widely as his parents danced with him, his father holding his right hand and Rose his left, the sun shining down upon them from a perfect blue sky.

"Georgie Porgie, pudding and pie," they sang to him, "kissed the girls and made them cry!"

And Georgie laughed with joy as bees buzzed and birds sang.

"They have forgotten you," said the voice of David's mother. *"This was once your room, but nobody comes in here now. Your father did, in the beginning, but then he resigned himself to the fact that you were gone and found pleasure instead in his other child and his new wife. She is pregnant again, although she does not yet know it. There will be a sister for Georgie, and then your father will have two children once more and there will be no need for memories of you."*

The voice seemed to come from everywhere and nowhere, from within David and from the hallway outside, from the floor beneath his feet and the ceiling above his head, from the stones in the walls and the books on the shelves. For a moment, David even saw her reflected in the glass of the window, a faded vision of his mother standing behind him and looking over his shoulder. When he turned around, there was nobody there, but still her reflection remained in the glass.

"It does not have to be that way," said his mother's voice. The lips of the image in the glass moved, but they appeared to be saying other words, for their motions did not quite match the words that David heard. *"Remain brave and strong for just a little longer. Find me here, and we can have our old life back again. Rose and Georgie will be gone, and you and I will take their places."*

Now the voices from the garden below had changed. They were no longer singing and laughing. When he looked down, David saw his father mowing the lawn and his mother clipping a rosebush with a pair of pruning shears, carefully beheading each branch and tossing the red flowers into a basket at her feet. And seated on a bench between them, reading a book, was David.

"You see? Do you see how it can be? Now come, we have been apart too long. It is time that we were together again. But be careful: she will be watching and waiting. When you see me, do not look left or right, but keep your eyes only on my face and everything will be well."

The image disappeared from the glass, and the figures vanished from the garden below. A cold wind arose, raising dust ghosts in the room, obscuring everything within. The dust made David cough, and his eyes watered. He backed out of the room and bent over in the hallway, hacking and spitting.

A noise came from nearby: the sound of a door slamming and locking from inside. He spun around, and a second door slammed and locked, then another. The door to every room that he had passed was shutting firmly. Now his bedroom door was suddenly shut in his face, and all of the doors ahead of him began to close as well. Only the torches on the walls lit his way, and suddenly they too began to be extinguished, starting with those nearest the stairs. There was now total darkness behind him, and it was advancing quickly. Soon, the entire hallway would be drowned in blackness.

David ran, trying desperately to stay ahead of the approaching shadows, his ears ringing with the sound of slamming doors. He was moving as quickly as he could, his feet slapping upon the hard stone floor, but the lights were dying faster than he could run. He saw the torches just behind him die, then the ones at either side, and finally those ahead fizzled out. He kept running, hoping that somehow he could catch up with them, that he would not be left alone in the dark. Then the last torches faded, and the darkness was complete.

"No!" shouted David. "Mum! Roland! I can't see. Help me!"

But nobody replied. David stood still, uncertain of what to do. He did not know what lay ahead, but he knew that the stairs were behind him. If he turned back, following the wall, he could find them again, but he would be abandoning his mother and Roland too, if he was still alive. If he went forward, he would be stumbling blindly into the unknown, easy prey for the 'she' of whom his mother's voice had spoken, the enchantress who guarded this place with thorns and creepers and who reduced men to husks in armor and heads on battlements.

And then David saw a tiny light in the distance, like a firefly suspended in the blackness, and his mother's voice said, *"David, don't be afraid. You're almost there. Don't give up now."*

He did as he was told, and the light grew stronger and brighter, until he saw that it was a lamp hanging high above his head. Slowly, the outline of an archway became visible to him. David drew nearer and nearer, so that at last he stood at the entrance to a great chamber, its domed ceiling supported by four enormous stone pillars. The walls and pillars were covered by thorned creepers far thicker than those that guarded the walls and gates of the fortress, the thorns so long and sharp that some were taller than David himself. Between each set of pillars a lamp hung from an ornate iron frame, and their light shone on chests of coins and jewelery, on goblets and gilded picture frames, on swords and shields, all gleaming with gold and precious stones. It was a treasure greater than most men could imagine, but David barely glanced at it. Instead, his attention was fixed on a raised stone altar at the center of the room. A woman lay upon the altar, still as the dead. She was dressed in a red velvet dress with her hands folded across her chest. As David looked more closely, he saw the rise and fall of her breathing. This, then, was the sleeping lady, the victim of the enchantress's spell.

David entered the chamber, and the flickering glow of the

lamps caught something bright and shiny high up on the thorned wall to his right. He turned, and his stomach cramped so hard at what he saw that he bent over in pain.

Roland's body was impaled upon one of the great thorns ten feet above the floor. The point had passed through his chest and erupted from his breastplate, destroying the image of the twin suns. There was a trace of blood upon his armor, but not very much. Roland's face was thin and gray, his cheeks hollow, and the skull sharp beneath the skin. Beside Roland's body was that of another, also wearing the armor of the twin suns: Raphael. Roland had discovered the truth about his friend's disappearance at last.

And they were not alone. The vaulted chamber was dotted with the remains of men, like drained flies set in a web of thorns. Some of them had been there for a very long time, for their armor had rusted to red and brown, and those that had heads were no more than skeletons.

David's anger overcame his fear, and his rage overcame any thoughts of flight. In that moment, he became more man than boy, and his passage into adulthood began in earnest. He walked slowly toward the sleeping woman, turning constantly in slow circles so that no hidden threat could creep up on him unawares. He remembered his mother's warning not to look right or left, but the sight of Roland impaled upon the wall made him want to confront the enchantress and kill her for what she had done to his friend.

"Come out," he shouted. "Show yourself!"

But nothing moved in the chamber, and no one answered his challenge. The only word he heard, half real, half imagined, was *"David,"* spoken in his mother's voice.

"Mum," he said, in reply. "I'm here."

He was now at the stone altar. A flight of five steps led up to the sleeping woman. He climbed them slowly, still aware of the unseen threat, the killer of Roland and Raphael and of all those men who hung, pierced and hollow, upon the walls. At last, he reached the altar and looked down upon the face of the sleeping woman. It was his mother. Her skin was very white, but there was a hint of pink at her cheeks, and her lips were full and moist. Her red hair glowed like fire against the stone.

"Kiss me," David heard her say, although her mouth remained still. *"Kiss me, and we will be together again."*

David placed his sword by her side and leaned over to kiss her cheek. His lips touched her skin. She was very cold, colder even than when she had lain in her open coffin, so cold that the touch of her was painful to him. It numbed his lips and stilled his tongue, and his breath turned to crystals of ice that sparkled like tiny diamonds in the still air. As he broke the contact with her, his name was called again, but this time it was a man's voice, not a woman's.

"David!"

He looked around, trying to find the source of the sound. There was movement upon the wall. It was Roland. His left hand waved feebly, then gripped the thorn that protruded from his chest, as though by doing so he might concentrate the last of his strength and say what needed to be said. His head moved, and with a final great effort he forced the words from his lips.

"David," he whispered. "Beware!"

Roland lifted his right hand, and his index finger pointed at the figure on the altar before it fell away. Then his body sagged on the thorn as the life passed from him at last.

David looked down at the sleeping woman, and her eyes opened. They were not the eyes of David's mother. Her eyes were green and loving and kind. These eyes were black, devoid of color, like lumps of coal set in snow. The face of the sleeping woman had also changed. She was no longer David's mother, although he still knew her. Now she was Rose, his father's lover. Her hair was black, not red, and it pooled like liquid night. Her lips opened, and David saw that her teeth were very white and very sharp, the canines longer than the rest. He took a step back, almost falling from the dais as the woman sat up on her stone bed. She stretched like a cat, her spine curving and her arms tensing. The shawl around her shoulders fell away, exposing an alabaster neck and the tops of her breasts. David saw drops of blood upon them, like a necklace of rubies frozen on her skin. The woman turned on the stone, allowing her gown to drape over the side. Those deep black eyes regarded David, and her pale tongue licked at the points of her teeth.

"Thank you," she said. Her voice was soft and low, but there was a sibilant undertone to her words, as though a snake had been given the power of speech. "Ssssuch a handssssome boy. Sssssuch a brave boy."

David retreated, but with each step he took the woman advanced a step to match it, so that the distance between them remained always the same.

"Am I not beautiful?" she asked. Her head tilted slightly, and her face looked troubled. "Am I not pretty enough for you? Come, kisssss me again."

She was Rose, but Not-Rose. She was night without the promise of dawn, darkness without light. David reached for his sword, then realized that it still lay on the altar. To get to it, he would have to find a way past the woman, and he knew instinctively that if he tried to slip by her, she would kill him.

She seemed to guess what he was thinking, for she glanced back at the sword. "You have no need of it now," she said. "Never hassss one ssso young come ssso far. Sssssso young, and ssso beautiful."

One slim finger, its nail etched in blood, touched itself to her lips.

"Here," she whispered. "Kissss me here."

David saw his reflection drown in her dark eyes, sinking in the depths of her, and knew what his fate would be. He spun on his heel and jumped the last steps, twisting awkwardly on his right ankle as he landed. The pain was bad, but he was not going to let it hinder him. On the floor ahead of him lay the sword of one of the dead knights. If he could just get to it—

A figure glided over his head, the hem of its gown brushing against his hair, and the woman appeared before him. Her bare feet were not touching the ground. She hung in the air, red and black, blood and night. She was no longer smiling. She opened her lips, exposing her fangs, and suddenly her mouth looked larger than before, with row upon row of sharp teeth like the inside of a shark's jaws.

Her hands reached for David. "I will have my kisss," she said, as her nails sank into his shoulders and her head moved toward David's lips.

David reached into the pocket of his jacket. His right hand sliced through the air, and the claw of the Beast tore a jagged red line across the woman's face. The wound gaped, but no blood flowed from it, for she had no blood in her veins. She shrieked and pressed her hand to the wound as David struck again, slashing from left to right and blinding her instantly. The woman attacked him with her fingernails, catching his hand and sending the Beast's claw flying from it. David ran for the doorway to the chamber, with no thought now but to get back to the pitch-black hallway and find his way to the stairs. But the creepers twisted and turned, blocking the way out and trapping him in the room with Not-Rose.

She still hung in the air, her hands now outstretched from her sides, her eyes and face ruined. David moved away from the entrance, trying to get to the fallen sword again. The woman's sightless eyes followed him.

"I can *sssssmell* you," she said. "You will pay for what you have done to me."

She flew toward David, her teeth snapping and her fingers clutching at the air. David darted to his right, then back to his left, in the hope that he could fool her and reach the sword, but she was too clever for him and cut him off. She moved back and forth before him, so quickly that she was little more than a blur in the air, always advancing, sealing off any avenue of escape and forcing him back against the thorns until at last she was only a few feet away from him. David felt sharp pains at his neck and back. He was standing against the tips of the thorns, long and sharp as spears. There was nowhere left for him to go. The woman's hand snatched at the air, missing his face by an inch.

"Now," she hissed, "you are mine. I will love you, and you will die loving me in return."

Her spine stretched, and her mouth opened so wide that her skull split almost in half, the rows of teeth braced to tear David's throat open. She shot forward, and David threw himself to the floor, waiting until she was almost upon him before he moved. Her dress covered his face, so that he heard but did not see what happened next. There was a sound like a rotten fruit being punctured, and a foot kicked once at his head, but only once.

David rolled out from beneath the folds of red velvet. The thorns had pierced the woman through the heart and the side. Her right hand too had been impaled, but her left hand was free. It trembled against a creeper, the only part of her that moved. David could see her face. She no longer looked like Rose. Her hair had turned to silver, and her skin was old and wrinkled. A dank, musty smell came from the wounds in her body. Her lower jaw hung loosely on her wrinkled chest. Her nostrils quivered as she smelled David, and she tried to speak. At first, her voice was so faint that he could not hear what she said. He leaned in closer, still wary of her even though he knew that she was dying. Her breath stank of putrefaction, but this time he understood her words.

"Thank you," she whispered, and then her body sagged against the thorns and crumbled to dust before his eyes.

And as she disappeared, the creepers began to wither and die, and the remains of the dead knights fell clattering to the ground. David ran to where Roland lay. His body had been almost drained of blood. David felt like crying for him, but no tears would come. Instead he dragged Roland's remains up the steps to the stone bed and, with some effort, laid him to rest upon it. He did the same for Raphael, placing his body by Roland's side. He put their swords upon their chests and folded their hands across the hilts, the way he had seen dead knights laid out in his books. He retrieved his own sword and placed it in its scabbard, then took one of the lamps from its stand and used it to find his way back to the stairs of the tower. The long corridor with its many rooms was now no more, and only dusty stones and crumbling walls remained in its place. When he got outside, he saw that here too, the creepers and thorns had withered away, and all that was left was an old fortress, ruined and decayed. Beyond its gates, Scylla stood waiting for him by the ashes of the fire. She neighed with joy as she saw him approach. David put his hand upon her brow and whispered in her ear, so that she might know what fate had befallen her beloved master. Then, finally, he climbed into the saddle and turned her toward the forest and the road east.

All was quiet as they passed through the trees, for the things that dwelled within them heard David coming and were afraid. Even the Crooked Man, who had returned to his perch among the topmost branches, now looked at the boy in a new way, and tried to work out how he might best use this latest development to his advantage.

XXVI

Of Two Killings and Two Kings

AVID AND SCYLLA followed the road to the east. David's eyes stared straight ahead, but they noticed little of what was before them. Scylla's head hung lower than it previously had, as though she too were mourning the passing of her master in her soft, dignified way. Snow sparkled in the eternal dusk, and icicles hung like frozen tears from the bushes and the trees.

Roland was dead. So too was David's mother. He had been a fool to imagine otherwise. Now, as the horse plodded through this cold, dark world, David admitted to himself, perhaps for the first time, that he had always known his mother was gone. He had just wanted to believe otherwise. It was like the routines that he had employed while she was ill in the hope that they might keep her alive. They were false hopes, dreams without foundation, insubstantial as the voice he had followed to this place. He could not change the world that he had left, and this world, while taunting him with the possibility that things could be different, had ultimately frustrated him. It was time to go home. If the king could not help him, then he might yet be forced to strike a bargain with the Crooked Man. All he had to do was speak Georgie's name aloud to him.

~ 259 ~

But hadn't the Crooked Man told him that everything could be restored to the way it was? That was a lie. His mother was dead, and the world of which she had been a part was gone forever. Even if he went back, it would be to a place in which she was only a memory. Home was now a place shared with Rose and Georgie, and the best would have to be made of that, for his sake as much as theirs. If the Crooked Man's promise could not be kept, then what others might he break?

It was as Roland had warned: *"He will say less than he means and conceal more than he reveals."*

Any deal made with the Crooked Man would be filled with potential traps and perils. David would just have to hope that the king was able and willing to help him, allowing him to avoid any further contact with the trickster. But what he had heard so far about the king had caused him doubt. Roland had clearly thought little of him, and even the Woodsman had admitted that the king's hold on his kingdom was not what it once was. Now, faced with the threat of Leroi and his wolf army, perhaps the king would be tested beyond endurance. His kingdom would be taken from him by force, and he would die in Leroi's jaws. With the burden of that knowledge on his shoulders, would he even have time for the problems of a boy lost in the world?

And what of the book itself, the Book of Lost Things? What could be contained in its pages that would help David to return home: a map to another hollow tree, perhaps, or a spell capable of magicking him back? But if the book had magical properties, then why couldn't the king use it to protect his kingdom? David hoped that the king wasn't like the Great Oz, all smoke and mirrors and good intentions, but without any real power to back him up.

So lost was David in his own thoughts, and so used was he to an empty road, that he failed to see the men until they were almost upon him. There were two of them, dressed mostly in rags, with scarves covering their faces so that only their eyes were visible. One carried a short sword, the other a bow with an arrow notched upon its string, ready to fire. They dashed from the undergrowth, casting aside the white furs with which they had camouflaged themselves, and stood in front of David, their weapons raised.

"Halt!" cried the man with the sword, and David stopped Scylla just a few feet from where they stood.

The one with the bow squinted down the length of his arrow, then eased the pressure on the string as he lowered the weapon.

"Why, it's just a boy," he said. His voice was hoarse and rumbled with menace. He lowered the scarf from his face, revealing a mouth distorted by a vertical scar that cut across his lips. His companion threw back the hood from his head. Most of his nose had been cut off. All that was left was a mess of scarred cartilage with two holes in the center.

"Boy or not, that's a fine horse he's riding," he said. "He has no business with such an animal. He probably stole it himself, so there's no sin in relieving him of what wasn't his to begin with."

He reached for Scylla's reins, but David pulled the horse back a step.

"I didn't steal her," he said softly.

"What?" said the thief. "What did you say, boy? We'll have none of your lip, or you won't live long enough to regret the day you met us."

He brandished his sword at David. It was primitive and crudely made, and David could see the marks of the whetstone upon its blade. Scylla neighed and stepped farther away from the threat.

"I said," David repeated, "that I didn't steal her, and she's not going anywhere with you. Now get away from us."

"Why, you little—"

The swordsman snatched at Scylla's reins once again, but this time David raised her up on her hind legs, then urged her onward and down. One of her hooves struck the swordsman on the forehead, and there was a hollow, cracking sound as the man fell dead to the ground. His fellow bandit was so shocked that he failed to respond quickly enough. He was still trying to lift his bow when David spurred Scylla, his own sword now drawn and extended. He slashed at the archer, and the very tip of his sword caught the man's throat, slicing through the rags to the flesh beneath. The bandit stumbled, and his bow fell. He raised his hand to his neck and tried to speak, but only a wet, gurgling sound emerged. Blood fountained through his fingers and scattered itself upon the snow. The front of his clothing was already drenched with red as he dropped to his knees beside his dead companion, the flow starting to ease as his heart began to fail.

David turned Scylla so that she was facing the dying man.

"I warned you!" shouted David. He was crying now, crying for Roland and his mother and his father, crying even for Georgie and Rose, for all of the things that he had lost, both those that could be named and those that could only be felt. "I asked you to leave us alone, but you wouldn't. Now look at what it's brought you. You idiots! You stupid, stupid men!"

The bowman's mouth opened and closed, and his lips formed words, but no sounds came out. His eyes were fixed on the boy. David saw them narrow, as if the bowman could not quite understand what was being said or what was happening to him as he knelt in the snow, his blood pooling around him.

Then, slowly, they grew wide and calm as death gave him an explanation.

David climbed down from Scylla's back and checked her legs to make sure that she had not injured herself during the confrontation. She seemed unhurt. There was blood on David's sword. He thought of wiping it clean upon the ragged clothing of one of the dead men, but he did not want to touch the bodies. Neither did he want to clean it on his own clothes, for then their blood would be on him. He opened his pack and found a piece of old muslin in which Fletcher had wrapped some cheese and used the material to get rid of the blood. He tossed the bloodied cloth onto the snow before kicking the bodies of the dead men into the ditch by the side of the road. He was too weary to try to hide them better. Suddenly, he felt a rumbling in his stomach. There was a sour taste in his mouth, and his skin was slick with sweat. He stumbled away from the bodies and vomited behind a rock, retching over and over until all that he had left to bring up was foul gas.

He had killed two men. He hadn't meant to, not really, but now they were dead because of him. The killings of the Loups and wolves at the canyon, even what he had done to the huntress in her cottage and the enchantress in her tower, had not affected him in this way. He had caused the deaths of the others, true, but now he had killed at least one of these men by tearing through his flesh with the point of a sword. Scylla's hooves had accounted for the other, but David had been in the saddle when it happened and had raised her up and urged her on. He hadn't even had to think about what he was doing; it had just come naturally to him, and it was that capacity for harm that frightened him more than anything else.

He wiped his mouth clean with snow, then remounted Scylla and urged her forward, leaving behind him the deed, if not the memory of it. As he rode, thick flakes began to descend, settling on his clothing and on Scylla's head and back. There was no wind. The snow fell straight and slow, adding another layer to the drifts and covering roads, trees, bushes, and bodies, the living and the dead as one beneath its veil. The corpses of the thieves were soon shrouded in white, and there they would have remained, unmourned and undiscovered, until the coming of spring, had not a wet muzzle traced their scent and revealed their remains. The wolf gave a low howl, and the forest came alive as the pack descended, tearing flesh and gnawing bones, the weak left to fight for scraps while the strong and fast filled their bellies. Yet there were too many now to be fed on so meager a meal. The pack had swollen so that it was many thousands strong: white wolves from the far north, who blended into the winter landscape so perfectly that only the darkness of their eyes and the redness of their jaws gave them away; black wolves from the east, said by old wives to be the spirits of witches and demons in the form of beasts; gray wolves from the forests to the west, bigger and slower than the others, who kept to their own and did not trust the others; and, finally, the Loups, who dressed like men and hungered like wolves and wanted to rule like kings. They stayed apart from the larger pack, watching from the edge of the forest as their primitive brethren snapped and fought over the entrails of the dead bandits. A female approached them from the road. In her jaws she held a scrap of muslin, marked with drying blood. The taste of the blood had made her mouth water, and it was all that she could do not to chew it and swallow it as she walked. Now she dropped it at the feet of her leader and stepped back obediently. Leroi lifted the rag to his nose and sniffed it. The smell of the dead men's blood was strong and sharp, but he could still detect the boy's scent beneath it.

Leroi had last smelled the boy in the courtyard of the fortress, led there by his scouts. They had refused to climb the stairs of the tower, disturbed by what they sensed within, but Leroi had ascended, more as a display of courage for his followers than out of any great desire to discover what lay above. With its enchantments vanquished, the tower was now merely an empty shell at the heart of an old fortress. All that remained of its former self was a stone chamber at the very top, littered with the remains of dead men and a scattering of dust that had once been something less than human. At its center was the raised stone dais, with the bodies of Roland and Raphael lying upon it. Leroi recognized Roland's scent, and knew that the boy's protector was now dead. He had been tempted to tear apart the bodies of the two knights, to desecrate their resting place, but he knew that this was what an animal would do, and he was no longer an animal. He left the bodies as they were and, although he would never have admitted it to his lieutenants, he was happy to depart the chamber and the tower. There were things that he did not understand there, and they made him uneasy.

Now he stood with the bloodied rag in his claws and felt a degree of admiration for the boy whom he was hunting. *How quickly you have grown,* thought Leroi. *Not so long ago you were a frightened child, and now you triumph where armed knights fail. You take the lives of men and wipe your blade clean to make it ready for the next killing. It is almost a pity that you have to die.*

Leroi was growing more like a man and less like a wolf with each day that passed, or so he told himself. He still had wiry hair upon his body, and his ears were pointed and his teeth sharp, but his muzzle was now little more than a swelling around his mouth, and the bones of his face were re-forming to make him look more human and less lupine. He rarely walked on all fours, except when the necessity for speed arose or when excitement at the detection of the boy's scent had briefly overwhelmed him. That was one of the benefits of having so many to call upon: while the horse's odor was strong, much stronger than that of the boy or that of the man, the recent snowfalls had meant that it was frequently lost to them, but by using large numbers of scouts, the scent was quickly found again each time. They had tracked him to the village, and Leroi had been tempted to attack it with the full strength of his pack, but they had picked up the spoor of the horse and the man heading east, and they knew then that the pair were no longer with the villagers. Some of his Loups had still counseled an assault on the village, for the pack was hungry, but Leroi knew that it would only waste valuable time. It suited him also to keep the appetite of the pack sharp, for hunger would increase their savagery when it came time to attack the king's castle. He recalled the man standing upon the village's defenses, defying Leroi even as those around him cowered. Leroi had admired the gesture, just as he admired many aspects of men's natures. This was one of the reasons was why he was so comfortable with his own transformation, but it would not prevent him from returning to the village and making an example of the man who had tried to face him down.

The pack had lost some ground when the boy and the man left the road, for Leroi had assumed that they would continue directly to the castle of the king, and half a day had been wasted before he realized his mistake. It was then only David's good fortune that had caused the pack to miss him as he left the Fortress of Thorns, for the wolves had been wary of the forest, uncertain of the hidden things that lived within the trees, and had skirted its deepest depths in their approach to the fortress. Once Leroi was sure that nobody remained alive inside, he sent a dozen scouts to follow David's trail through the forest while the main pack headed east toward the king's castle using a longer but safer route. When the pack was reunited with the scouts, only three remained alive. Seven had been killed by the creatures that lived within the trees. The other two—and this interested Leroi greatly—had been found with their throats cut and their snouts hacked off.

"The crooked one is protecting the boy," one of Leroi's most trusted lieutenants had growled upon hearing the news. He, too, was becoming more like a man, although in him the transformation was slower and less pronounced.

"He thinks that he has found a new king," replied Leroi. "But we are here to bring an end to the rule of the human kings. The boy will never claim the throne."

He barked an order, and his Loups began to gather the pack, snarling and biting at those who did not respond quickly enough. Their time was near. The castle was less than a day's march away, and once they reached it there would be meat enough for all and the bloody rule of the new king Leroi would begin.

Leroi might have been becoming something more than an animal and less than a man, but deep, deep inside he would always remain a wolf.

XXVII

Of the Castle, and
the King's Greeting

HE DAY PASSED, a poor, sluggish thing that departed almost gratefully as night took its place. David's spirits were low, and his back and legs ached from hours in the saddle. Still, he had managed to adjust the stirrups so that his feet fitted comfortably in them, and he had learned how to hold the reins properly from watching Roland, so he now looked more at ease on Scylla than ever before, even if the horse remained too big for him. The snow had dwindled to a few flurries, and soon would cease entirely. The land seemed to luxuriate in its silence and its whiteness, knowing that the snow had rendered it more beautiful than before.

They came to a bend in the road. Ahead of them, the far horizon was lit by a soft, yellow glow, and David knew that they were close to the king's castle. He felt a sudden surge of energy and urged Scylla on, even though they were both weary and hungry. Scylla broke into a trot, as though already smelling hay and fresh water and a warm barn in which to rest, but almost as quickly David reined her in again and listened carefully. He had heard something, like the sound of the wind, except that the night was still. Scylla seemed to sense it too, for she whinnied and pawed at the ground. David patted her flank, trying to calm her even as he felt himself grow tense.

"Hush, Scylla," he whispered.

The noise came again, clearer now. It was the howling of a wolf. There was no way of telling how near it was, for the snow muffled all sound, but it was close enough to be heard, and that was too close for David's liking. There was movement from the forest to his right, and he drew his sword, already imagining white teeth and a pink tongue and snapping jaws. Instead, the Crooked Man emerged. He had a slim, curved blade in his hand. David pointed his own sword at the approaching figure and stared down its length, the tip focused on the Crooked Man's throat.

"Put down your sword," said the Crooked Man. "You have nothing to fear from me."

But David kept his sword exactly where it was. He was pleased to see that his arm did not tremble. The Crooked Man, by contrast, took no pleasure in David's courage.

"Very well, then," he said. "As you wish. The wolves are coming. I don't know how long I can hold them off, but it should give you enough time to reach the castle. Stay on the road, and don't be tempted by shortcuts."

More howls came, closer now.

"Why are you helping me?" asked David.

"I've been helping you all along," replied the Crooked Man. "You were just too willful to understand. I have shadowed your path and saved your life, all so you could reach the castle. Now go to the king. He is expecting you. Go!"

And with that, the Crooked Man bounded away from David, skirting the edge of the forest, his blade making a whistling sound as he sliced at the air, already killing wolves in his mind. David

watched him until he was out of sight, then, with no other choice
but to do as he was advised, he urged Scylla toward the light
ahead. The Crooked Man watched him go from a hollow at the
base of an old oak. It had been so much more difficult than he had
anticipated, but the boy would soon be where he was supposed to
be, and the Crooked Man would be one step closer to his reward.

"Georgie Porgie, pudding and pie," he sang. He licked his lips.
"Georgie pudding, and Georgie pie." He giggled, then covered
his mouth to stifle the laugh. He was not alone. Harsh breathing
came from close by, and a plume of breath formed in the darkness. The Crooked Man curled up into a ball, only his knife hand
remaining outstretched, half buried beneath the snow.

And as the wolf scout passed by, he slit it from throat to tail,
and its entrails steamed in the chill night air.

The road twisted and turned, narrowing as David drew nearer to
his destination. Sheer faces of rock rose up on either side of him,
creating a canyon through which the pounding of Scylla's hooves
echoed, for the snow had not fallen as thickly here, the ground
sheltered by the walls above. Then David was clear of the canyon,
and before him stretched a valley with a river running through it.
By its banks, about a mile or so distant, stood a great castle with
high, thick walls and many towers and buildings. Lights glowed
in its windows, and fires were lit upon its battlements. David
could see soldiers on guard. As he watched, the portcullis was
raised and a group of twelve horsemen emerged. They crossed
the drawbridge and turned in David's direction, riding fast. Still
fearful of the wolves, David rode down to meet them. As soon as
they saw him, the horsemen urged their horses on until they
reached him and surrounded him, the men at the rear turning to
face the canyon, spears at the ready in case any threat should
emerge from that direction.

"We have been waiting for you," announced one of the men. He was older than the others, and he bore the scars of old battles upon his face. Gray-brown hair curled from beneath his helmet, and he wore a silver breastplate studded with bronze under his dark cloak. "We are to bring you to the safety of the king's chambers. Come now."

David rode with them, hemmed in on all sides by armed riders so that he felt at once both protected and a prisoner. They arrived at the drawbridge without incident and passed into the castle, the portcullis instantly lowering behind them. Servants came and helped David to dismount. They wrapped him in a cloak of soft, black fur and gave him a hot, sweet drink in a silver cup to warm him. One of them took Scylla by the reins. David was about to stop him when the leader of the horsemen intervened.

"They will take good care of your horse, and she will be stabled close to where you sleep. I am Duncan, Captain of the King's Guard. Have no fear. You are safe with us, an honored guest of the king."

He asked David to follow him. David did so, staying behind him as they left the outer courtyard and moved deeper into the castle. There were more people here than he had seen in his entire travels so far, and he was an object of interest to all of them. Serving girls stopped and whispered about him behind their hands. Old men bowed slightly as he passed, and small boys looked at him with something like awe.

"They have heard a great deal about you," said Duncan.

"How?" asked David.

But all Duncan would say was that the king had his ways.

Down stone corridors they went, past spitting torches and luxuriously furnished chambers. Now the servants were replaced by courtiers, serious men with gold around their necks and papers in their hands. They stared at David with a mixture of expressions: happiness, worry, suspicion, even fear. Finally, Duncan and David arrived at a pair of great doors, carved with images of dragons and doves. Soldiers stood guard at either side, each armed with a long pike. As David and Duncan approached, the soldiers opened the doors for them, revealing a large room lined with marble pillars, its floors covered with beautifully woven carpets. Tapestries hung from the walls, giving the chamber a feeling of warmth. They depicted battles and weddings, funerals and coronations. There were more courtiers here, and more soldiers, forming two lines between which David and Duncan passed, until they found themselves at the foot of a throne raised upon three stone steps. On the throne sat an old, old man. A gold crown lay on his brow, inset with red jewels, but it seemed to weigh heavily on him, and the skin was red and raw where the metal touched his forehead. His eyes were half closed, and his breathing was very shallow.

Duncan fell to one knee and bowed his head. He tugged at David's leg as a hint that he should do the same. David, of course, had never been before a king and was not sure how to behave, so he followed Duncan's example, only peering up from under the fringe of his hair so that he could see the old man.

"Your Majesty," said Duncan. "He is here."

The king stirred, and opened his eyes a little wider.

"Come closer," he said to David.

David wasn't sure if he was supposed to rise to his feet or stay kneeling and just shuffle along. He didn't want to offend anyone or get in any trouble.

"You may stand," said the king. "Come, let me see you."

David stood and approached the dais. The king beckoned him with a wrinkled finger, and David climbed the steps until he was facing the old man. With a great effort, the king leaned forward and gripped David's shoulder, the weight of his entire upper body seeming to rest upon the boy. He weighed hardly anything at all, and David was reminded of the drained husks of the knights in the Fortress of Thorns.

"You have come a long way," said the king. "Few men could have achieved what you have managed to accomplish."

David did not know how to respond. "Thank you" didn't seem right, and anyway he didn't feel particularly proud of himself. Roland and the Woodsman were both dead, and the bodies of the two thieves lay somewhere on the road, hidden by snow. He wondered if the king knew about them too. The king seemed to know a great deal for someone who was supposed to be losing control of his kingdom.

In the end, David settled upon saying, "I'm happy to be here, Your Majesty," and he imagined the ghost of Roland being impressed by this act of diplomacy.

The king smiled and nodded, as if it were not possible that someone could be *unhappy* to be in his company.

"Your Majesty," said David. "I was told that you could help me to get home. I was told that you had a book, and in it—"

The king raised a wrinkled hand, its back a chaos of purple veins and brown spots.

"All in good time," he said. "All in good time. For now, you must eat and you must rest. In the morning, we will talk again. Duncan will show you to your quarters. You will not be far from here."

With that, David's first audience with the king was over. He retreated backward from the high throne, because he thought that turning his back on the king might be considered rude. Duncan nodded at him approvingly, then rose and bowed to the king. He guided David to a small door to the right of the throne. From there, a set of stairs led up to a gallery overlooking the chamber, and David was shown into one of the rooms leading off it. The room was enormous, with a huge bed at one end, a table and six chairs in its center, a fireplace at the other end, and three small windows that overlooked the river and the road to the castle. A change of clothing lay upon the bed, and there was food on the table: hot chicken, potatoes, three kinds of vegetables, and fresh fruit for dessert. There was also a jug of water, and what smelled to David like hot wine in a stone pot. A large tub had been placed before the fire, with a pan of glowing coals beneath it to heat the water.

"Eat all you wish, and then sleep," said Duncan. "I will come for you in the morning. If there is anything that you need, ring the bell by your bedside. The door will not be locked, but please do not leave this room. You do not know the castle, and we would not wish you to get lost."

Duncan bowed to him, then left. David took off his shoes. He ate nearly all of the chicken and most of the fruit, and he tried the hot wine but didn't much care for it. In a little closet beside his bed he found a wooden bench with a round hole cut in it, which passed for a toilet. The smell was terrible, even with the bouquets of flowers and herbs that had been hung from hooks on the wall. David did what he had to do as quickly as possible, holding his breath for the entire time, then dashed out and closed the door firmly behind him before breathing again. He took off his clothes and sword and washed in the tub, then dressed himself in a stiff cotton nightshirt. Before he climbed into bed, he went to the door and opened it softly. The throne room beneath was now empty of guards, the king no longer present. However, a guard was walking along the gallery, his back to David, and David could see another guard on the opposite side. The thick walls blocked out all sound, so it was as if he and the guards were the only people alive in the castle. David closed the bedroom door and fell, exhausted, into bed. Within seconds, he was sound asleep.

*   *   *

David woke suddenly, and for a few moments he was unsure of where he was. He thought that he was back in his own bed, and he looked around for his books and his games, but they were nowhere to be seen. Then, quickly, everything came back to him. He sat up and saw that fresh wood had been stacked on the fire while he was sleeping. The remains of his supper and the plates that he had used had all been taken away. Even the tub and hot pan had been removed, all without waking him from his slumbers.

David had no idea how early or late it was, but he guessed that it was the middle of the night. The castle felt as if it was asleep, and when he glanced out of his window he saw a wan moon wreathed by wisps of cloud. Something had woken him. He had been dreaming of home, and in his dream he heard voices that did not belong in the house. At first, he had simply tried to incorporate them into his dream, the same way that the tolling of his alarm clock sometimes became the ringing of a telephone in his dream if he was very tired and very deep in sleep. Now, as he sat on his soft bed, surrounded by pillows, the low murmur of two men talking was clearer to him, and he was sure that he heard his name being spoken. He pushed back the covers on the bed and crept to the door. He tried listening at the keyhole, but the voices were too muffled to understand clearly, so he opened the door as quietly as he could and peered outside.

The guards who had been patrolling the gallery were gone. The voices were coming from the throne room below. Keeping to the shadows, David hid himself behind a large silver urn filled with ferns and looked down on the two men. One of them was the king, but he was not seated on his throne. He was sitting on the stone steps, wearing a purple dressing gown over a nightshirt of white and gold. His head was entirely bald on top and dotted with more brown spots. Lengths of white hair hung loosely over his ears and the collar of his gown, and he trembled in the cold of the great hall.

The Crooked Man sat upon the king's throne, his legs crossed and his fingers steepled before him. He seemed unhappy with something that the king had said, for he spit on the stone floor in disgust. David heard the spittle hiss and sizzle where it landed.

"It cannot be rushed," said the Crooked Man. "A few more hours will not kill you."

"Nothing, it seems, will kill me," said the king. "You promised an end to this. I need to rest, to sleep. I want to lie in my crypt and decay to dust. You promised me that I would be allowed to die at last."

"He thinks the book will help him," said the Crooked Man. "When he finds out that it has no value, he will listen to reason, and then we will both have our reward from him."

The king shifted position, and David saw that he had a book upon his lap. It was bound in brown leather and looked very old and ragged. The king's fingers brushed lovingly across its cover, and his face was a mask of sadness.

"The book has value to *me*," he said.

"Then you can take it to the grave with you," said the Crooked Man, "for it will be useless to anyone else. Until that time, leave it where its presence can taunt him."

The king stood painfully and tottered down the steps. He walked to a small alcove in the wall and laid the book carefully upon a gold cushion. David had not noticed it before because drapes had been drawn across it during his meeting with the king.

"Don't worry, Your *Majesty*," said the Crooked Man, his voice full of sarcasm. "Our bargain is almost concluded."

The king frowned. "It was no bargain," he said, "not for me, and not for the one whom you took to secure it."

The Crooked Man leaped from the throne and, in a single

bound, landed inches from the king. But the old man did not cower or try to move away.

"You concluded no bargain that you did not wish to conclude," said the Crooked Man. "I gave you what you desired, and I made clear what was expected of you in return."

"I was a child," said the king. "I was angry. I did not understand the harm that I was doing."

"And you think that excuses you? As a child you saw things only in black and white, good and bad, what gave you pleasure and what brought you pain. Now you see everything in shades of gray. Even the care of your own kingdom is beyond you, so unwilling are you to decide what is right and wrong or even to admit that you can tell the difference. You knew what you were agreeing to on the day that we made our bargain. Regrets have clouded your memory, and now you seek to blame me for your own weaknesses. Mind your tongue, old man, or else I will be forced to remind you of the power that I still wield over you."

"What can you do to me that you have not already done?" asked the king. "All that is left is death, and you continue to deny that to me."

The Crooked Man leaned so close to the king that their noses touched. "Remember, and remember well: there are easy deaths and there are hard deaths. I can make your passing as peaceful as an afternoon snooze, or as painful and lengthy as your withered body and brittle bones will allow. Never forget that."

The Crooked Man turned away and walked to the wall behind the throne. A tapestry of a unicorn hunt moved briefly in the torchlight, and then there was only the king, alone in his throne room. The old man went to the alcove, opened the book once more, and stared for a time at whatever was revealed in its pages, then closed it again and left through a doorway beneath the gallery. David was now alone. He waited for the guards to return, but they did not come. When five minutes had passed, and all remained quiet, he took the stairs down to the throne room and padded softly across the floor to where the book lay.

So this was the book of which the Woodsman and Roland had spoken. This was the Book of Lost Things. Yet the Crooked Man had declared it to be of no value, even though the king appeared to treasure it more than his crown. Perhaps the Crooked Man was wrong, thought David. Maybe he simply did not understand what was contained within its pages.

David reached out and opened the book.

XXVIII

Of the Book of Lost Things

HE FIRST PAGE to which David opened the book was decorated with a child's drawing of a big house: there were trees, and a garden, and long windows. A smiling sun shone in the sky, and stick figures of a man, a woman, and a little boy held hands beside the front door. David turned another page and found a ticket stub for a show at a London theater. Underneath it, a child's hand had written "My first play!" Across from it was a postcard of a seaside pier. It was very old and looked closer to brown-and-white than black-and-white. David turned more pages and saw flowers stuck down, and a tuft of dog hair ("Lucky, A Good Dog") and photographs and drawings and a piece of a woman's dress and a broken chain, painted to look like gold but with the base metal showing through. There was a page from another book, depicting a knight slaying a dragon, and a poem about a cat and a mouse, written in a boy's hand. The poem wasn't very good, but at least it rhymed.

David couldn't understand it. All of these things belonged in his world, not this one. They were tokens and souvenirs of a life not unlike his own. He read further, and came to a series of diary entries. Most of them were very short, describing days at school, trips to the seaside, even the discovery of a particularly large and hairy spider in a garden web. The tone of them changed as they went on, the entries growing longer and more detailed, but also bitter and angry. They spoke of the arrival of a little girl, a potential sister, into a family, and of a boy's rage at the attention being paid to the new arrival. There was regret, and nostalgia for a time when it had been just "me and my mummy and daddy." David felt a kinship with the boy, but also a dislike for him. His anger at the girl, and at his parents for bringing her into his world, was so intense that it veered into pure hatred.

"I would do anything to be rid of her," read one entry. "I would give away all of my toys, and every book that I ever owned. I would give up my savings. I would sweep the floors every day for the rest of my life. I would sell my soul if she would just GO AWAY!!!!"

But the final entry was the shortest of them all. It said simply: "I have decided. I will do it."

Glued to the last page was a photograph of a family, its four members standing beside a vase of flowers in a photographic studio. There was a father with a bald head and a pretty mother wearing a white dress decorated with lace. At her feet sat a boy dressed in a sailor suit, who scowled at the camera as though the photographer had just said something nasty to him. Beside him, David could just make out the hem of a dress and a pair of small black shoes, but the rest of the girl's image had been scraped away.

David turned back to the very first page of the book and saw what was written there. It read:

Jonathan Tulvey. His Book.

David closed the book with a snap and hastily stepped away from it. Jonathan Tulvey: Rose's great-uncle who had disappeared along with his little adopted sister and had never been seen again. This was Jonathan's book, a relic of his life. He remembered the old king, and the loving way in which he had touched the book.

"The book has value to me."

Jonathan was the king. He had made a bargain with the Crooked Man, and in return he had become the ruler of this land. Perhaps he had even passed through the same portal that David had used to come here. But what was the arrangement, and what had happened to the little girl? Whatever bargain he had made with the Crooked Man had cost him dearly in the end. The old king, pleading to be allowed to die, was living proof of this.

A sound came from above. David shrank back against the wall as the figure of a guard appeared on the gallery, resuming his position now that the chamber was empty once again. There was no way David could get back to his room without being seen. He looked around and tried to find another way out. He could take the doorway the king had used, but that would almost certainly mean being confronted by guards. There was also the tapestry on the wall behind the throne. Somehow, the Crooked Man had found a way out through there, and David doubted that there would be guards where the Crooked Man had gone. David was also curious. For the first time, he felt that he knew more than the Crooked Man or the king thought he knew. It was time to try to use that knowledge.

Silently, he made his way to the tapestry and lifted it back from the wall. Behind it was a door. David pushed down on the door handle, and it opened without a sound. Beyond lay a low-ceilinged passageway, lit by candles set in alcoves in the stonework. The roof of the passage was so low that it almost touched David's hair as he entered. He closed the door behind him and followed the passageway down, down, deep into the cold, dark places that lay beneath the castle. He passed disused dungeons, some still littered with bones, and a chamber that was filled with instruments of pain and torture: racks upon which to stretch prisoners until they screamed; thumbscrews with which to break their bones; spikes and spears and blades to pierce the flesh; and, in a far corner, an iron maiden, shaped like the mummies' coffins that David had seen in museums but with nails set into its lid so that anyone placed inside would face an agonizing death. It made David feel queasy, and he passed through the chamber as quickly as he could.

At last he came to an enormous room dominated by a great hourglass. Each bulb of the glass was as tall as a house, but the top bulb was almost empty. The wood and glass from which the hourglass had been constructed looked very old. Time, for someone or something, was draining away, and now it was almost gone.

Beside the hourglass room was a small chamber furnished with a simple bed, a stained mattress, and an old blanket resting upon it. On the wall across from the bed was an array of bladed weapons, daggers and swords and knives, all arranged in descending order of length. Another wall held a shelf covered in glass jars of different shapes and sizes. One of them seemed to glow faintly.

David's nose wrinkled at an unpleasant smell from close by. He turned to find the source and almost bumped his head against a garland of wolves' muzzles hanging by a rope from the ceiling above, twenty or thirty in all, some still damp with blood.

"Who are you?" said a voice, and David's heart came close to stopping from the shock of hearing it. He tried to find the source of the sound, but there was nobody there.

"Does he know you're here?" said the voice again. It was the voice of a girl.

"I can't see you," said David.

"But I can see you."

"Where are you?"

"I'm over here, on the shelf."

David followed the sound of the voice to the shelf of jars. There, in a green jar close to the edge, he saw a tiny little girl. Her hair was long and blond, and her eyes were blue. She shone with a pale light, and wore a simple white nightdress. There was a hole in the gown at her left breast, with a large chocolate-colored stain around it.

"You shouldn't be here," said the little girl. "If he finds you, he'll hurt you, just like he hurt me."

"What did he do to you?" asked David.

But the little girl only shook her head and clenched her lips tightly, as though trying not to cry.

"What's your name?" asked David, trying to change the subject.

"My name is Anna," said the little girl.

Anna.

"I'm David. How can I get you out of there?"

"You can't," said the girl. "You see, I'm dead."

David leaned in a little closer to the jar. He could see the girl's small hands touching against the glass, but they left no fingerprints upon it. Her face was white and her lips were purple, and dark rings surrounded her eyes. The hole in her nightdress was clearer now, and David thought that the stains surrounding it might be dried blood.

"How long have you been here?" he said.

"I've lost count of the years," she said. "I was very young when I came here. There was another little boy in this room when I arrived. I dream of him sometimes. He was like I am now, but he was very frail. He faded away when I was brought to this room, and I never saw him again. I've been growing weak, though. I'm afraid. I'm scared that what happened to him is going to happen to me. I'll disappear, and then no one will ever know what became of me."

She began to cry, but no tears fell, for the dead can no longer weep or bleed.

David placed his little finger against the jar, just where the girl's hand was touching it from the inside, so that only the glass separated them.

"Does anyone else know that you're here?" asked David.

She nodded. "My brother sometimes comes, but he's very old now. Well, I call him my brother, but he never was, not really. I just wanted him to be. He tells me that he's sorry. I believe him. I think he is sorry."

Suddenly, everything began to make awful sense to David.

"Jonathan brought you here, and he gave you to the Crooked Man," he said. "That was the bargain he made."

He sat down hard on the cold, uncomfortable bed.

"He was jealous of you," he continued, speaking more softly now, talking as much to himself as to the girl in the jar, "and the Crooked Man offered him a way to be free of you. Jonathan became king, and the one who preceded him, the old queen, was allowed to die. Perhaps, many years before, she had made a similar bargain with the Crooked Man, and the boy you saw in the jar when you came was her brother, or cousin, or some little boy next door who annoyed her so much that she dreamed of getting rid of him."

And the Crooked Man heard her dreams, because that was where he wandered. His place was the land of the imagination, the world where stories began. The stories were always looking for a way to be told, to be brought to life through books and reading. That was how they crossed over from their world into ours. But with them came the Crooked Man, prowling between his world and ours, looking for stories of his own to create, hunting for children who dreamed bad dreams, who were jealous and angry and proud. And he made kings and queens of them, cursing them with a kind of power, even if the real power lay always in his hands. And in return they betrayed the objects of their jealousy to him, and he took them into his lair deep beneath the castle . . .

David stood and returned to the girl in the jar.

"I know it's hard for you, but you have to tell me what happened to you when you came here. It's very important. Please, try."

Anna screwed her face up and shook her head. "No," she whispered. "It hurt. I don't want to remember it."

"You must," said David, and there was a new force to his voice. It sounded deeper, as though the man that he would become had briefly shown himself before his time. "If it's not to happen again, you have to tell me what he did."

Anna was trembling. Her lips were pressed as thin as paper, and her tiny fists were clenched so tightly that the bones threatened to break through her skin. At last, she released a moan of sorrow and anger and remembered pain, and the words poured out.

"We came through the sunken garden," she began. "Jonathan was always being so mean to me. He would tease me, when he spoke to me at all. He would pinch me and pull my hair. He would take me into the forest and try to lose me there, until I started to cry and he had to come back for me in case his parents heard me. He told me that if I ever said anything to them, he would give me away to a stranger. He said that they wouldn't believe me anyway because he was their real child and I wasn't. I was just a little girl that they'd taken pity on, and if I disappeared then they wouldn't be sad for very long.

"But sometimes he could be so kind and so sweet, as though he forgot that he was supposed to hate me and the real Jonathan shone through instead. Perhaps that was why I followed him down to the garden that night, because he'd been so nice to me that day. He'd bought me sweets with his own money, and he'd shared his pie with me after I dropped mine on the floor. He woke me in the night and told me that he had something to show me, something special and secret. Everyone else was asleep, and we sneaked down to the sunken garden, my hand in Jonathan's. He showed me a hollow place. I was scared. I didn't want to go inside. But Jonathan said that I'd see a strange land, a fabulous land, if I did. He went ahead, and I followed. At first, I couldn't see anything. There was only darkness and spiders. Then I saw trees and flowers, and smelled apple blossom and pine. Jonathan was standing in a clearing, dancing around in circles, laughing and calling to me to join him.

"So I did."

She fell silent for a moment. David waited for her to continue.

"There was a man waiting: the Crooked Man. He was sitting on a rock. He stared at me and licked his lips, then spoke to Jonathan.

" 'Tell me,' he said.

" 'Her name is Anna,' said Jonathan.

" 'Anna,' said the Crooked Man, as if he was trying my name out to see if he liked how it tasted. 'Welcome, Anna.'

"And then he leaped from the rock and wrapped me in his arms, and he began spinning round and round, just as Jonathan had done, but he spun so hard that he dug a hole in the ground and he dragged me down with him, through roots and dirt, past worms and beetles, into the tunnels that run beneath this world. He carried me for miles and miles, even though I cried and cried, until at last we came to these rooms.

"And then—"

She stopped.

"And then?" prompted David.

"He ate my heart," she whispered.

David felt himself grow pale. He was so sickened that he thought he might faint.

"He put his hand inside me, tearing at me with his nails, then pulled it out and ate it in front of me," she said. "And it hurt, it hurt so much. I was in such pain that I left my own body to escape it. I could see myself dying on the floor, and I was being lifted up, and there were lights and voices. Then glass closed around me, and I was trapped in this jar and placed on this shelf, and I've been here ever since. The next time I saw Jonathan, he had a crown on his head and he called himself the king, but he didn't look happy. He looked frightened and miserable, and he's stayed that way ever since. As for me, I never sleep because I am never tired. I never eat because I am never hungry. I never drink because I never feel thirst. I just stay here, with no way to tell how many days or years have passed, except when Jonathan comes and I see the ravages of time on his face. Mostly, though, *he* comes. He looks older now too. He's sick. As I fade, he grows weaker. I hear him talking in his sleep. He is looking for another now, someone to take Jonathan's place and someone to take mine."

David saw, once again, that hourglass in the room beyond, its top half nearly empty of grains. Was it counting down the days, the minutes, the hours, until the end of the Crooked Man's life? If he was allowed to take another child, would the hourglass be turned upside down so that the great count of his life could begin again? How many times had that glass been turned? There were many jars on the shelf, most of them thick with dust and mold. Had each one, at some point, held the spirit of some lost child?

A bargain: by naming the child to him, you doomed yourself. You became a ruler without power, haunted always by the betrayal of someone smaller and weaker than yourself, a brother, a sister, a friend whom you should have protected, someone who trusted you to stand up for them, who looked up to you, and who would, in turn, have been there for you as the years went by and childhood became adulthood. And once you had struck the bargain there was no way back, for who could return to their old life knowing the terrible thing that they had done?

"You're coming with me," said David. "I'm not leaving you alone here for a minute longer."

He lifted the jar from the shelf. There was a cork in the top, but David could not release it, no matter how hard he tried. His face grew puce from the effort, but all was in vain. He looked around and found an old sack in a corner.

"I'm going to put you in here," he said, "just in case someone sees us."

"That's all right," said Anna. "I'm not afraid."

David placed the jar carefully in the sack, then put the sack over his shoulder. Just as he was about to leave, something caught his eye in a corner of the room. It was his pajamas, his dressing gown, and a single slipper, the clothing discarded by the Woodsman before they had set out for the king. It seemed so long ago now, but here were tokens of the life that he had left behind. He did not like to think of them down here in the Crooked Man's lair. He gathered them up, went to the doorway, and listened carefully. There was no sound to be heard. David took a deep breath to calm himself, then started to run.

XXIX

Of the Crooked Man's Hidden Kingdom and the Treasures That He Kept There

HE CROOKED MAN'S LAIR was much larger, and much deeper, than David could have known. It ran far beneath the castle, and there were rooms that contained things much more terrifying than a collection of rusty torture implements or the ghost of a dead girl trapped in a jar. This was the heart of the Crooked Man's world, the place where all things were born and all things died. He was there when the first men came into the world, erupting into being along with them. In a way, they gave him life and purpose, and in return he gave them stories to tell, for the Crooked Man remembered every tale. He even had a story of his own, although he had changed its details in crucial ways before it could be told. In his tale it was the Crooked Man's name that had to be guessed, but that was his little joke. In truth, the Crooked Man had no name. Others could call him what they wished, but he was a being so old that the names given to him by men had no meaning for him: Trickster; the Crooked Man; Rumple—

Oh, but what was that name again? Never mind, never mind . . .

Only the names of children mattered to him, for there was a truth in the tale that the Crooked Man had given the world about himself: names did have a power, if they were used in the right way, and the Crooked Man had learned how to use them very well indeed. One enormous room in his lair was a testament to all that the Crooked Man knew: it was filled entirely with small skulls, each one bearing the name of a lost child, for the Crooked Man had struck many bargains for the lives of children. He could remember the faces and voices of every one, and sometimes, when he stood among their remains, he conjured up the memory of them so that the room was filled with their shades, a chorus of lost boys and girls weeping for their mummies and their daddies, a gathering of the forgotten and the betrayed.

The Crooked Man had treasures upon treasures, relics of stories told and stories yet to be told. A long crypt was used to store an array of thick glass cases, and in each case a body was suspended in yellowish liquid so that it would not decay. Come, look over here. Peer closely at this case, so close that your breath creates a little cloud of moisture upon the glass and you can stare into the milky eyes of the fat, bald man within. It's as if he himself is breathing, although he has not taken or released a breath in a very long time. See how his skin is burst and burned? See how his mouth and throat, his belly and lungs, are swollen and distended? Do you want to know his tale, for it is one of the Crooked Man's favorite stories. It is a nasty tale, a very nasty tale . . .

You see, the fat man's name was Manius, and he was very greedy. He owned so much land that a bird could take off from his first field and fly for a day and a night, yet still not reach the limits of Manius's property. He charged heavy rents to those who worked his fields and who lived in his villages. Even to set foot on his land was to invite a charge, and in this way he became very wealthy, but he never had enough and was always seeking new ways to increase his wealth. If he could have charged a bee to take pollen from a flower, or a tree to grow roots in his soil, then he would have done so.

One day, while Manius walked in the largest of his orchards, he saw a disturbance in the ground and out popped the Crooked Man, who was busy extending his network of tunnels under the earth. Manius challenged him, for he saw that the Crooked Man's clothes, although dirtied by the soil, had gold buttons and gold trim, and the dagger at his belt gleamed with rubies and diamonds.

"This is my land," he said. "All that is above it and all that is below belongs to me, and you must pay me for the right of passage beneath it."

The Crooked Man rubbed his chin thoughtfully. "That seems only fair," he said. "I will pay you a reasonable price."

Manius smiled and said, "I have ordered a banquet to be prepared for myself tonight. We will weigh all the food on the table before I eat, and all that is left when I am done. You will pay me in gold the weight of all that I have eaten."

"A bellyful of gold," said the Crooked Man. "It is agreed. I will come to you tonight, and I will give you all you can eat in gold."

They shook hands on the deal and parted. That night, the Crooked Man sat and watched as Manius ate and ate. He consumed two whole turkeys and a full ham, bowl upon bowl of potatoes and vegetables, whole tureens of soup, great plates of fruits and cakes and cream, and glass after glass of the finest wines. The Crooked Man carefully weighed it all before the meal began, and weighed the meager remains when the meal was over. The difference amounted to many, many pounds, or enough gold to purchase a thousand fields.

Manius belched. He felt very tired, so tired that he could barely keep his eyes open.

"Now where is my gold?" he asked, but the Crooked Man was growing blurry, and the room was spinning, and before he could hear the answer he was asleep.

When he awoke, he was chained to a wooden chair in a dark dungeon. His mouth was held open by a metal vise, and a bubbling cauldron was suspended above his head.

The Crooked Man appeared beside him. "I am a man of my word," he said. "Prepare to receive your bellyful of gold."

The cauldron tipped, and molten gold spilled into Manius's mouth and poured down his throat, scalding his flesh and burning his bones. The pain was beyond imagining, but he did not die, not immediately, for the Crooked Man had ways of delaying death to make his tortures last. The Crooked Man would pour a little gold, then allow it to cool before pouring a little more, and thus he continued until he had filled Manius so full of gold that it bubbled behind his back teeth. By then, of course, Manius was very dead indeed, for even the Crooked Man could not keep him alive indefinitely. Eventually, Manius took his place in the room full of glass cases, and the Crooked Man would come to look at him sometimes, and he would smile as he remembered this most splendid of tricks.

There were many such stories in the Crooked Man's lair: a thousand rooms, and a thousand stories for every room. One chamber housed a collection of telepathic spiders, very old, very wise, and very, very large, each one more than four feet across, with fangs so poisonous that a single drop of their venom, placed in a well, had once killed an entire village. The Crooked Man often used them to hunt those who strayed into his tunnels, and when the trespassers were found, the spiders would wrap them in silk and carry them back to their cobwebbed room, and there they would die very slowly as the spiders fed upon them, draining them drop by drop.

In one of the dressing rooms a woman sat facing a blank wall, endlessly combing her long, silver hair. Sometimes, the Crooked Man would take those who had angered him to visit the woman, and when she turned to look at them, they would see themselves reflected in her eyes, for her eyes were made of mirrored glass. And in those eyes they would be allowed to witness the moment of their deaths, so that they would know exactly when and how they would die. You might think that such knowledge would not be so terrible, and you would be wrong. We are not meant to know the time or the nature of our deaths (for all of us secretly hope that we may be immortal). Those who were given that knowledge found that they could not sleep or eat or enjoy any of the pleasures life had to offer them, so tormented were they by what they had seen. Their lives became a kind of living death, devoid of joy, and all that was left to them was fear and sadness, so that when at last the end came they were almost grateful for it.

A bedchamber contained a naked woman and a naked man, and the Crooked Man would bring children to them (not the special ones, the ones who gave him life, but the others, the ones he stole from villages or those who strayed from the path and became lost in the forest), and the man and the woman would whisper things to them in the darkness of their chamber, telling them things that children should not know, dark tales of what adults did together in the depths of the night while their sons and daughters were sleeping. In this way the children died inside. Forced into adulthood before they were ready, they had their innocence taken from them, and their minds collapsed under the weight of poisonous thoughts. Many grew up to become evil men and women, and so the corruption was spread.

One small, bright room was decorated only with a mirror,

plain and unadorned. The Crooked Man would steal husbands or wives from their marriage beds, leaving their spouses sleeping, and force the captives to sit before the mirror, and the mirror would reveal all of the bad secrets that their spouses kept hidden from them: all of the sins they had committed and all of the sins they wanted to commit; all of the betrayals already on their consciences and all of the betrayals that they might yet perpetrate. Then the captives would be returned to their beds, and when they awoke they would not remember the chamber, or the mirror, or their abduction by the Crooked Man. All they would recall was the knowledge that those whom they loved, and whom they thought loved them in return, were not as they had believed them to be, and in this way lives were ruined by suspicion and the fear of treachery.

There was a hall filled entirely with pools of what looked like clear water, and each pool showed a different part of the kingdom, so that little happened in the land beyond the castle that was not known to the Crooked Man. By diving into a pool, the Crooked Man could materialize in the place reflected in it. The air would ripple and shimmer, and suddenly an arm would appear, then a leg, and finally the face and hunched back of the Crooked Man, transported instantly from the depths beneath the castle to a room or a field far away. The Crooked Man's favorite torture was to take men or women, preferably those with large families, and hang them from chains in the room of pools. Then, while they watched, he would hunt down and kill their families before them, one by one. After each murder he would return to the room and listen to the pleas of his captives, but no matter how loudly they screamed and cried and begged for him to be merciful, he would not spare a single life. Finally, when all were dead, he would take the desolate men or women to his deepest, darkest dungeon, and there he would leave them to go mad with loneliness and grief.

Little evils, big evils, all were butter to the Crooked Man's bread. Through his network of tunnels and his room of pools, he knew more about his world than anyone else, and this knowledge gave him the power he required to rule the kingdom in secret. And all the time he haunted the shadows of another world, our world, and he made kings and queens of boys and girls and bound them to him by destroying their spirits and forcing them to betray children whom they should have protected. To those who threatened to rebel against him, he made promises that, someday, he would release them and the children they had sacrificed to him from their bargains, claiming that he could restore the frail figures in the jars to life if he chose (for most, like Jonathan Tulvey, very quickly realized their mistake in striking a bargain with the Crooked Man).

But there were some things that were beyond the Crooked Man's control. Bringing outsiders into the land changed it. They carried their fears with them, their dreams and their nightmares, and the land made them real. That was how the Loups had come into being. They were Jonathan's worst fear: from his earliest childhood, he had hated stories of wolves and of beasts that walked and talked like men. When the Crooked Man finally transported him into the kingdom, that fear followed, and the wolves began to transform. They alone did not fear the Crooked Man, as if some of Jonathan's secret hatred of the Crooked Man had found form in them. Now they presented the greatest threat to the kingdom, although it was one of which the Crooked Man hoped he could yet make use.

The boy called David was different from the others whom the Crooked Man had tempted. He had helped to destroy the Beast, and the woman who dwelled in the Fortress of Thorns. David did not realize it, but in a way they were *his* fears, and he had brought aspects of them into being. What had surprised the Crooked Man was the way in which the boy had dealt with them. His anger and grief had enabled him to do what older men had not managed to achieve. The boy was strong, strong enough to conquer his fears. He was also beginning to master his hatreds and jealousies. Such a boy, if he could be controlled, would make a great king.

But time was running out for the Crooked Man. He needed another child's life to drain. If he ate Georgie's heart, the infant's life span would become the Crooked Man's. If Georgie was destined to live to be one hundred years old, then the Crooked Man would be granted that hundred years instead and Georgie's spirit would remain trapped in one of the Crooked Man's jars, and he would absorb its light as he slept in his hard, narrow bed. All that was necessary was for the boy David to say the child's name aloud, to indulge his hatred and thus to damn them both.

The Crooked Man had less than one day of life left in his hourglass. He needed David to betray his half brother before midnight. Now, as he sat in his chamber of pools, he saw shapes appear on the hills around the castle, and for the first time in many decades he felt real fear, even as he put the finishing touches to his last, desperate plan.

For the wolves were gathering, and soon they would descend upon the castle.

While the Crooked Man was distracted by the approaching army, David, carrying Anna in her jar, made his way back through the warren of tunnels to the throne room. As they approached the door concealed by the tapestry, David could hear men shouting, and the running of feet and the clanking of weapons and armor. He wondered if his disappearance was the reason for the activity and tried to come up with the best way to explain his absence. He peered from behind the tapestry and saw Duncan standing nearby as he ordered men to the battlements and told others to make sure all entrances to the castle were secure. While the captain's back was turned, David slipped out and ran as quickly as he could to the stairs leading up to the gallery. If anyone saw him, they paid him no attention, and he knew then that he was not the cause of all this trouble. Once he was back in his bedroom, he closed the door and removed from his sack the jar containing Anna's ghost. Her light seemed to have grown dimmer in the short trip from the Crooked Man's lair to the castle itself, and she was slumped at the base of the glass, her face even paler than before.

"What's wrong?" David asked.

Anna held up her right hand, and David saw that it had faded to near-transparency.

"I feel weak," said Anna. "And I'm changing. I seem to be growing fainter."

David did not know what to say to console her. He tried to find somewhere to hide her, and decided eventually upon a shadowy corner of an enormous wardrobe, populated only by the husks of dead insects trapped in an ancient web.

But Anna cried out to him as he was about to place the jar in his chosen hiding place. "No," she said. "Please, not there. I've been trapped alone in the darkness for so many years, and I don't think I'm going to be in this world for much longer. Put me on the windowsill, so that I may look out and see trees and people. I'll be quiet, and no one will think of searching for me there."

So David opened one of the windows and saw that outside was a small, wrought-iron balcony. It was rusted in places and rattled when he touched it, but it would safely support the weight of the jar. He placed it carefully in one corner, and Anna moved forward and leaned against the glass.

For the first time since they had met, she smiled. "Oh," she said, "it's wonderful. Look at the river, and the trees beyond, and all of those people. Thank you, David. This is all that I wanted to see."

But David was not listening to her, for as she spoke howls rose from the hills above, and he saw black and white and gray shapes moving across the landscape, thousands upon thousands of them. There was a discipline and purpose about the wolves, almost like divisions of an army preparing for battle. Upon the highest point overlooking the castle, he saw clothed figures standing on their hind legs while more wolves ran to and fro, carrying messages back and forth between the Loups and the animals on the front line.

"What's happening?" asked Anna.

"The wolves have come," said David. "They want to kill the king and take over his kingdom."

"Kill Jonathan?" said Anna, and there was such horror in her voice that David looked away from the wolves and turned his attention back to the small, fading figure of the girl.

"Why are you so worried about him, after all that he's done to you?" he asked. "He betrayed you and let the Crooked Man feed on you, then left you to rot in a jar in a dungeon. How can you feel anything but hatred for him?"

Anna shook her head and, for a moment, she seemed much older than before. She may have been a girl in form, but she had existed for far longer than her appearance suggested, and in that dark place she had learned wisdom and tolerance and forgiveness.

"He's my brother," she stated. "I love him, no matter what he has done to me. He was young and angry and foolish when he made his bargain, and if he could turn back the clock and undo all that has been done, then he would. I don't want to see him hurt. And what will happen to all those people below if the wolves succeed and their rule replaces the rule of men and women? They will tear apart every living thing within these walls, and what little that is good here will cease to be."

As he listened to her, David wondered again how Jonathan

could have betrayed this girl. He must have been so angry and so sad, and that anger and sadness had consumed him.

David watched the wolves assemble, all with but one purpose: to take the castle and kill the king and everyone who stood by him. But the walls were thick and strong, and the gates were firmly closed against them. There were guards at the stinking holes where the waste left the castle, and armed men stood upon every roof and at every window. The wolves vastly outnumbered them, but they were outside and David could see no way for them to gain entry. As long as that situation continued, the wolves could howl all they wanted, and the Loups could send and receive as many messages as they chose. It would make no difference. The castle would remain impregnable.

XXX

Of the Crooked Man's Act of Betrayal

EEP BELOW THE GROUND, the Crooked Man watched the sands of his life trickle away, one by one. He was growing steadily weaker. His system was collapsing. His teeth were coming loose in his mouth, and there were weeping sores on his lips. Blood dripped from his twisted fingernails, and his eyes were yellow and rheumy. His skin was dry and flaking; long, deep cuts opened upon it when he scratched at it, revealing the muscles and tendons beneath. His joints ached, and his hair fell from his head in clumps. He was dying, yet he did not panic. There had been times in his long, dreadful life when he had been even closer than this to death, when it had seemed that he'd chosen the wrong child and there would be no betrayal and no new king or queen for him to manipulate like a puppet upon the throne. But, in the end, he had always found a way to corrupt them or, as he preferred to think of it, for them to corrupt themselves.

The Crooked Man believed that whatever evil lay in men was there from the moment of their conception, and it was only a matter of discovering its nature in a child. The boy David had as much rage and hurt as any child that the Crooked Man had yet encountered, but still he resisted his advances. It was time for one last gamble. For all he had achieved, and for all of the bravery that he had shown, the boy was still just a boy. He was far from home, separated from his father and the familiar things of his life. Somewhere inside, he was frightened and alone. If the Crooked Man could make that fear unbearable, then David would name the infant in his house and the Crooked Man would live on, and in time the search for David's replacement would commence. Fear was the key. The Crooked Man had learned that, faced with death, most men would do anything to stay alive. They would weep, beg, kill, or betray another to save their own skins. If he could make David afraid for his life, then he would give the Crooked Man what he desired.

So that strange, hunched being, old as the memory of men, left his lair of mirrored pools and hourglasses, of spiders and death-filled eyes, disappearing into the great network of tunnels that ran like a honeycomb beneath his realm. He passed below the castle buildings, under the walls, and into the countryside beyond.

And when he heard the howling of the wolves above him, he knew that he had reached his destination.

David had been reluctant to leave Anna, so weak did she seem. He was afraid that if he turned his back on her, she might disappear altogether. In turn, she who had been alone in the dark for so long was grateful for his company. She spoke to him of the long decades spent with the Crooked Man, of the awful things that he had done and the terrible tortures and punishments he had visited on those who had crossed him. David told her of his dead mother, and of the house that he now shared with Rose and Georgie, the same house in which Anna had once briefly lived after her own parents died. The little girl's aura seemed to grow brighter at the mention of her former home, and she quizzed David about the house and the village nearby and the changes that had occurred since she had left it. He told her of the war and of the great army marching across Europe, crushing all in its path.

"So you left behind one war, only to find yourself in the midst of another," she said.

David looked down on the columns of wolves moving purposefully across the valley and the hills. Their numbers seemed to swell with every passing minute, the ranks of black and gray positioning themselves to surround the castle. Like Fletcher before him, David was most disturbed by their order and discipline. It was a fragile thing, he suspected: without the Loups the wolf packs would scatter, fighting and scavenging their way back to their own territories, but for now the Loups had corrupted the natures of the wolves, just as their own natures had been corrupted. They believed themselves to be greater and more advanced than their brothers and sisters who walked on four legs, but in reality they were much worse. They were impure, mutations that were neither human nor animal. David wondered what the minds of the Loups were like as the two sides of their being fought constantly for supremacy. There had been a kind of madness in Leroi's eyes, of that much David was certain.

"Jonathan will not surrender to them," said Anna. "They cannot gain entry to the castle. They should simply disperse, but they won't. What are they waiting for?"

"An opportunity," said David. "Perhaps Leroi and his Loups have a plan, or maybe they're just hoping the king will make a mistake, but they can't turn back now. They will never assemble another army like this, and they won't be allowed to survive if they fail."

The door of David's bedroom opened, and Duncan, the Captain of the Guard, entered. David closed the window immedi-ately, just in case the Captain might spot Anna on the balcony.

"The king wishes to see you," he said.

David nodded. Even though he was safe within the castle walls, and surrounded by armed men, he first removed his sword and belt from where they hung on a bedpost, then cinched the belt around his waist. Doing this had become a routine with him, and now he did not feel properly dressed without the sword by his side. He was especially aware of his need for it after his foray into the lair of the Crooked Man. Down there in the trickster's chambers of pain and torture, he had realized how vulnerable he was without a weapon. David also knew that the Crooked Man was bound to notice that Anna was missing and was sure to come looking for her when he did. It would not take him long to work out that David was somehow involved, and the boy did not want to face the Crooked Man's anger without the sword to hand.

The captain did not object to the sword. In fact, he told David to bring all of his belongings with him. "You will not be return-ing to this room," he said.

It was all that David could do not to glance at the window behind which Anna was hidden.

"Why?" he asked.

"That's for the king to tell you," said Duncan. "We came for you earlier, but you were not to be found."

"I went for a walk," said David.

"You were told to remain here."

"I heard the wolves and wanted to find out what was going on. But everybody seemed to be rushing around, so I came back here."

"You need not fear them," said the captain. "These walls have never been breached, and no pack of animals is going to do what an army of men could not. Come, now. The king is waiting."

David packed his bag, added the clothing he had found in the Crooked Man's room, and followed the captain down to the throne room, casting one last look back at the window. Through the glass, he thought he could still see Anna's light shining faintly.

In the woods behind the wolves' lines, a flurry of snow shot into the air, followed by clumps of dirt and grass. A hole appeared, and from it emerged the Crooked Man. He held one of his curved blades at the ready, for this was a dangerous business. There was no way that he could strike a bargain with the wolves. Their leaders, the Loups, were aware of the Crooked Man's power and trusted him just as little as he trusted them. He had also been responsible for the deaths of too many of their number for them to forgive him so easily, or even to let him live long enough to plead for his life if one of the packs trapped him. Silently, he advanced until he saw a line of figures before him, all of them dressed in army uniforms scavenged from the bodies of dead soldiers. Some were smoking pipes while they stood over a map of the castle that had been drawn in the snow before them, trying to work out some way to gain entry. Already scouts had been dispatched to get close to the castle walls in order to discover if there were any cracks or fissures, any unguarded holes or portals, that might be of use to them. The gray wolves had been used as decoys and had died almost as soon as they came within reach of the defenders' arrows. The white wolves were harder to see, and although some of their number had also died, a few were able to approach close enough to the walls to conduct a minute examination, sniffing and digging in an effort to find a way through. Those that had survived to report back confirmed that the castle was as impregnable as it appeared to be.

The Crooked Man was close enough to hear the voices of the Loups and to smell the stink of their fur. Foolish, vain creatures, he thought. You may dress like men, and take on their manners and airs, but you will always stink like beasts and you will always be animals pretending to be what you are not. The Crooked Man hated them and hated Jonathan for conjuring them into being through the power of his imagination, creating his own version of the tale of the little girl in the red, hooded robe in order to give birth to them. The Crooked Man had watched with alarm as the wolves began to transform: slowly at first, their growls and snarls sometimes forming what might have been words, their front paws lifting into the air as they tried to walk like men. In the beginning it had seemed almost amusing to him, but then their faces had begun to change, and their intelligence, already quick and alert, had grown sharper yet. He had tried to get Jonathan to order a cull of the wolves throughout the land, but the king had acted too late. The first party of soldiers that he sent out to kill them were themselves slaughtered, and the villagers were too afraid of this new threat to do more than build higher walls around their settlements and lock their doors and windows at night. Now it had come to this: an army of wolves, led by creatures who were half man, half beast, intent upon seizing the kingdom for themselves.

"Come then," the Crooked Man whispered to himself. "If you want the king, take him. I am done with him."

The Crooked Man retreated, circling the generals, until he came to a she-wolf who was acting as a lookout. He made sure to stay downwind of her, judging his approach from the direction in which the lighter flakes of snow were blowing off the ground. He was almost upon her when she registered his presence, but by then her fate was sealed. The Crooked Man leaped, his blade already beginning its downward movement. As soon as he landed on the wolf, the knife sliced through her fur and deep into the flesh beneath, the Crooked Man's long fingers closing around her muzzle and snapping it tightly closed so that she could not cry out, not yet.

He could have killed her, of course, and taken her snout for his collection, but he did not. Instead, he cut her so deeply that she collapsed upon the ground and the snow around her grew red with her blood. He released his grip on her muzzle, and the wolf began to yelp and howl, alerting the rest of the pack to her distress. This was the dangerous part, the Crooked Man knew, riskier even than tackling the big she-wolf to begin with. He wanted them to see him, but not to get close enough to catch him. Suddenly, four massive grays appeared on the brow of a hill and howled a warning to the rest. Behind them came one of the despised Loups, dressed in all of the military finery he could muster: a bright red jacket with gold braid and buttons, and white trousers only partly stained by the blood of their previous owner. He wore a long saber on a black leather belt, and he was already drawing it as he stood and looked down upon the dying wolf and the being responsible for her pain.

It was Leroi, the beast who would be king, the most hated and feared of the Loups. The Crooked Man paused, tempted by the nearness of his greatest enemy. Although he was very ancient, and weakened by the dying of Anna's light and the slow slipping away of the grains of his life, the Crooked Man was still fast and strong. He felt certain that he could kill the four grays, leaving Leroi with only a captured sword with which to defend himself. If the Crooked Man killed Leroi, then the wolves would disperse, for he held their army together with the force of his will. Even the other Loups were not as advanced as he was, and they could be hunted down in time by the forces of the new king.

The new king! The reminder of what he had come to do brought the Crooked Man to his senses, even as more wolves and Loups appeared behind Leroi and a patrol of whites began to creep in from the south. For a moment, all was still as the wolves regarded their most despised foe standing over the dying she-wolf. Then, with a cry of triumph, the Crooked Man waved his bloody blade in the air and ran. Instantly, the wolves followed, pouring through the trees, their eyes bright with the thrill of the chase. One white wolf, sleeker and faster than the rest, separated itself from the pack, trying to cut off the Crooked Man's escape. The ground sloped down to where the Crooked Man was running, so that the wolf was about ten feet above him when its hind legs bent and it catapulted itself into the air, its fangs bared to tear out its quarry's throat. But the Crooked Man was too wily for it, and as it jumped he spun in a neat circle, his blade held high above his head, and sliced open the wolf from below. It fell dead at his feet, and the Crooked Man ran on. Thirty feet, now twenty, now ten. Ahead of him he could see the tunnel entrance, marked by earth and dirty snow. He was almost upon it when he saw a flash of red to his left and heard the *swish* of a sword slicing through the air. He raised his own blade just in time to block Leroi's saber, but the Loup was stronger than he had expected and the Crooked Man stumbled slightly, almost falling upon the ground. Had he done so all would have ended quickly, for Leroi was already preparing to deliver the death blow. Instead, the blade cut through the Crooked Man's garments, barely missing the arm beneath, but the Crooked Man pretended that a grave injury had been inflicted. He dropped his blade and staggered backward, his left hand clutched to the imaginary wound on his right arm. The wolves surrounded him now, watching the two combatants, howling their support for Leroi, willing him to finish the job. Leroi raised his head and snarled once, and all of the wolves fell quiet.

"You have made a fatal error," said Leroi. "You should have stayed behind the castle walls. We will breach them, in time, but you might have lived a little longer had you remained within their confines."

The Crooked Man laughed in Leroi's face, which was now, except for some unruly hairs and a slight snout, almost human in appearance.

"No, it is you who are mistaken," he said. "Look at you. You are neither man nor beast, but some pathetic creature who is less than both. You hate what you are and want to be what you cannot truly become. Your appearance may change, and you may wear all the fine clothes that you can steal from the bodies of your victims, but you will still be a wolf inside. Even then, what do you think will happen once your outer transformation is complete, when you start to resemble fully what once you hunted? You will look like a man, and the pack will no longer recognize you as its own. What you most desire is the very thing that will doom you, for they will tear you apart and you will die in their jaws as others have died in yours. Until then, half-breed, I bid you . . . farewell!"

And with that, he disappeared feet first into the mouth of the tunnel and was gone. It took Leroi a second or two to realize what had happened. He opened his mouth to howl in rage, but the sound that emerged was a kind of strangled cough. It was as the Crooked Man had said: Leroi's transformation was almost complete, and his wolf voice was now being replaced by the voice of a man. To hide his surprise at the loss of his howl, Leroi gestured at two of his scouts, indicating that they should proceed toward the tunnel mouth. They sniffed warily at the disturbed earth, then one swiftly poked its head inside, quickly pulling it back out in case the Crooked Man was waiting below. When nothing happened, it tried again, lingering longer. It sniffed the air in the tunnel. The Crooked Man's scent was present, but it was already growing fainter. He was running away from them.

Leroi got down on one knee and examined the hole, then

looked toward the hills behind which the castle lay. He considered his options. Despite his bluster, it was looking less and less likely that they would be able to find a way through the castle walls. If they did not attack soon, his wolf army would grow restless and hungrier than it already was. Rival packs would turn on one another. There would be fighting, and cannibalization of the weak. In their rage, they would rebel against Leroi and his fellow Loups. No, he needed to make a move, and make it quickly. If he could secure the castle, then his army could feed on its defenders while he and his Loups set about making plans for a new order. Perhaps the Crooked Man had simply overestimated his own abilities in using the tunnel to leave the castle and had taken an unnecessary risk in the hope of killing some wolves, maybe even Leroi himself. Whatever the reason, Leroi had been given the chance he had almost despaired of receiving. The tunnel was narrow, wide enough for only one Loup or wolf at a time. Still, it would allow a small force to enter the castle, and if they could get to the castle gates and open them from within, then the defenders would quickly be overwhelmed.

Leroi turned to one of his lieutenants. "Send skirmishers to the castle to distract the troops on the walls," he ordered. "Begin moving the main forces forward, and bring my best grays to me. Let the attack commence!"

XXXI

Of the Battle, and the Fate of Those Who Would Be King

HE KING was slumped on his throne, his chin upon his chest. He looked as though he was sleeping, but as David drew closer, he saw that the old man's eyes were open and staring blankly at the floor. The Book of Lost Things lay on his lap, the king's hand resting on its cover. Four guards surrounded him, one at each corner of the dais, and there were more at the doors and upon the gallery. As the captain approached with David, the king peered up, and the look on his face made David's stomach tighten. It was the face of a man who has been told that his one chance to avoid the executioner is to convince someone else to take his place, and in David the king seemed to see that very person. The captain stopped before the throne, bowed, and left them. The king ordered the guards to step away so that they could not hear what was being said, then tried to compose his features into an expression of kindness. His eyes gave him away, though: they were desperate and hostile and cunning.

"I had hoped," he began, "to speak with you under better circumstances. We find ourselves surrounded, but there is no reason to be afraid. They are mere beasts, and we will always be superior to them."

He crooked his finger at David. "Come closer, boy."

David ascended the steps. His face was now level with the king's. The king ran his fingers along the arms of the throne, pausing now and then to examine a particularly fine detail of its ornamentation, to caress lightly a ruby or an emerald.

"It is a wonderful throne, is it not?" he asked David.

"It's very nice," said David, and the king glanced sharply at him as though unsure of whether or not he was being mocked by the boy. David's face gave nothing away, and the king decided to let his answer pass without rebuke.

"From the earliest of times, the kings and queens of the realm have sat upon this throne and ruled the land from it. Do you know what they all had in common? I will tell you: they all came from your world, not this one. Your world, and mine. As one ruler dies, another crosses the boundary between the two worlds and assumes the throne. It is the way of things here, and it is a great honor to be chosen. That honor is now yours."

David did not reply, so the king continued.

"I am aware that you have encountered the Crooked Man. You should not let his appearance put you off. He means well, although he has a way of, um, *manipulating* the truth. He has been shadowing your path since you arrived here, and there were times when you were close to death and were saved only by his intervention. At first, I know that he offered to take you back to your home, but that was a lie. It is not in his gift or in his power to do so until you claim the throne. Once you have ascended to your rightful place, you may order him to do as you please. If you refuse the throne, he will kill you and seek another. That is how it has always been.

"You must accept what is being offered to you. If you do not like it, or find that it is not in you to rule, then you may order the Crooked Man to return you to your own land and the bargain will be concluded. You will be the king, after all, and he will be merely a subject. He asks only that your brother should come with you, that you might have company in this new world as you begin to rule. In time, he may even bring your father here, if you like, and imagine how proud *he* will be to see his firstborn seated on a throne, the king of a great realm! Well, what do you say?"

By the time the king had finished speaking, any pity that David might have felt for him had disappeared. Everything the king had said was a lie. He did not know that David had looked in the Book of Lost Things, that he had entered the Crooked Man's lair and met Anna there. David knew of hearts being consumed in the darkness, and the essence of children being kept in jars to fuel the life of the Crooked Man. The king, crushed by guilt and sorrow, wanted to be released from his bargain with the Crooked Man, and he would say anything to get David to take his place.

"Is that the Book of Lost Things in your hands?" asked David. "They say that it contains all kinds of knowledge, perhaps even magic. Is that true?"

The king's eyes glittered. "Oh, very true, very true. I will give it to you when I abdicate and the crown becomes yours. It will be my coronation gift. With it, you can order the Crooked Man to do your will, and he will have to obey. Once you are king, I will have no more use for it."

For a moment, the king looked almost regretful. Yet again, his fingers traveled across the cover of the book, smoothing down loose threads, exploring the places where the spine had begun to separate from the rest. It was like a living thing to him, as though his heart had also been removed from his body when he came to this land and it had taken the form of a book.

"And what will happen to you once I am king?" asked David.

The king looked away before he replied. "Oh, I will leave here and find some quiet place in which to enjoy my retirement," he said. "Perhaps I will even return to our world to see what has changed there since I left it."

But his words sounded hollow, and his voice cracked beneath the weight of his guilt and lies.

"I know who you are," said David softly.

The king leaned forward on his throne. "What did you say?"

"I know who you are," David repeated. "You are Jonathan Tulvey. Your adopted sister's name was Anna. You were jealous of her when she was brought to your home, and that jealousy never went away. The Crooked Man came and showed you how a life without her could be, and you betrayed her. You tricked her into following you through the sunken garden and into this place. The Crooked Man killed her and ate her heart, then kept her spirit in a glass jar. That book on your lap contains no magic, and its only secrets are yours. You are a sad, evil old man, and you can keep your kingdom and your throne. I don't want it. I don't want any of it."

A figure emerged from the shadows.

"Then you will die," said the Crooked Man.

He appeared much older than when David had last seen him, and his skin looked torn and diseased. There were wounds and blisters upon his face and hands, and he stank of his own corruption.

"You have been busy, I see," said the Crooked Man. "You have been sticking your nose in places where you had no business. You have taken something that belongs to me. Where is she?"

"She does not belong to you," said David. "She does not belong to anyone."

David drew his sword. This time, it shook a little as his hand trembled, but not very much.

The Crooked Man just laughed at him. "No matter," he said. "She had reached the end of her usefulness. Be careful lest the same can be said of you. Death is coming for you, and no sword can keep it away. You think you're brave, but let's see how brave you are when there is hot wolf breath and spittle upon your face and your throat is about to be ripped out. Then you will weep and wail and you will call for me, and perhaps I will answer. Perhaps . . .

"Tell me your brother's name and I will save you from all pain. I promise that I will not harm him. The land needs a king. If you agree to assume the throne, then I will let your brother live when I bring him here. I will find another to take his place, for there are sands in my hourglass yet. You will both abide here together, and you will rule justly and fairly. All this will come to pass. I give you my word. Just tell me his name."

The guards were watching David now, their own weapons unsheathed, ready to strike him down if he tried to hurt the king. But the king raised his hand to let them know that all was well, and they relaxed a little as they waited to see what would unfold.

"If you don't tell me his name, then I will cross back into your world and I will kill the infant in his bed," said the Crooked Man. "Even if it is the last thing that I do, I will leave his blood upon the pillows and the sheets. Your choice is simple: the two of you may rule together, or you may each die apart. There is no other way."

David shook his head. "No," he said. "I will not allow you to do it."

"Allow? *Allow?*" The Crooked Man's face contorted as he forced the word out. His lips cracked, and a little blood trickled from the splits, for he had only a little left to shed.

"Listen to me," he said. "Let me tell you the truth about the world to which you so desperately want to return. It is a place of pain and suffering and grief. When you left it, cities were being attacked. Women and children were being blasted to pieces or burned alive by bombs dropped from planes flown by men with wives and children of their own. People were being dragged from their homes and shot in the street. Your world is tearing itself apart, and the most amusing thing of all is that it was little better before the war started. War merely gives people an excuse to indulge themselves further, to murder with impunity. There were wars before it, and there will be wars after it, and in between people will still fight one another and hurt one another and maim one another and betray one another, because that is what they have always done.

"And even if you avoid warfare and violent death, little boy, what else do you think life has in store for you? You have already seen what it is capable of doing. It took your mother from you, drained her of health and beauty, and then cast her aside like the withered, rotten husk of a fruit. It will take others from you too, mark me. Those whom you care about—lovers, children—will fall by the wayside, and your love will not be enough to save them. Your health will fail you. You will become old and sick. Your limbs will ache, your eyesight will fade, and your skin will grow lined and aged. There will be pains deep within that no doctor will be able to cure. Diseases will find a warm, moist place inside you and there they will breed, spreading through your system, corrupting it cell by cell until you will pray for the doctors to let you die, to put you out of your misery, but they will not. Instead you will linger on, with no one to hold your hand or soothe your brow, as Death comes and beckons you into his darkness. The life you left behind is no life at all. Here, you can be king, and I will allow you to age with dignity and without pain, and when the time comes for you to die, I will send you gently to sleep and you will awaken in the paradise of your choosing, for each man dreams his own heaven. All I ask in return is that you name the child in your house to me, that you may have company in this place. Name him! Name him now before it's too late."

As he spoke, the tapestry behind the king shifted and billowed, and a gray shape materialized from behind it and pounced on the chest of the nearest guard. The wolf's head descended and twisted, and the guard's throat was torn apart. The wolf let out a great howl, even as the arrows fired down from the guards on the gallery pierced its heart. More wolves poured through the doorway, so many that the tapestry was torn from the wall and fell to the floor in a cloud of dust. The grays, the most loyal and ferocious of Leroi's troops, were invading the throne room. A horn sounded, and guards appeared from every doorway. A furious battle commenced, the guards slashing and spearing the wolves, trying to hold back their tide, while the wolves snapped and snarled, seeking any opening they could find in order to kill the men. They bit at legs and stomachs and arms, ripping bellies and opening throats. Soon the floor was awash with blood, channels of red flowing between the edges of the stones. The guards had formed a semicircle around the open doorway, but the sheer numbers of wolves were forcing them back.

The Crooked Man pointed at the teeming, fighting mass of men and animals. "See!" he shouted at David. "Your sword will not save you. Only I can do that. Tell me his name, and I will spirit you away from here in an instant. Speak, and save yourself!"

Now the grays had been joined by black wolves and white wolves. The wolf packs began working their way around the guards, invading rooms and hallways, killing everyone who stood against them. The king leaped from his throne and stared in horror at the wall of guards slowly being forced toward him by the pack.

The Captain of the Guard appeared at his right hand. "Come, Your Majesty," he said. "We must get you to safety."

But the king pushed him away and stared furiously at the Crooked Man. "You betrayed us," he said. "You betrayed us all."

The Crooked Man ignored him. His attention was focused only on David. "The name," he said again. "Tell me his name."

Behind him, the wolves broke the wall of men. Now there were newcomers among them who walked on their hind legs and wore the uniforms of soldiers. The Loups slashed at the guards with their swords, forcing a path through to the doors leading from the throne room. Two immediately disappeared down a hallway, followed by six wolves. They were making for the castle gates.

Then Leroi emerged. He looked out upon the carnage before him, and he saw the throne, *his* throne, and he found within himself one last lupine howl to signal his triumph. The king trembled at the sound, even as Leroi's eyes found his and the Loup moved forward to kill him. The Captain of the Guards was still trying to protect the king. He was keeping two grays at bay with his sword, but it was clear that he was tiring.

"Go, Your Majesty!" he shouted. "Go now!"

But the words were stopped in his throat as an arrow struck his chest, fired by one of Leroi's Loups. The captain fell to the floor, and the wolves descended upon him.

The king reached beneath the folds of his gown and withdrew an ornate gold dagger, then advanced upon the Crooked Man. "Foul thing," he cried. "After all that I did, after all that you made me do, you betrayed me at the last."

"I made you do nothing, Jonathan," replied the Crooked Man. "You did it because you wanted to. No one can make you do evil. You had evil inside you, and you indulged it. Men will always indulge it."

He lashed out at the king with his own blade, and the old man tottered and almost fell. Quick as a flash, the Crooked Man turned to grab David, but the boy stepped out of his path and slashed at him with his sword, opening a wound across the Crooked Man's chest that stank but did not bleed.

"You are going to die!" cried the Crooked Man. "Tell me his name, and you will live!"

He advanced on David, oblivious of his injury. David tried to stab at him again, but the Crooked Man avoided the blow and fought back, his nails tearing deep into David's arm. David felt as though he had been poisoned, for pain seeped into his arm, flowing through his veins and freezing his blood until it reached his hand and the sword fell from his numbed fingers. He was against a wall now, surrounded by fighting men and snarling wolves. Over the Crooked Man's shoulder, he saw Leroi advancing upon the king. The king tried to stab him with his dagger, but Leroi swatted it away, and it skidded across the stones.

"The name!" shrieked the Crooked Man. "The name, or I will leave you to the wolves."

Leroi picked up the king as if he were a doll, placing his hand beneath the old man's chin and tilting his head, exposing the king's neck. Leroi paused and looked at David. "You're next," he gloated, then opened his mouth wide, revealing his sharp white teeth. He bit into the king's throat, shaking him from side to side as he killed him. The Crooked Man's eyes opened wide in horror as the king's life drained away. A great patch of skin uncurled from the trickster's face like old wallpaper, exposing the gray, decaying flesh beneath.

"No!" he screamed, then reached out and grabbed David by the throat. "The name. You must tell me the name, or else we will both be lost."

David was very frightened, and knew that he was about to die.

"His name is—" he began.

"Yes!" said the Crooked Man, "Yes!" as the king's last breath bubbled in his throat and Leroi cast his dying body aside, wiping the old man's blood from his mouth while he advanced on David.

"His name is . . ."

"Tell me!" shrieked the Crooked Man.

"His name is 'brother,' " said David.

The Crooked Man's body collapsed in despair. "No," he moaned. "No."

Deep in the bowels of the castle, the last grains of sand trickled through the neck of the hourglass, and on a balcony far above, the ghost of a girl glowed brightly for a second, then faded away entirely. Had there been anyone there to see it happen, they would have heard her give a small sigh that was filled with joy and peace, for her torment had come to an end.

"No!" howled the Crooked Man, as his skin cracked and all of the foul gas began to burst forth from within. All was lost, all was lost. After time beyond measure and stories beyond telling, his life was at an end. And so furious was he that he dug his nails into his own scalp and began to tear it apart, ripping at skin and flesh. A deep cut appeared in his forehead, extending quickly down the bridge of his nose as he pulled at himself before bisecting his mouth. One half of his head was now in each of his hands, the eyes rolling wildly, yet still he tore, the great wound continuing through his throat and chest and belly until it reached his thighs, whereupon his body at last became two separate pieces and fell entirely apart. From the two halves of the Crooked Man crawled every nasty spineless thing that ever lived: bugs and beetles and centipedes, spiders and pale white worms, all of them twisting and writhing and scurrying upon the floor until they, too, grew still, as the final grain of sand fell through the neck of the hourglass and the Crooked Man died.

Leroi looked down upon the mess, grinning. David had started to close his eyes, preparing to die, when Leroi suddenly shuddered. He opened his mouth to speak, and his jaw fell away and landed upon the stones at his feet. His skin began to crumble and flake like old plaster. He tried to move, but his legs would no longer support him. Instead, they broke at the knees, so that he fell forward on the ground, cracks appearing across his face and the backs of his hands. He tried to scrape at the ground, but his fingers shattered like glass. Only his eyes remained as they had been, but they were now filled with confusion and pain.

David watched Leroi dying. He alone understood what was happening.

"You were the king's nightmare, not mine," he said. "When you killed him, you killed yourself."

Leroi's eyes blinked uncomprehendingly, then ceased all movement. He became merely the broken statue of a beast, now without another's fear to animate it. Tiny fissures covered his entire body, and then he collapsed into a million pieces and was gone forever.

All around the throne room, the other Loups were crumbling to dust, and the common wolves, deprived of their leaders, began to retreat through the tunnel as more guards entered the throne room, their shields raised to form a wall of steel through which the tips of spears poked like the spines of a hedgehog. They ignored David as he picked up his sword and ran through the hallways of the castle, past frightened servants and bewildered courtiers, until he found himself in the open air. He climbed to the highest battlement and stared out over the landscape beyond. The wolf army had descended into confusion. Allies were turning on one another now, fighting, biting, the fast climbing over the slow in their urge to retreat and return to their old territories. Already great columns of wolves were fleeing for the hills. All that was left of the Loups were columns of dust that swirled for a moment, then were scattered to the four winds.

David felt a hand upon his arm and looked around to see a familiar face.

It was the Woodsman. There was wolf blood on his clothing and his skin. It dripped from the blade of his ax and pooled darkly on the floor.

David could not speak. He just dropped his sword and pack and hugged the Woodsman tightly. The Woodsman laid a hand on the boy's hand and stroked his hair gently.

"I thought you were dead," sighed David. "I saw the wolves drag you away."

"No wolf will take my life," he said. "I managed to fight my way to the horse breeder's cottage. I barricaded the door, then fell unconscious from my wounds. It was many days before I was well enough to follow your trail, and I could not get through the ranks of the wolves until now. But we must leave this place quickly. It will not stand for much longer."

David felt the battlements shake beneath his feet. A gap opened in the wall beneath his feet. Others appeared in the main buildings, and bricks and mortar began to tumble down to the cobblestones below. The labyrinth of tunnels beneath the castle was collapsing, and the world of kings and crooked men was coming apart.

The Woodsman led David down into the courtyard, where a horse was waiting, and told him to climb on, but David instead found Scylla in her barn. The horse, frightened by the sounds of battle and the howling of the wolves, whinnied with relief at the sight of the boy. David patted her forehead and whispered calming words to her, then mounted her and followed the Woodsman from the castle. Guards on horseback were already harassing the fleeing wolves, forcing them farther and farther away from the scene of the battle. A steady flow of people was moving through the main gates, servants and courtiers loaded down with whatever food or riches they could carry as they abandoned the castle before it fell into ruins around their ears. David and the Woodsman took a route that led them away from the confusion, pausing only when they were safely away from wolves and men, and stood upon the brow of a hill overlooking the castle. From there, they watched as it collapsed upon itself until all that was left was a hole in the ground marked by wood and brick and a cloud of filthy, choking dust. Then they turned their backs upon it and rode together for many days until they came at last to the forest where David had first entered this world. Now there was only one tree marked with twine, for all of the Crooked Man's magic had been undone with his death.

The Woodsman and David dismounted before the great tree.

"It is time," the Woodsman said. "Now you must go home."

XXXII

Of Rose

AVID STOOD in the middle of the forest, staring at the length of twine and the hollow in the tree that had now revealed itself once more. One of the trees nearby had recently been scored by the claws of an animal, and bloody sap dripped from the wound in its trunk, staining the snow beneath. A breeze stirred its neighbors so that their branches caressed its crown, calming it and reassuring it, making it aware of their presence. The clouds above were beginning to part, and sunlight speared through the gaps. The world was changing, transformed by the end of the Crooked Man.

"Now that it is time to leave, I'm not sure I want to go," said David. "I feel that there's more to see. I don't want things to go back to the way they were."

"There are people waiting for you on the other side," said the Woodsman. "You have to return to them. They love you, and without you their lives will be poorer. You have a father and a brother, and a woman who would be a mother to you, if you let her. You must go back, or else their lives will be blighted by your absence. In a way, you have already made your decision. You rejected the Crooked Man's bargain. You chose to live not here but in your own world."

David nodded. He knew that the Woodsman was right.

"There will be questions asked if you return as you are," said the Woodsman. "You must leave all that you are wearing behind, even your sword. You will have no need for it in your own world."

David took from his saddlebag the package containing his tattered pajamas and dressing gown and put them on behind a bush. His old clothes felt strange on him now. He had changed so much that they seemed as if they belonged to a different person, one who was vaguely familiar to him but younger and more foolish. They were the clothes of a child, and he was a child no longer.

"Tell me something, please," said David.

"Whatever you wish to know," said the Woodsman.

"You gave me clothing when I came here, the clothes of a boy. Did you ever have children?"

The Woodsman smiled. "They were all my children," he said. "Every one that was lost, every one that was found, every one that lived, and every one that died: all, all were mine, in their way."

"Did you know that the king was false when you began to lead me to him?" asked David. It was a question that had been troubling him ever since the Woodsman had reappeared. He could not believe this man would willingly lead him into danger.

"And what would you have done had I told you what I knew, or what I suspected, of the king and the trickster? When you came here, you were consumed by anger and grief. You would have given in to the blandishments of the Crooked Man, and then all would have been lost. I had hoped to guide you to the king myself, and on the journey I would have tried to help you see danger that you were in, but that was not to be. Instead, while others aided you along the way, it was your own strength and courage that brought you at last to an understanding of your place in this world and your own. You were a child when first I found you, but now you are becoming a man."

He stretched out his hand to the boy. David shook it, then released it and hugged the Woodsman. After a moment, the Woodsman returned the gesture, and they stayed that way, garlanded with sunlight, until the boy stepped away.

Then David went to Scylla and kissed the horse's brow. "I shall miss you," he whispered to her, and the horse neighed softly and nuzzled at the boy's neck.

David walked to the old tree and looked back at the Woodsman. "Can I ever come back here?" he asked, and the Woodsman said something very strange in reply.

"Most people come back here," he said, "in the end."

He raised his hand in farewell, and David took a deep breath and stepped into the trunk of the tree.

At first, he could smell only musk and earth and the dry decay of old leaves. He touched the inside of the tree and felt the roughness of its bark against his fingers. Although the tree was huge, he could not go for more than a few steps before striking the interior. His arm still hurt from where the Crooked Man had pierced him with his nails. He felt claustrophobic. There appeared to be no way out, but the Woodsman would not have lied to him. No, there must have been some mistake. He decided to step back outside again, but when he turned around, the entrance was gone. The tree had sealed itself up entirely, and now he was trapped inside. David began to shout for help and bang his fists against the wood, but his words simply echoed around him, bouncing back in his face, mocking him even as they faded.

But suddenly there was light. The tree was sealed, yet there was still illumination coming from above. David looked up and saw something sparkling like a star. As he watched, it grew and grew, descending toward where he stood. Or perhaps he was rising, ascending to meet it, for all of his senses were confused. He heard unfamiliar sounds—metal upon metal, the squeaking of wheels—and caught a sharp chemical smell from close by. He was seeing things—the light, the grooves and fissures of the tree trunk—but gradually he became aware that his eyes were closed. If that was the case, then how much more could he see once his eyes were open?

David opened his eyes.

He was lying on a metal bed in an unfamiliar room. Two large windows looked out on a green lawn where children walked with nurses by their sides or were wheeled in chairs by white-clad orderlies. There were flowers by his bedside. A needle was embedded in his right forearm, connected by a tube to a bottle on a steel frame. There was a tightness around his head. He reached up to touch it with his fingers and felt bandages instead of hair. He turned slowly to the left. The movement caused his neck to ache, and his head began to pound. Beside him, asleep in a chair, was Rose. Her clothes were wrinkled, and her hair was greasy and unwashed. A book lay upon her lap, its pages marked by a length of red ribbon.

David tried to speak, but his throat was too dry. He tried again and emitted a hoarse croak. Rose opened her eyes slowly and stared at him in disbelief.

"David?" she said.

He still couldn't speak properly. Rose poured water from a jug into a glass and placed it against his lips, supporting his head so he could drink more easily. David saw that she was crying. Some of her tears dripped onto his face as she took the glass away, and he tasted them as they fell into his mouth.

"Oh, David," she whispered. "We were so worried."

She placed the palm of her hand against his cheek, stroking him gently. She couldn't stop crying, but he could see that she was happy despite her tears.

"Rose," said David.

She leaned forward. "Yes, David, what is it?"

He took her hand in his.

"I'm sorry," he said.

And then he fell back into a dreamless sleep.

XXXIII

Of All That Was Lost and All That Was Found

I N THE DAYS that followed, David's father would often talk about how close David had come to being taken from them: of how they could find no trace of him in the aftermath of the crash, of how they'd been convinced that he had been burned alive in the wreckage, then, when no sign of him was discovered, fearful that he might have been abducted from them; how they had searched the house and gardens and forest, finally scouring the fields for him, assisted by their friends, by the police, even by passing strangers troubled by their pain; how they had returned to his room in the hope that he might have left some hint as to where he was going; how they had at last found a hidden space behind the wall of the sunken garden, and there he was, lying in the dirt, having somehow crawled through a crack in the stonework and then become trapped in the hollow by the falling rubble.

The doctors said that he had taken another of his fits, perhaps as a result of the trauma of the crash, and this one had caused him to lapse into a coma. David had stayed in a deep sleep for many days, until the morning when he awoke and spoke Rose's name. And even though there were aspects of his disappearance that could not be fully explained—what he had been doing out in the garden to begin with, and how he had come by some of the marks on his body—they were just glad to have him back, and no word of blame or anger was ever directed at him. Only much later, when he was out of danger and back in his own room, did Rose and his father, when they were alone in their bed at night, remark upon how much the incident had changed David, making him both quieter and more thoughtful of others; more affectionate toward Rose, and more understanding of her own difficulties in trying to find a place for herself in the lives of these two men, David and his father; more responsive to sudden noises and potential dangers, yet also more protective of those who were weaker than he, and of Georgie, his half brother, in particular.

The years went by, and David grew both too slowly and too quickly from a boy to a man: too slowly for him but too quickly for his father and Rose. Georgie grew too, and he and David remained as close as siblings can be, even after Rose and their father went their separate ways, as grown-ups will sometimes do. They divorced amicably, and neither of them ever married again. David went to university, and his father found a little cottage by a stream where he could fish upon his retirement. Rose and Georgie lived together in the big old house, and David visited them as often as he could, either alone or with his father. If time permitted, he would step into his old bedroom and listen for the sound of the books whispering to one another, but they were always silent. If the weather was good, he would descend to the remains of the sunken garden, repaired somewhat since the crash of the plane but still not quite as it once was, and stare silently at the cracks in its walls, but he never tried to enter it again and no one else did either.

But as time progressed, David discovered that about one thing at least the Crooked Man had not lied: his life was filled with great grief as well as great happiness, with suffering and regret as well as triumphs and contentment. David lost his father when he was thirty-two, his father's heart failing as he sat by the stream with a fishing rod in his hands, the sun shining upon his face so that, when he was found by a passerby hours after his death, his skin was still warm. Georgie attended the funeral in his army uniform, for another war had commenced to the east and Georgie was anxious to do his duty. He traveled to a land far from this one, and there he died alongside other young men whose dreams of honor and glory ended upon a muddy battlefield. His remains were shipped home and buried in a country churchyard beneath a small stone cross bearing his name, the dates of his birth and death, and the words "Beloved Son and Brother."

David married a woman with dark hair and green eyes. Her name was Alyson. They planned a family together, and the time came for Alyson to give birth to their child. But David was anxious for them both, for he could not forget the words of the Crooked Man: *"Those whom you care about—lovers, children—will fall by the wayside, and your love will not be enough to save them."*

There were complications during the birth. The son, whom they named George in honor of his uncle, was not strong enough to live, and in giving brief life to him Alyson lost her own, and so the Crooked Man's prophecy came to pass. David did not marry again, and he never had another child, but he became a writer and he wrote a book. He called it *The Book of Lost Things,* and the book that you are holding is the book that he wrote. And when children would ask him if it was true, he would tell them that, yes, it was true, or as true as anything in this world can be, for that was how he remembered it.

And they all became his children, in a way.

As Rose grew older and weaker, David looked after her. When Rose died, she left her house to David. He could have sold it, for by then it was worth a great deal of money, but he did not. Instead, he moved in and set up his little office downstairs, and he lived there contentedly for many years, always answering his door to the children who called—sometimes with their parents, sometimes alone—for the house was very famous, and a great many boys and girls wanted to see it. If they were very good, he would take them down to the sunken garden, although the cracks in the stonework had long been repaired, for David did not want children crawling in there and getting into trouble. Instead, he would talk to them of stories and books, and explain to them how stories wanted to be told and books wanted to be read, and how everything that they ever needed to know about life and the land of which he wrote, or about any land or realm that they could imagine, was contained in books.

And some of the children understood, and some did not.

In time, David himself grew frail and ill. He was no longer able to write, for his memory and eyesight were failing him, or even to walk very far to greet the children as once he had. (And this, too, the Crooked Man had told him, just as surely as if David had stared into the mirrored eyes of the lady in the dungeons.) There was nothing that the doctors could do for him except try to ease his pain a little. He hired a nurse to look after him, and his friends came to spend time by his side. As the end drew near, he requested that a bed be made up for him in the great library downstairs, and each night he slept surrounded by the books he had loved as a boy and as a man. He also quietly asked his gardener to perform one simple task for him, and to tell no one else of it, and the gardener did as he requested, for he loved the old man very much.

And in the deepest, darkest hours of the night, David would lie awake and listen. The books had started whispering again, yet he felt no fear. They spoke softly, offering words of comfort and grace. Sometimes they told the stories that he had always loved, but now his own was among them.

One night, when his breathing had grown very shallow and the light in his eyes had begun to dim at last, David rose from his bed in the library and slowly made his way to the door, pausing only to pick up a book along the way. It was an old leather-bound album, and in it were photographs and letters, cards and trinkets, drawings and poems, locks of hair and a pair of wedding rings, all of the relics of a life long lived, except this time the life was his. The whispering of the books grew louder, the voices of the tomes rising in a great chorus of joy, for one story was about to end and a new story would soon be born. The old man caressed their spines in farewell as he passed from the room, then left the library and the house for the last time to walk through the damp grass to where the sunken garden lay.

In one corner, a hole had been opened by the gardener, big enough to accommodate a grown man. David got down on his hands and knees and painfully crawled into the space until he found himself in the cavity behind the brickwork. Then he sat in the darkness and waited. At first nothing happened, and he had to struggle to keep his eyes from closing, but after a time he saw a light growing, and felt a cool breeze upon his face. He smelled tree bark and fresh grass and flowers in bloom. A hollow opened before him, and he stepped through it and found himself in the heart of a great forest. The land had changed forever. There were no longer beasts like men or unformed nightmares that waited for their chance to trap the unwary. There was no more fear, no more endless twilight. Even the childlike flowers were gone, for the blood of children was no longer shed in shadowy places and their souls were at rest. The sun was setting, but it was a beautiful sight, lighting the sky with purple and red and orange as the long day came to its peaceful close.

A man was standing before David. He carried an ax in one hand and in the other a garland of flowers, gathered by him as he walked through the forest and bound together with lengths of long grass.

"I came back," said David, and the Woodsman smiled.

"Most people do, in the end," he replied, and David wondered at how like his father the Woodsman was, and how he had failed to notice it before.

"Come along," said the Woodsman. "We've been waiting for you."

And David saw himself reflected in the Woodsman's eyes, and there he was no longer old but a young man, for a man is always his father's child no matter how old he is or how long they have been apart.

David followed the Woodsman down forest paths, through glades and over brooks, until they came at last to a cottage with smoke rising lazily from its chimney. A horse stood in a small field nearby, nibbling contentedly at the grass, and as David approached, it raised its head and neighed in delight, shaking its mane as it trotted across the field to greet him. David walked to the fence and bowed his head to Scylla's. Scylla closed her eyes as he kissed her brow, then shadowed his footsteps as he approached the house, sometimes nudging gently at his shoulder as though to remind him of her presence.

The door of the cottage opened, and a woman appeared. She had dark hair and green eyes. In her arms she held a baby boy, barely out of the womb, who clutched at her blouse as she walked, for a lifetime was but a moment in that place, and each man dreams his own heaven.

And in the darkness David closed his eyes, as all that was lost was found again.

A Conversation with John Connolly

It's a terrible question to ask, but where did the idea for *The Book of Lost Things* come from?

I can probably give you a terrible answer to that question, then, because I don't know. I've tried to analyze some of the elements that went into its creation in the notes that follow, but they really don't explain how it came into being. I wanted to write about childhood and grief, about that transition from childhood to adulthood, but I suppose I knew that I would end up mining my own childhood for much of the novel, and that was colored by books and stories. Thinking about it now, I delved very deeply into my past, and into my own fears as both a child and an adult. I'm surprised by what came out, and I can't help but feel that the book gives form to a great deal of material that was sitting around in my subconscious. I just hope that others will see echoes of themselves in it. I think that they will. After all, I know the elemental stories that provide the backbone of the book have survived for a reason, and if they had that kind of impact on me then they will probably have had a similar impact on others.

You've made it quite clear that you don't consider this to be a children's book, yet it's a book that many children might well enjoy. Can you elaborate a little on that?

I think that it's a book about childhood, or more specifically that period or moment when a child becomes very aware of the reality of the world in which he lives: that it is difficult, that it owes no debt to the souls who inhabit it, that it is likely to be filled with a certain amount of pain and loss, and that, ultimately, human beings are powerless against the force of mortality. Something is lost at that moment. I don't want to call it innocence, because I find it hard to remember when I was ever innocent, even as a child. There is always an awareness in children of their own vulnerability, however deeply buried it may be, and I think that is what the great folktales and fairy tales tap into. Yet they are also very affirmative, positive stories, in that their ultimate message is that these challenges can and must be overcome as part of the transition from childhood to adulthood.

So you're right: an older child could certainly read the book, but I think a child will read it differently from an adult, and that has been my experience of the book's reception so far. Adults have been far more aware of the theme of loss in the book, and its final chapter will resonate more with adults than with children. In fact, I've been very surprised by some of the interpretations that readers have drawn from it. Elements of it are quite deliberately ambiguous, so it's not entirely unexpected, but I suppose what has pleased me most is that adults have applied their own experiences to the book, and that has affected the way in which they read it and understand it.

How autobiographical is it?

Well, I never entirely retreated into a world of my own creation, but I did use books both as a means of escape and then, gradually, to help me understand the world, which is something that I still do. There are elements of David's character that are very similar to mine as a child: the love of books, obviously, but also some of his fears about his parents and their mortality, which I think is common to a lot of children. The description of David's encounter with the psychiatrist is pretty much drawn from memory. My parents took me to a psychiatrist when I was twelve or thirteen, and it wasn't a very satisfactory experience for anyone involved. I can clearly recall his frustration as I painstakingly drew the pictures he had asked me to draw. He eventually concluded that I was a worrier, which wasn't entirely helpful. It was a little bit like going to the doctor and being told that you were ill, but without any attempt being made to actually diagnose the problem. After all, I would hardly have been at a psychiatrist's office if I weren't worried about something.

David's obsessive compulsive disorder is something that I suffered from for a time, although not to a debilitating degree. I think it was a product of my fears for my family's safety, and a desire to feel that I could exercise some kind of control over the world that they inhabited. It went away after a few years as I gradually matured, but I still think that, on some level, it was not an unnatural reaction to the adult world.

There is a particular fascination with fairy tales and folktales in the book. Why is that?

Because they're so elemental, I suppose. I was always interested in something that the Brothers Grimm wrote in the introduction to one of their collections. They said that every society, and every age, produced its own version of the same tales. I think I saw some similarities between the earlier tales and elements of mystery and supernatural fiction, which was why they found their way into my earlier books too. In *The Book of Lost Things,* they become the building blocks for the creation of the world into which David retreats after the death of his mother. They are the first stories, the essence of later tales, and so he returns to them and, over the course of the book, learns from the variations upon them that he himself composes in his imagination.

The Book of Lost Things will, I suppose, be described in some areas as a complete departure for you after the mystery novels and supernatural stories for which you're best known. Do you agree?

Not entirely. I think it just finds a new way to approach some of the themes that have always interested me, particularly the overcoming of grief and loss, and a fascination with the ways in which children contain the seeds of the adults they will become, and the manner in which childhood trauma can affect that adult in later life. That's clear right from the book's dedication: "For in every adult dwells the child that was, and in every child lies the adult that will be."

The interest in folktales and fairy tales that was present in the earlier books is simply made explicit here. *Every Dead Thing* used images of child-stealing and the wicked witch in connection with the killer Adelaide Modine, and much of *Dark Hollow* was based on the tropes and conventions of fairy tales: the dark woods, the hidden child, the ogre in the forest. Equally, some of the stories from *Nocturnes* could have found a home in *The Book of Lost Things,* particularly "The Erlking" or "The New Daughter." Structurally, too, the book echoes elements of the earlier books. Right from the beginning I've used tales told within tales to further the action, or to provide the reader with information about the characters' pasts. In *The Book of Lost Things,* the stories have a subtler function. While they appear to be told to David, it is in fact David who chooses both the tales and the tellers, instinctively recognizing in the stories a lesson about how he can overcome the difficulties in which he finds himself emotionally.

It is a book that, from the beginning, endorses the act of reading as a means of engaging with the realities of our existence.

Well, David, the child at the heart of the book, creates a world out of the books and stories he has read. He finds a way to externalize his fears and his demons through stories, and in that way he can begin to deal with them.

I think the act of reading imbues the reader with a sensitivity toward the outside world that people who don't read can sometimes lack. I know it seems like a contradiction in terms; after all, reading is such a solitary, internalizing act that it appears to represent a disengagement from day-to-day life. But reading, and particularly the reading of fiction, encourages us to view the world in new and challenging ways. I have always believed that fiction acts as a prism, taking the reality of our existence and breaking it down into its constituent parts, allowing us to see it in a completely different form. It allows us to inhabit the consciousness of another, which is a precursor to empathy, and empathy is, for me, one of the marks of a decent human being.

Can you see yourself returning to the world of this book?

I don't know. In one way, there's just so much to explore in these tales, and I've only just scratched the surface, but perhaps there are other ways to examine them and to come to an understanding of them. There is a kind of perfect unity to *The Book of Lost Things*. It begins as it should begin, and it ends exactly how it should end—for me at least. I think that these old stories will always influence me, but for now, *The Book of Lost Things* can stand on its own. I've written the best book that I could possibly write at this stage, being the person and writer that I am. I can live with what I've done here.

*Of Fairy Tales, Dark Towers, and
Other Such Matters*

Some Notes on *The Book of Lost Things*

RUMPELSTILTSKIN

*In truth, the Crooked Man had no name. Others could call him what they
wished, but he was a being so old that the names given to him by men had
no meaning for him: Trickster; The Crooked Man; Rumpel—*
    Oh, but what was that name again? Never mind, never mind . . .
                    —*The Book of Lost Things,* Chapter XXIX

OF "RUMPELSTILTSKIN"

The most important figure in *The Book of Lost Things,* apart from
David himself, is the Crooked Man. In the novel, he owes part of
his ancestry to Rumpelstiltskin, the dwarf who spins straw into
gold for a poor miller's daughter, but who demands her firstborn
child in return, and only by guessing his name can she thwart
him. But the Crooked Man is also referred to as a "trickster" in
the book, and that name carries with it a certain amount of
mythological baggage.

Tricksters are rule-breakers, such as the Norse god Loki (who
tricks the blind Hod into killing his twin brother, Balder, with a
sprig of mistletoe), Reynard the Fox in French folktales, or the
raven and the coyote in Native American stories. That rule-
breaking usually takes the form of theft or, as the name suggests,
trickery.

The trickster is an important archetype, a mischievous, sometimes malicious creature who survives the challenges of the world
through deceit. Despite the damage he causes, he leads those who
encounter him to confront their own deficiencies and the defi-

ciencies of the society in which they exist. In other words, even as he tears things down, he leads to the creation of other, better structures in their place. In a sense, he represents the part of the human psyche that is unrestricted by convention, the imaginative capability that enables us to confront, and overcome, our problems.

The trickster is also a shape-shifter, Joseph Campbell's *Hero with a Thousand Faces* given form. He is a survivor, being born and reborn, and in that way he symbolizes a creation mythology that links into Christianity and the possibility of eternal life. Symbols of clocks and time adhere to the trickster (an hourglass in the case of *The Book of Lost Things*). He is also associated with storytelling, which, in *The Book of Lost Things,* gives him much of his power.

ORIGINS

While the best-known version of "Rumpelstiltskin" remains that of the Brothers Grimm (first published by them in 1812), there are English, Italian, and Swedish variations as well, and the character has gone by many names: Titeliture, Panzimanzi, Whuppity Stoorie, and Purzinigele among them. In certain rural communities spinning was a marital test, and the Grimms altered some aspects of their source material to give their version of the tale a unique, er, spin, if you will excuse the dreadful pun. In some oral versions of the tale, the girl's problem is not that she cannot fulfil her promise to spin gold from straw, but that she can spin *only* gold. Looked at in a certain way (admittedly only by excluding Rumpelstiltskin's desire for the girl's child), it is possible to see the dwarf as a benevolent figure, and some versions of the tale allow him to escape without harm in the end.

"Rumpelstiltskin" is also slightly problematical in that there is a great deal of deception and greed at work here, even in characters for whom we may be supposed to feel a degree of affection. It is, after all, the poor miller who gets his daughter into all this trouble to begin with by lying to the king, and the king himself is greedy enough to want to put his wife-to-be to work on increasingly larger amounts of straw. In fact, it could be argued that the only person in the story who is not guilty of deceit on some level is Rumpelstiltskin himself, who is up front about his demands at all times, and even feels enough pity for the girl to engage in a guessing game at the end, though he has no obligation other than to adhere to the original agreement.

In *The Book of Lost Things,* the Crooked Man is a considerably more malevolent version of this character, albeit with many of the traits identifiable from the trickster myths. Nevertheless, even in his malevolence it is he who ultimately forces David to recognize his responsibilities toward the infant, Georgie, who has invaded his life.

Variations on the tale can be found in Emma Donoghue's *Kissing the Witch* ("The Tale of the Spinster"), William Hathaway's *Disenchantments* ("Rumpelstiltskin"), and Anne Sexton's *Transformations* ("Rumpelstiltskin").

Rumpelstiltskin

The Brothers Grimm

Once there was a miller who was poor, but who had a beautiful daughter. Now it happened that he had to go and speak to the king, and in order to make himself appear important he said to him: "I have a daughter who can spin straw into gold." The king said to the miller: "That is an art which pleases me well, if your daughter is as clever as you say, bring her tomorrow to my palace, and I will put her to the test."

And when the girl was brought to him he took her into a room which was quite full of straw, gave her a spinning-wheel and a reel, and said: "Now set to work, and if by tomorrow morning early you have not spun this straw into gold during the night, you must die." Thereupon he himself locked up the room, and left her in it alone. So there sat the poor miller's daughter, and for the life of her she could not tell what to do. She had no idea how straw could be spun into gold, and she grew more and more frightened, until at last she began to weep.

But all at once the door opened, and in came a little man.

"Good evening, mistress miller," he said. "Why are you crying so?"

"Alas," answered the girl, "I have to spin straw into gold, and I do not know how to do it."

"What will you give me if I do it for you?" asked the dwarf.

"My necklace," said the girl.

The little man took the necklace, seated himself in front of the wheel, and *whirr, whirr, whirr,* three turns, and the reel was full, then he put another on, and *whirr, whirr, whirr,* three times round, and the second was full too. And so it went on until the morning, when all the straw was spun, and all the reels were full of gold.

By daybreak the king was already there, and when he saw the gold he was astonished and delighted, but his heart became only more greedy. He had the miller's daughter taken into another room full of straw, which was much larger, and commanded her to spin that also in one night if she valued her life. The girl knew not how to help herself, and was crying, when the door opened again, and the little man appeared, and said:

"What will you give me if I spin that straw into gold for you?"

"The ring on my finger," answered the girl.

The little man took the ring, again began to turn the wheel, and by morning had spun all the straw into glittering gold.

The king rejoiced beyond measure at the sight, but still he had not gold enough, and he had the miller's daughter taken into a still larger room full of straw, and said: "You must spin this, too, in the course of this night, but if you succeed, you shall be my wife."

Even if she be a miller's daughter, thought he, I could not find a richer wife in the whole world. When the girl was alone the dwarf came again for the third time, and said: "What will you give me if I spin the straw for you this time also?"

"I have nothing left that I could give," answered the girl.

"Then promise me, if you should become queen, to give me your first child."

Who knows whether that will ever happen, thought the miller's daughter, and, not knowing how else to help herself in this strait, she promised the dwarf what he wanted, and for that he once more spun the straw into gold.

And when the king came in the morning, and found all as he had wished, he took her in marriage, and the pretty miller's daughter became a queen. A year after, she brought a beautiful child into the world, and she never gave a thought to the dwarf. But suddenly he came into her room, and said: "Now give me what you promised."

The queen was horror-struck, and offered the dwarf all the riches of the kingdom if he would leave her the child. But the dwarf said: "No, something alive is dearer to me than all the treasures in the world."

Then the queen began to lament and cry, so that the dwarf pitied her. "I will give you three days," said he. "If by that time you find out my name, then shall you keep your child."

So the queen thought the whole night of all the names that she had ever heard, and she sent a messenger over the country to inquire, far and wide, for any other names that there might be. When the dwarf came the next day, she began with Caspar, Melchior, Balthazar, and said all the names she knew, one after another, but to every one the little man said: "That is not my name." On the second day she had inquiries made in the neighborhood as to the names of the people there, and she repeated to the dwarf the most uncommon and curious. "Perhaps your name is Shortribs, or Sheepshanks, or Laceleg," she said, but he always answered: "That is not my name."

On the third day the messenger came back again, and said: "I have not been able to find a single new name, but as I came to a high mountain at the end of the forest, where the fox and the hare bid each other good night, there I saw a little house, and before the house a fire was burning, and round about the fire quite a ridiculous little man was jumping; he hopped upon one leg and shouted—

"Today I bake, tomorrow brew,
the next I'll have the young queen's child.
Ha, glad am I that no one knew
that Rumpelstiltskin I am styled."

You may imagine how glad the queen was when she heard the name. And when soon afterwards the little man came in, and asked, "Now, mistress queen, what is my name?" at first she said:

"Is your name Conrad?"

"No."

"Is your name Harry?"

"No."

"Perhaps your name is Rumpelstiltskin?"

"The devil has told you that! The devil has told you that," cried the little man, and in his anger he plunged his right foot so deep into the earth that his whole leg went in, and then in rage he pulled at his left leg so hard with both hands that he tore himself in two.

THE WATER OF LIFE

This new world was too painful to cope with. . . . This world was not like the world of his stories. In that world, good was rewarded and evil was punished. If you kept to the path and stayed out of the forest, then you would be safe. If someone was sick, like the old king in one of the tales, then his sons could be sent out into the world to seek the remedy, the Water of Life, and if just one of them was brave enough and true enough, then the king's life could be saved. David had been brave. His mother had been braver still. In the end, bravery had not been enough. This was a world that did not reward it. The more David thought about it, the more he did not want to be part of such a world.

—*The Book of Lost Things,* Chapter II

OF "THE WATER OF LIFE"

It's easy to see why this is such a potent tale for David, even though it is referred to only in passing in *The Book of Lost Things.* The loss of a parent is a child's greatest fear. In David's case, that fear is made real when his mother dies, and he realizes the disparity between the tale he has read and the reality of human mortality. Yet this tale is also referenced in the book because of the king's response to his sons when they beg to be allowed to find the water of life: "I would rather die." In his reply is a recognition of the natural order of things, that the old should pass on eventually and the young survive. Much of the trouble that follows is caused by the usurpation of this natural order.

Finally, there is the theme of fraternal arrogance and betrayal.

David is guilty of the former at times in the novel, based largely on his inability to come to terms with the intrusion of Rose and his half-brother, Georgie, into his family life. This in turn raises the possibility of betrayal, which the Crooked Man recognizes and uses against David throughout *The Book of Lost Things*.

The Water of Life

The Brothers Grimm

There was once a King who had an illness, and no one believed that he would come out of it with his life. He had three sons who were much distressed about it, and went down into the palace-garden and wept. There they met an old man who inquired as to the cause of their grief. They told him that their father was so ill that he would most certainly die, for nothing seemed to cure him. Then the old man said, "I know of one more remedy, and that is the water of life; if he drinks of it he will become well again; but it is hard to find." The eldest said, "I will manage to find it," and went to the sick King, and begged to be allowed to go forth in search of the water of life, for that alone could save him.

"No," said the King, "the danger of it is too great. I would rather die."

But he begged so long that the King consented. The prince thought in his heart, "If I bring the water, then I shall be best beloved of my father, and I shall inherit the kingdom."

So he set out, and when he had ridden forth a little distance, a dwarf stood there in the road who called to him and said, "Whither away so fast?"

"Silly shrimp," said the prince, very haughtily, "it is nothing to do with you," and rode on. But the little dwarf had grown angry, and had wished an evil wish. Soon after this the prince entered a ravine, and the further he rode the closer the mountains drew together, and at last the road became so narrow that he could not advance a step further; it was impossible either to turn his horse or to dismount from the saddle, and he was shut in there as if in prison. The sick King waited long for him, but he came not.

Then the second son said, "Father, let me go forth to seek the water," and thought to himself, "If my brother is dead, then the kingdom will fall to me."

At first the King would not allow him to go either, but at last he yielded, so the prince set out on the same road that his brother had taken, and he too met the dwarf, who stopped him to ask whither he was going in such haste?

"Little shrimp," said the prince, "that is nothing to thee," and rode on without giving him another look. But the dwarf bewitched him, and he, like the other, rode into a ravine, and could neither go forwards nor backwards. So fare haughty people.

As the second son also remained away, the youngest begged to be allowed to go forth to fetch the water, and at last the King was obliged to let him go. When he met the dwarf and the latter asked him whither he was going in such haste, he stopped, gave him an explanation, and said, "I am seeking the water of life, for my father is sick unto death."

"Dost thou know, then, where that is to be found?"

"No," said the prince.

"As thou hast borne thyself as is seemly, and not haughtily like thy false brothers, I will give thee the information and tell thee how thou mayst obtain the water of life," said the dwarf. "It springs from a fountain in the courtyard of an enchanted castle, but thou wilt not be able to make thy way to it, if I do not give thee an iron wand and two small loaves of bread. Strike thrice with the wand on the iron door of the castle and it will spring open: inside lie two lions with gaping jaws, but if thou throwest a loaf to each of them, they will be quieted. Then hasten to fetch some of the water of life before the clock strikes twelve, else the door will shut again, and thou wilt be imprisoned."

The prince thanked him, took the wand and the bread, and set out on his way. When he arrived, everything was as the dwarf had said. The door sprang open at the third stroke of the wand, and when he had appeased the lions with the bread, he entered the castle, and came to a large and splendid hall, wherein sat some enchanted princes whose rings he drew off their fingers. A sword and a loaf of bread were lying there, which he carried away. After this, he entered a chamber, in which was a beautiful maiden who rejoiced when she saw him, kissed him, and told him that he had delivered her, and should have the whole of her kingdom, and that if he would return in a year their wedding should be celebrated; likewise she told him where the spring of the water of life was, and that he was to hasten and draw some of it before the clock struck twelve.

Then he went onwards, and at last entered a room where there was a beautiful newly made bed, and as he was very weary, he felt inclined to rest a little. So he lay down and fell asleep. When he awoke, it was striking a quarter to twelve. He sprang up in a fright, ran to the spring, drew some water in a cup which stood near, and hastened away. But just as he was passing through the iron door, the clock struck twelve, and the door fell to with such violence that it carried away a piece of his heel. He, however, rejoicing at having obtained the water of life, went homewards, and again passed the dwarf. When the latter saw the sword and the loaf, he said, "With these thou hast won great wealth; with the sword thou canst slay whole armies, and the bread will never come to an end." But the prince would not go home to his father without his brothers, and said, "Dear dwarf, canst thou not tell me where my two brothers are? They went out before I did in search of the water of life, and have not returned."

"They are imprisoned between two mountains," said the dwarf. "I have condemned them to stay there, because they were so haughty."

Then the prince begged until the dwarf released them; but he warned him, however, and said, "Beware of them, for they have bad hearts." When his brothers came, he rejoiced, and told them how things had gone with him, that he had found the water of life and had brought a cupful away with him, and had rescued a beautiful princess, who was willing to wait a year for him, and then their wedding was to be celebrated and he would obtain a great kingdom. After that they rode on together, and chanced upon a land where war and famine reigned, and the King already thought he must perish, for the scarcity was so great.

Then the prince went to him and gave him the loaf, wherewith he fed and satisfied the whole of his kingdom, and then the prince gave him the sword also wherewith he slew the hosts of his enemies, and could now live in rest and peace. The prince then took back his loaf and his sword, and the three brothers rode on. But after this they entered two more countries where war and famine reigned and each time the prince gave his loaf and his sword to the Kings, and had now delivered three kingdoms, and after that they went on board a ship and sailed over the sea.

During the passage, the two eldest conversed apart and said, "The youngest has found the water of life and not we. For that our father will give him the kingdom which belongs to us, and he will rob us of all our fortune." They then began to seek revenge, and plotted with each other to destroy him. They waited until they found him fast asleep, then they poured the water of life out of the cup, and took it for themselves, but into the cup they poured salt sea-water.

Now therefore, when they arrived home, the youngest took his cup to the sick King in order that he might drink out of it, and be cured. But scarcely had he drunk a very little of the salt sea-water than he became still worse than before. And as he was lamenting over this, the two eldest brothers came, and accused the youngest of having intended to poison him, and said that they had brought him the true water of life, and handed it to him. He had scarcely tasted it, when he felt his sickness departing, and became strong and healthy as in the days of his youth.

After that they both went to the youngest, mocked him, and said, "You certainly found the water of life, but you have had the pain, and we the gain; you should have been sharper, and should have kept your eyes open. We took it from you whilst you were asleep at sea, and when a year is over, one of us will go and fetch the beautiful princess. But beware that you do not disclose aught of this to our father; indeed he does not trust you, and if you say a single word, you shall lose your life into the bargain, but if you keep silent, you shall have it as a gift."

The old King was angry with his youngest son, and thought he had plotted against his life. So he summoned the court together and had sentence pronounced upon his son, that he should be secretly shot. And once when the prince was riding forth to the chase, suspecting no evil, the King's huntsman had to go with him, and when they were quite alone in the forest, the huntsman looked so sorrowful that the prince said to him, "Dear huntsman, what ails you?"

The huntsman said, "I cannot tell you, and yet I ought."

Then the prince said, "Say openly what it is, I will pardon you."

"Alas!" said the huntsman, "I am to shoot you dead. The King has ordered me to do it."

Then the prince was shocked, and said, "Dear huntsman, let

me live; there, I give you my royal garments; give me your common ones in their stead."

The huntsman said, "I will willingly do that, indeed I should not have been able to shoot you." Then they exchanged clothes, and the huntsman returned home; the prince, however, went further into the forest. After a time three wagons of gold and precious stones came to the King for his youngest son, which were sent by the three Kings who had slain their enemies with the prince's sword, and maintained their people with his bread, and who wished to show their gratitude for it.

The old King then thought, "Can my son have been innocent?" and said to his people, "Would that he were still alive, how it grieves me that I have suffered him to be killed!"

"He still lives," said the huntsman. "I could not find it in my heart to carry out your command," and told the King how it had happened. Then a stone fell from the King's heart, and he had it proclaimed in every country that his son might return and be taken into favour again.

The princess, however, had a road made up to her palace which was quite bright and golden, and told her people that whosoever came riding straight along it to her, would be the right wooer and was to be admitted, and whoever rode by the side of it, was not the right one, and was not to be admitted. As the time was now close at hand, the eldest thought he would hasten to go to the King's daughter, and give himself out as her deliverer, and thus win her for his bride, and the kingdom to boot.

Therefore he rode forth, and when he arrived in front of the palace, and saw the splendid golden road, he thought, it would be a sin and a shame if he were to ride over that, and turned aside, and rode on the right side of it. But when he came to the door, the servants told him that he was not the right man, and was to go away again. Soon after this the second prince set out, and when he came to the golden road, and his horse had put one foot on it, he thought, it would be a sin and a shame to tread a piece of it off, and he turned aside and rode on the left side of it, and when he reached the door, the attendants told him he was not the right one, and he was to go away again.

When at last the year had entirely expired, the third son likewise wished to ride out of the forest to his beloved, and with her forget his sorrows. So he set out and thought of her so incessantly, and wished to be with her so much, that he never noticed the golden road at all. So his horse rode onwards up the middle of it, and when he came to the door, it was opened and the princess received him with joy, and said he was her deliverer, and lord of the kingdom, and their wedding was celebrated with great rejoicing. When it was over she told him that his father invited him to come to him, and had forgiven him. So he rode thither, and told him everything; how his brothers had betrayed him, and how he had nevertheless kept silence. The old King wished to punish them, but they had put to sea, and never came back as long as they lived.

LITTLE RED RIDING HOOD

Once upon a time, there was a girl who lived on the outskirts of the forest. She was lively and bright, and she wore a red cloak, for that way if she ever went astray she could easily be found . . .
—*The Book of Lost Things,* Chapter IX

OF "LITTLE RED RIDING HOOD"

The Woodsman tells David this story to explain the origin of the Loups, itself the French word for wolves and one half of the French word for werewolf, *loup-garou,* so the Woodsman's story brings together one fairy tale and one legend. The strong presence of the Loups in *The Book of Lost Things* is due in part to Jonathan Tulvey's fear of wolves, which is communicated to David, but also because, of all the wild animals that might stalk the forests in his imagination, wolves are surely the worst and seem to exercise a particularly strong grasp on human fears. The threat they evoke is that of being devoured, of being consumed by another. We tend to sentimentalize other animals, such as bears (an error brilliantly pointed up in Werner Herzog's documentary *Grizzly Man*), but wolves tend not to be perceived in the same way. They hunt as a pack. They are intelligent. They are perceived as potentially dangerous. That it should be the myth of the werewolf, a man overcome by the wolf within, that persists rather than, say, a story of a man becoming like a bear or a boar—both more dangerous to humans in their way—says a great deal about our attitude not only toward these animals but toward the potential of the beast within us all. And in Leroi, the king of the Loups, half-man, half-beast, the Big Bad Wolf who talks and schemes finds a new form and purpose.

The sexual undertones to "Little Red Riding Hood," explored to varying degrees by different interpreters of the tale, are made quite explicit in *The Book of Lost Things*. In fact, the Red Riding Hood figure becomes the sexual aggressor, seducing the wolf who does his best to avoid contact with her. As elsewhere in the book, this can be seen as a reflection of David's own dawning sexual awareness but also as his understanding of the sexual nature of the relationship between his father and Rose. Early in the book, he hears Rose laugh in a "low, throaty way" as a prelude to sex, and later the Crooked Man uses images of them together in an effort to fuel David's anger.

ORIGINS

Stories and myths of consumption have an ancient history. The mythological figure of Cronos swallows his children, only for them to return miraculously from his belly, with a stone replacing each swallowed child. An eleventh-century Latin story, "Fecunda ratis," tells of a little girl in a red cap found in a pack of wolves. The first literary adaptation of the Riding Hood tale comes from Perrault in 1697. That version tends not to be terribly popular now, since it ends with Red Riding Hood being devoured by the wolf and, unlike in the more familiar versions, staying inside it to be digested. The Grimms made further changes to their source material, because in earlier versions Red Riding Hood is portrayed as a clever young woman who uses her intelligence to outwit the wolf, even stripping naked in one telling in order to distract him, then going outside to relieve herself before promptly running away. The Grimms made the story more of a cautionary tale about a little girl who, despite stern injunctions to the contrary, strays from the path, distracted by flowers and butterflies, thereby allowing the wolf the time it needs to act against her and her grandmother. Arguably, they also removed much of the obvious eroticism apparent in earlier versions, although it doesn't take a great deal of imagination to inject it right back in again. (Incidentally, the Little Red Riding Hood Project—www.usm.edu/english/fairy tales/lrrh/lrrhhome.htm—at the University of Southern Mississippi's website contains an archive of sixteen versions of the tale, as well as a range of images, that provides an opportunity to examine a number of other approaches to the story.)

Bruno Bettelheim, in *The Uses of Enchantment,* is quite dismissive of Perrault's version, arguing that in his desire to teach a moral lesson, he turns the wolf from a ravenous beast into little more than a metaphor with hair. Nobody warns Perrault's Red Riding Hood not to stray from the path, and Perrault's moral can best be summarized as "Be careful when talking to strange men." In fact, just in case the moral isn't clear enough, Perrault provides a little poem at the end of the tale, to clarify things for the reader.

From this story one learns that children,
Especially young girls,
Pretty, well bred, and genteel,
Are wrong to listen to just anyone,
And it's not at all strange,
If a wolf ends up eating them.
I say a wolf, but not all wolves
Are exactly the same.
Some are perfectly charming,
Not loud, brutal, or angry

But tame, pleasant, and gentle,
Following young ladies into their homes, into their chambers,
But watch out if you haven't learned that tame wolves
Are the most dangerous of all.

So now you know. While there is a warning in the Grimms' tale, it is implicit rather than explicit, rearing its head only in the mother's warning to her daughter. Applying the sexual interpretation that has fueled so many versions of the tale, both old and modern, the real danger faced by Red Riding Hood is her sexuality, a consequence of which is her ambivalent response to the wolf's overtures. (The Grimms produced a second version that contains an addition in which Red Riding Hood again encounters a wolf on her way to her grandmother's house, but this time runs straight to the older woman, and together they repel the wolf's advances, eventually drowning him in a water trough to dampen his ardor.)

One of the most notable modern adaptations of the tale is contained in Angela Carter's wonderful collection *The Bloody Chamber,* which in turn inspired Neil Jordan's film *The Company of Wolves.* Another unusual film version of the tale is the 1996 movie *Freeway,* with Reese Witherspoon as a runaway in a red jacket menaced by a serial killer.

Little Red Riding Hood

The Brothers Grimm

Once upon a time there was a sweet little girl. Whoever laid eyes upon her could not help but love her. But it was her grandmother who loved her most. She could never give the child enough. Once she made her a present, a small, red velvet cap, and since it was so becoming and the girl insisted on always wearing it, she was called Little Red Riding Hood.

One day her mother said to her, "Come, Little Red Riding Hood, take this piece of cake and bottle of wine and bring them to your grandmother. She's sick and weak, and this will strengthen her. Get an early start, before it becomes hot, and when you're out in the woods, be nice and good and don't stray from the path, otherwise you'll fall and break the glass, and your grandmother will get nothing. And when you enter her room, don't forget to say good morning, and don't go peeping in all the corners."

"I'll do just as you say," Little Red Riding Hood promised her mother.

Well, the grandmother lived out in the forest, half an hour from the village, and as soon as Little Red Riding Hood entered the forest, she encountered the wolf. However, Little Red Riding Hood did not know what a wicked sort of an animal he was and was not afraid of him.

"Good day, Little Red Riding Hood," he said.

"Thank you kindly, wolf."

"Where are you going so early, Little Red Riding Hood?"

"To Grandmother's."

"What are you carrying under your apron?"

"Cake and wine. My grandmother's sick and weak, and yesterday we baked this so it will help her get well."

"Where does your grandmother live, Little Red Riding Hood?"

"Another quarter of an hour from here in the forest. Her house is under the three big oak trees. You can tell it by the hazel bushes," said Little Red Riding Hood.

The wolf thought to himself, This tender young thing is a juicy morsel. She'll taste even better than the old woman. You've got to be real crafty if you want to catch them both. Then he walked next to Little Red Riding Hood, and after a while he said, "Little Red Riding Hood, just look at the beautiful flowers that are growing all around you! Why don't you look around? I believe you haven't even noticed how lovely the birds are singing. You march along as if you were going straight to school, and yet it's so delightful out here in the woods!"

Little Red Riding Hood looked around and saw how the rays of the sun were dancing through the trees back and forth and how the woods were full of beautiful flowers. So she thought to herself, If I bring Grandmother a bunch of fresh flowers, she'd certainly like that. It's still early, and I'll arrive on time. So she ran off the path and plunged into the woods to look for flowers. And each time she plucked one, she thought she saw another even prettier flower and ran after it, going deeper and deeper into the forest. But the wolf went straight to the grandmother's house and knocked at the door.

"Who's out there?"

"Little Red Riding Hood. I've brought you some cake and wine. Open up."

"Just lift the latch," the grandmother called. "I'm too weak and can't get up."

The wolf lifted the latch, and the door sprang open. Then he went straight to the grandmother's bed without saying a word and gobbled her up. Next he put on her clothes and her nightcap, lay down in her bed, and drew the curtains.

Meanwhile, Little Red Riding Hood had been running around looking for flowers, and only when she had as many as she could carry did she remember her grandmother and continue on the way to her house again. She was puzzled when she found the door open, and as she entered the room, it seemed so strange inside that she thought, Oh, goodness, how frightened I feel today, and usually I like to be at Grandmother's. She called out, "Good morning!"

But she received no answer. Next she went to the bed and drew back the curtains.

There lay her grandmother with her cap pulled down over her face giving her a strange appearance. "Oh, Grandmother, what big ears you have!"

"The better to hear you with."

"Oh, Grandmother, what big hands you have!"

"The better to grab you with."

Grandmother, what a terribly big mouth you have!"

"The better to eat you with!"

No sooner did the wolf say that than he jumped out of bed and gobbled up poor Little Red Riding Hood. After the wolf had satisfied his desires, he lay down in bed again, fell asleep, and began to snore very loudly.

The huntsman happened to be passing by the house and thought to himself: "The way the old woman's snoring, you'd better see if anything's wrong." He went into the room, and when he came to the bed, he saw the wolf lying in it.

"So I've found you at last, you old sinner," said the huntsman. "I've been looking for you for a long time."

He took aim with his gun, and then it occurred to him that the wolf could have eaten the grandmother and that she could still be saved. So he did not shoot but took some scissors and started cutting open the sleeping wolf's belly. After he made a couple of cuts, he saw the Little Red Riding Hood shining forth, and after he made a few more cuts, the girl jumped out and exclaimed, "Oh, how frightened I was! It was so dark in the wolf's body."

Soon the grandmother came out. She was alive but could hardly breathe. Little Red Riding Hood quickly fetched some large stones, and they filled the wolf's body with them. When he awoke and tried to run away, the stones were too heavy so he fell down at once and died. All three were quite delighted. The huntsman skinned the fur from the wolf and went home with it. The grandmother ate the cake and drank the wine that Little Red Riding Hood had brought, and soon she regained her health. Meanwhile, Little Red Riding Hood thought to herself, Never again will I stray from the path by myself and go into the forest when my mother has forbidden it.

HANSEL AND GRETEL

Once upon a time there were two children, a boy and a girl . . .
—*The Book of Lost Things,* Chapter XI

OF "HANSEL AND GRETEL"

This has always been one of my favorite fairy tales, so it was natural that it should find its place in *The Book of Lost Things.* But, like each of the stories, whether told by Roland or the Woodsman, or referred to explicitly or obliquely in the text, it was selected because it has a particular relevance to David or his circumstances.

In this case, the obvious reference point is desertion and, more particularly, the child's fear of being deserted by his parents. I have a clear memory of myself as a young child, returning home from school one day—I can't have been more than seven, and it is a reflection of the changes in our times that few parents would now be willing to let their seven-year-old son walk twenty minutes to school by himself—to find that my house had gone. Quite simply, the house that I had left that morning was no longer there. What had happened (and forgive me if this makes me sound like an unusually silly child) was that my parents had decided to have the exterior of the house painted, so that the door, the gables, and the guttering were no longer the old color familiar to me. In addition, the painters had removed the house number so as not to stain the metal with paint. I knew my house primarily by its color: it was a red house, on a street where each house was identical in construction and only the colors made one house distinct from another. The red house was gone, and another had taken its place. For a few minutes, I was in shock, and only the appearance of my next-door neighbor, Mrs. Curran, confirmed to me that, abandoned though I was, I was not going to be entirely alone in the world. It was she who explained to me what had occurred, but I can still recall that day quite clearly, and the sense that one of my worst fears had, however briefly, come to pass.

So abandonment is a theme here. In *The Book of Lost Things,* David has already been deserted by one parent, in a sense—his mother has died—and he fears that he is being rejected by his father and his father's new partner in favor of their infant child. (To some degree, this is reflected in the alteration of the parental roles in David's version of the tale: it is the father figure who betrays the children, not the mother.) But there is another message here for David: it concerns the importance of independence, and the realization that, at some point, children will have to make their own way in the world, whether that independence is forced on them through bereavement, or slowly gained as the child progresses toward adulthood. This is the principal point at which the tale in *The Book of Lost Things* deviates from the original story. In the traditional story, Hansel and Gretel succeed by combining their efforts and their strengths. They overcome the witch, and in that way they survive. But in *The Book of Lost Things,* Hansel is weaker and more fearful than Gretel. While she understands the necessity of self-sufficiency if they are to survive, her brother does not. Gretel grows up and achieves what most young children doubt they will ever manage to create for themselves: an existence independent of their parents in which they meet and overcomes the challenges that the adult world will place before them. Hansel, by contrast, fails to mature. Instead, even after the witch (an alternative mother figure) is vanquished, he continues to seek a substitute, and in that way dooms himself.

ORIGINS

"Hansel and Gretel" is a German folktale, but it has analogues in other cultures and is part of a tradition of tales best summarized as "The Children and The Ogre," in which children enter the lair of an ogre and turn the tables upon it, often escaping with gold or treasure. It was first published by the Brothers Grimm in 1812, and was sourced from their neighbor, Dortchen Wild, who later became Wilhelm Grimm's wife. The Grimms consistently revised many of the stories in their collections, and almost half a century passed between their original version of the tale and the final version that appeared in 1857. During that time, the children were given names for the first time, their mother became their stepmother, and reasons were given for their abandonment.

It may be the case that the Grimms were particularly fond of this story, as it had echoes in their own life: an absent, long-dead father (abandonment), their affection for their mother, and their own closeness as brothers. It is, after all, one of the few fairy tales that is about sibling love rather than sibling rivalry (as in "Cinderella," for example). It also has a certain grounding in the realities of the time: there were famines in nineteenth-century Germany, cities and towns had their share of abandoned children, and maternal mortality, particularly during or after childbirth, meant that stepmothers were ubiquitous. Similarly, the threat posed by the woods and forests was very real, and a child who became lost in them would have little chance of survival.

Variations on the tale by modern writers can be found in Robert Coover's *Pricksongs & Descants* ("The Gingerbread House"); Garrison Keillor's *Happy to Be Here* ("My Stepmother,

Myself"); Emma Donoghue's *Kissing the Witch* ("The Tale of the Cottage"); and Anne Sexton's 1971 book of poems, *Transformations* ("Hansel and Gretel").

Hansel and Gretel

The Brothers Grimm

At the edge of a great forest dwelt a poor woodcutter with his wife and his two children. The boy was called Hansel and the girl Gretel. The woodcutter was very poor, and once when great famine fell on the land, he could no longer procure even daily bread. Now when he thought over this by night in his bed, and tossed about in his anxiety, he groaned and said to his wife: "What is to become of us? How are we to feed our poor children, when we no longer have anything even for ourselves?" "I'll tell you what, husband," answered the woman, "early tomorrow morning we will take the children out into the forest to where it is the thickest; there we will light a fire for them, and give each of them one more piece of bread, and then we will go to our work and leave them alone. They will not find the way home again, and we shall be rid of them." "No, wife," said the man, "I will not do that; how can I bear to leave my children alone in the forest—the wild animals would soon come and tear them to pieces." "O, you fool!" said she, "then we must all four die of hunger, you may as well plane the planks for our coffins," and she left him no peace until he consented. "But I feel very sorry for the poor children, all the same," said the man.

The two children had also not been able to sleep for hunger, and had heard what their stepmother had said to their father. Gretel began to cry, and said to Hansel: "Now all is over with us." "Be quiet, Gretel," said Hansel, "do not distress yourself, I will soon find a way to help us." And when the old folks had fallen asleep, he got up, put on his little coat, opened the door below, and crept outside. The moon shone brightly, and the white pebbles which lay in front of the house glittered like real silver pennies. Hansel stooped and stuffed the little pocket of his coat with as many as he could get in. Then he went back and said to Gretel: "Be comforted, dear little sister, and sleep in peace, God will not forsake us," and he lay down again in his bed. When day dawned, but before the sun had risen, the woman came and awoke the two children, saying: "Get up, you sluggards! We are going into the forest to fetch wood." She gave each a little piece of bread, and said: "There is something for your dinner, but do not eat it up before then, for you will get nothing else." Gretel took the bread under her apron, as Hansel had the pebbles in his pocket. Then they all set out together on the way to the forest. When they had walked a short time, Hansel stood still and peeped back at the house, and did so again and again. His father said: "Hansel, what are you looking at there and staying behind for? Pay attention, and do not forget how to use your legs." "Ah, father," said Hansel, "I am looking at my little white cat, which is sitting up on the roof, and wants to say good-bye to me." The wife said: "Fool, that is not your little cat, that is the morning sun which is shining on the chimneys." Hansel, however, had not been looking back at the cat, but had been constantly throwing one of the white pebbles out of his pocket on the road.

When they had reached the middle of the forest, the father said: "Now, children, pile up some wood, and I will light a fire that you may not be cold." Hansel and Gretel gathered brushwood together, as high as a little hill. The brushwood was lighted, and when the flames were burning very high, the woman said: "Now, children, lay yourselves down by the fire and rest, we will go into the forest and cut some wood. When we have done, we will come back and fetch you away."

Hansel and Gretel sat by the fire, and when noon came, each ate a little piece of bread, and as they heard the strokes of the wood-axe they believed that their father was near. It was not the axe, however, but a branch which he had fastened to a withered tree which the wind was blowing backwards and forwards. And as they had been sitting such a long time, their eyes closed with fatigue, and they fell fast asleep. When at last they awoke, it was already dark night. Gretel began to cry and said: "How are we to get out of the forest now?" But Hansel comforted her and said: "Just wait a little, until the moon has risen, and then we will soon find the way." And when the full moon had risen, Hansel took his little sister by the hand, and followed the pebbles which shone like newly coined silver pieces, and showed them the way.

They walked the whole night long, and by break of day came once more to their father's house. They knocked at the door, and when the woman opened it and saw that it was Hansel and Gretel, she said: "You naughty children, why have you slept so long in the forest—we thought you were never coming back at all!" The father, however, rejoiced, for it had cut him to the heart to leave them behind alone.

Not long afterwards, there was once more great dearth throughout the land, and the children heard their stepmother saying at night to their father: "Everything is eaten again, we have one half loaf left, and that is the end. The children must go, we will take them farther into the wood, so that they will not find their way out again; there is no other means of saving ourselves!" The man's heart was heavy, and he thought: "It would be better for you to share the last mouthful with your children." The woman, however, would listen to nothing that he had to say, but scolded and reproached him. He who says A must say B, likewise, and as he had yielded the first time, he had to do so a second time also.

The children, however, were still awake and had heard the

conversation. When the old folks were asleep, Hansel again got up, and wanted to go out and pick up pebbles as he had done before, but the woman had locked the door, and Hansel could not get out. Nevertheless he comforted his little sister, and said: "Do not cry, Gretel, go to sleep quietly, the good God will help us."

Early in the morning came the woman, and took the children out of their beds. Their piece of bread was given to them, but it was still smaller than the time before. On the way into the forest Hansel crumbled his in his pocket, and often stood still and threw a morsel on the ground. "Hansel, why do you stop and look round," said the father, "go on." "I am looking back at my little pigeon which is sitting on the roof, and wants to say good-bye to me," answered Hansel. "Fool!" said the woman, "that is not your little pigeon, that is the morning sun that is shining on the chimney." Hansel, however, little by little, threw all the crumbs on the path.

The woman led the children still deeper into the forest, where they had never in their lives been before. Then a great fire was again made, and the mother said: "Just sit there, you children, and when you are tired you may sleep a little; we are going into the forest to cut wood, and in the evening when we are done, we will come and fetch you away." When it was noon, Gretel shared her piece of bread with Hansel, who had scattered his by the way. Then they fell asleep and evening passed, but no one came to the poor children. They did not awake until it was dark night, and Hansel comforted his little sister and said: "Just wait, Gretel, until the moon rises, and then we shall see the crumbs of bread which I have strewn about, they will show us our way home again." When the moon came they set out, but they found no crumbs, for the many thousands of birds which fly about in the woods and fields had picked them all up.

Hansel said to Gretel: "We shall soon find the way," but they did not find it. They walked the whole night and all the next day too from morning till evening, but they did not get out of the forest, and were very hungry, for they had nothing to eat but two or three berries, which grew on the ground. And as they were so weary that their legs would carry them no longer, they lay down beneath a tree and fell asleep.

It was now three mornings since they had left their father's house. They began to walk again, but they always came deeper into the forest, and if help did not come soon, they must die of hunger and weariness. When it was midday, they saw a beautiful snow-white bird sitting on a bough, which sang so delightfully that they stood still and listened to it. And when its song was over, it spread its wings and flew away before them, and they followed it until they reached a little house, on the roof of which it alighted; and when they approached the little house they saw that it was built of bread and covered with cakes, but that the windows were of clear sugar. "We will set to work on that," said Hansel, "and have a good meal. I will eat a bit of the roof, and you Gretel, can eat some of the window, it will taste sweet." Hansel reached up above, and broke off a little of the roof to try how it tasted, and Gretel leant against the window and nibbled at the panes. Then a soft voice cried from the parlour:

Nibble, nibble, gnaw,
Who is nibbling at my little house?

The children answered:

The wind, the wind,
The heaven-born wind,

and went on eating without disturbing themselves. Hansel, who liked the taste of the roof, tore down a great piece of it, and Gretel pushed out the whole of one round windowpane, sat down, and enjoyed herself with it. Suddenly the door opened, and a woman as old as the hills, who supported herself on crutches, came creeping out. Hansel and Gretel were so terribly frightened that they let fall what they had in their hands. The old woman, however, nodded her head, and said, "Oh, you dear children, who has brought you here? Do come in, and stay with me. No harm shall come to you." She took them both by the hand, and led them into her little house. Then good food was set before them, milk and pancakes, with sugar, apples, and nuts. Afterwards two pretty little beds were covered with clean white linen, and Hansel and Gretel lay down in them, and thought they were in heaven.

The old woman had only pretended to be so kind; she was in reality a wicked witch, who lay in wait for children, and had only built the little house of bread in order to entice them there. When a child fell into her power, she killed it, cooked and ate it, and that was a feast day with her. Witches have red eyes, and cannot see far, but they have a keen scent like the beasts, and are aware when human beings draw near. When Hansel and Gretel came into her neighbourhood, she laughed with malice, and said mockingly: "I have them, they shall not escape me again!" Early in the morning before the children were awake, she was already up, and when she saw both of them sleeping and looking so pretty, with their plump and rosy cheeks, she muttered to herself: "That will be a dainty mouthful" Then she seized Hansel with her shrivelled hand, carried him into a little stable, and locked him in behind a grated door. Scream as he might, it would not help him. Then she went to Gretel, shook her till she awoke, and cried: "Get up, lazy thing, fetch some water, and cook something good for your brother, he is in the stable outside, and is to be made fat. When he is fat, I will eat him." Gretel began to weep bitterly, but it was all in vain, for she was forced to do what the wicked witch commanded.

And now the best food was cooked for poor Hansel, but Gretel got nothing but crab-shells. Every morning the woman crept to the little stable, and cried: "Hansel, stretch out your finger that I may feel if you will soon be fat." Hansel, however, stretched out a little bone to her, and the old woman, who had dim eyes, could not see it, and thought it was Hansel's finger, and was astonished that there was no way of fattening him. When four weeks had gone by, and Hansel still remained thin, she was seized with impatience and would not wait any longer. "Now, then, Gretel," she cried to the girl, "stir yourself, and bring some water. Let Hansel be fat or lean, tomorrow I will kill him, and cook him." Ah, how the poor little sister did lament when she had to fetch the water, and how her tears did flow down her cheeks! "Dear God, do help us," she cried. "If the wild beasts in the forest had but devoured us, we should at any rate have died together." "Just keep your noise to yourself," said the old woman, "it won't help you at all."

Early in the morning, Gretel had to go out and hang up the cauldron with the water, and light the fire. "We will bake first," said the old woman, "I have already heated the oven, and kneaded the dough." She pushed poor Gretel out to the oven, from which flames of fire were already darting. "Creep in," said the witch, "and see if it is properly heated, so that we can put the bread in." And once Gretel was inside, she intended to shut the oven and let her bake in it, and then she would eat her, too. But Gretel saw what she had in mind, and said: "I do not know how I am to do it; how do I get in?" "Silly goose," said the old woman. "The door is big enough; just look, I can get in myself!" and she crept up and thrust her head into the oven. Then Gretel gave her a push that drove her far into it, and shut the iron door, and fastened the bolt. Oh then she began to howl quite horribly, but Gretel ran away, and the godless witch was miserably burnt to death.

Gretel ran like lightning to Hansel, opened his little stable, and cried: "Hansel, we are saved! The old witch is dead!" Then Hansel sprang like a bird from its cage when the door is opened. How they did rejoice and embrace each other, and dance about and kiss each other! And as they had no longer any need to fear her, they went into the witch's house, and in every corner there stood chests full of pearls and jewels. "These are far better than pebbles!" said Hansel, and thrust into his pockets whatever could be got in, and Gretel said: "I, too, will take something home with me," and filled her pinafore full. "But now we must be off," said Hansel, "that we may get out of the witch's forest."

When they had walked for two hours, they came to a great stretch of water. "We cannot cross," said Hansel, "I see no footplank, and no bridge." "And there is also no ferry," answered Gretel, "but a white duck is swimming there; if I ask her, she will help us over." Then she cried:

> *Little duck, little duck, dost thou see,*
> *Hansel and Gretel are waiting for thee?*
> *There's never a plank, or bridge in sight,*
> *Take us across on thy back so white."*

The duck came to them, and Hansel seated himself on its back, and told his sister to sit by him. "No," replied Gretel, "that will be too heavy for the little duck; she shall take us across, one after the other." The good little duck did so, and when they were once safely across and had walked for a short time, the forest seemed to be more and more familiar to them, and at length they saw from afar their father's house. Then they began to run, rushed into the parlour, and threw themselves round their father's neck. The man had not known one happy hour since he had left the children in the forest; the woman, however, was dead. Gretel emptied her pinafore until pearls and precious stones ran about the room, and Hansel threw one handful after another out of his pocket to add to them. Then all their troubles were at an end, and they lived together in perfect happiness.

THE THREE BILLY-GOATS GRUFF

David had never imagined that he might see a troll, although he had always been fascinated by them. In his mind, they existed as shadowy figures who dwelled beneath bridges, testing travelers in the hope of eating them when they failed. The figures that climbed over the lip of the canyon, flaming torches in their hands, were not quite what he had expected. They were smaller than the Woodsman but very broad, and their skin was like that of an elephant, tough and wrinkled. Raised plates of bone, like those on the backs of some dinosaurs, ran along their spines, but their faces were similar to those of apes; very ugly apes, admittedly, and ones that seemed to be suffering from severe acne, but apes nonetheless. Each troll took up a position in front of one of the bridges and smiled grimly. They had small red eyes that glowed sinisterly in the gathering darkness . . .

—*The Book of Lost Things,* Chapter XII

OF TROLLS AND "THE THREE BILLY GOATS GRUFF"

The tale of "The Three Billy Goats Gruff" is probably one of the first fairy stories I can remember being told. Its appeal to children is obvious: it's structurally simple, quite repetitive, and easy to recall. I always remembered it as being slightly sinister, though, in that the goats seem to sell out one another rather easily, and I had to take it on trust that they knew that the final billy goat was strong enough to tackle the troll. All told, it doesn't teach children very much, apart from the fact that it's a good idea to hang around with someone bigger than you in order to deal with potential bullies, and it's okay to sell out your friends if the need arises. A friend of mine was most aggrieved at this interpretation, because her mother had told her that the moral of the story was that the strong should protect the weak. If that is the case, then surely the largest billy goat would lead the way. It also suggests a somewhat misplaced faith in the ability of trolls to grasp the concept of delayed gratification. (There is also the possibility that the goats deliberately put themselves in harm's way knowing that the biggest of their number will be able to annihilate any troll they encounter and thus they seem to resemble a hairier version of Charles Bronson in *Death Wish,* dispensing vigilante justice just as Bronson did with muggers in New York through the judicious application of a sock filled with rolled-up coins.)

Nevertheless, I always loved the image of the troll beneath the bridge, and the threat of being consumed that it represented. *The Book of Lost Things* takes the conventions of the bridge, the challenge (in this case a riddle), and the trolls and uses them in quite a traditional way. The virtue of the original tale lies in its simplicity: a threat and a challenge to be overcome through superior wit.

The Three Billy Goats Gruff

Traditional

Once upon a time there were three billy goats, who were to go up to the hillside to make themselves fat, and the name of all three was "Gruff."

On the way up was a bridge over a cascading stream they had to cross; and under the bridge lived a great ugly troll, with eyes as big as saucers, and a nose as long as a poker.

So first of all came the youngest Billy Goat Gruff to cross the bridge.

Trip, trap, trip, trap! went the bridge.

"Who's that tripping over my bridge?" roared the troll.

"Oh, it is only I, the tiniest Billy Goat Gruff, and I'm going up to the hillside to make myself fat," said the billy goat, with such a small voice.

"Now I'm coming to gobble you up," said the troll.

"Oh, no! Pray don't take me. I'm too little, that I am," said the billy goat. "Wait a bit till the second Billy Goat Gruff comes. He's much bigger."

"Well, be off with you," said the troll.

A little while after came the second Billy Goat Gruff to cross the bridge.

Trip, trap, trip, trap, trip, trap, went the bridge.

"Who's that tripping over my bridge?" roared the troll.

"Oh, it's the second Billy Goat Gruff, and I'm going up to the hillside to make myself fat," said the billy goat, who hadn't such a small voice.

"Now I'm coming to gobble you up," said the troll.

"Oh, no! Don't take me. Wait a little till the big Billy Goat Gruff comes. He's much bigger."

"Very well! Be off with you," said the troll.

But just then up came the big Billy Goat Gruff .

Trip, trap, trip, trap, trip, trap! went the bridge, for the billy goat was so heavy that the bridge creaked and groaned under him.

"Who's that tramping over my bridge?" roared the troll.

"It's I! The big Billy Goat Gruff," said the billy goat, who had an ugly hoarse voice of his own.

"Now I'm coming to gobble you up," roared the troll.

"Well, come along! I've got two spears,
And I'll poke your eyeballs out at your ears;
I've got besides two curling stones,
And I'll crush you to bits, body and bones."

That was what the big billy goat said. And then he flew at the troll, and poked his eyes out with his horns, and crushed him to bits, body and bones, and tossed him out into the cascade, and after that he went up to the hillside. There the billy goats got so fat they were scarcely able to walk home again. And if the fat hasn't fallen off them, why, they're still fat; and so,

Snip, snap, snout.
This tale's told out.

SNOW WHITE AND THE SEVEN DWARFS

*"Huh," said the dwarf, apparently satisfied, and started walking again.
"Everybody's heard of her: 'Ooooh, Snow White who lives with the
dwarfs, eats them out of house and home. They couldn't even kill her right.'
Oh yes, everybody knows about Snow White."*

"Er, kill her?" asked David.

*"Poisoned apple," said the dwarf. "Didn't go too well. We underesti-
mated the dose."*

—*The Book of Lost Things,* Chapter XIII

OF "SNOW WHITE AND THE SEVEN DWARFS"

David's encounter with the dwarfs remains the lightest scene in
the book, and deliberately so, although in its very avoidance of the
darker aspects of the story it raises questions about David's deepest fears. This is, after all, a tale in which a wicked, jealous stepmother plots to kill and eat a child, and it might therefore be
expected that David's imagination would put a darker spin on it.
Yet, for most of those who read the story as children, or more particularly for those who can recall the Disney movie, it is the dwarfs
who are perhaps the most memorable feature of the tale. True, the
witch/stepmother is a terrifying character, and many of us can
recite her incantation to her mirror at the drop of a hat, but there
is comfort in the dwarfs and the promise of help and protection,
however limited, that they might offer. When I was writing the
book, I wondered if David might choose to set aside the issue of
the stepmother entirely and concentrate instead on the dwarfs.

Their personalities, though, have been altered slightly by their proximity to a history of communism on David's bookshelves, a book that David has tried and failed to understand, giving up after only a couple of pages. One of the themes of *The Book of Lost Things* is the way in which stories and books feed into one another, in much the same way that I, as a writer, have been influenced by the books that I have read. In that sense, *The Book of Lost Things* is a narrative constructed not only from the books David has encountered, but also from the books and stories that have influenced me.

ORIGINS

This is probably one of the most widely circulated of fairy tales, with versions in Asia, Africa, Scandinavia, South America, and Europe, leading to minor changes to elements of the story. The Grimms, for example, have the wicked stepmother consulting a mirror, but in other cultures she talks to the sun, the moon, even an omniscient trout. Similarly, the dwarfs are replaced in some versions by robbers, bears, monkeys, old women, and brothers, enabling us to view the musical *Seven Brides for Seven Brothers* as a riff on the tale, with Snow White represented by the first bride and a succession of others following in her footsteps. While the stepmother is responsible for the assassination attempts in the most famous tellings of the tale, in others she entrusts the task to a crooked physician, or sends a beggar in her stead. The instruments of assassination have included poisoned grapes, wine, letters, flowers, darts, slippers and soap.

Clearly, on one level, "Snow White" is a tale of mother-daughter conflict, and it is interesting that in many versions of the story it is Snow White's mother who is envious of the young woman's beauty. The Grimms, it is fair to say, were rather sentimental about motherhood, almost certainly because of their own upbringing, and tended to change mothers to stepmothers at every available opportunity. And if it is true that the tale of Snow White is one of the most well known of fairy tales then it is also true that it is one of those that have been most frequently sanitized over the years, cleansed of the mother/stepmother's cannibalistic urges (Disney contents itself with an order to remove Snow White's heart; the Grimms go for lungs and liver, or the heart in some alternative translations; while the Spanish up the ante with a request for a bottle of Snow White's blood, stoppered with her toe) and varying her eventual demise from the "fall" in Disney to the more traditional red-hot iron shoes, which the wicked queen is forced to wear and dance in until she dies.

Bruno Bettelheim, unsurprisingly, has a great time with "Snow White" in his book *The Uses of Enchantment.* He is particularly hard on the dwarfs, regarding their presence as a bowdlerization of the original tale and ultimately dismissing them as "permanently arrested on a pre-oedipal level," which, while possibly true, rather takes a lot of the fun out of the whole affair. Nevertheless, the oedipal nature of the conflict in the story—a mother's envy of her daughter's budding sexuality—has provided ample fodder for other writers to explore the tale's darker implications in greater depth, from Anne Sexton and Robert Coover to Tanith Lee and Donald Barthelme.

There are also clear echoes of other tales here. The theme of abandonment in a forest, encountered in "Hansel And Gretel," emerges once again, but for different reasons, and in the dwarfs' responses to Snow White's presence one can hear the Three Bears' similar exclamations of displeasure at Goldilocks's trespass, which is why she is also referenced by the dwarfs in *The Book of Lost Things.*

Snow White and the Seven Dwarfs

The Brothers Grimm

Once upon a time in the middle of winter, when the flakes of snow were falling like feathers from the sky, a queen sat at a window sewing, and the frame of the window was made of black ebony. And whilst she was sewing and looking out of the window at the snow, she pricked her finger with the needle, and three drops of blood fell upon the snow. And the red looked pretty upon the white snow, and she thought to herself, "Would that I had a child as white as snow, as red as blood, and as black as the wood of the window-frame."

Soon after that she had a little daughter, who was as white as snow, and as red as blood, and her hair was as black as ebony; and she was therefore called Little Snow-white. And when the child was born, the Queen died.

After a year had passed the King took to himself another wife. She was a beautiful woman, but proud and haughty, and she could not bear that anyone else should surpass her in beauty. She had a wonderful looking-glass, and when she stood in front of it and looked at herself in it, and said—

"Looking-glass, Looking-glass, on the wall,
Who in this land is the fairest of all?"

the looking-glass answered—

"Thou, O Queen, art the fairest of all!"

Then she was satisfied, for she knew that the looking-glass spoke the truth.

But Snow-white was growing up, and grew more and more beautiful; and when she was seven years old she was as beautiful as the day, and more beautiful than the Queen herself. And once when the Queen asked her looking-glass—

"Looking-glass, Looking-glass, on the wall,
Who in this land is the fairest of all?"

it answered—

"Thou art fairer than all who are here, Lady Queen.
But more beautiful still is Snow-white, as I ween."

Then the Queen was shocked, and turned yellow and green with envy. From that hour, whenever she looked at Snow-white, her heart heaved in her breast, she hated the girl so much.

And envy and pride grew higher and higher in her heart like a weed, so that she had no peace day or night. She called a huntsman, and said, "Take the child away into the forest; I will no longer have her in my sight. Kill her, and bring me back her heart as a token." The huntsman obeyed, and took her away; but when he had drawn his knife, and was about to pierce Snow-white's innocent heart, she began to weep, and said, "Ah dear huntsman, leave me my life! I will run away into the wild forest, and never come home again."

And as she was so beautiful the huntsman had pity on her and said, "Run away, then, you poor child." "The wild beasts will soon have devoured you," thought he, and yet it seemed as if a stone had been rolled from his heart since it was no longer needful for him to kill her. And as a young boar just then came running by he stabbed it, and cut out its heart and took it to the Queen as proof that the child was dead. The cook had to salt this, and the wicked Queen ate it, and thought she had eaten the heart of Snow-white.

But now the poor child was all alone in the great forest, and so terrified that she looked at every leaf of every tree, and did not know what to do. Then she began to run, and ran over sharp stones and through thorns, and the wild beasts ran past her, but did her no harm.

She ran as long as her feet would go until it was almost evening; then she saw a little cottage and went into it to rest herself. Everything in the cottage was small, but neater and cleaner than can be told. There was a table on which was a white cover, and seven little plates, and on each plate a little spoon; moreover, there were seven little knives and forks, and seven little mugs. Against the wall stood seven little beds side by side, and covered with snow-white counterpanes.

Little Snow-white was so hungry and thirsty that she ate some vegetables and bread from each plate and drank a drop of wine out of each mug, for she did not wish to take all from one only. Then, as she was so tired, she laid herself down on one of the little beds, but none of them suited her; one was too long, another too short, but at last she found that the seventh one was right, and so she remained in it, said a prayer and went to sleep.

When it was quite dark the owners of the cottage came back; they were seven dwarfs who dug and delved in the mountains for ore. They lit their seven candles, and as it was now light within the cottage they saw that someone had been there, for everything was not in the same order in which they had left it.

The first said, "Who has been sitting on my chair?"

The second, "Who has been eating off my plate?"

The third, "Who has been taking some of my bread?"

The fourth, "Who has been eating my vegetables?"

The fifth, "Who has been using my fork?"

The sixth, "Who has been cutting with my knife?"

The seventh, "Who has been drinking out of my mug?"

Then the first looked round and saw that there was a little hole on his bed, and he said, "Who has been getting into my bed?" The others came up and each called out, "Somebody has been lying in my bed too." But the seventh when he looked at his bed saw little Snow-white, who was lying asleep therein. And he called the others, who came running up, and they cried out with astonishment, and brought their seven little candles and let the light fall on little Snow-white. "Oh, heavens! oh, heavens!" cried they, "what a lovely child!" and they were so glad that they did not wake her up, but let her sleep on in the bed. And the seventh dwarf slept with his companions, one hour with each, and so got through the night.

When it was morning little Snow-white awoke, and was frightened when she saw the seven dwarfs. But they were friendly and asked her what her name was. "My name is Snow-white," she answered. "How have you come to our house?" said the dwarfs. Then she told them that her stepmother had wished to have her killed, but that the huntsman had spared her life, and that she had run for the whole day, until at last she had found their dwelling. The dwarfs said, "If you will take care of our house, cook, make the beds, wash, sew, and knit, and if you will keep everything neat and clean, you can stay with us and you shall want for nothing." "Yes," said Snow-white, "with all my heart," and she stayed with them. She kept the house in order for them; in the mornings they went to the mountains and looked for copper and gold, in the evenings they came back, and then their supper had to be ready. The girl was alone the whole day, so the good dwarfs warned her and said, "Beware of your stepmother, she will soon know that you are here; be sure to let no one come in."

But the Queen, believing that she had eaten Snow-white's

heart, could not but think that she was again the first and most beautiful of all; and she went to her looking-glass and said—

"Looking-glass, Looking-glass, on the wall,
Who in this land is the fairest of all?"

and the glass answered—

"Oh, Queen, thou art fairest of all I see,
But over the hills, where the seven dwarfs dwell,
Snow-white is still alive and well,
And none is so fair as she."

Then she was astounded, for she knew that the looking-glass never spoke falsely, and she knew that the huntsman had betrayed her, and that little Snow-white was still alive.

And so she thought and thought again how she might kill her, for so long as she was not the fairest in the whole land, envy let her have no rest. And when she had at last thought of something to do, she painted her face and dressed herself like an old peddler, and no one could have known her. In this disguise she went over the seven mountains to the seven dwarfs, and knocked at the door and cried, "Pretty things to sell, very cheap, very cheap." Little Snow-white looked out of the window and called out, "Good-day my good woman, what have you to sell?" "Good things, pretty things," she answered; "stay-laces of all colours," and she pulled out one which was woven of bright-coloured silk. "I may let the worthy old woman in," thought Snow-white, and she unbolted the door and bought the pretty laces. "Child," said the old woman, "what a fright you look; come, I will lace you properly for once." Snow-white had no suspicion, but stood before her, and let herself be laced with the new laces. But the old woman laced so quickly and so tightly that Snow-white lost her breath and fell down as if dead. "Now I am the most beautiful," said the Queen to herself, and ran away.

Not long afterwards, in the evening, the seven dwarfs came home, but how shocked they were when they saw their dear little Snow-white lying on the ground, and that she neither stirred nor moved, and seemed to be dead. They lifted her up, and, as they saw that she was laced too tightly, they cut the laces; then she began to breathe a little, and after a while came to life again. When the dwarfs heard what had happened they said, "The old peddler was no one else than the wicked Queen; take care and let no one come in when we are not with you."

But the wicked woman when she had reached home went in front of the glass and asked—

"Looking-glass, Looking-glass, on the wall,
Who in this land is the fairest of all?"

and it answered as before—

"Oh, Queen, thou art fairest of all I see,
But over the hills, where the seven dwarfs dwell,
Snow-white is still alive and well,
And none is so fair as she."

When she heard that, all her blood rushed to her heart with fear, for she saw plainly that little Snow-white was again alive. "But now," she said, "I will think of something that shall put an end to you," and by the help of witchcraft, which she understood, she made a poisonous comb. Then she disguised herself and took the shape of another old woman. So she went over the seven mountains to the seven dwarfs, knocked at the door, and cried, "Good things to sell, cheap, cheap!" Little Snow-white looked out and said, "Go away; I cannot let any one come in." "I suppose you can look," said the old woman, and pulled the poisonous comb out and held it up. It pleased the girl so well that she let herself be beguiled, and opened the door. When they had made a bargain the old woman said, "Now I will comb you properly for once." Poor little Snow-white had no suspicion, and let the old woman do as she pleased, but hardly had she put the comb in her hair than the poison in it took effect, and the girl fell down senseless. "You paragon of beauty," said the wicked woman, "you are done for now," and she went away.

But fortunately it was almost evening, when the seven dwarfs came home. When they saw Snow-white lying as if dead upon the ground they at once suspected the stepmother, and they looked and found the poisoned comb. Scarcely had they taken it out when Snow-white came to herself, and told them what had happened. Then they warned her once more to be upon her guard and to open the door to no one.

The Queen, at home, went in front of the glass and said—

"Looking-glass, Looking-glass, on the wall,
Who in this land is the fairest of all?"

then it answered as before—

"Oh, Queen, thou art fairest of all I see,
But over the hills, where the seven dwarfs dwell,
Snow-white is still alive and well,
And none is so fair as she."

When she heard the glass speak thus she trembled and shook with rage. "Snow-white shall die," she cried, "even if it costs me my life!"

Thereupon she went into a quite secret, lonely room, where no one ever came, and there she made a very poisonous apple. Outside it looked pretty, white with a red cheek, so that everyone who saw it longed for it; but whoever ate a piece of it must surely die.

When the apple was ready she painted her face, and dressed herself up as a countrywoman, and so she went over the seven mountains to the seven dwarfs. She knocked at the door. Snow-white put her head out of the window and said, "I cannot let any one in; the seven dwarfs have forbidden me." "It is all the same to me," answered the woman, "I shall soon get rid of my apples. There, I will give you one."

"No," said Snow-white, "I dare not take anything." "Are you afraid of poison?" said the old woman; "look, I will cut the apple in two pieces; you eat the red cheek, and I will eat the white." The apple was so cunningly made that only the red cheek was poisoned. Snow-white longed for the fine apple, and when she saw that the woman ate part of it she could resist no longer, and stretched out her hand and took the poisonous half. But hardly had she a bit of it in her mouth than she fell down dead. Then the Queen looked at her with a dreadful look, and laughed aloud and said, "White as snow, red as blood, black as ebony-wood! This time the dwarfs cannot wake you up again."

And when she asked of the Looking-glass at home—

"Looking-glass, Looking-glass, on the wall,
Who in this land is the fairest of all?"

it answered at last—

"Oh, Queen, in this land thou art fairest of all."

Then her envious heart had rest, so far as an envious heart can have rest. The dwarfs, when they came home in the evening, found Snow-white lying upon the ground; she breathed no longer and was dead. They lifted her up, looked to see whether they could find anything poisonous, unlaced her, combed her hair, washed her with water and wine, but it was all of no use; the poor child was dead, and remained dead. They laid her upon a bier, and all seven of them sat round it and wept for her, and wept three days long.

Then they were going to bury her, but she still looked as if she were living, and still had her pretty red cheeks. They said, "We could not bury her in the dark ground," and they had a transparent coffin of glass made, so that she could be seen from all sides, and they laid her in it, and wrote her name upon it in golden letters, and that she was a king's daughter. Then they put the coffin out upon the mountain, and one of them always stayed by it and watched it. And birds came too, and wept for Snow-white; first an owl, then a raven, and last a dove.

And now Snow-white lay a long, long time in the coffin, and she did not change, but looked as if she were asleep; for she was as white as snow, as red as blood, and her hair was as black as ebony.

It happened, however, that a king's son came into the forest, and went to the dwarfs' house to spend the night. He saw the coffin on the mountain, and the beautiful Snow-white within it, and read what was written upon it in golden letters. Then he said to the dwarfs, "Let me have the coffin, I will give you whatever you want for it." But the dwarfs answered, "We will not part with it for all the gold in the world." Then he said, "Let me have it as a gift, for I cannot live without seeing Snow-white. I will honour and prize her as my dearest possession." As he spoke in this way the good dwarfs took pity upon him, and gave him the coffin.

And now the King's son had it carried away by his servants on their shoulders. And it happened that they stumbled over a tree-stump, and with the shock the poisonous piece of apple which Snow-white had bitten off came out of her throat. And before long she opened her eyes, lifted up the lid of the coffin, sat up, and was once more alive. "Oh, heavens, where am I?" she cried. The King's son, full of joy, said, "You are with me," and told her what had happened, and said, "I love you more than everything in the world; come with me to my father's palace, you shall be my wife."

And Snow-white was willing, and went with him, and their wedding was held with great show and splendour. But Snow-white's wicked stepmother was also bidden to the feast. When she had arrayed herself in beautiful clothes she went before the Looking-glass, and said—

"Looking-glass, Looking-glass, on the wall,
Who in this land is the fairest of all?"

the glass answered—

"Oh, Queen, of all here the fairest art thou,
But the young Queen is fairer by far as I trow."

Then the wicked woman uttered a curse, and was so wretched, so utterly wretched, that she knew not what to do. At first she would not go to the wedding at all, but she had no peace, and must go to see the young Queen. And when she went in she knew Snow-white; and she stood still with rage and fear, and could not stir. But iron slippers had already been put upon the fire, and they were brought in with tongs, and set before her. Then she was forced to put on the red-hot shoes, and dance until she dropped down dead.

GOLDILOCKS

"Hang on," said David. "Goldilocks ran away from the bears' house and never went back there again."

He stopped talking. The dwarfs were now looking at him as if he might have been a little slow.

"Er, didn't she?" he added.

—*The Book of Lost Things,* Chapter XIII

OF "GOLDILOCKS"

This tale is referred to by the dwarfs in their conversation with David, and it is made quite clear to him that Goldilocks came to a bad end, as befits an amateur burglar and food thief who makes the mistake of falling asleep in a houseful of bears. While it's little more than a dark joke, it does point up David's naiveté at this stage in the tale. Bears are cuddly, dwarfs are not murderous, and Snow White is pretty and gay. Probably.

ORIGINS

This story first found its way into print in 1837, in the form of a prose story entitled "The Three Bears," told by the poet Robert Southey (1774–1843) in his collection *The Doctor*. Goldilocks is not yet present, and instead her place is taken by a little old woman. Later versions replaced the old woman with a girl named Silver-hair, with Goldilocks eventually making her first appearance in the volume *Old Nursery Stories and Rhymes* (1904). Southey may have based his tale on an earlier source, possibly part of an oral tradition, but the story has now become so firmly entrenched in the popular imagination that Southey's involvement has largely been forgotten.

The Three Bears

Robert Southey

A tale which may content the minds of learned men and grave philosophers.
—Gascoyne

Once upon a time there were Three Bears who lived together in a house of their own in a wood. One of them was a Little, Small, Wee Bear, and one was a Middle-sized Bear, and the other was a Great, Huge Bear. They had each a pot for their porridge; a little pot for the Little, Small, Wee Bear, and one was a middle-sized pot for the Middle Bear, and a great pot for the Great, Huge Bear. And they had each a chair to sit in; a little chair for the Little, Small, Wee Bear, and a middle-sized chair for the Middle Bear and a great chair for the Great, Huge Bear. And they had each a bed to sleep in; a little bed for the Little, Small, Wee Bear, and a middle-sized bed for the Middle Bear, and a great bed for the Great, Huge Bear.

One day, after they had made the porridge for their breakfast, and poured it into their porridge-pots, they walked out into the wood while the porridge was cooling, that they might not burn their mouths by beginning too soon to eat it. And while they were walking, a little old Woman came to the house. She could not have been a good, honest old Woman; for first she looked in at the window, and then she peeped in at the key-hole; and see-ing nobody in the house, she lifted the latch. The door was not fastened, because the Bears were good Bears, who did nobody any harm, and never suspected that anybody would harm them. So the little old Woman opened the door and went in; and well she was when she saw the porridge on the table. If she had been a good little old Woman, she would have waited till the Bears came home, and then, perhaps, they would have asked her to breakfast; for they were good Bears—a little rough or so, as the manner of Bears is, but for all that very good-natured and hospitable. But she was an impudent, bad old Woman, and set about helping herself.

So first she tasted the porridge of the Great, Huge Bear, and that was too hot for her; and she said a bad word about that. And then she tasted the porridge of the Middle Bear, and that was too cold for her; and she said a bad word about that too. And then she went to the porridge of the Little, Small, Wee Bear and tasted that; and that was neither too hot nor too cold, but just right; and she liked it so well she ate it all up: but the naughty old Woman said a bad word about the little porridge-pot, because it did not hold enough for her.

Then the little old Woman sat down in the chair of the Great, Huge Bear, and that was too hard for her. And then she sat down in the chair of the Middle Bear, and that was too soft for her. And then she sat down in the chair of the Little, Small, Wee Bear, and that was neither too hard nor too soft, but just right. So she seated herself in it and there she sat till the bottom of the chair came out, and down came hers, plump upon the ground. And the naughty old Woman said a wicked word about that too.

Then the little old Woman went upstairs into the bed-chamber in which the Three Bears slept. And first she lay down upon the bed of the Great, Huge Bear, but that was too high at the head for her. And she lay down upon the bed of the Middle Bear, and that was too high at the foot for her. And then she lay down upon the bed of the Little, Small, Wee Bear, and that was neither too high at the head nor at the foot, but just right. So she covered herself up comfortably, and lay there till she fell fast asleep.

By this time the Three Bears thought their porridge would be cool enough; so they came home to breakfast. Now, the little old Woman had left the spoon of the Great, Huge Bear standing in his porridge.

"Somebody has been at my porridge!" said the Great, Huge Bear, in his great, rough, gruff voice. And when the Middle Bear looked at his he saw that the spoon was standng in it too. They were wooden spoons; if they had been silver ones, the naughty old Woman would have put them in her pocket.

"Somebody has been at my porridge!" said the Middle Bear in his middle voice.

Then the Little, Small, Wee Bear looked at his, and there was the spoon in the porridge-pot, but the porridge was all gone.

"Somebody has been at my porridge, and has eaten it all up!" said the Little, Small, Wee Bear, in his little, small, wee voice.

Upon this the Three Bears, seeing that someone had entered their house, and eaten up the Little, Small, Wee Bear's breakfast, began to look about them. Now, the little old Woman had not put the hard cushion straight when she rose from the chair of the Great, Huge Bear.

"Somebody has been sitting in my chair!" said the Great, Huge Bear, in his great, rough, gruff voice.

And the little old Woman had squatted down the soft cushion of the Middle Bear.

"Somebody has been sitting in my chair!" said the Middle Bear, in his middle voice.

And you know what the little old Woman had done to the third chair.

"Somebody has been sitting in my chair, and has sat the bottom of it out!" said the Little, Small, Wee Bear, in his little, small, wee voice.

Then the Three Bears thought it necessary that they should make farther search; so they went upstairs into their bed-chamber. Now, the little old Woman had pulled the pillow of the Great, Huge Bear out of its place.

"Somebody has been lying in my bed!" said the Great, Huge Bear in his great, rough, gruff voice.

And the little old Woman had pulled the bolster of the Middle Bear out of its place.

"Somebody has been lying in my bed!" said the Middle Bear, in his middle voice.

And when the Little, Small, Wee Bear came to look at his bed, there was the bolster in its place; and the pillow in its place upon the bolster; and upon the pillow was the little old Woman's ugly, dirty head—which was not in its place, for she had no business there.

"Somebody has been lying in my bed and here she is!" said the Little, Small, Wee Bear, in his little, small, wee voice.

The little old Woman had heard in her sleep the great, rough, gruff voice of the Great, Huge Bear; but she was so fast asleep that it was no more to her than the roaring of wind or the rumbling of thunder. And she had heard the middle voice of the Middle Bear, but it was only as if she had heard someone speaking in a dream. But when she heard the little, small, wee voice of the Little, Small, Wee Bear, it was so sharp and so shrill that it awakened her at once. Up she started; and when she saw the Three Bears on one side of the bed, she tumbled herself out at the other, and ran to the window.

Now, the window was open, because the Bears, like good, tidy Bears, as they were, always opened their bed-chamber window when they got up in the morning. Out the little old Woman jumped; and whether she broke her neck in the fall, or ran into the wood and was lost, or found her way out of the wood and was taken up by the constable and sent to the House of Correction for a vagrant as she was I can not tell. But the Three Bears never saw anything more of her.

THE THREE ARMY-SURGEONS

"And then I had some good fortune. Three surgeons were traveling through the forest, and I came upon them and captured them and brought them here. They told me of a salve that they had created, one that could fuse a severed hand back upon its wrist, or a leg to its torso. I made them show me what they could do. I cut the arm from one of them and the others repaired it, just as they said they could. Then I cut another in half, and his friends made him whole again. Finally, I severed the head of the third, and they fixed it again upon his neck.

"And they became the first of my new prey . . ."

—The Book of Lost Things, Chapter XVI

OF "THE THREE ARMY-SURGEONS"

I have a drawing on my wall entitled *Rabbit* by an artist named David Morris. (It can be viewed at www.davidmorris.info/index.html.) It depicts a rabbit-headed child and a child-headed rabbit peering from behind a pair of trees. Along with the recurring images of hunters and hunting in the stories of the Brothers Grimm, and the story entitled "The Tale of the Three Army-Surgeons," the drawing provided inspiration for the section of *The Book of Lost Things* in which David meets the huntress. How did the child come to have the head of the rabbit, I wondered, and vice versa? I then considered how David might outwit the huntress. In part, he learns from the story of Hansel and Gretel, told to him earlier by the Woodsman, because, like Gretel, he spots a way to use his apparent innocence to trick the woman who threatens him. But David is more cunning than Gretel: he exploits the vanity of the huntress, and her desire to be supreme among all the predators of the forest, by telling her of centaurs.

I can find very little background about this story, and to be honest, the only element of it that I wanted to use explicitly in *The Book of Lost Things* was the application of the salve to cure wounds. The story clearly has things to say about the hubris of the medical profession and the manner in which surgeons market their skills, which was probably particularly relevant to those in the early nineteenth century who had reason to fear physicians as much as need them.

Nevertheless, the story also raises some interesting questions about what we might now term "body horror." After all, at its heart is the idea of being taken over by "the Other," something beyond oneself. Each of the surgeons finds that his individuality, even his consciousness, is under threat because of the addition of elements of beings alien to him. It's not difficult, then, to see the influence of this tale on, say, Mary Shelley's *Frankenstein* (particularly the use of body parts stolen from a dead criminal who has died on the gallows), or to find echoes of it in films such as *Invasion of the Body Snatchers, The Hands of Orlac,* or David Cronenberg's *The Fly.*

These ideas feed into the later stages of David's battle with the huntress, when she is finally confronted by the outcasts resulting from her experiments (and I feel certain that something of my own memories of H. G. Wells's *The Island of Doctor Moreau* crept in here as well). The question that this encounter poses, though, is what leads those wretched creatures to turn so viciously upon her, their animal side or the part of them that is still a child?

OF HUNTERS AND HUNTRESSES AND FATHER FIGURES

In many fairy tales, a male figure appears who can be viewed as an unconscious representation of the father. It is typically a hunter or a man of the woods, and in The *Book of Lost Things* it is the Woodsman whom David first encounters upon entering the new world and in whom, at the novel's end, he recognizes aspects of his own father. The Woodsman, though, is flawed by a lack of knowledge and a reluctance, as David sees it, to share information about certain aspects of his life. He also proves unable to protect David from the wolves, and the boy has to rely on his own courage instead—although the Woodsman's willingness to sacrifice himself for the boy hints at the understanding David will achieve at the end of the novel.

Roland, too, is an alternative father figure, although his devotion to his "quest" and to the absent Raphael means that he is an even less reliable figure than the Woodsman. Fletcher, the de facto leader of the villagers later in the book, provides another version of the father figure for David, although one who is compromised by caution and who, like his peers, refuses to acquiesce entirely to Roland's plan of action against the Beast. The King, too, tries to pretend to be a father figure to David, but he also attempts to appeal to him as an equal, or one who would be an equal if he accepted the throne.

So again and again we encounter male figures who fail to be the protectors David needs. In part, this is because of the distrust he feels with regard to his own father, and his sense of betrayal at his father's new relationship, a relationship apparently consummated not long after the death of David's mother. In this we might ask if David does not have some legitimate cause for grievance. How long is it appropriate for someone to grieve for a lost spouse? The speed with which David's father takes up with Rose, and her presence at the hospital in which his mother is dying, might suggest that the seeds of this relationship were sown while his mother was still alive. Clearly, David recognizes this at some level, and his father's failure to address it adequately suggests a weakness to his character. But again and again in fairy tales we encounter weak father figures: the lying miller and greedy king of "Rumpelstiltskin"; the father who colludes in the abandonment of his children in "Hansel and Gretel"; the king who is unable to recognize the threat posed by his wife to his daughter in "Snow White"; and the hunter who subsequently fails both to fulfill the queen's wish to kill Snow White or to protect her instead. David's father, then, is one of a long line of weak men.

Yet one of the most terrifying and callous characters in the book is the huntress, a woman who essentially usurps the role traditionally given to men in fairy tales. She is the anti-protector, a parent-hunter who, instead of keeping the wild animals from the child's door, captures those animals and uses them to undermine the child's identity, fusing it with that of a creature of the forest in order to hunt down and kill the resulting hybrid. Again, she is a symbol of the female threat that dominates David's life in the form of his own stepmother, but she is perhaps worse than that, for if the traditional father figure cannot protect his child, then what will take his place but a being prepared to exploit that vulnerability to its ultimate end? Like the man who dwelt by railway tracks, the man responsible for the death of Billy Golding, she is a child killer.

Finally, this raises one final question, for there are two children whose fate is never properly uncovered in *The Book of Lost Things*. Their shades haunt David—quite literally in the case of the spirit of Anna encountered toward the book's end. David, through his imagination, creates one version of what might have happened to them but, if we accept that the world he enters is entirely a product of his imagination (and I am by no means suggesting that this is the only option), then what *did* happen to Jonathan and Anna? In his meditation on the terrible death of Billy Golding, David offers a possibility that is frighteningly probable, a possibility that colors every subsequent event in the book.

The Three Army-Surgeons

The Brothers Grimm

Three army-surgeons who thought they knew their art perfectly were travelling about the world, and they came to an inn where they wanted to pass the night. The host asked whence they came, and whither they were going?

"We are roaming about the world and practicing our art."

"Just show me what you can do," said the host.

Then the first said he would cut off his hand, and put it on again early next morning; the second said he would tear out his heart, and replace it next morning; the third said he would cut out his eyes and heal them again next morning.

"If you can do that," said the innkeeper, "you have learned everything."

They, however, had a salve, with which they rubbed themselves, which joined parts together, and they carried with them everywhere the little bottle in which it was. Then they cut the hand, heart and eyes from their bodies as they had said they would, and laid them all together on a plate, and gave it to the innkeeper. The innkeeper gave it to a servant who was to set it in the cupboard, and take good care of it.

The girl, however, had a lover in secret, who was a soldier.

When the innkeeper, the three army-surgeons, and everyone else in the house were asleep, the soldier came and wanted something to eat. The girl opened the cupboard and brought him some food, and forgot to shut the cupboard-door again. She seated herself at the table by her lover, and they chattered away together. While she sat so contentedly there, thinking of no ill luck, the cat came creeping in, found the cupboard open, took the hand and heart and eyes of the three army-surgeons, and ran off with them.

When the soldier had done eating, and the girl was taking away the things and going to shut the cupboard, she saw that the plate which the innkeeper had given her to take care of was empty. Then she said to her lover, "Ah, miserable girl, what shall I do? The hand is gone, the heart and the eyes are gone too, what will become of me in the morning?"

"Be easy," said he, "I will help thee out of thy trouble. There is a thief hanging outside on the gallows. I will cut off his hand. Which hand was it?"

"The right one."

Then the girl gave him a sharp knife, and he went and cut the poor man's right hand off, and brought it to her. After this he caught the cat and cut its eyes out, and now nothing but the heart was wanting.

"Have you not been butchering, and are not the dead pigs in the cellar?" said he.

"Yes," said the girl.

"That's good," said the soldier, and he went down and fetched a pig's heart. The girl placed all together on the plate, and put it in the cupboard, and when after this her lover took leave of her, she went quietly to bed.

In the morning when the three army-surgeons got up, they told the girl she was to bring them the plate on which the hand, heart, and eyes were lying. Then she brought it out of the cupboard, and the first fixed the thief's hand on and smeared it with his salve, and it grew to his arm directly. The second took the cat's eyes and put them in his own head. The third fixed the pig's heart firm in the place where his own had been, and the innkeeper stood by, admired their skill, and said he had never yet seen such a thing as that done, and would sing their praises and recommend them to everyone. Then they paid their bill and departed.

As they were on their way, the one with the pig's heart did not stay with them at all, but wherever there was a corner he ran to it, and rooted about in it with his nose as pigs do. The others wanted to hold him back by the tail of his coat, but that did no good. He tore himself loose, and ran wherever the dirt was thickest.

The second also behaved very strangely; he rubbed his eyes, and said to the others, "Comrades, what is the matter? I don't see at all. Will one of you lead me, so that I do not fall."

Thus with difficulty they travelled on till evening, when they reached another inn. They went into the bar together, and there at a table in the corner sat a rich man counting money. The one with the thief's hand walked round about him, made a sudden movement twice with his arm, and at last when the stranger turned away, he snatched at the pile of money, and took a handful from it. One of them saw this, and said, "Comrade, what art thou about? Thou must not steal. Shame on thee!"

"Eh," said he, "but how can I stop myself? My hand twitches, and I am forced to snatch things whether I will or not."

After this, they lay down to sleep, and while they were lying there it was so dark that no one could see his own hand. All at once the one with the cat's eyes awoke, aroused the others, and said. "Brothers, just look up, do you see the white mice running about there?" The two sat up, but could see nothing. Then said he, "Things are not right with us, we have not got back again what is ours. We must return to the innkeeper, for he has deceived us."

They went back therefore, the next morning, and told the host they had not got what was their own again; that the first had a thief's hand, the second cat's eyes, and the third a pig's heart. The innkeeper said that the girl must be to blame for that, and was going to call her, but when she had seen the three coming, she had run out by the backdoor, and not come back. Then the three said he must give them a great deal of money, or they would set his house on fire. He gave them what he had, and whatever he could get together, and the three went away with it. It was enough for the rest of their lives, but they would rather have had their own proper organs.

THE GOOSE-GIRL

When the story was done, Roland looked at David.

"What did you think of my tale?" he asked.

*David's brow was furrowed. "I think I read a story like it once before,"
he said. "But my story was about a princess, not a prince. The ending was
the same, though."*

"And did you like the ending?"

*"I did when I was little. I thought that was what the false prince
deserved. I liked it when the bad were punished to death."*

"And now?"

"It seems cruel."

*"But he would have done the same to another, had it been in his power
to do so."*

"I suppose so, but that doesn't make the punishment right."

"So you would have shown mercy?"

"If I was the true prince, then, yes, I think so."

"But would you have forgiven him?"

David thought about the question.

*"No, he did wrong, so he deserved some punishment. I would have
made him herd the pigs and live the way the true prince had been forced to
live, and if he ever hurt one of the animals, or hurt another person, then the
same thing would be done to him."*

Roland nodded approvingly. "That is a fit punishment, and merciful."

—The Book of Lost Things, *Chapter XIX*

*   *   *

OF "THE GOOSE-GIRL"

The version of this tale told by the Brothers Grimm, and reprinted here, is one of a number of variations found in Europe and elsewhere. Once among the most famous of their tales, it has now fallen from favor somewhat, perhaps because of its simplicity. There are no dwarfs, no ogres, no witches. It is a story of betrayal, and of equanimity in the face of suffering. Traditionally, the main figure, the "goose girl" of the title, is female, but Roland, in his telling of the tale to David, changes the main character's sex to male in order to make it more relevant to David's situation. There are models for this in some of the earlier variations, such as the English story "Roswal and Lillian."

One interpretation of the tale sees it as a lesson in the inability of parents to ensure their child's development to maturity. All of the earthly goods entrusted by the old queen to her daughter are not enough to keep her safe. Much of what befalls her is due to her own carelessness and lack of maturity, and the story makes clear the difficulties and challenges that a child may face on the road to adulthood. It also makes clear the importance of being true to oneself, and the danger of usurping another's position to obtain advancement.

The story that Roland tells David, though, is much simpler. On one level, the story can be interpreted as a "cuckoo in the nest" tale. Clearly, that is how David sees his half-brother, Georgie, and Roland recognizes the boy's anger at the newcomer. The changes he makes to the tale become most obvious and relevant at the end: where both tales end with a gruesome punishment, Roland invites David to find an alternative by questioning him about the justice or otherwise of the retribution visited upon the impostor. (Still, it is worth noting that in both versions of the tale the wrongdoer imposes the sentence to be visited upon himself/herself, an indication both that the evil person's intentions undo him/her in the long run and that evil is a matter of choice.) That David suggests a more merciful alternative is an indication that he is already, at some level, beginning to come to terms with Georgie's presence and with his own duty toward a being who is more vulnerable and less powerful than he is.

In general, though, I was reluctant throughout the book to "sanitize" the old tales in any way, and they remain "red in tooth and claw." Children understand the nature of punishment, and it is reassuring to them to know that evil is punished as evil should be. Equally, to remove the violence and threat from the stories is to take away much of their potency, as well as to undermine the messages they communicate about the sometimes troubling and terrifying nature of the world children inhabit.

The Goose-Girl

The Brothers Grimm

There was once upon a time an old Queen whose husband had been dead for many years, and she had a beautiful daughter. When the princess grew up she was betrothed to a prince who lived at a great distance. When the time came for her to be married, and she had to journey forth into the distant kingdom, the aged Queen packed up for her many costly vessels of silver and gold, and trinkets also of gold and silver; and cups and jewels—in short, everything which appertained to a royal dowry, for she loved her child with all her heart. She likewise sent her maid-in-waiting, who was to ride with her, and hand her over to the bridegroom, and each had a horse for the journey, but the horse of the King's daughter was called Falada, and could speak. So when the hour of parting had come, the aged mother went into her bedroom, took a small knife and cut her finger with it until it bled, then she held a white handkerchief to it into which she let three drops of blood fall, gave it to her daughter and said, "Dear child, preserve this carefully, it will be of service to you on your way."

So they took a sorrowful leave of each other; the princess put the piece of cloth in her bosom, mounted her horse, and then went away to her bridegroom. After she had ridden for a while she felt a burning thirst, and said to her waiting-maid. "Dismount, and take my cup which thou hast brought with thee for me, and get me some water from the stream, for I should like to drink." "If you are thirsty," said the waiting-maid, "get off your horse yourself, and lie down and drink out of the water, I don't choose to be your servant." So in her great thirst the princess alighted, bent down over the water in the stream and drank, and was not allowed to drink out of the golden cup. Then she said, "Ah, Heaven!" and the three drops of blood answered, "If thy mother knew this, her heart would break." But the King's daughter was humble, said nothing, and mounted her horse again. She rode some miles further, but the day was warm, the sun scorched her, and she was thirsty once more, and when they came to a stream of water, she again cried to her waiting-maid, "Dismount and give me some water in my golden cup," for she had long ago forgotten the girl's ill words. But the waiting-maid said still more haughtily, "If you wish to drink, drink as you can, I don't choose to be your maid." Then in her great thirst the King's daughter alighted, bent over the flowing stream, wept and said, "Ah, Heaven!" and the drops of blood again replied, "If thy mother knew this, her heart would break." And as she was thus drinking and leaning right over the stream, the handkerchief with the three drops of blood fell out of her bosom, and floated away with the water without her observing it, so great was her trouble. The waiting-maid, however, had seen it, and she rejoiced to think that she had now power over the bride, for since the princess had lost the drops of blood, she had become weak and powerless. So now when she wanted to mount her horse again, the one that was called Falada, the waiting-maid said, "Falada is more suitable for me, and my nag will do for thee," and the princess had to be content with that. Then the waiting-maid, with many hard words, bade the princess exchange her royal apparel for her own shabby clothes; and at length she was compelled to swear by the clear sky above her, that she would not say one word of this to anyone at the royal court, and if she had not taken this oath she would have been killed on the spot. But Falada saw all this, and observed it well.

The waiting-maid now mounted Falada, and the true bride the bad horse, and thus they travelled onwards, until at length they entered the royal palace. There were great rejoicings over her arrival, and the prince sprang forward to meet her, lifted the waiting-maid from her horse, and thought she was his consort. She was conducted upstairs, but the real princess was left standing below. Then the old king looked out of the window and saw her standing in the courtyard, and saw how dainty and delicate and beautiful she was, and instantly went to the royal apartment, and asked the bride about the girl she had with her who was standing down below in the courtyard, and who she was? "I picked her up on my way for a companion; give the girl something to work at, that she may not stand idle." But the old King had no work for her, and knew of none, so he said, "I have a little boy who tends the geese, she may help him." The boy was called Conrad, and the true bride had to help him to tend the geese. Soon afterwards the false bride said to the young King, "Dearest husband, I beg you to do me a favor." He answered. "I will do so most willingly." "Then send for the knacker, and have the head of the horse on which I rode here cut off, for it vexed me on the way." In reality, she was afraid that the horse might tell how she had behaved to the King's daughter. Then she succeeded in making the King promise that it should be done, and the faithful Falada was to die; this came to the ears of the real princess, and she secretly promised to pay the knacker a piece of gold if he would perform a small service for her. There was a great dark-looking gateway in the town, through which morning and evening she had to pass with the geese: would he be so good as to nail up Falada's head on it, so that she might see him again, more than once. The knacker's man promised to do that, and cut off the head, and nailed it fast beneath the dark gateway.

Early in the morning, when she and Conrad drove out their flock beneath this gateway, she said in passing, "Alas, Falada, hanging there!"

Then the head answered,

Alas, young Queen, how ill you fare!
If this your tender mother knew,
Her heart would surely break in two.

Then they went still further out of the town, and drove their geese into the country. And when they had come to the meadow, she sat down and unbound her hair which was like pure gold, and Conrad saw it and delighted in its brightness, and wanted to pluck out a few hairs. Then she said,

Blow, blow, thou gentle wind, I say,
Blow Conrad's little hat away,
And make him chase it here and there,
Until I have braided all my hair,
And bound it up again.

And there came such a violent wind that it blew Conrad's hat far away across country, and he was forced to run after it. When he came back she had finished combing her hair and was putting it up again, and he could not get any of it. Then Conrad was angry, and would not speak to her, and thus they watched the geese until the evening, and then they went home.

Next day when they were driving the geese out through the dark gateway, the maiden said, "Alas, Falada, hanging there!"

Falada answered,

Alas, young Queen, how ill you fare!
If this your tender mother knew,
Her heart would surely break in two.

And she sat down again in the field and began to comb out her hair, and Conrad ran and tried to clutch it, so she said in haste,

Blow, blow, though gentle wind, I say,
Blow Conrad's little hat away,
And make him chase it here and there,
Until I have braided all my hair,
And bound it up again.

Then the wind blew, and blew his little hat off his head and far away, and Conrad was forced to run after it, and when he came back, her hair had been put up a long time, and he could get none of it, and so they looked after their geese till evening came.

But in the evening after they had got home, Conrad went to the old King, and said, "I won't tend the geese with that girl any longer!" "Why not?" inquired the aged King. "Oh, because she vexes me the whole day long." Then the aged King commanded him to relate what it was that she did to him. And Conrad said,

"In the morning when we pass beneath the dark gateway with the flock, there is a sorry horse's head on the wall, and she says to it, "Alas, Falada, hanging there!" And the head replies,

Alas, young Queen, how ill you fare!
If this your tender mother knew,
Her heart would surely break in two.

And Conrad went on to relate what happened on the goose pasture, and how when there he had to chase his hat.

The aged King commanded him to drive his flock out again next day, and as soon as morning came, he placed himself behind the dark gateway, and heard how the maiden spoke to the head of Falada, and then he too went into the country, and hid himself in the thicket in the meadow. There he soon saw with his own eyes the goose-girl and the goose-boy bringing their flock, and how after a while she sat down and unplaited her hair, which shone with radiance. And soon she said,

Blow, blow, thou gentle wind, I say,
Blow Conrad's little hat away,
And make him chase it here and there,
Until I have braided all my hair,
And bound it up again.

Then came a blast of wind and carried off Conrad's hat, so that he had to run far away, while the maiden quietly went on combing and plaiting her hair, all of which the King observed. Then, quite unseen, he went away, and when the goose-girl came home in the evening, he called her aside, and asked why she did all these things. "I may not tell you that, and I dare not lament my sorrows to any human being, for I have sworn not to do so by the heaven which is above me; if I had not done that, I should have lost my life." He urged her and left her no peace, but he could draw nothing from her. Then said he, "If thou wilt not tell me anything, tell thy sorrows to the iron-stove there," and he went away. Then she crept into the iron-stove, and began to weep and lament, and emptied her whole heart, and said, "Here am I deserted by the whole world, and yet I am a King's daughter, and a false waiting-maid has by force brought me to such a pass that I have been compelled to put off my royal apparel, and she has taken my place with my bridegroom, and I have to perform menial service as a goose-girl. If my mother did but know that, her heart would break."

The aged King, however, was standing outside by the pipe of the stove, and was listening to what she said, and heard it. Then he came back again, and bade her come out of the stove. And royal garments were placed on her, and it was marvellous how beautiful she was! The aged King summoned his son, and revealed to him that he had got the false bride who was only a waiting-maid, but that the true one was standing there, as the sometime goose-girl. The young King rejoiced with all his heart when he saw her beauty and youth, and a great feast was made ready to which all the people and all good friends were invited. At the head of the table sat the bridegroom with the King's daughter at one side of him, and the waiting-maid on the other, but the waiting-maid was blinded, and did not recognize the princess in her dazzling array. When they had eaten and drunk, and were merry, the aged King asked the waiting-maid as a riddle, what a person deserved who had behaved in such and such a way to her master, and at the same time related the whole story, and asked what sentence such a one merited? Then the false bride said: "She deserves no better fate than to be stripped entirely naked, and put in a barrel which is studded inside with pointed nails, and two white horses should be harnessed to it, which will drag her along through one street after another, till she is dead." "It is thou," said the aged King, "and thou hast pronounced thine own sentence, and thus shall it be done unto thee." And when the sentence had been carried out, the young King married his true bride, and both of them reigned over their kingdom in peace and happiness.

BEAUTY AND THE BEAST

At that moment, the mirror on the wall to his right shimmered and grew transparent, and through the glass he saw the shape of a woman. She was dressed all in black and was seated on a great throne in an otherwise empty room. Her face was veiled, and her hands were covered in velvet gloves.

"Can I not look upon the face of the one who has saved my life?" asked Alexander.

"I choose not to allow it," the Lady replied.

— *The Book of Lost Things,* Chapter XX

OF "BEAUTY AND THE BEAST"

Roland's telling of this tale was a comparatively late addition to *The Book of Lost Things,* and it is a story that relates more to his own quest than to David's. With it, I think he finds a way to put into words the fear he feels at what awaits him in the Fortress of Thorns, but—and here it should be remembered that even this tale is a product of David's imagination, and is influenced by his emotions—the threat posed is once again female, although by this stage David's responses to his situation are becoming more complex. While there is evil in this tale, it does not emanate from the female character. It is the male character who is at fault. Guilty of arrogance and vanity, he is punished for his sins.

*　　*　　*

ORIGINS

The story of "Beauty and the Beast" has its roots in Apuleius's "Cupid and Psyche," from *The Golden Ass* (A.D. 2). The story came to prominence in the fifteenth century, when it was printed in Latin and dispersed throughout Europe, then subsequently translated into other languages for public performance, with each culture feeding a little of its own distinctive aspects back into the tale, so that a family of tales arose from the original story. The version of the story that is regarded as canonical was penned by Mme (Jeanne-Marie) Leprince de Beaumont in 1757 for her *Magasin des enfants* (or *Young Misses Magazine,* as it came to be translated), although earlier versions were written by Giambattista Basile, Perrault, and Giovanni Straparola. In 1740, Mme de Villeneuve published a novel, *Les Contes marins, ou la jeune Américaine,* that contained a version of "Beauty and the Beast," reprinted below.

The story, with reference to its origins in Apuleius, can be taken as a tale of the harnessing of female sexuality, or, perhaps, of male sexuality, given the transformation from beast to handsome male that occurs in the more moralistic versions of the tale; although it may also be taken as a recognition of the reality of sex in a loving relationship, the literal "beast with two backs." Robert Graves saw it as a "philosophical allegory of the progression of the rational soul towards intellectual love," while in medieval times it may have found its soul mates among tales of companion love, in particular those that advocated a woman's tolerance of an ugly male who could support her.

Worth looking at in relation to this tale, as with many of the others mentioned in this section, are Marina Warner's two excellent works *No Go the Bogeyman* (1998) and *From the Beast to the Blonde: On Fairy Tales and Their Tellers* (1994).

Beauty and the Beast

Jeanne-Marie Leprince de Beaumont

There was once a very rich merchant, who had six children, three sons, and three daughters; being a man of sense, he spared no cost for their education, but gave them all kinds of masters. His daughters were extremely handsome, especially the youngest. When she was little everybody admired her, and called her "The little Beauty"; so that, as she grew up, she still went by the name of Beauty, which made her sisters very jealous.

The youngest, as she was handsomer, was also better than her sisters. The two eldest had a great deal of pride, because they were rich. They gave themselves ridiculous airs, and would not visit other merchants' daughters, nor keep company with any but persons of quality. They went out every day to parties of pleasure, balls, plays, concerts, and so forth, and they laughed at their youngest sister, because she spent the greatest part of her time in reading good books.

As it was known that they were great fortunes, several eminent merchants made their addresses to them; but the two eldest said they would never marry, unless they could meet with a duke, or an earl at least. Beauty very civilly thanked them that courted her, and told them she was too young yet to marry, but chose to stay with her father a few years longer.

All at once the merchant lost his whole fortune, excepting a small country house at a great distance from town, and told his children with tears in his eyes, they must go there and work for their living. The two eldest answered that they would not leave the town, for they had several lovers, who they were sure would be glad to have them, though they had no fortune; but the good ladies were mistaken, for their lovers slighted and forsook them in their poverty. As they were not beloved on account of their pride, everybody said: they do not deserve to be pitied, we are very glad to see their pride humbled, let them go and give themselves quality airs in milking the cows and minding their dairy. But, added they, we are extremely concerned for Beauty, she was such a charming, sweet-tempered creature, spoke so kindly to poor people, and was of such an affable, obliging behaviour. Nay, several gentlemen would have married her, though they knew she had not a penny; but she told them she could not think of leaving her poor father in his misfortunes, but was determined to go along with him into the country to comfort and attend him. Poor Beauty at first was sadly grieved at the loss of her fortune; "but," said she to herself, "were I to cry ever so much, that would not make things better, I must try to make myself happy without a fortune."

When they came to their country house, the merchant and his three sons applied themselves to husbandry and tillage; and Beauty rose at four in the morning, and made haste to have the house clean, and dinner ready for the family. In the beginning she found it very difficult, for she had not been used to work as a servant, but in less than two months she grew stronger and healthier than ever. After she had done her work, she read, played on the harpsichord, or else sung whilst she spun.

On the contrary, her two sisters did not know how to spend their time; they got up at ten, and did nothing but saunter about the whole day, lamenting the loss of their fine clothes and acquaintance. "Do but see our youngest sister," said they, one to the other, "what a poor, stupid, mean-spirited creature she is, to be contented with such an unhappy dismal situation."

The good merchant was of quite a different opinion; he knew very well that Beauty outshone her sisters, in her person as well as her mind, and admired her humility and industry, but above all her humility and patience; for her sisters not only left her all the work of the house to do, but insulted her every moment.

The family had lived about a year in this retirement, when the merchant received a letter with an account that a vessel, on board of which he had effects, was safely arrived. This news had liked to have turned the heads of the two eldest daughters, who immediately flattered themselves with the hopes of returning to town, for they were quite weary of a country life; and when they saw their father ready to set out, they begged of him to buy them new gowns, head-dresses, ribbons, and all manner of trifles; but Beauty asked for nothing for she thought to herself, that all the money her father was going to receive, would scarce be sufficient to purchase everything her sisters wanted.

"What will you have, Beauty?" said her father.

"Since you have the goodness to think of me," answered she, "be so kind to bring me a rose, for as none grows hereabouts, they are a kind of rarity." Not that Beauty cared for a rose, but she asked for something, lest she should seem by her example to condemn her sisters' conduct, who would have said she did it only to look particular.

The good man went on his journey, but when he came there, they went to law with him about the merchandise, and after a great deal of trouble and pains to no purpose, he came back as poor as before.

He was within thirty miles of his own house, thinking on the pleasure he should have in seeing his children again, when going through a large forest he lost himself. It rained and snowed terribly; besides, the wind was so high, that it threw him twice off his horse, and night coming on, he began to apprehend being either starved to death with cold and hunger, or else devoured by the wolves, whom he heard howling all round him, when, on a sudden, looking through a long walk of trees, he saw a light at some distance, and going on a little farther perceived it came from a place illuminated from top to bottom. The merchant returned God thanks for this happy discovery, and hastened to the place, but was greatly surprised at not meeting with any one in the outer courts. His horse followed him, and seeing a large stable open, went in, and finding both hay and oats, the poor beast, who was almost famished, fell to eating very heartily; the merchant tied him up to the manger, and walking towards the house, where he saw no one, but entering into a large hall, he found a good fire, and a table plentifully set out with but one cover laid. As he was wet quite through with the rain and snow, he drew near the fire to dry himself. "I hope," said he, "the master of the house, or his servants will excuse the liberty I take; I suppose it will not be long before some of them appear."

He waited a considerable time, until it struck eleven, and still nobody came. At last he was so hungry that he could stay no longer, but took a chicken, and ate it in two mouthfuls, trembling all the while. After this he drank a few glasses of wine, and growing more courageous he went out of the hall, and crossed through several grand apartments with magnificent furniture, until he came into a chamber, which had an exceeding good bed in it, and as he was very much fatigued, and it was past midnight, he concluded it was best to shut the door, and go to bed.

It was ten the next morning before the merchant waked, and as he was going to rise he was astonished to see a good suit of clothes in the room of his own, which were quite spoiled; certainly, said he, this palace belongs to some kind fairy, who has seen and pitied my distress. He looked through a window, but instead of snow saw the most delightful arbours, interwoven with the beautifullest flowers that were ever beheld. He then returned to the great hall, where he had supped the night before, and found some chocolate ready made on a little table. "Thank you, good Madam Fairy," said he aloud, "for being so careful, as to provide me a breakfast; I am extremely obliged to you for all your favors."

The good man drank his chocolate, and then went to look for his horse, but passing through an arbor of roses he remembered Beauty's request to him, and gathered a branch on which were several; immediately he heard a great noise, and saw such a frightful Beast coming towards him, that he was ready to faint away.

"You are very ungrateful," said the Beast to him, in a terrible voice; "I have saved your life by receiving you into my castle, and, in return, you steal my roses, which I value beyond any thing in the universe, but you shall die for it; I give you but a quarter of an hour to prepare yourself, and say your prayers."

The merchant fell on his knees, and lifted up both his hands. "My lord," said he, "I beseech you to forgive me, indeed I had no intention to offend in gathering a rose for one of my daughters, who desired me to bring her one."

"My name is not My Lord," replied the monster, "but Beast; I don't love compliments, not I. I like people to speak as they think; and so do not imagine, I am to be moved by any of your flattering speeches. But you say you have got daughters. I will forgive you, on condition that one of them come willingly, and suffer for you. Let me have no words, but go about your business, and swear that if your daughter refuse to die in your stead, you will return within three months."

The merchant had no mind to sacrifice his daughters to the ugly monster, but he thought, in obtaining this respite, he should have the satisfaction of seeing them once more, so he promised, upon oath, he would return, and the Beast told him he might set out when he pleased, "but," added he, "you shall not depart empty handed; go back to the room where you lay, and you will see a great empty chest; fill it with whatever you like best, and I will send it to your home," and at the same time Beast withdrew.

"Well," said the good man to himself, "if I must die, I shall have the comfort, at least, of leaving something to my poor children." He returned to the bedchamber, and finding a great quantity of broad pieces of gold, he filled the great chest the Beast had mentioned, locked it, and afterwards took his horse out of the stable, leaving the palace with as much grief as he had entered it with joy. The horse, of his own accord, took one of the roads of the forest, and in a few hours the good man was at home.

His children came round him, but instead of receiving their embraces with pleasure, he looked on them, and holding up the branch he had in his hands, he burst into tears. "Here, Beauty," said he, "take these roses, but little do you think how dear they are like to cost your unhappy father," and then related his fatal adventure. Immediately the two eldest set up lamentable outcries, and said all manner of ill-natured things to Beauty, who did not cry at all.

"Do but see the pride of that little wretch," said they; "she would not ask for fine clothes, as we did; but no truly, Miss wanted to distinguish herself, so now she will be the death of our poor father, and yet she does not so much as shed a tear."

"Why should I," answered Beauty, "it would be very needless, for my father shall not suffer upon my account, since the monster will accept one of his daughters, I will deliver myself up to all his fury, and I am very happy in thinking that my death will save my father's life, and be a proof of my tender love for him."

"No, sister," said her three brothers, "that shall not be, we will go find the monster, and either kill him, or perish in the attempt."

"Do not imagine any such thing, my sons," said the merchant. "Beast's power is so great, that I have no hopes of your overcoming him. I am charmed with Beauty's kind and generous offer, but I cannot yield to it. I am old, and have not long to live, so can only lose a few years, which I regret for your sakes alone, my dear children."

"Indeed father," said Beauty, "you shall not go to the palace without me, you cannot hinder me from following you." It was to no purpose all they could say. Beauty still insisted on setting out for the fine palace, and her sisters were delighted at it, for her virtue and amiable qualities made them envious and jealous.

The merchant was so afflicted at the thoughts of losing his daughter, that he had quite forgot the chest full of gold, but at night when he retired to rest, no sooner had he shut his chamber door, than, to his great astonishment, he found it by his bedside; he was determined, however, not to tell his children, that he was grown rich, because they would have wanted to return to town, and he was resolved not to leave the country; but he trusted Beauty with the secret, who informed him that two gentlemen came in his absence, and courted her sisters; she begged her father to consent to their marriage, and give them fortunes, for she was so good, that she loved them and forgave heartily all their ill usage. These wicked creatures rubbed their eyes with an onion to force some tears when they parted with their sister, but her brothers were really concerned. Beauty was the only one who did not shed tears at parting, because she would not increase their uneasiness.

The horse took the direct road to the palace, and towards evening they perceived it illuminated as at first. The horse went of himself into the stable, and the good man and his daughter came into the great hall, where they found a table splendidly served up, and two covers. The merchant had no heart to eat, but Beauty, endeavouring to appear cheerful, sat down to table, and helped him. "Afterwards," thought she to herself, "Beast surely has a mind to fatten me before he eats me, since he provides such plentiful entertainment." When they had supped they heard a great noise, and the merchant, all in tears, bid his poor child farewell, for he thought Beast was coming. Beauty was sadly terrified at his horrid form, but she took courage as well as she could, and the monster asked her if she came willingly. "Ye–e–es," said she, trembling.

The beast responded, "You are very good, and I am greatly obliged to you; honest man, go your ways tomorrow morning, but never think of coming here again."

"Farewell Beauty, farewell Beast," answered he, and immediately the monster withdrew. "Oh, daughter," said the merchant, embracing Beauty, "I am almost frightened to death, believe me, you had better go back, and let me stay here."

"No, father," said Beauty, in a resolute tone, "you shall set out tomorrow morning, and leave me to the care and protection of providence." They went to bed, and thought they should not close their eyes all night; but scarce were they laid down, than they fell fast asleep, and Beauty dreamed a fine lady came and said to her, "I am content, Beauty, with your good will, this good action of yours in giving up your own life to save your father's shall not go unrewarded." Beauty waked, and told her father her dream, and though it helped to comfort him a little, yet he could not help crying bitterly, when he took leave of his dear child.

As soon as he was gone, Beauty sat down in the great hall, and fell a crying likewise; but as she was mistress of a great deal of resolution, she recommended herself to God, and resolved not to be uneasy the little time she had to live; for she firmly believed Beast would eat her up that night.

However, she thought she might as well walk about until then, and view this fine castle, which she could not help admiring; it was a delightful pleasant place, and she was extremely surprised at seeing a door, over which was written, "Beauty's Apartment." She opened it hastily, and was quite dazzled with the magnificence that reigned throughout; but what chiefly took up her attention, was a large library, a harpsichord, and several music books. "Well," said she to herself, "I see they will not let my time hang heavy upon my hands for want of amusement." Then she reflected, "Were I but to stay here a day, there would not have been all these preparations." This consideration inspired her with fresh courage; and opening the library she took a book, and read these words, in letters of gold:

Welcome Beauty, banish fear,
You are queen and mistress here.
Speak your wishes, speak your will,
Swift obedience meets them still.

"Alas," said she, with a sigh, "there is nothing I desire so much as to see my poor father, and know what he is doing." She had no sooner said this, when casting her eyes on a great looking glass, to her great amazement, she saw her own home, where her father arrived with a very dejected countenance. Her sisters went to meet him, and notwithstanding their endeavours to appear sorrowful, their joy, felt for having got rid of their sister, was visible in every feature. A moment after, everything disappeared, and Beauty's apprehensions at this proof of Beast's complaisance.

At noon she found dinner ready, and while at table, was entertained with an excellent concert of music, though without seeing anybody. But at night, as she was going to sit down to supper, she heard the noise Beast made, and could not help being sadly terrified. "Beauty," said the monster, "will you give me leave to see you sup?"

"That is as you please," answered Beauty trembling.

"No," replied the Beast, "you alone are mistress here; you need only bid me gone, if my presence is troublesome, and I will immediately withdraw. But, tell me, do not you think me very ugly?"

"That is true," said Beauty, "for I cannot tell a lie, but I believe you are very good natured."

"So I am," said the monster, "but then, besides my ugliness, I have no sense; I know very well, that I am a poor, silly, stupid creature."

"'Tis no sign of folly to think so," replied Beauty, "for never did fool know this, or had so humble a conceit of his own understanding."

"Eat then, Beauty," said the monster, "and endeavour to amuse yourself in your palace, for everything here is yours, and I should be very uneasy, if you were not happy."

"You are very obliging," answered Beauty, "I own I am pleased with your kindness, and when I consider that, your deformity scarce appears."

"Yes, yes," said the Beast, "my heart is good, but still I am a monster."

"Among mankind," says Beauty, "there are many that deserve that name more than you, and I prefer you, just as you are, to those, who, under a human form, hide a treacherous, corrupt, and ungrateful heart."

"If I had sense enough," replied the Beast, "I would make a fine compliment to thank you, but I am so dull, that I can only say, I am greatly obliged to you."

Beauty ate a hearty supper, and had almost conquered her dread of the monster; but she had like to have fainted away, when he said to her, "Beauty, will you be my wife?"

She was some time before she dared answer, for she was afraid of making him angry, if she refused. At last, however, she said trembling, "No, Beast." Immediately the poor monster went to sigh, and hissed so frightfully, that the whole palace echoed. But Beauty soon recovered her fright, for Beast having said, in a mournful voice, "Then farewell, Beauty," left the room; and only turned back, now and then, to look at her as he went out.

When Beauty was alone, she felt a great deal of compassion for poor Beast. "Alas," said she, "'tis thousand pities, anything so good natured should be so ugly."

Beauty spent three months very contentedly in the palace. Every evening Beast paid her a visit, and talked to her, during supper, very rationally, with plain good common sense, but never with what the world calls wit; and Beauty daily discovered some valuable qualifications in the monster, and seeing him often had so accustomed her to his deformity, that, far from dreading the time of his visit, she would often look on her watch to see when it would be nine, for the Beast never missed coming at that hour. There was but one thing that gave Beauty any concern, which was, that every night, before she went to bed, the monster always asked her, if she would be his wife. One day she said to him, "Beast, you make me very uneasy, I wish I could consent to marry you, but I am too sincere to make you believe that will ever happen; I shall always esteem you as a friend, endeavour to be satisfied with this."

"I must," said the Beast, "for, alas! I know too well my own misfortune, but then I love you with the tenderest affection. However, I ought to think myself happy, that you will stay here; promise me never to leave me."

Beauty blushed at these words; she had seen in her glass, that her father had pined himself sick for the loss of her, and she longed to see him again. "I could," answered she, "indeed, promise never to leave you entirely, but I have so great a desire to see my father, that I shall fret to death, if you refuse me that satisfaction."

"I had rather die myself," said the monster, "than give you the least uneasiness. I will send you to your father, you shall remain with him, and poor Beast will die with grief."

"No," said Beauty, weeping, "I love you too well to be the cause of your death. I give you my promise to return in a week. You have shown me that my sisters are married, and my brothers gone to the army; only let me stay a week with my father, as he is alone."

"You shall be there tomorrow morning," said the Beast, "but remember your promise. You need only lay your ring on a table before you go to bed, when you have a mind to come back. Farewell, Beauty." Beast sighed, as usual, bidding her good night, and Beauty went to bed very sad at seeing him so afflicted. When she waked the next morning, she found herself at her father's, and having rung a little bell, that was by her bedside, she saw the maid come, who, the moment she saw her, gave a loud shriek, at which the good man ran up stairs, and thought he should have died with joy to see his dear daughter again. He held her fast locked in his arms above a quarter of an hour. As soon as the first transports were over, Beauty began to think of rising, and was afraid she had no clothes to put on; but the maid told her, that she had just found, in the next room, a large trunk full of gowns, covered with gold and diamonds. Beauty thanked good Beast for his kind care, and taking one of the plainest of them, she intended to make a present of the others to her sisters. She scarce had said so when the trunk disappeared. Her father told her that Beast insisted on her keeping them herself, and immediately both gowns and trunk came back again.

Beauty dressed herself, and in the meantime they sent to her sisters who hastened thither with their husbands. They were both of them very unhappy. The eldest had married a gentleman, extremely handsome indeed, but so fond of his own person, that he was full of nothing but his own dear self, and neglected his wife. The second had married a man of wit, but he only made use of it to plague and torment everybody, and his wife most of all. Beauty's sisters sickened with envy, when they saw her dressed like a princess, and more beautiful than ever, nor could all her obliging affectionate behaviour stifle their jealousy, which was ready to burst when she told them how happy she was. They went down into the garden to vent it in tears; and said one to the other, in what way is this little creature better than us, that she should be so much happier? "Sister," said the oldest, "a thought just strikes my mind; let us endeavour to detain her above a week, and perhaps the silly monster will be so enraged at her for breaking her word, that he will devour her."

"Right, sister," answered the other, "therefore we must show her as much kindness as possible." After they had taken this resolution, they went up, and behaved so affectionately to their sister, that poor Beauty wept for joy. When the week was expired, they cried and tore their hair, and seemed so sorry to part with her, that she promised to stay a week longer.

In the meantime, Beauty could not help reflecting on herself, for the uneasiness she was likely to cause poor Beast, whom she sincerely loved, and really longed to see again. The tenth night she spent at her father's, she dreamed she was in the palace garden, and that she saw Beast extended on the grass lawn, who seemed just expiring, and, in a dying voice, reproached her with her ingratitude. Beauty started out of her sleep, and burst into tears. "Am I not very wicked," said she, "to act so unkindly to Beast, that has studied so much, to please me in everything? Is it his fault if he is so ugly, and has so little sense? He is kind and good, and that is sufficient. Why did I refuse to marry him? I should be happier with the monster than my sisters are with their husbands; it is neither wit, nor a fine person, in a husband, that makes a woman happy, but virtue, sweetness of temper, and complaisance, and Beast has all these valuable qualifications. It is true, I do not feel the tenderness of affection for him, but I find I have the highest gratitude, esteem, and friendship; I will not make him miserable, were I to be so ungrateful I should never forgive myself." Beauty having said this, rose, put her ring on the table, and then laid down again; scarce was she in bed before she fell asleep, and when she waked the next morning, she was overjoyed to find herself in the Beast's palace.

She put on one of her richest suits to please him, and waited for evening with the utmost impatience, at last the wished-for hour came, the clock struck nine, yet no Beast appeared. Beauty then feared she had been the cause of his death; she ran crying and wringing her hands all about the palace, like one in despair; after having sought for him everywhere, she recollected her dream, and flew to the canal in the garden, where she dreamed she saw him. There she found poor Beast stretched out, quite senseless, and, as she imagined, dead. She threw herself upon him without any dread, and finding his heart beat still, she fetched some water from the canal, and poured it on his head. Beast opened his eyes, and said to Beauty, "You forgot your promise, and I was so afflicted for having lost you, that I resolved to starve myself, but since I have the happiness of seeing you once more, I die satisfied."

"No, dear Beast," said Beauty, "you must not die. Live to be my husband; from this moment I give you my hand, and swear to be none but yours. Alas! I thought I had only a friendship for you, but the grief I now feel convinces me, that I cannot live without you." Beauty scarce had pronounced these words, when she saw the palace sparkle with light; and fireworks, instruments of music, everything seemed to give notice of some great event. But nothing could fix her attention; she turned to her dear Beast, for whom she trembled with fear; but how great was her surprise! Beast was disappeared, and she saw, at her feet, one of the loveliest princes that eye ever beheld; who returned her thanks for having put an end to the charm, under which he had so long resembled a Beast. Though this prince was worthy of all her attention, she could not forbear asking where Beast was.

"You see him at your feet," said the prince. "A wicked fairy had condemned me to remain under that shape until a beautiful virgin should consent to marry me. The fairy likewise enjoined me to conceal my understanding. There was only you in the world generous enough to be won by the goodness of my temper, and in offering you my crown I can't discharge the obligations I have to you."

Beauty, agreeably surprised, gave the charming prince her hand to rise; they went together into the castle, and Beauty was overjoyed to find, in the great hall, her father and his whole family, whom the beautiful lady, that appeared to her in her dream, had conveyed thither.

"Beauty," said this lady, "come and receive the reward of your judicious choice; you have preferred virtue before either wit or beauty, and deserve to find a person in whom all these qualifications are united. You are going to be a great queen. I hope the throne will not lessen your virtue, or make you forget yourself. As to you, ladies," said the fairy to Beauty's two sisters, "I know your hearts, and all the malice they contain. Become two statues, but, under this transformation, still retain your reason. You shall stand before your sister's palace gate, and be it your punishment to behold her happiness; and it will not be in your power to return to your former state, until you own your faults, but I am very much afraid that you will always remain statues. Pride, anger, gluttony, and idleness are sometimes conquered, but the conversion of a malicious and envious mind is a kind of miracle."

Immediately the fairy gave a stroke with her wand, and in a moment all that were in the hall were transported into the prince's dominions. His subjects received him with joy. He married Beauty, and lived with her many years, and their happiness— as it was founded on virtue—was complete.

SLEEPING BEAUTY

"I had a friend," [Roland] said, without looking at David. "His name was Raphael. He wanted to prove himself to those who doubted his courage and spoke ill of him behind his back. He heard the tale of a woman bound to sleep by an enchantress in a chamber filled with treasures, and he vowed to release her from her curse."

—*The Book of Lost Things,* Chapter XIX

Now David could see why [the fortress] had appeared blurred from a distance. It was completely covered by brown creepers that wound around the central tower and covered the walls and battlements, and from the creepers emerged dark thorns, some easily a foot long and thicker than David's wrist . . .

—*The Book of Lost Things,* Chapter XXIV

OF "SLEEPING BEAUTY"

In *The Book of Lost Things,* the tale of Sleeping Beauty is conflated by David with other sources, including Browning's poem "Childe Roland to the Dark Tower Came," to lead him to the Fortress of Thorns and the sleeping woman within. She is ostensibly the object of Roland's quest, but in reality Roland is seeking Raphael, his soul mate. It is David who gives ultimate form to the woman in the tower, who is both his own mother and Rose, the woman who would be his mother, but also an embodiment of all David's fears, a female figure even more threatening than the Beast he faces earlier in the book.

The sexual elements of the original tale, which have been softened somewhat in later retellings, resurface here, a manifestation of David's own dawning sexuality, and a recognition of his confused feelings toward Rose (and are perhaps a nod to the oedipal interpretations placed on many such stories by Bruno Bettelheim). Clearly, the story of the sleeping princess can be taken as an allegory of the journey from childhood to womanhood: the pricking of the thumb to draw blood, presaging menstruation; the period of dormancy, of waiting for the first sexual awakening; and the arrival of that awakening in the form of a sexual relationship, symbolized in some tales by a kiss and in others by an act far more intimate.

ORIGINS

"Briar Rose," or "Sleeping Beauty," as it is often better known, appeared in many different forms before it was eventually set down by the Brothers Grimm. A brief summary would include versions by Perrault and Basile, as well as appearances in the fourteenth-century Catalan *Frayre de Joy e Sor de Placer,* and in the sixteenth-century French *Perceforest.*

In early versions of the tale, the sleeping girl was raped by her discoverer (in Basile's tale, the king who discovers her "plucks from her the fruits of love") and awoke with the birth of her baby: quite literally, a sexual awakening. Later tellers of the tale opted for an awakening that was slightly less abrupt, most famously the kiss in the tale told by the Brothers Grimm.

Earlier versions also extended the tale, including the details of the princess's marriage, her encounter with a cannibalistic mother-in-law, and the mother-in-law's eventual demise in a vat of snakes. Throughout, though, Sleeping Beauty remains one of the most passive of fairy tale heroines, and it is hardly surprising that the tale has proved tempting for those who might seek to reinterpret it. As with other tales included in *The Book of Lost Things,* Emma Donoghue, Anne Sexton, and Robert Coover have all reworked the story to different ends.

Little Briar Rose

The Brothers Grimm

A long time ago there were a King and Queen who said every day, "Oh, if only we had a child!" but they never had one. But it happened that once when the Queen was bathing, a frog crept out of the water on to the land, and said to her, "Your wish shall be fulfilled; before a year had gone by you shall have a daughter."

What the frog had said came true, and the Queen had a little girl who was so pretty that the King could not contain himself for joy, and ordered a great feast. He invited not only his kindred, friends and acquaintance, but also the Wise Women, in order that they might be kind and well-disposed towards the child. There were thirteen of them in his Kingdom, but as he had only twelve golden plates for them to eat out of, one of them had to be left at home.

The feast was held with all manner of splendour, and when it came to an end the Wise Women bestowed their magic gifts upon the baby: one gave virtue, another beauty, a third riches, and so on with everything in the world that one can wish for.

When eleven of them had made their promises, suddenly the thirteenth came in. She wished to avenge herself for not having been invited, and without greeting, or even looking at any one, she cried with a loud voice, "The King's daughter shall in her fifteenth year prick herself with a spindle, and fall down dead." And, without saying a word more, she turned round and left the room.

They were all shocked but the twelfth, whose good wish still

John Connolly

remained unspoken, came forward, and as she could not undo the evil sentence, but only soften it, she said, "It shall not be death, but a deep sleep of a hundred years, into which the princess shall fall."

The King, who would fain keep his dear child from the misfortune, gave orders that every spindle in the whole kingdom should be burnt. Meanwhile the gifts of the Wise Women were plenteously fulfilled on the young girl, for she was so beautiful, modest, good-natured, and wise, that every one who saw her was bound to love her.

It happened that on the very day when she was fifteen years old the King and Queen were not at home, and the maiden was left in the palace quite alone. So she went round into all sorts of places, looked into rooms and bedchambers just as she liked, and at last came to an old tower. She climbed up the narrow winding-staircase, and reached a little door. A rusty key was in the lock, and when she turned it the door sprang open, and there in a little room sat an old woman with a spindle, busily spinning her flax.

"Good day, old dame," said the King's daughter; "what are you doing there?" "I am spinning," said the old woman, and nodded her head. "What sort of thing is that, that rattles round so merrily?" said the girl, and she took the spindle and wanted to spin too. But scarcely had she touched the spindle when the magic decree was fulfilled, and she pricked her finger with it.

And, in the very moment when she felt the prick, she fell down upon the bed that stood there, and lay in a deep sleep. And this sleep extended over the whole palace; the King and Queen who had just come home, and had entered the great hall, began to go to sleep, and the whole court with them. The horses, too, went to sleep in the stable, the dogs in the yard, the pigeons upon the roof, the flies on the wall; even the fire that was flaming on the hearth became quiet and slept, the roast meat left off frizzling, and the cook, who was just going to pull the hair of the scullery boy, because he had forgotten something, let him go, and went to sleep. And the wind fell, and on the trees before the castle not a leaf moved again.

But round about the castle there began to grow a hedge of thorns, which every year became higher, and at last grew close up around the castle and all over it, so that there was nothing of it to be seen, not even the flag upon the roof. But the story of the beautiful sleeping "Briar-rose," for so the princess was named, went about the country, so that from time to time kings' sons came and tried to get through the thorny hedge into the castle.

But they found it impossible, for the thorns held fast together, as if they had hands, and the youths were caught in them, could not get loose again, and died a miserable death.

After long, long years a King's son came again to that country, and heard an old man talking about the thorn-hedge, and that a castle was said to stand behind it in which a wonderfully beautiful princess, named Briar-rose, had been asleep for a hundred years; and that the King and Queen and the whole court were asleep likewise. He had heard, too, from his grandfather, that many kings' sons had already come, and had tried to get through the thorny hedge, but they had remained sticking fast in it, and had died a pitiful death. Then the youth said, "I am not afraid, I will go and see the beautiful Briar-rose." The good old man might dissuade him as he would, he did not listen to his words.

But by this time the hundred years had just passed, and the day had come when Briar-rose was to awake again. When the

King's son came near to the thorn-hedge, it was nothing but large and beautiful flowers, which parted from each other of their own accord, and let him pass unhurt, then they closed again behind him like a hedge. In the castle-yard he saw the horses and the spotted hounds lying asleep; on the roof sat the pigeons with their heads under their wings. And when he entered the house, the flies were asleep upon the wall, the cook in the kitchen was still holding out his hand to seize the boy, and the maid was sitting by the black hen which she was going to pluck.

He went on farther, and in the great hall he saw the whole of the court lying asleep, and up by the throne lay the King and Queen.

Then he went on still farther, and all was so quiet that a breath could be heard, and at last he came to the tower, and opened the door into the little room where Briar-rose was sleeping. There she lay, so beautiful that he could not turn his eyes away; and he stooped down and gave her a kiss. But as soon as he kissed her, Briar-rose opened her eyes and awoke, and looked at him quite sweetly.

Then they went down together, and the King awoke, and the Queen, and the whole court, and looked at each other in great astonishment. And the horses in the courtyard stood up and shook themselves; the hounds jumped up and wagged their tails; the pigeons upon the roof pulled out their heads from under their wings, looked round, and flew into the open country; the flies on the wall crept again; the fire in the kitchen burned up and flickered and cooked the meat; the joint began to turn and frizzle again, and the cook gave the boy such a box on the ear that he screamed, and the maid plucked the fowl ready for the spit.

And then the marriage of the King's son with Briar-rose was celebrated with all splendour, and they lived contented to the end of their days.

ROBERT BROWNING AND "CHILDE ROLAND TO THE DARK TOWER CAME"

Some of the poems weren't too bad, once he gave them a chance. One was about a knight—except in the poem he was called a "Childe"—and his search for a dark tower and whatever secret it contained. The poem didn't really seem to end properly, though. The knight reached the tower and, well, that was it. David wanted to know what was in the tower, and what happened to the knight now that he'd reached it, but the poet obviously didn't think that was important. It made David wonder about the kind of people who wrote poems.

—*The Book of Lost Things,* Chapter III

The smell from the battlefield was making David queasy, and it added to his sense that the old man was not to be trusted. Now the way he spoke of the "she" who had done this, and the manner in which he smiled at the mention of her, made it very clear to David that the men who had died here had died very badly indeed.

"And who is 'she'?" asked Roland.

"She is the Beast . . ."

—*The Book of Lost Things,* Chapter XVIII

A faint light appeared in the topmost window of the tower and then was blocked as a figure passed before the opening. It paused and seemed to stare down upon the man and boy below, then disappeared.

—*The Book of Lost Things,* Chapter XXIV

*   *   *

OF "CHILDE ROLAND . . ."

Robert Browning (1812–1889) is one of my favorite poets, although I discovered him quite late as part of my English degree at Trinity College, Dublin. His character poems are perhaps the most striking, and I still find it hard to see the art of Andrea del Sarto and Fra Lippo Lippi without comparing both artists to their depiction in Browning's poems of the same name, derived in part from the study of Vasari and his *Lives of the Artists.*

Still, it was "Childe Roland to the Dark Tower Came" that impacted upon me the most, perhaps because it is so rich in imagery and uses the structure of the quest—a structure that is, I think, among the most elementally appealing to readers. (It also clearly provides the basis for Stephen King's *Dark Tower* sequence of seven novels, with the gunslinger Roland at their heart.) Nevertheless, like David, I can recall being slightly frustrated by the ending of the poem. While I understood the logic behind it—or at least could justify it by my understanding that the terror to be faced in the tower is individual to each of us or represents something far deeper than can be expressed in animate form—I had been raised on stories that were not so open-ended. Now I realize that it hardly matters what may lie in the tower. What matters is that Roland is prepared to confront it. We all, in our way, have such a fear to face. Perhaps, in the end, the great terror at the base of the tower will be our own mortality.

The poem was first published in the 1855 volume *Men and Women,* and, per Browning's own note beneath the title, it takes its title and inspiration from the song sung by Edgar in Shakespeare's *King Lear,* when he pretends to be a madman. The most relevant lines from *King Lear,* spoken by the Fool, are:

Childe Rowland to the dark tower came;
His word was still, Fie, fo, and fum,
I smell the blood of a British man.

There are also obvious nods to earlier figures, such as the hero of the Scottish ballad "Childe Roland" and the twelfth-century French "Song of Roland." Browning's use of allegory in the poem also suggests the influence of Bunyan's *Pilgrim's Progress,* and the images of gothic horror echo the style of the Romantics. It's also likely that Browning had read the great Middle English narrative poem *Sir Gawain and the Green Knight.*

"Childe," incidentally, is an aristocratic title, referring to a young man who has yet to be knighted, which echoes David's predicament: he is a young man who has not yet begun to reach adulthood. Meanwhile, Roland, David's protector in *The Book of Lost Things,* is also ambiguous about his own status.

But what of the poem's impact on David's imagination, and in turn upon the landscape of *The Book of Lost Things*? Images of towers recur in the novel: from the ruined church in the forest, through to the steeple at the heart of the fortified village, and finally to the tower that dominates the Fortress of Thorns. ("The round squat turret, blind as the fool's heart" to quote Browning.) The tower is one of the most important symbols in the book, and its importance derives in large part from David's reading of the poem. Although it frustrates him, at some unconscious level he does understand its meaning, even though he tries earlier in the story to put a shape on his fear in the form of the Beast. In the tower David, like Roland, will face his worst fear, the apotheosis of the threatening female figures that appear again and again in the novel, just as they appear in the old fairy tales so beloved of the boy.

There are other images from the poem that appear in *The Book of Lost Things*: the "hoary cripple" becomes the old man who appears to David and Roland at the battlefield, which is also referred to in the poem. ("The fight must so have seemed in that fell cirque. / What penned them there, with all the plain to choose?") The knights who have preceded Roland and died in their quest also assume a more concrete form in the book.

Ultimately, though, it is unclear if the narrative encountered in the poem is meant to be taken as real or imagined. If imagined, then the narrator has externalized a landscape ravaged by his own memories, fears, and desires, in much the same way that David creates the landscape in *The Book of Lost Things* in order to come to terms with his own demons.

Childe Roland to the Dark Tower Came
 (See Edgar's song in *Lear*)
My first thought was, he lied in every word,
That hoary cripple, with malicious eye
Askance to watch the working of his lie
On mine, and mouth scarce able to afford
Suppression of the glee that pursed and scored
Its edge, at one more victim gained thereby.

What else should he be set for, with his staff?
What, save to waylay with his lies, ensnare
All travellers who might find him posted there,
And ask the road? I guessed what skull-like laugh
Would break, what crutch 'gin write my epitaph
For pastime in the dusty thoroughfare,

If at his counsel I should turn aside
Into that ominous tract which, all agree,

Hides the Dark Tower. Yet acquiescingly
I did turn as he pointed: neither pride
Nor hope rekindling at the end descried,
So much as gladness that some end might be.

For, what with my whole world-wide wandering,
What with my search drawn out thro' years, my hope
Dwindled into a ghost not fit to cope
With that obstreperous joy success would bring,
I hardly tried now to rebuke the spring
My heart made, finding failure in its scope.

As when a sick man very near to death
Seems dead indeed, and feels begin and end
The tears and takes the farewell of each friend,
And hears one bid the other go, draw breath
Freelier outside ("since all is o'er," he saith,
"And the blow fallen no grieving can amend;")

While some discuss if near the other graves
Be room enough for this, and when a day
Suits best for carrying the corpse away,
With care about the banners, scarves and staves:
And still the man hears all, and only craves
He may not shame such tender love and stay.

Thus, I had so long suffered in this quest,
Heard failure prophesied so oft, been writ
So many times among "The Band"—to wit,
The knights who to the Dark Tower's search addressed
Their steps—that just to fail as they, seemed best,
And all the doubt was now—should I be fit?

So, quiet as despair, I turned from him,
That hateful cripple, out of his highway
Into the path he pointed. All the day
Had been a dreary one at best, and dim
Was settling to its close, yet shot one grim
Red leer to see the plain catch its estray.

For mark! no sooner was I fairly found
Pledged to the plain, after a pace or two,
Than, pausing to throw backward a last view
O'er the safe road, 'twas gone; grey plain all round:
Nothing but plain to the horizon's bound.
I might go on; nought else remained to do.

So, on I went. I think I never saw
Such starved ignoble nature; nothing throve:
For flowers—as well expect a cedar grove!
But cockle, spurge, according to their law
Might propagate their kind, with none to awe,
You'd think; a burr had been a treasure trove.

No! penury, inertness and grimace,
In some strange sort, were the land's portion. "See
Or shut your eyes," said Nature peevishly,
"It nothing skills: I cannot help my case:
'Tis the Last Judgment's fire must cure this place,
Calcine its clods and set my prisoners free."

If there pushed any ragged thistle-stalk
Above its mates, the head was chopped; the bents
Were jealous else. What made those holes and rents

In the dock's harsh swarth leaves, bruised as to baulk
All hope of greenness? 'tis a brute must walk
Pashing their life out, with a brute's intents.

As for the grass, it grew as scant as hair
In leprosy; thin dry blades pricked the mud
Which underneath looked kneaded up with blood.
One stiff blind horse, his every bone a-stare,
Stood stupefied, however he came there:
Thrust out past service from the devil's stud!

Alive? he might be dead for aught I know,
With that red gaunt and colloped neck a-strain,
And shut eyes underneath the rusty mane;
Seldom went such grotesqueness with such woe;
I never saw a brute I hated so;
He must be wicked to deserve such pain.

I shut my eyes and turned them on my heart.
As a man calls for wine before he fights,
I asked one draught of earlier, happier sights,
Ere fitly I could hope to play my part.
Think first, fight afterwards—the soldier's art:
One taste of the old time sets all to rights.

Not it! I fancied Cuthbert's reddening face
Beneath its garniture of curly gold,
Dear fellow, till I almost felt him fold
An arm in mine to fix me to the place
That way he used. Alas, one night's disgrace!
Out went my heart's new fire and left it cold.

Giles then, the soul of honour—there he stands
Frank as ten years ago when knighted first.
What honest men should dare (he said) he durst.
Good—but the scene shifts—faugh! what hangman hands
Pin to his breast a parchment? His own bands
Read it. Poor traitor, spit upon and curst!

Better this present than a past like that;
Back therefore to my darkening path again!
No sound, no sight as far as eye could strain.
Will the night send a howlet or a bat?
I asked: when something on the dismal flat
Came to arrest my thoughts and change their train.

A sudden little river crossed my path
As unexpected as a serpent comes.
No sluggish tide congenial to the glooms;
This, as it frothed by, might have been a bath
For the fiend's glowing hoof—to see the wrath
Of its black eddy bespate with flakes and spumes.

So petty yet so spiteful! All along
Low scrubby alders kneeled down over it;
Drenched willows flung them headlong in a fit
Of mute despair, a suicidal throng:
The river which had done them all the wrong,
Whate'er that was, rolled by, deterred no whit.

Which, while I forded,—good saints, how I feared
To set my foot upon a dead man's cheek,
Each step, or feel the spear I thrust to seek

For hollows, tangled in his hair or beard!
—It may have been a water-rat I speared,
But, ugh! it sounded like a baby's shriek.

Glad was I when I reached the other bank.
Now for a better country. Vain presage!
Who were the strugglers, what war did they wage,
Whose savage trample thus could pad the dank
Soil to a plash? Toads in a poisoned tank,
Or wild cats in a red-hot iron cage—

The fight must so have seemed in that fell cirque.
What penned them there, with all the plain to choose?
No foot-print leading to that horrid mews,
None out of it. Mad brewage set to work
Their brains, no doubt, like galley-slaves the Turk
Pits for his pastime, Christians against Jews.

And more than that—a furlong on—why, there!
What bad use was that engine for, that wheel,
Or brake, not wheel—that harrow fit to reel
Men's bodies out like silk? with all the air
Of Tophet's tool, on earth left unaware,
Or brought to sharpen its rusty teeth of steel.

Then came a bit of stubbed ground, once a wood,
Next a marsh, it would seem, and now mere earth
Desperate and done with; (so a fool finds mirth,
Makes a thing and then mars it, till his mood
Changes and off he goes!) within a rood—
Bog, clay and rubble, sand and stark black dearth.

Now blotches rankling, coloured gay and grim,
Now patches where some leanness of the soil's
Broke into moss or substances like boils;
Then came some palsied oak, a cleft in him
Like a distorted mouth that splits its rim
Gaping at death, and dies while it recoils.

And just as far as ever from the end!
Nought in the distance but the evening, nought
To point my footstep further! At the thought,
A great black bird, Apollyon's bosom-friend,
Sailed past, nor beat his wide wing dragon-penned
That brushed my cap—perchance the guide I sought.

For, looking up, aware I somehow grew,
'Spite of the dusk, the plain had given place
All round to mountains—with such name to grace
Mere ugly heights and heaps now stolen in view.
How thus they had surprised me,—solve it, you!
How to get from them was no clearer case.

Yet half I seemed to recognise some trick
Of mischief happened to me, God knows when—
In a bad dream perhaps. Here ended, then,
Progress this way. When, in the very nick
Of giving up, one time more, came a click
As when a trap shuts—you're inside the den!

Burningly it came on me all at once,
This was the place! those two hills on the right,
Crouched like two bulls locked horn in horn in fight;
While to the left, a tall scalped mountain . . . Dunce,

Dotard, a-dozing at the very nonce,
After a life spent training for the sight!

What in the midst lay but the Tower itself?
The round squat turret, blind as the fool's heart
Built of brown stone, without a counterpart
In the whole world. The tempest's mocking elf
Points to the shipman thus the unseen shelf
He strikes on, only when the timbers start.

Not see? because of night perhaps?—why, day
Came back again for that! before it left,
The dying sunset kindled through a cleft:
The hills, like giants at a hunting, lay
Chin upon hand, to see the game at bay,—
"Now stab and end the creature—to the heft!"

Not hear? when noise was everywhere! it tolled
Increasing like a bell. Names in my ears
Of all the lost adventurers my peers,—
How such a one was strong, and such was bold,
And such was fortunate, yet each of old
Lost, lost! one moment knelled the woe of years.

There they stood, ranged along the hillsides, met
To view the last of me, a living frame
For one more picture! in a sheet of flame
I saw them and I knew them all. And yet
Dauntless the slug-horn to my lips I set,
And blew. "Childe Roland to the Dark Tower came."

CENTAURS

"I was thinking about what you said last night," said David carefully, "about how all children dream of being animals."

"And is it not true?" asked the huntress.

"I think so," said David. "I always wanted to be a horse."

The huntress looked interested.

"And why a horse?"

"In the stories that I read when I was little, I came across a creature called a centaur. It was half horse and half man. Instead of a horse's neck, it had the torso of a man, so it could hold a bow in its hands. It was beautiful and strong, and it was the perfect hunter because it combined all of the strength and speed of a horse with the skill and cunning of a man. You were fast on your mount yesterday, but you were still not one with your horse. I mean, doesn't your horse trip sometimes, or move in ways that you hadn't expected? My father used to ride as a boy, and he told me that even the finest of horsemen can be unsaddled. If I was a centaur, then I would be the best of both horse and man in one, and if I hunted, then nothing would ever be able to escape me."

—*The Book of Lost Things,* Chapter XVII

OF CENTAURS

What is interesting about the myth of the centaur is its very vagueness, as evidenced by the short section from Graves's *Greek Myths* included here. Nevertheless, David is right in finding something fascinating about the combination of man and beast represented by the centaur, and it's possible, given the sexual undercurrents that run through this section, that the centaur's appeal for the huntress is more complex than a desire merely to hunt more efficiently.

ORIGINS

Horses were sacred to the moon, and hobbyhorse dances, designed to make rain fall, have apparently given rise to the legend that the Centaurs were half horse, half man. The earliest Greek representation of Centaurs—two men joined at the waist to horses' bodies—is found on a Mycenaean gem from the Heraeum at Argos; they face each other and are dancing. A similar pair appear on a Cretan bed seal; but since there was no native horse cult in Crete, the motif has evidently been imported from the mainland. In archaic art, the satyrs were also pictured as hobbyhorse men, but later as goats. Centaurus will have been an oracular hero with a serpent's tail, and the story of Boreas's mating with mares is therefore attached to him.

—*The Greek Myths,* Robert Graves

HARPIES

David's book of Greek myths, meanwhile, was the same size and color as
a collection of poetry nearby, and he would sometimes pull out the poems
instead of the myths.

—*The Book of Lost Things,* Chapter III

[David] saw a shape, much larger than any bird that he had ever seen,
gliding through the air, supported by the updrafts from the canyon. It had
bare, almost human, legs, although its toes were strangely elongated and
curved like an eagle's talons. Its arms were outstretched, and from them
hung the great folds of skin that served as its wings. Its long white hair
flowed in the wind . . .

It had a female form: old, and with scales instead of skin, yet still female
for all that. He risked another look and saw the creature descending now in
diminishing circles.

"Harpies," said David.

—*The Book of Lost Things,* Chapter XII

OF HARPIES

My first memory of harpies is from Ray Harryhausen's film *Jason
and the Argonauts,* where stop-motion terrors in female form tormented the blind Phineus. In *The Book of Lost Things,* harpies are
one of a number of evil female figures that derive in part from
David's own misplaced hatred for his stepmother, Rose, but they
also take their place in the tradition of such figures in fairy tales.
Evil is often presented as uniquely female in such stories. For

critics such as Bruno Bettelheim, female evil was based in part on the oedipal conflicts he perceived at the heart of these tales, but it may also be the case that there is nothing more terrifying to a child than a threatening female, or mother, figure. In general, it's probably fair to say that children are more frightened of their fathers than of their mothers, with fathers representing authority figures and traditionally assuming the responsibility for discipline. For a child to be turned upon by a woman is perhaps more unsettling because it is so unexpected, even unnatural, to the extent that Shakespeare's Lady Macbeth demands to be "unsex(ed)" in order to become a murderous party to her husband's ambitions.

The harpies are a comparatively simple version of what David perceives as the female threat to his happiness. While the story of Phineus is perhaps the most well known of the Greek myths, I've included some other references from Graves as well:

Nereus, Phorcys, Thaumas, Eurybia, and Ceto were all children born to Pontus by Mother Earth; thus the Phorcids and Nereids claim cousinhood with the Harpies. These are the fair-haired and swift-winged daughters of Thaumas by the Ocean-nymph Electra, who snatch up criminals for punishment by the Erinnyes, and live in a Cretan cave.

According to others, however, it was Tantalus who stole the golden mastiff (the guardian of Zeus as an infant), and Pandereus to whom he entrusted it and who, on denying that he had ever received it was destroyed, together with his wife, by the angry gods, or turned into stone. But Pandereus's orphaned daughters Merope and Cleothera, whom some call Cameiro and Clytie, were reared by Aphrodite on curds, honey, and sweet wine. Hera endowed them with beauty and more than human wisdom;

Artemis made them grow tall and strong; Athene instructed them in every known handicraft. It is difficult to understand why these goddesses showed such solicitude, or chose Aphrodite to soften Zeus's heart towards those orphans and arrange good marriages for them—unless, of course, they had themselves encouraged Pandereus to commit the theft. Zeus must have suspected something, because while Aphrodite was closeted with him on Olympus, the Harpies snatched away the three girls, with his consent, and handed them over to the Erinnyes, who made them suffer vicariously for their father's sins.

The Argonauts put to sea again on the next day, and came to Salmydesseus in Eastern Thrace, where Phineus, the son of Agenor, reigned. He had been blinded by the gods for prophesying the future too accurately, and was also plagued by a pair of Harpies; loathsome, winged female creatures who, at every meal, flew into the palace and snatched victuals from his table, befouling the rest, so that it stank and was inedible. One Harpy was called Aellopus, and the other Ocypete. When Jason asked Phineus for advice on how to win the golden fleece, he was told: "First rid me of the Harpies!" Phineus's servants spread the Argonauts a banquet, upon which the Harpies immediately descended, playing their usual tricks. Calais and Zetes, however, the winged sons of Boreas, arose sword in hand, and chased them into the air and far across the sea. Some say they caught up with the Harpies at the Strophades islands, but spared their lives when they turned back and implored mercy; for Iris, Hera's messenger, intervened, promising that they would return to their cave in Cretan Dicte and never again molest Phineus. Others say Ocypete made terms at these islands, but that Aellopus flew on, only to be drowned in the Peloponnesian river Tigris, now called Harpys after her.

Sirens were carved on funereal monuments as death angels chanting dirges to lyre music, but were also credited with erotic designs on the heroes whom they mourned; and, since the soul was believed to fly off in the form of a bird, were pictured, like the Harpies, as birds of prey waiting to catch and secure it.

—*The Greek Myths,* Robert Graves

THE DEATH OF MANIUS

There was . . . a book about the Roman Empire that had some very inter-
esting drawings in it and seemed to take a lot of pleasure in describing the
cruel things that the Romans did to people and that other people did to the
Romans in return.

—The Book of Lost Things, Chapter III

Come, look over here. Peer closely at this case, so close that your breath cre-
ates a little cloud of moisture upon the glass and you can stare into the
milky eyes of the fat, bald man within. It's as if he himself is breathing,
although he has not taken or released a breath in a very long time. See how
his skin is burst and burned? See how his mouth and throat, his belly and
lungs, are swollen and distended? Do you want to know his tale, for it is
one of the Crooked Man's favorite stories. It is a nasty tale, a very nasty
tale . . .

    You see, the fat man's name was Manius, and he was very greedy . . .
                        —The Book of Lost Things, Chapter XXIX

OF MANIUS

I came across this story quite recently, while reading Tom Holland's excellent history of the Roman Republic, *Rubicon.* There is
an unsettling, fairy tale element to the story of Manius, both in
the end that he meets and in the early life of Mithridates, his
nemesis, that appeared to suit *The Book of Lost Things.* Also, it
seemed the kind of story that would strike a boy like David as
being particularly memorable, a prime example of, as he puts in,

"the cruel things that the Romans did to people and that other people did to the Romans in return . . ."

Not long afterwards he [King Mithridates VI, Eupator of Pontus] captured Manius Aquillius, one of the ambassadors and the one who was most to blame for this war. Mithridates led him around, bound on an ass, and compelled him to introduce himself to the public as "maniac." Finally, at Pergamon, Mithridates poured molten gold down his throat, thus rebuking the Romans for their bribe-taking.

History of Rome: The Foreign Wars, Appian of Alexandria

Looking to widen their activities, Roman business interests began casting greedy eyes on Pontus, a kingdom on the Black Sea coast in the north of what is now Turkey. In the summer of 89 the Roman commissioner in Asia, Manius Aquillius, trumped up an excuse for an invasion. Rather than risk his own troops' lives, he preferred to order a client-king to do the fighting for him—having assumed, with fatal complacency, that any fallout from such a provocation would be easily containable. But the King of Pontus, Mithridates, was no ordinary opponent. His biography, carefully honed by a genius for propaganda, read like a fairy tale. Persecuted by his wicked mother as a child, the young prince had been forced to take refuge in a forest. Here he had lived for seven years, outrunning deer and outfighting lions. Nervous that his mother might still try to have him murdered, Mithridates had also developed an obsessive interest in toxicology, taking repeated antidotes until he was immune to poison. Not the kind of boy, in short, to let family stand in the way of a throne. Duly returning to his capital at the head of a conquering army, Mithridates had his mother killed, and then, just for good measure, his brother and sister too. More than twenty years later he remained as power hungry and ruthless as ever—far too much, certainly, for a reluctant Roman poodle. The invasion was contemptuously repelled.

Next, however, came a more fateful step. Mithridates had to decide whether to take the attack to Rome herself. Superpowers were not taken on lightly, but war with the Republic was a challenge for which Mithridates had been preparing all his reign. Like any ambitious despot, he had worked hard to beef up his offensive capabilities, and his army was shiny new—literally so, since its weapons were embossed with gold and its armour with bright jewels. But if Mithridates liked to make a splash, he also enjoyed playing at cloak and dagger: travelling undercover through Asia, he had seen enough to convince him of the provincials' hatred of Rome. This, more than anything, was what persuaded him to take the plunge. Crossing into the province of Asia, he found the garrisons protecting it scanty and ill-prepared, and the Greek cities eager to hail him as a saviour. In a matter of weeks Roman power in the province had totally collapsed, and Mithridates found himself standing on the shore of the Aegean Sea.

As a matricidal barbarian he was hardly the kind of champion the Greeks would normally have taken to their hearts. But better a matricidal barbarian than the *publicani*—the longing for freedom was so desperate, and the loathing of Rome so visceral, that the provincials were determined to go to any lengths to dispose of their oppressors. In the summer of 88, when Rome's chains had already been thrown off, they were to demonstrate this in a horrific explosion of violence. Aiming to bind the Greek cities to him irrevocably, Mithridates wrote to them, ordering the massacre of every Roman and Italian left in Asia. The Greeks followed his instructions with savage relish. Victims were rounded up and slaughtered by hired assassins, hacked to pieces as they clung to sacred statues, or shot as they attempted to escape into the sea. Their bodies were left to rot unburied outside the city walls.

Eighty thousand men, women and children were said to have been killed on that single, deadly night.

As a blow to the Roman economy, this was calculated and devastating; but as a blow to Roman prestige it was far worse. Mithridates had already shown himself a master of propaganda, resurrecting the Sibyl's prophecies and throwing in some new ones of his own in order to make them appear more relevant to himself. The common theme was the appearance of a great king from the East, an instrument of divine retribution sent to humble the arrogant and grasping superpower. The mass slaughter of businessmen was only one way in which Mithridates chose to dramatise this. Even more calculated for effect was the execution of Manius Aquillius, the Roman commissioner who had provoked Mithridates into war in the first place. Falling ill at just the wrong moment, the unfortunate Aquillius was captured and dragged back to Pergamum, shackled all the way to a seven-foot barbarian. After tying him to an ass and parading him through jeering crowds, Mithridates next ordered some treasure melted down. When all had been prepared, Aquillius's head was jerked back, his mouth forced open, and the molten metal poured down his throat. "Warmongers against every nation, people and king under the sun, the Romans have only one abiding motive—greed, deep-seated, for empire and riches." This had been the verdict of Mithridates on the Republic and now, in the person of her legate in Asia, he exacted symbolic justice. Manius Aquillius choked to death on gold."

—*Rubicon,* Tom Holland